THE ROOTS OF WRATH

By B.T. Narro

Jon Oklar:
Book 4

Cover and Map by Beatriz Garrido

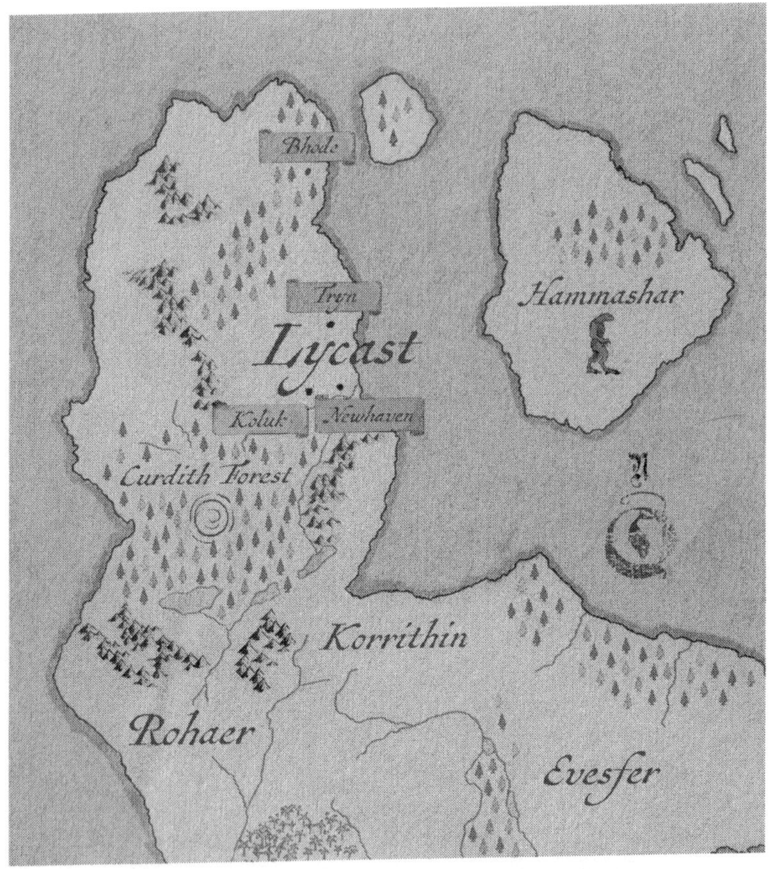
Bhode
Tryn
Lycast
Koluk
Newhaven
Curdith Forest
Hammashar
Korrithin
Rohaer
Evesfer

CHAPTER ONE

I thought it was strange that Eden had given me a note. It was the morning after Valinox snuck his invisible self and another invisible sorcerer on his back—a sorcerer I'd never even seen before—into my room. There they waited for me to be alone so they could murder me. They would've succeeded had Aliana not sensed their presence and Hadley not disrupted all mana with a curse. I killed the sorcerer Valinox brought, and Valinox jumped through my large window to flee. I spent the night in Michael's room afterward.

Eden had been waiting outside my room for me to return from my morning bath. That's when she handed me the slip of paper and walked away without offering a single word of explanation.

The note read, *"After breakfast, I want you to enter my room and take my Induct stone of dteria away from me. No matter what I say, you must leave my room with it in your possession. Bring it to Barrett. He knows what to do."*

"What's that?" Michael asked as he read over my shoulder. I hadn't heard him coming up behind me. "Did I see Eden give that to you?"

"Yes, but she didn't explain anything about it." Seeing as how Eden hadn't mentioned keeping this between us, I let Michael read it.

"What's an Induct stone?" he asked.

"I have no idea."

"Maybe something Valinox gave her."

A silence passed.

"Do you trust her?" he asked.

"I thought I did, but now I'm not so sure."

"She's driving me mad, Jon," Michael told me candidly.

"How?" I had barely seen them speak to each other since we had returned to the castle from Koluk.

"Because she looks better than ever, but…you know what she did."

"Oh." I was a little disappointed. I thought he might've been disturbed about something I hadn't heard about yet, something Eden did while in Valinox's company.

I figured I wasn't the only one who was a little worried that she might turn against us again. She had fed sensitive information about us to Valinox and nearly killed Remi with a dagger to her neck.

We had forgiven her for this, mostly because we had seen her attempt to kill Valinox later. Plus, she would've died from his retribution had I not healed her afterward. However, the dteria that now empowered her could also have corrupted her in ways we had yet to see.

My stomach rumbled loudly enough to draw Michael's eyes down to it. He laughed and put up his hands defensively. "I won't keep you from your breakfast any longer, Jon Oklar."

"It's fine," I muttered as I started down the hall with Michael following. He always made me out to be some kind of food-crazed beast. Sure, I ate fast and sometimes audibly enjoyed my meals, but I was more of a slave to sorcery than to food.

"For I am not brave enough to stand between Jon

Oklar and his breakfast!" Michael announced. "In fact, I daresay no man is brave enough to come between Jon and his food. Like a bear out of hibernation, Jon Oklar trudges toward his certain meal—"

"That's enough," I said.

The board creaked underneath my foot.

"The ground quivers beneath the massive weight of his thumping footfalls!" Michael went on.

To my displeasure, my stomach grumbled again, even louder this time.

"Beware!" Michael decreed. "There is a growl in his belly, and I daresay it is the very sound of a void that cannot be filled!"

"I daresay you shut up," I muttered.

There was a chuckle from behind us. We stopped and looked back. Hadley was a few steps away, quiet as a mouse until now.

I had thought Hadley was beautiful since she met me at Kataleya's mansion, despite showing up with matted, unwashed hair and covered in dirty layers of clothing. Today, she looked even lovelier than usual. She wore a green tunic with a gray shirt underneath that covered her arms. A wide belt across her slender abdomen pulled together the loose fabric of her attire and accentuated her curves. She had a warm smile on her pouty lips, white teeth bright beneath dark eyes that always seemed to stir something in me.

"Is this a morning routine?" she asked playfully.

"Yes," Michael answered. "Every morning, Jon threatens to tear down the very walls of this castle unless he's had his breakfast. If only Valinox had put himself between Jon and his breakfast, the evil demigod probably wouldn't be here today."

"How are you, Hadley?" I asked. "Feel free to ignore Michael, by the way."

She chuckled. "Good. You seem well, considering what happened last night."

I wasn't really, though. I wouldn't soon forget that I had almost died. I didn't know what the sleeping arrangements would be from now on, but I didn't want to sleep alone until we found some way of destroying the gem that had allowed Valinox to carry someone into the castle with both of them cloaked by invisibility.

I looked forward to speaking to the king so I could hear his plan on the matter. But Michael was right, even if he tended to exaggerate things. More than anything, I was looking forward to breakfast. I would keep up my brave face for now. Besides, it was always better to be positive so long as I could be realistic.

"Valinox almost lost his life, even if I did as well," I said. "He might be more hesitant to come back now."

"How many more of those curse stones do you have?" Michael asked Hadley.

"The curse is called mana break. There are four left. I have one, Eden has one, the king's councilman has one, and Reuben has one. I think you should ask Reuben for his, Jon, because you are more of a target than he is."

There was still the question of whether I could activate the curse without assistance. It required a spell of ordia, a school of magic that did not come easily to me. I hadn't gotten the chance to attempt to use the one Hadley had given me, which she had activated to save my life. Before that, Valinox had enclosed dteria all around me, preventing me from casting anything as he and his sorcerer tried to suffocate me.

"I'll ask him," I said.

The three of us headed down the hall and toward the stairs.

"Jon, how would you feel about going to the forest with me today, if we're allowed?" Hadley asked. "I need to search for more ingredients. We could use Aliana's help as well to track down animals, unless Reuben can do it."

I wanted to go with Hadley no matter where she was headed, my feelings for her stronger every time I saw her. However, I didn't have the luxury of time. As I thought of how to answer, Michael spoke up.

"I'm not sure I would trust Reuben's skill for a task like that. No one knows how much he's really able to track."

"Then this might be a good chance for him to work on it," Hadley said.

I asked, "How important is it that you find these ingredients?"

"I really can't say. It depends on many things that are still unknown." We headed down the stairs and out of the apartments. It was just a short walk to the great hall, where our meals were served in the dining area.

"I'm not sure I can go into the forest today," I said, knowing she was still waiting for an answer. "I need to train as much as possible."

"They say the forest is the best place to learn spells," she countered. "I figured you and the other sorcerers have trained there in the past and experienced this personally."

"We have," I agreed, "but it doesn't sound like I'll have much time to train if I'm hunting with you and Reuben."

"Oh, you won't need to stay with us. I only want you

to be close enough in case...of danger."

I tried to think of what she was referring to specifically and soon realized there were many sources of danger to worry about. Valinox wasn't the only one after us. So were an entire army of sorcerers. They were just starting north now, no longer impeded by a snowstorm made by Failina—the demigod of erto. But there could be others who were already here. The king of Rohaer had sent several groups earlier that we had encountered and, not so easily, disposed of. There might be more stalking us.

Then there were the dangers of the forest itself. The creatures there were aggressive and deadly. I could've lost my life to one of them, a cantar, when it had attacked me, Aliana, and Eden soon after I had learned my first spell.

"I'd be happy to go if I'm able to train while there," I answered Hadley.

"Oh good. Now we just have to convince the king. Would you like to speak to him on my behalf? He seems to favor you."

"I'll see if I can arrange a meeting after breakfast, but first I'll have to visit Eden in her room."

"If Jon's not going to be hunting with you," Michael interjected, "you'll definitely want Aliana over Reuben. He's not any good with a bow like she is."

"Hadley can shoot just fine," I said, then shared a quick look with her.

"How do you know...? Oh, the battle," Michael realized. "I saw that fire mage's corpse with an arrow in it and wondered who shot her. That was you?" he asked Hadley.

"Well, she was going to cast at—"

"Hold on," Michael interrupted. He stopped and turned around. We had entered the great hall but were still a room away from the dining quarters. He had a serious look as he faced Hadley. I thought for a moment that he might tell a joke, but his tone soon made it clear that this was not a joking matter.

"You shouldn't provide an excuse for killing that sorcerer. You know what Rohaer wants. Their army isn't going to stop murdering until there's too few of us to stand against them, and then there will be no one to stop them from wreaking havoc on all of Lycast. If there's one less of them, then all the better. I've heard how Jon talks about killing them with reluctance and guilt, and I hear it from you now as well. It's not just a necessary evil. It's glory and honor. It's something to be proud of. You shot that fire mage dead, and you probably saved many people from burning to death."

She gave a nod. "You're right."

"Jon?" Michael waited for me to agree.

I was still hesitant, however.

"Valinox carried someone into your room and tried to suffocate you so you couldn't scream for help," Michael argued. "And you're a damn healer, Jon. They must know how many lives you could save, not just of those who fight, but of everyone in Dorrinthal. And they *still* want you dead. It's time to let go of your hesitance, don't you think?"

"I don't have hesitance. I just can't be enthusiastic about something that bothers me. It's like asking you to be enthusiastic about the cold."

"I would be if warmth was trying to kill me!" he said with a bit of a laugh.

It prompted me to chuckle as well. "I know you have

a good point, so I'll try."

"Jon," spoke a familiar voice behind me. "Can I have a quick word?"

I turned to see the princess standing in the entrance room of the great hall. There were a couple of guards behind her, as there always were these days.

"Sure," I said as Hadley and Michael left us.

Callie Lennox had turned fifteen recently. Her birthday reminded me that I had one coming up soon as well. I would be nineteen. I would think this age difference between us would mean something to her father, the king, but I was starting to get the idea that he might one day compel me to marry his daughter. I didn't know why else he would give me an emerald bracelet and tell me to gift it to her on her birthday, claiming it was from me.

Kataleya had warned me this might be the case. She had told me I should make a decision between Callie and Hadley before I hurt someone. Somehow, Kataleya knew my feelings for Hadley without me sharing them with anyone. It might've had something to do with how difficult it was to keep my feelings out of my expressions, or perhaps it had more to do with the fact that Hadley was just that beautiful.

"We'll just be a moment," Callie told her guards as she had me follow her out into the courtyard. From the tone of her voice, it sounded like something was wrong.

We stopped near the well, out of earshot of the castle workers using the courtyard to go between buildings within the castle grounds.

"I heard what happened last night," Callie said with a touch to my arm. "Are you all right?"

"Yeah, thanks to the other sorcerers. Did your

father talk to you this morning?"

"He did, but not about you." She looked toward the keep. "I have to keep this brief. He mentioned Trevor Chespar to me in a way that makes me think he's considering sending me off to marry this man I haven't ever met."

"What did he say?"

"He said, 'What do you think about the Chespars, Callie, especially their firstborn, Trevor?' "

"Oh." That sounded pretty clear to me. I felt bad for Callie, seeing how worried she looked, but I was a little relieved. Kataleya had said that the king was most likely considering Trevor as a potential husband for his daughter. Kataleya's family, the Yorns, have been working with the Chespars for a while now.

I didn't know exactly what it meant for noble families to be working together, but I was aware that these days they were training an army that was supposed to assist the king in this war. Kataleya expressed fears to me that her father might've been considering using these armed forces to lead a revolt against the king and take the crown for himself. He was murdered by his cousin before any of that could happen, but the noble family of the Chespars remained intact and was possibly even more of a threat to the crown now that Kataleya's father was gone. Therefore, a marriage joining the king's family to the Chespars could prevent a revolt.

I, however, still had trouble believing the Chespars would revolt anytime soon. The odds of us beating Rohaer in this war were substantially unfavorable. If there was going to be a revolt, it would have to be after the dust settled from this war, otherwise the Chespars would be decimated by Rohaer.

"My father told me earlier that I could marry whomever I wanted," Callie continued. "I asked him if this was still the case. He said he would like me to choose someone beneficial to our family, and soon. He recommended considering Trevor Chespar."

"You might want to talk to Kataleya," I suggested. "I don't know Trevor, but she does."

She shook her head. "That's not...no. What I wanted to ask was if my father mentioned anything about this to you. I know you two talk. I thought, perhaps, he might've suggested other options for marriage that he's keeping from me." She had a hinting tone.

I didn't have a way with words as so many of my friends did, notably Kataleya, Hadley, and even Michael. So I had absolutely no idea how to go about addressing this issue.

The way her gaze always seemed intent on my eyes was no different now compared to when I usually spoke with her. She was not a shy girl but confident and outspoken.

Callie's father had talked to me about Trevor, and so had Kataleya. But wasn't Callie asking if I might be a candidate for marriage?

"I don't think I can help you. He didn't mention anything to me about you or marriage," I was glad to tell her truthfully.

She studied me for a moment, possibly determining my honesty. Then she seemed disappointed as she looked down for a breath.

"I don't want to marry Trevor." Her head popped up again as she showed me a frown.

I understood that notion very well, as I would hate

to be forced into a marriage also. I wondered if she could read this from the look I gave her.

"I'm sorry I can't do more to help," I said.

She seemed to notice something behind me and quickly told me, "Maybe you can, if you suggest someone more suited for me."

"Callie," the king intoned as I heard him walking up. "I'd like to speak to Jon."

"Yes, Father. I will be in the dining hall with Mother." She shot me a pointed look before scurrying off, as if reminding me to heed her words. I wasn't prepared to help her with this issue, though, and I imagined I wouldn't be any time in the near future.

The king was quite tall, standing about an inch above me. There was concern in his eyes as he spoke. "I was awakened with the news of what happened last night. However, I didn't come to see you right away because I knew you would be safe sleeping in Michael's room and we could speak in the morning. I hope you understand."

"I do, sire."

"Destroying the gem that allows Valinox to remain invisible is our highest priority right now. I want you to know that. Your safety is just as important to me as my family's. I'm not going to let anything happen to you."

Again, I found myself wondering if there was more to his words. "I appreciate that. What's the plan, sire?"

He gave a sigh. "I need to speak with Souriff again. There's little we can do without her help, but she has refused to take a callring with her because she thinks it brings her shame to be called upon by mortals, so I must wait until she visits. In the meantime, you and Eden are Valinox's most bothersome targets. Neither of you should ever be alone. You should always have enough help around to face Valinox and another invisible sorcerer if he returns with one. Do you believe that you and Michael could manage this at night, or shall I have a guard sleeping in the same room as the two of you?"

"We should be fine so long as Aliana is close enough to sense Valinox and his sorcerer once their cloaking spell comes to an end."

"That was the other matter I wanted to address. She told me that you asked, last night, if she sensed anyone in your room, and she did not. It was soon after that she did sense someone. Is that when the cloaking spell came to an end?"

"Yes."

"So the invisibility spell must not only work on our eyes but our mana as well. Aliana also mentioned that she only sensed one other person with you, even though Valinox and his sorcerer made three." There seemed to be a question to his tone.

"Valinox has a natural resistance that makes it impossible, or perhaps just difficult, for Aliana to sense him even when the cloaking spell is not active. The same thing happened when she tried to sense Eslenda when we first saw the elf in the forest. Aliana's spell didn't work."

I wondered what had happened to Eslenda. She had returned to the castle with us after the battle but had left the next morning. I hoped she and the king had contact, but his majesty was in contact with many people I wasn't aware of. It wasn't my job to know of everything, and I was thankful for that. I had enough going on without keeping track of all of our possible allies.

"So it does seem crucial for Aliana to be nearby," the

king said. "Your window will be repaired before nightfall. You and Michael will share your room from now on, while Aliana and Eden will share Aliana's room next to yours. That is how it must be until we find a way to counter the permanent illusion. I'm also providing bells in each of your rooms. They are to be wrung loudly if Valinox comes back. Lastly, I'm putting a couple of armed guards in the hall outside your rooms. If it's deemed necessary that they guard you through the night in your room, I will arrange that, but I believe now it will just make it more difficult for you to sleep."

I agreed; I didn't like the idea of someone watching me while I slept. "Thank you, sire, but what about you?" I had to assume Nykal was as much of a target as I was.

"A sorcerer will be here today, a fire mage who won't leave my side."

"Are you sure he or she can be trusted?"

"I will earn his trust, as I have yours and everyone else's. But in the meantime, I will have his loyalty through an oath."

"Is he coming from the army of the Chespars?" I asked.

The king didn't look too pleased by my question. "Kataleya has been speaking with you, I see."

"She shared her concerns about her father and was looking for advice."

"I'm already taking care of it. Your added worries couldn't possibly help at this point. I want you thinking more about yourself from now on."

I decided to trust him in that regard. Besides, he already had Kataleya looking out for him. She was better than I was at knowing what to do in these political affairs.

"Then in regard to myself, sire, a few of us would like to visit Curdith Forest today."

"Jennava will be in charge of your training regimen from now on, so it is up to her. Leon will focus on combat while he is further trained on battle tactics. He seems to have a knack for it, from what I've heard, but he'll need to be an expert."

I had heard from my peers that Leon was not only an unstoppable force on the battlefield, but he seemed to have eyes in the back of his head. I hadn't spent much time fighting near him, but the others had. They all had experiences to share of Leon helping them, possibly even saving their lives.

"Have breakfast and inform the others of their new sleeping arrangements," the king told me. "When I have figured out what to do about Valinox, you will be among the first to find out."

I gave a quick bow and then headed into the dining hall.

I was the last one to join the table of the other sorcerers—my peers. There was too much chatter for my ears to pick out anything specific. I noticed Eden at the far end, her head down as she ate. I let my gaze linger to see if she might look up and give me some kind of clue as to what was going to happen in her room after breakfast, but it seemed clear to me that she didn't want to address it.

I took the open bench next to Michael on the other side of the group from Eden. Charlie still hadn't returned from Koluk. I was hoping he would soon, and with armor for us. Someone had taken my measurements the last time I had spoken to the king, before today. I already had a new sword made out of Valaer steel. I looked forward to the armor the king had promised me as well.

Then again, did he expect me to wear the armor throughout the day, up until the last moments before I got into bed? That sounded terribly uncomfortable, and I wasn't sure it would even help. Had I been wearing a helmet when Valinox surprised me, he or his dteria sorcerer would've suffocated me just the same as if I didn't have one. The armor wasn't going to save me from a surprise attack, but it should help in battle so long as it wasn't too cumbersome.

I didn't fear battle. I trusted myself as I did Leon and most of my peers. I did fear, however, something happening to one of my friends and me being too late to heal them.

I had no idea what our next task would be for the king. Rohaer was hundreds of miles away. It would take them a while to get here, but I figured the king would do a lot more than order his army to be trained as we waited for them to arrive.

I noticed Hadley's eyes on me, a questioning expression on her face. She sat across from me, next to Remi.

"The king's fine with it so long as Jennava is," I told her.

"Then I'll ask her." Hadley got up and walked over to the other table, where Jennava and Leon ate separately from everyone else.

"Ask her what?" Reuben wondered. He was on the other side of Michael.

"Do you want to go to the forest and help us hunt? Hadley needs ingredients, and we figured you do too."

"Why not Aliana?" he asked.

I noticed the ranger looking up at the sound of her

name. She sat across from Eden on the other side of the table, Kataleya beside her.

"It's fine if you don't want to come," I told Reuben.

"What's going on?" Aliana asked.

Everyone quieted.

Remi spoke. "Hadley and I are going into the forest with Jon. Reuben, we thought you might want to practice your tracking skill there where it's most likely to improve. There's no better place than the forest."

"What about Valinox?" Reuben asked.

"That's why Jon and I are going," the fire mage answered him.

"What will the rest of us be doing?" Aliana asked. I was a little surprised that she'd asked me.

"I don't know," I said.

"You don't know or you don't want to share?" Reuben asked.

Now everyone stared at me. They seemed to assume that I knew more than they did, and perhaps that was usually right. The king did speak to me more often than he did the other sorcerers. My friends probably didn't know that he often didn't share much with me, though. Usually the only thing I found out was something they would learn a moment later, after the king was done discussing it with me.

"I don't know anything about what we're doing today, but the king did tell me that some of us are going to have different sleeping arrangements." I looked at Michael. "We'll be sharing my room." Then I glanced across the table. "Aliana, Eden will be staying with you. That way you can sense if Valinox brings another sorcerer into either of our rooms. The king says he's also going to have a couple of armored guards in the hall."

Aliana had a sideways look at Eden, who barely lifted her gaze from her plate. She seemed embarrassed as she met Aliana's gaze, looking away quickly.

"I'm sorry you have to share a room with me," Eden muttered.

"It's fine," Aliana said, and sounded like she meant it.

It was Michael who seemed the most displeased by the news, as he glowered at me. "How long are we expected to be sharing your bed?"

The beds were gigantic. It was almost like no one else was there, with Michael and me on either end last night. "You can sleep on the floor if you don't like it," I jested.

"Pffft."

Hadley returned, and Jennava was with her.

"Reuben, we need to know something." Jennava spoke somewhat sternly, considering she usually had quite a friendly demeanor. "If our sorcerers go with you into the forest without Aliana, will you be able to track anything for Hadley to shoot?"

"I can, but I still don't understand why Aliana doesn't go with us."

"Because this is your chance to improve," Jennava answered. "You spend most of your time working on enchanting and practicing your swordsmanship."

"I practice my spell of earth as well," Reuben said with a bit of an attitude. "I don't need extra time in the forest. You should just take Aliana."

"I'd like to go," Aliana chimed in.

"You can, Aliana," Jennava said. "But Reuben, I'm trying to understand where your skill level is at. We need to know going forward."

He raised his voice. "I'm never going to be as good a ranger as Aliana. Is that what you want to hear? I'm never going to be as good of an enchanter as Eden, either. And I'm never going to be as good a swordsman as Jon, all right! Now will you leave it alone?"

A tense silence passed.

"The hell are you complaining about?" Leon shouted as he got up from his table and marched over. "I've seen you stand against Rohaer's best and come out without a scratch on you. You compare yourself to Aliana, but she tracks like her skill was bestowed from Basael himself. Then you compare yourself to Eden, and she's been enchanting for years before you could even reach the notes of ordia. Then you compare yourself to Jon!" Leon laughed snidely. "Jon was born in Bhode with nothing to do but swordfight with his father, one of the best swordsmen in Lycast. Of course you're not going to be better than these three people at what *they're* best at, but you're the only one of the group who can do all three. So I ask you again. What the hell are you complaining about? Take this chance to improve one of your three skills and stop being such a daisy about it."

Reuben had a quiet voice as he replied. "I just don't see the point in learning to track with Aliana here."

"Have you ever thought that you and Aliana might not always be next to each other as this war presses on? Hmm? Have you ever thought that having two trackers might be extremely valuable to all of us?"

Reuben didn't reply as he looked down. It seemed pretty clear to me that Reuben just wanted to be the best at something. The rest of us were, mostly because we didn't have overlapping skills like Reuben did. The king had probably arranged that purposefully, recruiting each of us not so much because we were all incredibly talented right away but because we were different from each other. We filled a role.

Michael was the only wind mage, Kataleya the only water mage, and Remi the only fire mage. The three of them specialized in erto, though Kataleya and I had both learned a simple fire spell since we'd come here. Considering how often we burned ourselves, I didn't think we'd ever have as much control over fire as Remi did.

Charlie was the only metal mage, which meant he specialized in the single note of mtalia. Similar to Charlie, Aliana couldn't reach any other notes besides her specialty, llB, which was earth.

Eden had specialized in ordia long before coming to the castle, with a focus on enchanting. Thinking of that reminded me that Reuben, on the day we all first met, had announced that he would also specialize in ordia but wanted to be a harbinger, like Barrett—the king's councilman. Reuben wanted to create magical contracts like the ones we signed when we took an oath to protect the king. I hadn't heard anything about his progress. Perhaps he had given it up for now, because Barrett already filled that role and we didn't need two harbingers.

The more I thought about this, the more I realized that Reuben had probably struggled with figuring out his identity. It must be clear to him that he was recruited mostly because his family was rich. I imagined this had been getting to him more and more as he had expected to show improvement more than the rest of us, when really his skills with sorcery hadn't seemed to change all that much since he'd come here.

"I'll go to the forest," he mumbled. "But don't expect tracking like Aliana's. My range is short."

"That's fine," Hadley said. "I can't curse the animals from very far anyway."

I could see by everyone's expression—except Eden's—that I wasn't the only one who was confused by Hadley's statement.

"You don't need their hair or blood to curse them?" I asked.

"Always I do, but in this case the hair is on the target still, not in my hand. I can use and dissolve the hair with my curse without actually holding it. It's because of this that witches are prone to accidents when they are first learning the craft, often cursing ourselves. I used to do it all the time."

We all looked at Eden. She had cursed herself with the same curse that she had performed on Aliana. After, both of them had verbally attacked Kataleya. I never heard Eden give an explanation about this, but that didn't mean she had kept it from her closer friends. I had always figured Valinox had wanted her to practice cursing, and Eden had told Kataleya and Aliana the specifics of the demigod's request. I had also hoped she had apologized to them personally.

Kataleya, as if sensing our thoughts, said, "Eden already apologized."

"Profusely," Aliana added.

Eden blushed. She seemed to be having trouble meeting all of our gazes.

"Oh, I didn't know the same had happened to Eden," Hadley said.

Wanting to change the subject, I asked, "So you can curse anyone without taking one of their hairs or some of their blood?"

"I can, but the curse is weaker the farther I am away," Hadley replied. "That doesn't matter much when I'm cursing small animals. I can cause them to be drowsy or have a false sense of security from up to fifty yards away."

"Oh shit." Michael spoke with dread. "What can you do to people, then?"

It sounded like he had something in mind. When he noticed many of us staring at him he spoke defensively.

"Whatever she can do, Valinox can do worse. It's good to know."

"He's got a point," Leon said. "Maybe the next time Valinox strikes, it will be through a curse."

"There isn't much that curses can't do," Hadley said. "But certain curses are stronger than others. I wouldn't worry too much about Valinox using a curse as a means of an attack, though. He would have to have the target's hair or blood in hand to perform a curse as debilitating as knocking them unconscious. Blood is always stronger. Without either, he might just be able to harmlessly sway your mood."

I noticed many gazes on me after her comment.

Leon asked me, "Is there any chance he got some of your blood?"

"No. He was too busy fighting, then running."

"But none of it ended up on him?" Leon pressed.

I tried to think back to how much blood I had spilled when he had run his blade down my spine. I was too busy trying to catch my breath after he cracked my ribs to really tell.

"I'm not sure," I answered.

"It shouldn't matter," Hadley said. "Even when Jon

fought Gourfist and got a whole lot of Gourfist's blood on his clothes, I was only able to squeeze out enough for one spell. So it's unlikely that Valinox was able to collect enough of Jon's blood."

Michael chuckled. "Is that all you were able to squeeze out of Jon?"

"Shut up," Leon said with a smack to Michael's chest. "This situation is shit," he complained. "We hardly know what we're going to be fighting against. How many witches do you think they have, Hadley?"

"The king of Rohaer had several lesser witches when I left two years ago, but they didn't have the gift like I do. They could still be too weak to pose a threat to us."

"What about other kinds of mages?" Leon asked. "Fire, wind, water, and what about rangers and metal mages?"

"I'm afraid I can't help you. I wasn't privy to the kind of information."

Leon drew a long breath. He took a quick glance around. There was no one near our section of the table. "Then we have to hope the king's spy gets back to us."

"He has a spy?" Michael asked cheerfully.

"He does. A man in the army who is loyal to us, I think. I've never met him."

"Finally, some good news," Michael said.

"If all of you are done eating," Jennava said, "we should be leaving soon. There's time for chatting on the way to the forest."

"Your instructor's right," Leon said. "No time to waste."

It sounded like he was perfectly fine with the new arrangements.

"Unless any of you have pressing business to attend to," Jennava said, "then you're all to spend the day in the forest. It's unlikely we're going to have much time to train before the king sends us off. We have to make the most of today."

"Where are we going?" I asked.

"Nobody knows yet, but I'm sure you'll all be needed."

I caught Eden's gaze. I was about to nod to tell her that I remembered her note, but she looked away as if wanting to avoid the issue completely.

CHAPTER TWO

Most everyone returned to the apartments, as was common after breakfast. I would take my sword made out of Valaer steel, but I had no armor yet. With Remi and Hadley there, I felt I would probably be safe. With more of us around, we would be even safer.

I had looked forward to training today. My power with dvinia had surprised me recently. I was beginning to wonder if I could do more than just lift myself into the air. Perhaps I could start attempting to fly today. I figured learning to do so would be a slow and painful process. It was better to start sooner rather than later.

It would be good to know if the dark mages in Rohaer could lift themselves, or if they chose not to train this ability at all. It was no wonder that the dark mages in Lycast had practically been able to fly. They'd had Cason around to heal their injuries, a necessity to improving such a skill. But there had been no news of a healer in Rohaer, which may have made it too difficult for dark mages there to train this skill. Otherwise, many of them would be taken out of the fight with broken bones. This was why Cason was so valued by Valinox, and why Valinox had gone to such great lengths to protect him.

The door to Eden's room was closed when I arrived. I knocked on it. "It's Jon," I said.

She opened the door. It might've been the first time

in a while that Eden stared right at me. She looked different, mostly because of her hair. She usually wore it in a stylish fashion, her dark brown locks combed over to fall loosely down one side of her head, some often resting on the front of her shoulder. But now it was messy and shorter than I remembered. I didn't know when she had cut it, but it had to be recently.

She had large, beautiful eyes of hazel, and thick eyelashes, dark. However, the whites of her eyes were bloodshot near the corners. She had always appeared delicate, but now she seemed tough, angry. These moods didn't seem to sit right on her face.

"I changed my mind. Go away," she said, using a tone as if I was nothing but a bother.

She started to close the door, but I put my foot in front of it. It banged loudly against my boot.

"What are you doing?" she complained loudly.

I figured many of my peers, who had gone to their rooms to pack for the forest, had heard both the door striking my boot and Eden's following question. I knew this might not look good for me in their eyes, but seeing Eden this way made me realize why she had come to me in the first place. She needed my help. I wasn't going to leave.

I pushed past Eden, shoving her out of the way in the process, and shut the door behind us, mostly to give her privacy. I had a feeling she was going to need it.

"Get out of my room, Jon," she said as she balled her fists.

"Where is the Induct stone?" I asked. In the note, she had told me to take it from her. It must be infused with dteria and altering her mind.

"Get out!" she yelled.

"I'm not leaving until I have it."

There was a gentle knock on the door. "Is everything all right?" Aliana asked from the other side.

I quickly locked the door just as I heard her turning the doorknob. "We're fine," I said. "Eden just needs help with something."

"I do not," she countered as she started for the door.

With my outstretched arm, I barred her from accessing it. She tried to get around me, but she was much smaller. I didn't even need the use of my other hand as she started to struggle to get past me.

"Eden," I whispered. "I know why you came to me. You're losing this fight against dteria. You need someone to take the Induct stone you mentioned. I'm now certain that it holds dteria just like a moonstone, only it's probably stronger. Make this easier on both of us and get it for me."

"I changed my mind, all right, Jon? It happens sometimes," she said snidely. "Maybe you're too stupid to know that."

"I'm not leaving," I told her forcefully. "Not without the Induct stone."

My instincts took over as she swung at me, and I blocked her thin arm by holding mine up. She tried to strike me with her other hand, but I grabbed her wrist. She was very easy to detain.

"I can do this all day," I said.

"Let go of me!" she yelled.

"Jon, what are you doing to her?" Aliana asked. She tried the doorknob again.

Then I heard other voices muttering in the hall.

"This is looking bad for both of us," I told Eden quietly. "Just tell me where the Induct stone is and we can end this."

"You're a bastard," she seethed. "You're not getting my stone. You just want it for yourself."

"Are you even hearing yourself? Hell, Eden, I thought you were better at resisting dteria than this. You're worse than a drunk being thrown out of a tavern."

"I'm fine unless someone is trying to take my stone like you are!"

"Jon?" Michael asked with too hard knocks on the door. "Let us in."

"I *can* let them in," I told Eden. "But then everyone is going to see you like this. I know you were trying to avoid that by coming to me. You knew I would do the right thing, no matter how difficult you made it. But I can let them in," I repeated. "I can let everyone see you like this. No one's going to trust you for a long time if they do, and you know that. You don't want that."

"Just get out of here," she said through gritted teeth.

"You have another choice. You can keep your voice down and tell me where the Induct stone is, and we can talk our way out of this after."

She thrashed against my hold of her wrists. "Tell them whatever you want. I'm not giving it to you. Let me go!"

"I'm not leaving until I have it!" I said, frustration getting the better of me.

"Then I'll make you leave!" She squirmed violently and got a hand free, then she aimed it and hit me with a strong spell of dteria.

It surprised me too much for me to be ready; I couldn't believe she would cast at me—indoors, nonetheless! I was thrown back and hit the door. Eden ran toward me, her gaze on the lock. I found the four familiar notes of dvinia, readied a fifth note of G, and targeted Eden. My mana wrapped around her waist. Then I forced it up into the air with the power of my mind.

She came up off the floor, her feet flailing. She aimed her hand at me again and struck me with dteria once more, knocking me into the door. I heard a small commotion outside, but I couldn't pay much attention as I focused. Using my mana, I tossed Eden onto her bed and morphed the dvinia to pin her against the mattress.

"Eden, calm down!"

"Fuck you!"

*****

The sorcery wrestling match went on for a few long minutes, but I had her overpowered the entire time. It was a terrible feeling to fight against one of my peers, but Eden made no attempts to curb her aggression until she was too exhausted to continue. I had held her against her own bed for the better part of it, though my mana had slipped off during one of her forceful blasts of dteria that had struck me in the stomach.

She finally seemed to have given up, both of us sweaty and drawing quick breaths. I didn't hear much from my friends outside anymore. I hoped that Michael, who had seen the note, might've pieced together what was actually happening here and explained it to the rest of them.

Eden lay on her bed as I stumbled around her room, trying to feel for dteria. Eventually, I realized there was probably a reason I hadn't felt it yet. It was sealed away where the mana would be kept out of the air. I went to her wooden chest near her desk and tried to open it, but it was locked.

Still exhausted, I went over to where Eden lay in a ball on her bed. "Where's the key?" I asked.

"Fuck off," she grumbled between gasps for breath.

I started patting down the pockets of her pants and soon found something inside. She tried to grab my hand as I reached into her pocket, but I pinned her arms back with my other hand and retrieved the key.

She must've regained some strength, because the next thing I knew, she was jumping on my back as I was walking away from her bed.

"You can't have it!" she shouted as she wrapped her arm around my neck.

It squeezed a choking sound out of my throat before she sealed off my air completely. Would she actually choke me to death if she could?

I was sick of this...and I knew I could heal her later.

I flipped her over me, slamming her back onto the floor with nearly all my strength.

I think the only reason she didn't scream in pain was because she was just too exhausted. She did groan and squirm, though, tears falling from her eyes. I felt pity for Eden, for so many reasons.

I unlocked her wooden chest and was taken aback by an offensive magical odor. The dteria was a pungent stench to my mana, eliciting a similar reaction in my body as if I was hit by a pungent odor of rotting meat. I had grown to be more disgusted by dteria as my sensitivity to mana had increased. Eden should not have kept an Induct stone in her possession for so long.

I didn't even want to touch it, but she had told me to bring it to Barrett. I had come this far, and I wasn't going to give up now.

"My fucking tailbone," she grumbled as she cried. "I think you broke it."

"I would heal you now," I told Eden as I stepped around her writhing body. "But then you'd make it nearly impossible for me to get this to Barrett. I'll heal you when I come back."

I did not look forward to seeing my friends as I unlocked the door and opened it. Michael and Aliana were the closest to the door, though everyone else stood nearby. I knew what they saw didn't look good for me. Eden and I were both drenched in sweat. Her room was in disarray, especially the covers of her bed. She lay near it on the floor, twisting in obvious pain.

I held up the black stone. "I have to get this to Barrett. I'll be back to heal Eden after."

Fortunately, my peers seemed to understand. They parted for me as a few of them nodded.

I hurried to the keep. Once I was inside, I was tempted to lift myself up the floors rather than run up the stairs, but I didn't trust my spell to hold me while I carried this Induct stone of dteria. It pulled my mana down to lower frequencies.

I was glad to find that Barrett wasn't meeting with the king but was in his own study on the second floor of the keep. He was guarded just like the king and the king's family, with two armored men outside his door. They let me pass without delay.

Still catching my breath, I set the Induct stone on his desk and stepped back.

"Why are you delivering this and not Eden?" Barrett asked.

"Can you do something about it so I can focus?" I

requested.

He moved his palm over the black stone and closed his eyes. I hadn't really looked at his face until now. There was a bruise on his cheek as if he'd been punched.

Barrett made a grabbing motion. The stone lost its black color as I felt dense dteria in the air. I made a wide wall of dvinia and moved it across the room from the desk toward the door, careful not to bump into anything. It wasn't long after that the feeling of dteria went away.

"Eden needed my help," I said, answering his earlier question.

"That is disappointing."

"Why? Better yet, why didn't someone help her sooner?"

"Jennava tried to get her to disenchant this Induct stone yesterday, but she couldn't convince Eden to do it. Then Jennava and Leon tried together, and still Eden refused. Eventually, they brought me with them to disenchant the gem against Eden's will, and that's how I got this." He pointed at the bruise on his cheek.

"Would you like me to heal it for you?"

"Yes."

I moved around his desk. "Why didn't you call for me?"

"It wasn't a priority until recently."

Wasn't a priority? What did that say about what they thought of Eden?

I reached up and put my hand over his cheek. It just took a moment to heal his bruise, Barrett wincing until I was done.

"By the looks of you," he said, "I'm sure it took considerable force for you to get this from Eden."

I didn't answer, as I was starting to get the feeling that he and our instructors were quickly losing hope in Eden. "She came to me for help this morning, and she's going to be a lot better now that this cursed stone is no longer in her possession."

"It wasn't cursed but enchanted, and I'm going to leave it up to Eden to enchant it again, this time for you."

"Enchant it with what?" I had been told that there was no way to create an essence of dvinia, which was the only school of magic I would be using for a while.

He held up the stone. It was no longer black but translucent. "I can feel that this Induct stone is a lot like a moonstone in that it can hold a spell. However, the limitations of this Induct stone feel different than a moonstone. I'm almost certain that it can hold a spell of dvinia." He handed it to me. "Take it to Eden to be primed. If she refuses, then bring it up with Jennava or Leon."

An essence of dvinia seemed too good to be true, but Barrett seemed certain.

"Go on, now," the councilman said. "The others must be waiting for you before they leave for the forest."

I had other questions, though. "Wait a minute. I've never even heard of an Induct stone before. Do you know how Eden got it?"

"I had never seen one before now. Eden informed us that there are many of them near the center of Curdith Forest. We believe it was created when something came from the stars and struck the forest, which caused the Day of Death."

"So she picked this up from the ground when Valinox brought her there to open the portal to Fyrren?"

"Yes. He turned one into an essence of dteria for her to hold onto so the creatures wouldn't attack her. There's something about the powerful scent of dteria that turns them into friends, most likely Airinold's doing and a discussion for another time. Valinox took the stone away from Eden later, but she found another and turned it into a second essence of dteria."

Now I remembered her talking about using an essence of dteria to get through the forest to reach us in time for the battle, but she hadn't mentioned anything about an Induct stone. I wondered if even then she didn't want to part with it.

I needed to know something else. "Are you suggesting that Eden is becoming corrupted?"

"She is, Jon. It's not a question but a fact. The only unknown that remains is if she can control herself and keep from continuing down this path. Eden might be your friend, but she has proven to be traitorous in the past. She might do so again. Jennava and Leon are keeping a close watch on her, as should you. If she becomes more dangerous, she will need to be removed."

"You mean put in the dungeons?"

"That is one option," he said in a dark tone.

I shuddered at the thought of them executing Eden.

"Does Eden know she is being watched this way?" I asked.

"That is something we have been struggling with, whether to tell her. For the safety of the rest of us, we, for now, will keep her uninformed." He tossed his hand. "It should be clear enough to her anyway that we know she is struggling with corruption. This is the punishment Leon issued her upon her re-acceptance. She is to learn how to use dteria without it controlling her. If she cannot do that, then we must protect everyone else. She will have to pull herself together or face the consequences."

I didn't know how to respond.

Barrett continued. "Leon and Jennava have both struggled with the corruption of dteria in the past and have told me they are confident they can get Eden through this difficult period, but it seems that Eden has reached out to you, at least in this one matter. She might do so again. Be careful, Jon. She might eventually give in completely and decide to take you out as a means of winning over Valinox as she had once before."

"She wouldn't do that."

He showed me a look as if I were a child who couldn't comprehend the complexity of the situation. "You don't know people who have gone down this path of dteria, but I do. In fact, Cason was one of them. He used to be a completely different young man before he started dabbling with dteria. It changed him just as it has changed thousands of others. Right now, Eden would not kill you, but that might change as well."

"Then why not make her give up dteria completely?" I questioned. "There's no reason she has to keep at it."

"Because our demands would do nothing. She has gone too far to give it up so suddenly. She needs to learn how to control it before she can stop casting, or it will permanently control her. There is a limit to the amount of dteria that every dark mage can be exposed to before they cross this threshold. Eden seemed to be well before the threshold before she came into contact with the powerful Induct stone, but now she's far past it. If she doesn't learn to control dteria like Jennava has, then she will become a danger to anyone who wants to stop her from using it."

"I'm not telling you to demand that she stop. I'm saying you can force her to stop by punishing her every time she casts. She wasn't this crazy until very recently. It can't take too long to correct."

Barrett studied me for a moment before replying. "We believe she can control it." He paused as if choosing his words carefully. "At the same time, her skill with dteria could prove extremely useful."

I was stunned. "So you're basically saying that if Eden stops using dteria you'll throw her out of the castle, but if she uses it too much and loses control, you'll kill her?"

"Killing her would be extreme, but if it's necessary then it must be done. None of us wants that, Jon, and we will do everything in our power to prevent it." Barrett sighed as he studied my reaction. I was certain I appeared angry. "She *agreed* to this punishment upon returning," he continued. "She almost killed Remi Ryler. You shouldn't soon forget that. You were punished for doing a lot less, don't you remember? You are all here in service to the king. You are to train and become as powerful as you can so that we can stand against Rohaer. I could go on, but that should be more than enough for you to see that you are in no position to change the king's mind."

So this was the king's decision, not Barrett's or anyone else's. "What if Eden refuses to use dteria any longer?" I asked.

"Then she will likely be replaced with another sorcerer who is more suited to provide us with what we need in the upcoming months."

I couldn't believe it. "Are you forgetting about her enchanting skill? Reuben just admitted this morning that he'll never be as good as she is."

"There is not enough time for her to learn any level three or higher enchanting skills, and we do not have the resources for her level one and two skills to make much of a difference."

I remembered Eden telling me, when she had increased the durability of my last sword, that enchantments could be measured in levels. She had performed a level one enchantment and had admitted that I probably wouldn't notice the difference after my sword was enchanted.

"But she will eventually be a powerful enchanter, most likely. That must mean something to the king," I argued.

"It is not a priority. The focus lies on winning this war. You must understand that by now, Jon. If the existence of another person decreases our chances of winning, then we must remove that person. I thought that was the whole reason behind all of your actions? You will always do what is in the best interests of the kingdom. Or is that just something you have claimed?"

"This is different. This is someone who's trying to do good."

"Do you know who else wanted to do good? He was a young sorcerer who Nykal looked after when no one else would."

"Cason," I grumbled.

"Nykal and I both tried to stop him from using dteria. We gave him many chances. He lied to us many times, or maybe he just lied to himself. It doesn't matter. What does is that we let it go on too long. He should've been stopped before he became so powerful. Many lives were lost recently because he wasn't. Your friend Calvin was one of them."

He paused as if to give me a chance to reply, but I was still trying to let go of my anger before I responded.

"I need to know you are with us on this," Barrett said, "in case Eden or Hadley become corrupted."

"Hadley?" I blurted in shock. "She has shown no signs of the dteria changing her. Curses are different. They don't require much force behind the spell, and it's the force—the amount—of dteria that makes the difference." I spoke confidently, but this was something I had only theorized in order to explain how Hadley seemed unaffected by the corruption.

"Yes, that is what we believe," I was glad to hear him say, "but the king and I have little experience with witches. You and the other sorcerers must keep an eye on both young women."

I shook my head. "Hadley's been using curses for years. Dteria would've changed her by now if it was going to."

"How can you be sure? Maybe it's just a slower process when using a small amount, as needed for cursing."

He had a point. I couldn't be sure given that logic, but I felt connected to Hadley in ways I couldn't quite explain. I knew and trusted her. She did not have a dark side within her.

At least he hadn't issued any kind of warning about my feelings getting in the way of good judgement. He and the king probably didn't know that I was interested in her.

"Take the Induct stone back to Eden," the councilman said. "Tell her to prime the stone so you can use it as an essence of dvinia. It's up to you and your instructors to be vigilant for now. Just remember that there have been many times throughout history when friendship has been beaten by dteria."

I felt like I was returning to a different world when I left the keep and headed back to the apartments. I had faced soldiers, mostly men, whose minds had been twisted from years of dteria use, but I had never gotten to know someone before they started using dteria and watched it change them. It was as disturbing as watching an illness slowly destroy a person's health, like what had happened to my father.

I was as certain as I could be that Hadley was not at all affected by corruption, but Eden…I still wasn't sure if she would get over this, even with our help.

Most of my peers were in the courtyard. They looked ready to go to the forest, all carrying a bag on their back. I assumed the wonderful castle staff had provided them with dried lunches and there was one waiting for me once I was ready to go.

Hopefully this won't take long.

Aliana was the only one remaining in Eden's room when I returned. Eden stood near her desk, a hand on the top of her chair for support. Her tunic was still wet with sweat, as was my thin shirt.

"Can I speak to Eden alone?" I asked Aliana.

She eyed the translucent stone in my hand for a moment before she walked past me. "We're waiting to go."

"I know," I said. "But it's important I do this now."

Aliana closed the door as she left. Eden, a hand on her lower back, looked sadder than anything else. It was as if she'd lost something important to her. I approached her.

"I'm going to heal you."

She didn't speak or acknowledge me. I put my hand over hers on her lower back. She snatched it out of the way.

I had done considerable damage to her by flipping her over me and slamming her into the floor. There were very few things as draining as casting my healing spell. It felt like I was carrying a heavy load while trying to run upstairs for each moment that the spell went on. Fortunately, I repaired the damage quickly. Eden, however, was not very tolerant of pain. She had jammed a book into her mouth and bit down to keep from screaming. There were teeth marks on it when I was done.

I pulled out the nearby chair from her desk. "Sit," I said.

She did, though she still wouldn't look at me.

I crouched in front of her. "Listen, Eden. What I'm about to tell you is very important."

"I don't care."

"What? How can you not?"

"Because I know what you're going to say. You're going to tell me that I have to stop letting dteria control me, but you don't know what it's like. It's impossible. I thought it would be easy, but that was before I came into possession of the Induct stone. Now it's too late to go back."

She still wouldn't look at me. A tear slid down her cheek.

"It's pointless, Jon. Just turn me over to the king before I hurt someone."

"I'm not going to do that. You're nowhere near as gone as others."

"I wasn't until recently. I'm telling you, there's no

point. I have to cast. It's like I'm dying of hunger and there's a delicious piece of food already at the back of my throat and I'm not supposed to swallow it. I try not to, but the feeling never goes away until I eventually do. There's always more hunger. It doesn't stop, no matter how long I go without casting."

"You remember that Leon and I faced Cason in the street not far from this castle?"

She nodded.

"Leon told Cason that he just needed to stop casting for a while and eventually his mind would return to how it was before it became affected by dteria. Leon wouldn't lie, especially not to Cason. There was no reason to then. And if that's true for Cason, then it should be even easier for you. I'm sure you're just not going long enough without casting. How long have you had that Induct stone nearby?"

"About a week. I didn't notice how much it was changing me until I started thinking about getting rid of it."

"Now it's gone, so you don't have to worry about that anymore. You have a whole group of people who want to help you through this. All you need to do is try your best."

"You don't know how hard it is. Even right now I want to throw you across the room." She formed a sick grin as she glanced up. Then she shook her head and appeared frustrated with herself. "I've already shamed myself in front of Jennava, Leon, and Barrett, and now you as well."

"What did you tell the other sorcerers after I left?" I asked.

"I didn't say much. I just told them you are helping

me and that everyone should stay away from me for now. I think some of the girls were upset I didn't go to them, but I knew they wouldn't have been able to take the Induct stone by force. I would've probably hurt them very badly if they had tried. Only you could do it."

"You should stop trying to hide this. Fight it openly like Leon did when he was using it to help us resist."

She showed me a look of betrayal. "You sound like them. You'd rather I lose myself to the dteria than give it up completely and become weak."

"No, I'd rather you give it up and become weak, but there's a problem with that. They will replace you with someone else because apparently your enchanting skill isn't enough of a priority. But if you think that's the only way to stop dteria from taking control of you, then we can help you do that. You just have to ask yourself what you think you can do. Remember, Eden, that you have Leon and Jennava—two people who have used dteria and learned to control it."

"I'm not giving up dteria. There's no way."

"Then you'd better learn to control it, or it's going to get you killed."

I was glad when I didn't see surprise register on her face. In fact, she nodded. "That's exactly why I gave you that note this morning. I knew they would have me executed, maybe soon, especially after I punched Barrett for trying to take the Induct stone away."

"That was quite a bruise you left on his face," I said as a joke to lighten the mood.

But her face twisted as she smiled. "It's what he gets," she said and jumped up from the chair. "I should've done worse to you for taking it away."

She picked me up with dteria as I rolled my eyes.

"Really?" I said.

She threw me across the room. I landed on my feet and slid to a stop. "Oh come on, Eden. This isn't amusing."

She picked me up again and threw me against the door. It hurt, but I refused to show any evidence of pain. She picked me up once more. I put my hands over my hips, on top of the cushiony energy wrapped around my waist.

"What is the point of this?" I asked.

"Shut up!" She threw me against the door again. Her face showed rage as she pulled her hand through the air, dragging me across her room toward her. I stumbled over with a lazy expression.

"You know I'll just heal any injury you cause me," I told her as I crossed by.

She seemed to put all of her strength into one last throw, picking me up high from the floor and tossing me sideways toward her hearth. I caught myself with dvinia and pushed the other way with my mind, stopping in the air and landing on my feet.

She showed exhaustion through heavy breaths as I walked back toward her. "Are you done?" I asked.

She looked like herself again, though defeated and embarrassed, as her arms hung loosely.

"They're waiting for us," I said as I picked up the Induct stone which had fallen to the floor. "Barrett said you could prime this for me. I don't know what that means, but I suggest you do it."

She took a moment to catch her breath, barely looking up at me. "You're not angry for what I just did?"

"No, just annoyed. I understand what you're going through. Everyone will, so stop fussing about it."

She showed a hint of a smile. "Maybe you're right." She reached out and took the Induct stone from me. Her expression changed again as she looked at the translucent stone.

"Eden," I warned. "Don't go backward."

"I don't think I can prime this for you without wanting to keep it for myself." She turned away as she handed it to me blindly. "Have Reuben do it. I bet he can by now."

"It's better that you do it, and that I tell Barrett and the others that you did."

She looked back at me from the sides of her eyes. "I can't."

That was the last thing I could handle. Apparently I had a threshold just like Eden did.

I grabbed her by her shoulders and gave her a shake. "Stop telling me you can't do something and do it! I know you can. Just prime the goddamn stone and let's get the hell out of here!"

"You don't understand," she mumbled to the floor.

"Of course I do. We all must do things we don't want. You'd better start taking responsibility for yourself and have some self-control, or this is going to end badly." I stepped back and snatched the stone out of her hand, gesturing at her with it. "I tried to be nice to you, but it's not getting us anywhere. This is going to be hard for a long time, but then it will get easier. You'd better get used to that right now and stop this attitude of giving up, or soon you'll find that everyone else will give up on you as well. Where is your fighting spirit?" I gave a harsh shove to her shoulder. "Fight this! Don't you think I would? Don't you think everyone else would? Why are you any different?" I shoved her again. "Fight it!"

She drew a sharp breath." You're right. Give me that." She took back the stone. She mumbled a few uncouth things directed at dteria as she seemed to have an internal battle, gritting her teeth and waving her hand over the stone. Then she pushed it back against my stomach. "Keep this fucking thing away from me now."

She collected a bag and hurried toward the door.

"Wait, no one told me what priming a stone means," I complained. "What do I do with it now?"

"Just push a dense cluster of dvinia against it until it can hold no more." She opened the door to leave.

I hurried after her. I still had to collect my pack from my room. "How do I know when it can hold no more?"

"With ordia, and you'd better not ask me to help you."

"How long will it take?" I stopped outside my room as she hurried down the hall.

"I don't know. Just shut up about it or I'm going to take it back from you." She spun around. "I'm serious, Jon. Keep that away from me until I have better control over dteria. That Induct stone is extremely powerful." I saw another change come over her as she looked down at it in my hands as if it was a meal she was craving. Her mouth twisted, and so did her body as she turned away from me and seemed to force her legs to move down the stairs.

I looked at the Induct stone again. I had done all of this just to help Eden, but now I couldn't help but imagine what I might be capable of with a stone like this in my possession.

CHAPTER THREE

All of us, except Leon, headed to the forest. I walked with Michael and Reuben, a little ways behind the larger group of girls ahead of us, with Jennava at the front. Michael asked me what happened, and I could hear the girls asking Eden the same thing.

"She's struggling with dteria, but she wanted to give me this." I showed them the Induct stone.

A few more questions led to me telling them everything I knew about Induct stones, which I admitted was not a lot, and how I was now supposed to infuse —I guessed that was the right word—this stone with dvinia.

"If it's anything like a moonstone," Reuben said, "it's not going to stay primed for long. You'd better start now before the opening to lock in a spell closes. It won't last for more than an hour."

I spent the rest of the long walk through the city and into the forest casting my spell of Grab and pushing the dvinia against the Induct stone. I heard bits and pieces of Michael and Reuben arguing about whether Michael's "tender care" would do anything to help Eden out of her dteria craze. I was just glad we could discuss it openly. Eden's chances of getting through it were much better this way than if she had to struggle in private.

I had never held any spell for an hour straight, but I was pleased with my ability to maintain it. There were two parts to spellcasting. The most difficult was forming the spell initially, splitting my mana into the five different notes required for the complicated spell. I had done it so many times by now, however, that it was like swinging a sword, second nature to me.

The second part was what really drained my mana —and my stamina—and that was maintaining the spell. I thought of casting as a lot like lifting something above my head and holding it there. The act of lifting it high up was much more complicated, but it wasn't as demanding as keeping it up. With my mana already split into the five different frequencies that it took to cast the spell, I just had to continue feeding more mana into the Grab spell to keep it together.

It begged the question: Was it possible to maintain two spells at once? I wondered this more as I maintained the Grab spell on the way to the forest.

By the time we made it to the edge of the woods, I felt that the Induct stone couldn't take anymore dvinia. It wasn't that it had absorbed everything I casted. On the contrary, only a small portion of mana was taken into the stone during each moment that I had kept the spell up. But my casting had gone on for so long that I knew that the stone now held onto a huge amount of mana that was already shaped into the spell of my wish. I could feel it the same way I could feel heat in the air.

"How is this supposed to help?" I asked, figuring Reuben might know. "If the dvinia is trapped in the stone, what could that do for me?"

"You're thinking about it the wrong way. Imagine your spell is opening a door. The essence is a key. It can get you through much easier."

I frowned. "It's already easy for me to cast my spell.

I thought this would give me more power."

"It also does that."

"But how?" I asked, though I didn't doubt him. I could already feel that the next time I casted my spell, it would be far more powerful than it had been before. I needed to understand why.

"It just does," Reuben said.

"You obviously don't know," Michael commented.

"Do *you*?" Reuben countered.

"Of course not, but I'm not pretending like I do."

It seemed that Kataleya heard us. She slowed and joined our group at the back. "There's a second part to essences that explains how the added power works," she explained. "There's mana all around us that normally we can't feel. The essence converts that mana to your own in the form of the locked spell."

It was like a light had gone on. "Oh, so that's why these essences can pull on the frequency of our natural mana, because this other form of mana is actually... meddling with ours?" I didn't know the right word, but I figured Kataleya did.

"It's more like two sounds mixing together. The new sound could distract you and make you lose focus of the one you're used to, and eventually you'll start noticing the new one just as much as the old."

That worried me. "Eden said this Induct stone is very powerful. Does that mean it could alter my natural mana?"

"Nothing can alter your mana that we know of, but it can distract you like I said. It can make you have a more difficult time using other frequencies, like the low notes necessary for ordia. However, I wouldn't worry. Enough time away from the essence should remove the distraction completely."

Michael asked, "What about this other mana that we can't feel?"

Kataleya raised an eyebrow. "What about it?"

"Why the hell can't we feel it if it's there?"

She formed a cunning smile. "Actually, that's quite interesting to consider, isn't it?"

Michael scratched his head. "I don't know, Kat. Why don't you tell me how interesting it is?"

"When all of us were younger, we couldn't feel our own mana. Now we can. I would think this implies that the same could happen to the mana around us. After enough time, or perhaps after we become more in touch with our mana, we might have access to a large amount of energy. Imagine how much more powerful it could make our spells."

"What about Leon?" I asked. "Or Eslenda. Maybe they already have access to this mana."

"It would explain why they are so much stronger than the rest of us," Kataleya agreed. She had clearly already thought of this.

"Speaking of," I said, "I still don't know what Jennava specializes in. I've never seen her cast."

"Because it's dteria," Kataleya said. "She doesn't want to use it unless absolutely necessary."

Oh. I wondered how strong she was with it.

Reuben asked, "There's nothing else she can cast?"

"I believe she has a wide range and can cast a number of erto spells, but she doesn't have a strong grasp on any of them."

"What about ice?" I asked. I had only met one ice mage, a vain woman who surprised me by actually putting herself at risk to fight back against Cason and the other dark mages who had attacked the castle. I wondered if I might see her again or meet the other sorcerers who used their casting to make a living. As of recently, I had felt like there were too few of us trying to make a difference in this war.

They won't join unless the king is offering to pay them handsomely. He hadn't in the past, because their services had been too expensive considering that most of us seemed to be better fighters than they were. Now that our enemies from Rohaer were coming, however, the king might be more desperate.

"I don't think Jennava can use ice," Kataleya said.

I had learned the spell Fire after a whole day of practicing nothing else. I could make flames at will, but I didn't have much control over them like I did with dvinia. I had only used the spell while traveling, to start my campfires, and once against Gourfist to set his feathers on fire. I knew I would be seeing the beast again before this was over, perhaps sooner rather than later.

The main spell of ice was lC, lE, lG. The lowercase "L" stood for "Lower" because these notes were lower in frequency than higher versions of the same notes.

Considering the lowest frequency I could reach was lC, I could potentially cast a spell of ice. I figured if I did take the day to learn the spell, I wouldn't be able to do much with it besides make a cluster of ice that I supposed I could propel at an enemy. That wouldn't do very much good, so I hadn't taken the time to practice.

The purpose of ice seemed to be more practical rather than a tactic used for combat. Seeing as how snow wasn't common here like it was in Bhode, I assumed ice mages did very well for themselves by offering their services of encasing perishable food in ice.

I was still interested in learning all the spells I could—ice, fire, water, and wind—but no spell in these schools compared to what I could potentially do with dvinia…and what I would attempt very soon.

I looked at the Induct stone in my hand. It was no longer translucent but white like snow. If Kataleya was correct, then this glorified essence would grant me additional mana that I normally wouldn't have access to.

To practice my new spell safely, I should be in the forest. That had to do with Valinox. If he was around, he was less likely to see me here among the greenery. But with all the tree branches and the canopy above, I was as impeded here as I was protected.

"Jon, you have that look again," Michael said with an uneasy tone.

"What look?"

"Like you're about to do something dangerous, and no one's going to be able to stop you."

"You're right." Sometimes I didn't like how well Michael seemed to know me. "Everyone, wait a moment," I announced. The group ahead of us turned around and allowed us to catch up.

"What is it?" Jennava asked.

"It's time I start practicing what I came here to do." I tried to keep a plain expression, but the thrill in my heart pulled up the corners of my mouth. "I'm going to try to stay in sight, but it won't be easy. Are all of you planning to continue southwest?"

Jennava frowned at me. "I was going to split the groups, Jon, to increase our ability to hunt and scavenge. I was going to put you in charge of one with Reuben, Hadley, and Eden. They might need your assistance."

"There isn't going to be a better time to fly."

Her frown deepened. "Why do you speak of flying like you are going to be soaring around like a bird?"

"Because that's exactly what I'm planning."

"It's too dangerous. You have to work your way up to that."

"I have been," I said. "I have been lifting myself and others for a long time now. I know I have it in me to fly. We all know the best place to learn something new is Curdith Forest because of the natural dvinia of the land. It empowers our mana."

"No one has confirmed that it is natural dvinia and not something else, but you are right that the forest is the best place to improve any skill." Jennava had her hands on her hips. She glanced around, then gave a resigned sigh. "Fine, I will keep you out of the groups and reorganize them so that they both have adequate protection. One will head south while the other heads west. Perhaps you can check on both of them so long as you don't hurt yourself. Always stay close enough where we can hear you and you can hear us."

"Got it." I took that as permission to leave. I didn't want to wait a moment longer.

Here near the outskirts of the forest, there was more room between the trees. There were even a few beaten paths. We weren't the only ones who went into the forest, given how close the capital was, though I didn't see anyone else in this moment.

With a clear route in front of me, I picked myself up with dvinia. It was easy, practiced, like lifting a heavy stone. I felt great power at my disposal with my new Induct stone, like I could throw myself as fast as I could loose an arrow from a bow.

I had always been careful in the past, usually lifting myself slowly. Not this time.

I threw myself up and outward with about half my strength. The forest blurred around me as wind took my breath away.

I felt my eyes open wide as I realized that I was going too fast. I cursed in fear as I tried to throw myself the other way with the dvinia still wrapped around my waist, but my momentum was too fast.

There was no hope to land on my feet as I slammed into the ground. Rolling across sticks and roots hurt like hell, but I was more worried about tears in my clothing. I tried to stop myself with my hands and feet, but it was no use. I could only curse my stupidity inwardly and wait until it was over.

My back struck a rock. I already had my healing spell ready. Nothing was broken. It wasn't too bad. I was back on my feet and completely better in a few moments. Then I checked my clothing.

"Dammit." There was a rip across the knee of my pants and dirt stains across other places.

"I'm all right," I called to everyone watching me. I was maybe fifty yards from them, too far to see their expressions. I imagined they were shocked and perhaps even worried by my violent spill.

Jennava yelled something that sounded like, "Be more careful!"

"I will!"

I turned the other way. This time I would toss myself far enough that, when I inevitably fell, they wouldn't see me embarrass myself.

I picked myself up again and threw myself forward. The incredible feeling of hurtling through the air pulled a happy shriek out of my throat. This time I was ready for the speed. I slowed myself quickly and pulled up with my dvinia as gravity threatened to take me to the ground.

I was still going faster than I could sprint when I landed, my leg struggling to keep up. But I held myself up with dvinia to ensure I wouldn't fall. A tree came at me fast. I tried to use my leg muscles to veer out of the way, but I stumbled and was about to dive headfirst into the trunk.

My quick reflexes kicked in as I lurched to the side using dvinia. Another tree! This time my shriek was not one of fun. I barely got my arms up before I struck the tree trunk.

I looked down to see cuts running along my arms and small holes in the sleeves of my shirt. But the worst was the sharp stinging across my forehead.

My clothes were always getting ruined. "Dammit!" I yelled.

I healed myself, wiped the flakes of bark off my face and arms, then turned to look behind me. I could faintly make out Michael running toward me.

"You good, Jon?" I heard him yell.

"Fine!" I yelled back. "Absolutely fine!"

He stopped there. He seemed to be watching me, no doubt worried.

I was beginning to wonder if maybe the forest was not the best place to practice after all, but I already felt much stronger. The Induct stone and the natural mana of the forest made me feel as though I could fly, really fly, like a bird.

Or like a demigod.

I knew I shouldn't stray too far from my group. I especially shouldn't leave the cover of the forest, but this feeling was overpowering. I already was figuring out the excuse I would tell them when I returned.

"Imagine you could fly," I would tell my friends. "Imagine you could soar, but the trees kept getting in your way. Could you really wait until tomorrow to try it?"

Sure, some of them would still disagree, and Jennava might scold me, but that was a problem for later.

I looked back at the group one last time, reminding myself which direction they would be walking deeper into the forest. I did plan to return to them soon. First, I had to try this with all of my ability, just once.

Maybe twice.

I took myself farther away with another toss of my body, which was beginning to feel rather light when I held it with dvinia. I didn't put as much force into the launch as before because I was sick of running into things.

I landed just fine this time. I turned right and headed north through the forest, picking myself up and giving my light self a good toss. I hurtled through the air and landed safely again, further getting used to the feeling. As I learned to control it, it felt almost like I was jumping fifty yards at a time. Each landing was easier than the last. I hardly even felt myself tiring. Soon I came to the spot I had planned to reach, the northern edge of the forest.

There was nothing but open land in front of me. I was completely free.

A moment of hesitation stopped me as I was about to fly. A tiny voice told me not to do this. A couple things could lead to my death here. Valinox could spot me if he was nearby, or I could hit my head on the way down and fall unconscious. None of my friends would know to look for me here. I should at least go back and tell Jennava I would be out here.

But then she would try to stop me. Besides, what could they do for such an injury even if they were around? And I should be able to flee from Valinox.

I was just going to try this twice. Maybe three times. I would be safe. The tiny voice that tried to stop me was the same one that tried to convince me not to leave Bhode and travel south after my father died. It was pure fear.

I don't have time to listen to fear.

But something else came to mind that made me hesitate, not fear but a real reason to wait. If I was really going to throw myself as high and far as I could, I had to squeeze the dvinia around my body even harder. Otherwise it would slip up from my waist when I threw it with my mind. It would then strike the underside of my arms probably with enough force to dislocate both my shoulders at the same time.

I didn't see how this was supposed to work, though. Could I ever hold myself tightly enough to use the full power of my mind? The force of my Grab spell was already tight and uncomfortable when hurling myself with half my mind's power.

I couldn't see any other way around it; I was going to have to change the way I held my body. This required widening the grip of dvinia so that it supported me from my hips nearly down to my knees.

I still wasn't used to the feeling of lifting myself with my mind. It made me feel young and light, like when I was a boy and my father would throw me into the air.

I smiled as I remembered him fondly.

For practice, I tossed myself using my new method. I flew up high enough to break a leg if I was to fall and then let my spell come apart naturally as I released my mind's hold. I trusted myself as I fell quickly, forming a wide blanket of dvinia like a sheet ready to catch my sitting form.

I pulled up on my spell as I hit it with my body, the dvinia slowing my fall until I was close enough to the ground to get my feet out underneath me.

It had been so easy that I was certain I could do it if I was falling at twice, even three times the speed.

I wrapped dvinia around my waist again. With the Induct stone resting in my pocket, I felt stronger than I ever had in my life.

It's time to fly.

I hurled myself as high and as far as I could.

I tried to gasp for breath, but I couldn't breathe. The feeling was too intense to even shriek. I wondered how fast I was going as the wind screeched in my ears.

Up and up I went, higher than I'd ever been before. I passed trees that looked like small bushes below me. I finally felt myself starting to slow and arc downward a bit, but I still had a good hold of the dvinia around my waist. I hurled myself forward again.

Breathless again, I wanted to scream but couldn't.

Eventually I started to slow once more. I was panting from the excitement. I hooted with glee.

I threw myself up and outward a third time, using all the force I could muster. The wind pulled at me so hard I was pretty sure I felt the tears in my clothing widening. It was difficult to keep my concentration as I yelped with joy. I didn't wait until I slowed, hurling myself a fourth time to see what speed I could reach.

It was easy to maintain altitude and speed without tiring. However, there did seem to be a limit as to how fast I could go, as I tried to throw myself in the direction I was already going a fifth time. I barely felt the difference, and by then, the sound of the wind was hurting my ears.

I still found it difficult to breathe, gasping here and there to make up for the breaths I couldn't take in, but soon I realized that drawing in air through my nose while relaxed and blowing it out through my mouth made the process simple.

I could maintain a very fast speed without much trouble. I just had to keep pulling myself up here and there with a few pushes forward in between.

I'm actually flying! I hadn't experienced anything like this in my life. Feeling weeps of joy bubbling up from my chest, I stopped propelling myself with my mind and let gravity take over.

I was already crying before I landed. This was going to change everything.

Perhaps I was vain, but the next thought that went through my mind was that I couldn't wait to show this off to my peers. I wiped my eyes and looked around.

"My god, I've gone far!" It had to be over a mile away from where I'd come out of the trees.

I didn't want to stop and go back into the forest because I couldn't fly like this with all the trees around me. I stood there, knowing I should head back but refusing to move.

I wanted to try other methods of flight. What if

I spread my arms and tilted my body horizontally to really feel like a bird? Perhaps I could go faster because the wind wouldn't whip against my entire body, but I didn't trust myself to take on a difficult and unpracticed maneuver like that without supervision. How else could I alter my flying skill to improve it? Maybe if I lay on a sheet of dvinia? No, it would be too easy to slip off.

Perhaps the first method was best. I couldn't think about it any longer without trying it again.

I felt fresh, like I had only taken a short jog. I could soar much farther before stopping next time, but which direction should I choose? I looked back at the forest again. I had already decided I wasn't going to return just yet. Where else could I go?

A great idea came to me.

CHAPTER FOUR

It didn't take too long before I returned to Curdith Forest. Here, I could no longer fly safely, with all the trees around, but I could still perform the fifty-yard jumps as I had on my way out of the forest. It didn't take more than a minute to find one group of my peers. I accidentally startled them as I landed loudly behind Michael, Reuben, and Hadley. They jumped as they shot alarmed looks over their shoulders.

"I'm sorry about that," I said as I quickly swung my backpack around and opened it up. "I have something for you, Michael." I handed him a biscuit from a bakery he'd mentioned a while ago. He'd said that the biscuits there were the one thing he would miss when we left Koluk. It was flaky and still warm.

"Uh, thanks?" he said as he took it with confusion and had a bite.

He must've thought that I had brought it with me. I stared at him and waited, a smirk growing on my mouth.

He seemed to realize something was amiss. He looked at the biscuit again.

"Wait, is this—?" But the sound of him choking interrupted his statement.

He coughed as he spat up the biscuit while I slapped him on the back a few times.

Reuben pointed at the biscuit in Michael's hand.

"Nox's blade, is that from that bakery in Koluk that Michael likes?"

"It is," I said.

"Seriously?" Michael asked, as Hadley gasped and covered her mouth.

"I'm serious."

"It's still warm!" He held it out for Reuben and Hadley as they poked it.

"By the devil's tail," Hadley said. "You just went all the way to Koluk and returned?"

"I sure did," I said with a proud smile. "How long was I gone?"

"Maybe thirty minutes?" Michael asked as he looked at the others.

"Well, I practiced for about five minutes before I started heading there."

"So twenty-five minutes?" Reuben said with wide eyes. "That's more than twenty miles from here, Jon!"

"And twenty miles back," I added.

"Good god!" Michael said. "Can you take me next time?"

We all chuckled.

"No, I'm serious," Michael said. "Can you take someone on your back?"

"Oh, um." I tried to imagine Michael on my back. He didn't look very light. He was somewhat tall, like me, with broad shoulders. He had a defined chest and toned arms from all of his sword practice.

"Get on and let's see," I said.

"Really?" I couldn't tell if he was excited or scared. He sounded to be both.

"I'll just take us a little bit into the air to see how it feels."

"Shouldn't you start with someone lighter?" Hadley offered. She was much shorter than Michael, thin as well.

"If we're volunteering, then I'd like to go too," Reuben said.

"Ladies first," I said as I stood in front of Hadley with my back ready.

"Here," she told Michael as she handed him her bow and quiver. Then she put her hands on my shoulders, but she didn't jump up. I looked back to see her with a fearful expression.

"We did see you fall a number of times, in dramatic fashion," she said as her hands slid off my shoulders. "And your clothes! Look at them. I hadn't really noticed until now."

"I stopped falling soon after I left the forest."

"But you haven't tried with anyone on your back yet," she said.

"If you don't want to go first, I will," Michael said.

"No, I should go first, being much lighter than you." She bent her knees as if to jump up, but she didn't. "You will be careful, Jon?"

"I will…at first," I mumbled after she hopped on my back.

"Jon!" she complained. "Be careful!"

"Hold on!"

I took off through the forest. Hadley gasped in my ear as she clutched me tightly. It was a tad more difficult to get us going, but I felt that I could still make it high into the air and even all the way to Koluk with her on my back, if I wanted.

I pushed us faster and higher, keeping my eyes out for branches.

"Watch out!" she yelled as I jolted out of the way of a tree then dipped down beneath a branch.

There was a small clearing in the canopy ahead. I flew almost straight up into the air to reach it.

"Too high! That's too high!"

"Just hold on!"

She screamed in my ear. "We're not going to make it through there!"

"We are. Just keep close to me."

She squeezed me tighter. I pushed us upward, up and up. The trees of Curdith Forest were very tall, but it didn't matter. We broke out from the forest through the gap in the canopy.

I finally stopped pushing and let us slowly come to a stop in the sky above the treetops. There I held us. I wouldn't be able to maintain this hold for long. It was easier to put my strength into tossing us in a direction and guiding us using momentum. I was waiting for Hadley to react, but she didn't say anything.

I looked back at her to find that she had closed her eyes, though she was beginning to squint one open.

She gasped and squeezed me, shutting her eyes again.

"It's okay," I said. "I won't drop us."

Slowly her eyes came open. "By the devil's tail," she whispered as I felt her hold relax somewhat. "This is something else, Jon. You are a marvel."

"I could take us a little farther if you'd like."

"No, please get us down!" she said with a frightened laugh.

*****

We joined with the second group soon after I took Michael and Reuben on a little trip above the forest. After Jennava scolded me for going off on my own, I spent the next couple of hours taking each of my friends up and around one by one. Eden was the only one who didn't volunteer. Even Jennava wanted a turn. She claimed it was because we might be using this technique as a form of transport, and she needed to see how efficient and dangerous it was, but we all knew that she also wanted to see what it felt like. Who didn't wish to fly? Besides, she didn't seem mad at me, just concerned I would endanger myself again. She made me promise to inform her if I wanted to go off on my own again.

It was good practice for me to carry others, not just because I agreed with Jennava that we might use this technique for transport, but because it seemed to be the quickest way for me to strengthen my spell. The additional weight on my mind proved challenging, but I felt my skill growing quickly.

Eventually we stopped for lunch. We sat in a loose circle as we ate dried food from our bags. My flights had proven to be a huge distraction—no one had caught or slain any creature of the forest—but no one was complaining, either.

I sat near Michael and Hadley. I heard Reuben and Kataleya nearby, as they spoke about the Chespars and the other nobles, mostly expressing concerns to each other.

"Say, Hadley," Michael said in a quiet voice. "If curses can make people feel things they wouldn't normally feel, can they cause an attraction?"

"Yes," Hadley answered quickly.

"How would it work?" Michael asked. "Would you need the hairs of both the person you're cursing and the person you're making them attracted to?"

"You would, and having two targets would make the curse more difficult and weaker than if it only had one target." She glanced over at him. "So it would be easier to make one person attracted to another than to make both attracted."

"I see."

Hadley stared at him a moment longer. "Why do you ask?"

Michael gave a quick look at Eden that appeared to satisfy Hadley's curiosity.

"I highly doubt Eden's skill with curses could ever lead you to have a false attraction toward her," Hadley whispered. "Besides, the attraction would change drastically when the curse went away. It might even turn into disgust for a short time. You would know if you'd been cursed."

"That's good, I guess," he muttered. He didn't sound too pleased by her answer.

I figured he was looking for an easy explanation for his feelings for Eden, which probably had not changed even after her betrayal had come out. Michael didn't seem to want these feelings, which made sense to me. Eden scared me a bit. Perhaps she scared Michael as well.

She sat mostly on her own, some distance between Remi and Aliana on one side, Reuben and Kataleya on the other. I was a little surprised to hear Kataleya laughing, especially because it must've been something Reuben said, as he held a smile.

"Jon," Hadley said. "How much of your ability to fly

has to do with that Induct stone?"

"I was already able to throw myself with almost the same power before I had the Induct stone. I had just never tried it before. I think what the stone mostly does is increase my ability to continue casting without feeling tired, so long as it's the Grab spell. It feels like another sorcerer is helping me every time I cast it."

"Then I think it's worthwhile to calculate the risk versus benefit of obtaining more Induct stones for the other sorcerers."

"Hey, that's a good point," Michael said. "Why don't you fly to the center of the forest and get some more, Jon?" he asked facetiously. "Try not to wake Gourfist while you're there."

"I'm serious," Hadley said. "It's not as if a separate trip needs to be made for every Induct stone." She held up a finger. "One trip, and you could equip almost every sorcerer in the army with an Induct stone, after they had been primed and infused, of course."

Michael put his hand over his chin. Eventually he opened his palms in a shrug. "But Gourfist...Hadley. Gourfist."

"How long would it take for a group of us to reach the center of the forest? Eden came from there. She might know. Eden—?" Hadley started to call to her, but Michael interrupted.

"She didn't fly back from the center," he said. "She rode cantars nearly to Koluk, which is much closer to the center than we are here. It's not like all of us could ride the beasts of the forest."

"Eden, will you join us?" Hadley asked.

Eden lumbered over. I caught her glancing at the Induct stone sitting beside me, making me want to hide it from view, but I didn't. I wanted to give her a chance to control herself.

Hadley's beckoning of Eden had drawn the attention of everyone else. Reuben asked, "What's going on?"

"We were discussing how much extra mana Jon receives from the Induct stone."

"While casting the spell infused in the stone," I added, realizing then that I was against the idea of traveling to the center of the forest. As good as it sounded to equip our sorcerers with a stone like this one, I couldn't fathom safely getting there with a large enough group to take on Gourfist.

"Yes, while casting the specific spell trapped inside," Hadley agreed. "Obtaining more of them would be extremely beneficial to our cause. I was wondering, Eden, how many did you see on the ground near the portal to Fyrren?"

"There were a lot," she said. "A hundred, I would guess, maybe more."

"It would just take one trip," Hadley said. "I thought we could put our minds together and figure out how we might do it."

Kataleya had a crinkle across her forehead "You're talking about killing Gourfist to get more Induct stones?"

"I am."

"But Gourfist could be the only thing stopping Valinox from killing us directly," Kataleya said.

"The demigods on our side—Souriff and Failina—could fight just as viciously once Gourfist is gone. It is only fear of retribution that is stopping them."

"Says you," Reuben argued. "Souriff admitted herself that she is unlikely to kill any of our enemies, even if Valinox shows that he can do it without punishment. This sounds like a terrible idea. Think about the time it would take to get there and the men we might lose in the fight. What if Valinox brought his best fighter to the bout with Gourfist and ambushed us while we dealt with that four-footed, multiclawed, beast-of-an-eagle? With an invisible demigod behind us, and the transformed one in front of us, that might be the end of everything."

Eden gasped. "With Gourfist gone, we would be able to get to Nijja."

"Oh!" Remi said as she pointed at Eden. "That's right!"

I hadn't seen the enchanter and the fire mage this animated in some time.

"What does that mean for us?" Michael asked.

"Nijja should be able to disenchant the gem Valinox took from her, the one that maintains his invisibility spell," Eden answered. "Then we could hide her from Valinox to keep him from forcing her to make another for him."

"You talked about this with Remi?" Aliana asked.

"It came up recently," Remi said. "I was wondering if Eden could disenchant the gem."

"I had tried last night when he attacked Jon, but the enchantment is too strong."

"But the room was cursed," Hadley said. "No spells could be cast anyway."

"I'm not sure what to tell you," Eden said. "My disenchant spell went through. It just didn't work."

"That is fascinating," Hadley said. "I'm not sure why that would be, but that's a matter for later. I agree that Nijja should be able to dissolve her own enchantment, but would she have to be close to Valinox to do it?"

"That's the best part about it," Eden said. "An enchanter like her should be able to disenchant the gem from many miles away."

"The hardest part would be convincing her to come with us out of Fyrren," Remi added.

Jennava finally stepped in. "And hiding her after, like you mentioned, Eden. Well, you met her. Do you believe she could be convinced of these things?"

"Not by us, surely. We would need Souriff to agree to go with us. That means killing Gourfist with her help and going into Fyrren. But Fyrren is a very dangerous place. I nearly died there when a swarm of camouflaged snakes attacked me. It would probably be better to have Souriff go alone once we take care of Gourfist. I don't know if she would be up for any of that."

I said, "Valinox probably could tell when we awaken Gourfist. He might come with his strongest sorcerer, like Reuben suggests."

"We still haven't discussed the difficulty of getting there," Reuben added. "Eden, what would a trip like that look like for us?"

"I imagine it would take a week, and it would not be safe. There were huge beasts close to the center. I'm not sure we would be able to fight against all of them in our way."

Kataleya asked Eden, "Don't you think it's worth it to put an end to Valinox's invisibility spell?"

She shook her head. "I think it's better if Jon, Souriff, and Failina take the people they can carry to the center and fight Gourfist on their own."

"That's only if we can reach the demigods and convince them to help us," Jennava said. "We still haven't met Failina, and Souriff does things on her own."

We all fell silent.

"I will speak to the king about it tonight," Jennava said. "If all of you are done eating, we need to make the most of this time."

"Jennava?" I tried. "Is the king going to send us to intercept Rohaer in the near future?"

"Like the rest of you, I have not been made aware of his plans yet. The specific tasks involving us are most likely still in the making."

Kataleya said, "The king will not let our enemies step foot in Lycast. It would be detrimental to allow Rohaer to pillage our cities and set up strongholds. The only real question is if the king has the power to force his nobles' armies to take the front line, because he definitely won't want to send off his troops—and that includes us—to stand as the first line of defense."

I noticed Reuben and Aliana looking at each other as if there was something each of them wanted to say.

"Go ahead," Aliana urged him.

Reuben addressed us. "The king spoke to me a while ago about this. He enlisted the help of my father to make our own stronghold, but not in any town. They've been building one in the forest, close to the only road between Lycast in Rohaer. It won't be much longer before it's well-equipped. I believe that is where the king will station most, if not all, of his troops soon enough, and we might go with them. Rohaer is bound to cross by it."

I didn't understand something. "Wouldn't it take a long time to build a stronghold from nothing?"

"It's only made of wood, Jon," Reuben said. "Not stone, and it *has* been in the works for a long time now."

"He received help from my father as well," Aliana said.

I had almost forgotten about Aliana's father, a rich noble who had wanted his identity to remain hidden from his illegitimate daughter. Was he still in the dungeons beneath the castle? He had been put there after we figured out he had been working with Cason—something he had eventually admitted to.

"I've been talking with my father from time to time." Aliana spoke mostly to the ground. "The king has wanted me to ingratiate myself with him to turn him to our side. I'm still not sure he can be trusted, but he is helping by using his own coin."

"But he's still in the dungeons?" I asked, then noticed Hadley shoot Aliana a look of surprise. *That's right, she wasn't here when it happened.*

Aliana must've noticed Hadley as well, because she spoke to her directly. "I never knew who my father was until recently. It turned out he was working against the king, but he was caught."

"I see," Hadley replied. "I'm sorry for my reaction."

"It's fine. I'm not close with him," Aliana said.

"Aliana, Kataleya, and I are quite knowledgeable about the nobilities' roles in this war," Reuben said. "All noble families are invested, some more than others, but Kataleya and I agree that most are looking at this war as an opportunity. Someone is likely to betray the king, either during or after the war."

"It might even be my family," Kataleya said.

Now this didn't surprise me because Kataleya had spoken to me about this, but I could see others among us who were hearing it for the first time.

"It has only recently come to my attention,"

Kataleya continued, "that my father might've been planning a revolt against our king. He wanted me to marry Trevor Chespar so that our families could unite. Our armies, together, are stronger than the army of the king. Trevor has still shown interest in me after hearing about the death of my father, but I don't know if he's part of the plan or if all of it is in my imagination. I'm fairly certain I will have to investigate it and most definitely speak to my mother about it, which means I'll probably be leaving for a time."

"So you're certain now you're going?" I asked.

"The only thing that would change my mind would be if Trevor marries the king's daughter, which would put everyone's worries to rest."

"I thought she was going to marry Jon," Remi said to my surprise.

"What?" I said. "Why did you think that?"

"You're not going to marry her?" Remi asked.

"I'm not involved with her romantically. Not at all. We're just friends."

Remi seemed surprised, but I was even more surprised. Why was she looking at me like I was a fool?

"Jon's weighing his options," Kataleya said as if to answer everyone's silent question.

"So he could marry the princess?" Aliana asked. "I mean, it's been offered to him?"

"Wait a minute," but I spoke at the same time as Jennava.

"I don't think it's right for all of you to be prying into these affairs," she scolded. "This is Jon's life."

"But these affairs do pertain to us," Reuben argued. "We are going to be the ones fighting against a revolt. The princess' hand in marriage could tell us which noble family we won't have to worry about. If Jon's going to marry her, we should know so we can better prepare for the Chespars to make a play for the crown."

"I'm not marrying the princess," I said a little angrily. "Let me be clear about something. I haven't seen her as more than a friend at any point since coming to the castle. Nothing has ever happened between us. I wouldn't let it."

"That's obviously not what we're discussing," Reuben said with a roll of his eyes. "Everyone knows that many betrothals, like one to Callie Lennox right now, don't have to do with anything but politics. Do you believe Trevor Chespar would marry her for love and companionship? Of course not. But he might marry her anyway, and then your chances of ever being a noble will be gone."

"I don't care about that."

"Well that's good," Reuben spoke quickly. "It would be better for all of us if you let Trevor marry her, but personally I think you're wasting an opportunity that you will never see again."

"Can we drop this?" I asked.

"Yes, enough of this," Jennava announced. "We came here for the necessities required for enchanting and cursing, and so far we have nothing to show for our efforts."

As she split us into two groups again, I noticed Hadley eyeing me. She diverted her gaze when I looked over, but I could almost read her thoughts.

Sure enough, she volunteered to join Remi's group this time. I saw the two of them walking close when we separated, and I was just about certain that Hadley was asking Remi what she saw that made Remi think I would marry the princess.

I still felt the same way about Hadley as when I was first getting to know her. She made my blood run hot, but both Kataleya and Reuben had now advised me to consider marrying into the Lennox family. It seemed like most of my peers had already assumed I would be interested in such a marriage.

Part of me didn't even want to think about it. More than anything, I just wanted to win the war against Rohaer. But another part of me knew that I should consider it. Marrying into the king's family was an opportunity I might never have again because Callie would probably be married before the war was over, and there would be no family more powerful than the Lennoxes if we won.

But why did I care about joining a powerful family? Until now, it had never been a desire that even crossed my mind. It wasn't long ago that I was living in Bhode with hardly anything to my name. I had just wanted to learn sorcery; that was all. Now I found myself thinking about the riches and political sway that came with being a noble. I had never thought myself to be greedy before, but was I wrong?

No, the answer came quickly. I wanted these things because recently I had seen what kind of world I was really living in. If I was never going to be a noble myself, then I would always be answering to one of them, if not the king. If I wanted more for myself, I would have to seriously consider marrying the princess.

As all these thoughts ran through my head, I walked with Michael, Reuben, and Kataleya, all of us quiet. Hadley had passed her bow and quiver to me now that she had joined Aliana's group.

"There's something ahead," Reuben said as he pointed.

"How far?" Michael asked.

"We should be able to see it soon."

We pushed through some thick shrubbery and spotted a deer grazing. The animal heard us and darted off before I could ready an arrow.

It was the first time I had seen Reuben use his tracking skill. I was glad he had not only matured emotionally but had grown as a sorcerer. I wondered how well he handled the sword now. I had seen brief glimpses of him and Michael fighting against Rohaer's sorcerers and swordsmen during our last battle, but it was a chaotic scene without time to notice much besides the happy fact they could keep themselves alive.

Unfortunately, it probably wouldn't be long before I had a much better opportunity to see just how well they fared. My pulse increased as I thought about one of my friends being killed before my eyes. It seemed more possible than ever.

I couldn't let that happen. "Reuben, Michael, how do the both of you feel about some sword practice with me tomorrow? We've never really had the chance."

"Sure thing," Michael said facetiously, "as long as you're not going off to fight Gourfist, or if something else comes up."

"He has a point, Jon," Reuben said. "You have enough to worry about without adding us to your list. Besides, Leon is actually a decent teacher."

I didn't know how to respond to that. I really wanted to help them improve if I could, but maybe Leon had it covered. Mostly, I just wanted to spend more time with them. It had been too long since we'd done something fun, and there were few things I enjoyed more than sparring.

"There's something else this way," Reuben said.

We continued on as if I'd never mentioned training with them.

CHAPTER FIVE

Our group managed to hunt down five creatures during the next few hours. Reuben told us that each one would fetch many ingredients, given how all of their claws and teeth could be used, in addition to other parts. I thought we had done a fine job tracking and shooting them, but when we met with the other group soon later and heard they had hunted down a dozen more than us, I was sure I wasn't the only one in our group who felt a little bad about it.

Reuben was mostly quiet during the walk back. Before we'd left, he'd said his tracking skill would never be as good as Aliana's, but Leon had implied that was because she was exceptional. It didn't look as if this made much of a difference to Reuben, though. I didn't know what to tell him to make him feel better. He was still very useful. Every sorcerer was.

"You're getting better every day, aren't you?" Kataleya asked Reuben in a clear attempt to brighten his mood.

"Slowly."

"That's better than nothing," she said. "You're already at a level that will help us."

"I can barely sense anything past thirty yards. How is that going to help us before it's time to fight?"

"We won't be fighting anyone for a while," Kataleya said. "There's time to improve."

Speaking of, I was itching to fly again. I couldn't get the feeling out of my mind. It seemed like a waste to walk back without practicing.

I moved over to walk beside Jennava and explained what I planned to do.

"I've been thinking about this," she replied. "Rather than flying on your own, it's more likely that you will be carrying someone most of the time. That's what you should be practicing now, but I don't want you going so high with anyone on your back anymore. Not until we develop a harness to make sure your passenger stays on."

Everything she said made sense, but I wasn't going to be walking all the way back to the castle when I could be flying. "But I want to practice more in the meantime. I—"

"Yes, you can go ahead of us. Keep in mind that you are vulnerable in the air if Valinox is nearby. This is a skill worth practicing even considering the risk, but try not to stray too far from Newhaven at any given time."

"I'll stay close to the capital," I said, then took a running start. I wrapped dvinia around me with my spell of Grab and picked myself up.

With little caution, I heaved myself up higher and higher, dodging tree branches and trunks alike.

"Jon, be care—!"

I couldn't hear Jennava anymore as I broke through the canopy. I hurled myself outward and breathed in the rushing air. Letting out a sigh of relief, I was already becoming addicted to the feeling. I didn't ever want to walk anywhere again.

I soared higher into the sky and took in the beautiful sight of Lycast. Beneath me, the forest came to an end, met by a river and a short bridge. A path broke out and led to the main road into Newhaven. The city looked small from up here, though growing ever bigger as I zoomed toward it. I spotted the castle near the center. I planned to land within the tall walls, but not before I enjoyed this a little while longer.

I could get there in less than a minute. Meanwhile, it was going to take the rest of my group an hour to get back.

Past the capital, to the east, lay the vast ocean. To the south stood the mountains where Leon had taken me and the others when I had first learned the spell of dvinia. Deeper south, toward the higher peaks, was where Souriff and I had faced Valinox and Cason. The other way, to the north, lay the long road between the capital and Tryn, the city where I had first stopped after my trip from Bhode. It was in Tryn where I had sought out a sorcerer to explain the energy I felt buzzing in my mind and eventually met Barrett.

I took myself higher into the sky, looking far north toward my hometown. All I could make out from here was the snowy forest that surrounded Bhode. It was difficult to keep myself suspended compared to tossing myself intermittently, which gave my mind chances to recuperate. For now, however, I held myself high up and looked straight south.

Rohaer would come for us from this direction. I wondered where their army was right now. I could see straight down the road, as it snaked between the mountains and the forest, though it did turn eventually around the tall, rocky slopes that ran south for hundreds of miles. The forest grew deep into Rohaer territory. My gaze could follow it long past where the road turned out of view. It was huge in its entirety.

I couldn't see any of the towns that lay near the road between the kingdoms, but I knew they were somewhere in the far distance behind the hills and trees. I wondered what might become of them as Rohaer's army headed past them to get to us. I imagined the king didn't want to find out. He would want us to stop the army before they entered our kingdom.

Beginning to tire, I wanted to let myself down. But I was just a mile away from the castle. I could make it.

Just as I was about to hurl myself that way, something startled me.

"Follow me," said someone right behind me.

"Ah!" I yelled.

With my concentration broken, my spell came apart. I fell as I screamed in horror.

However, I was so high up that I had plenty of time to compose myself. Catching myself seemed too difficult. Instead, I wrapped dvinia around my body and used my momentum to guide myself forward instead of down, pulling up hard as I sped through the air.

Eventually I arced enough to gain height once more, my speed starting to slow. Now immensely tired and hovering only about as high as the tall trees of the forest nearby, I looked around for the woman whose voice I had heard.

She breezed over to me through the air. I felt power emanating from her and knew right away that she had to be Failina, the demigod of erto.

Failina looked very different from her sister, Souriff. Her hair was short and layered, rising up above her head and slightly falling to the side. The color was hard to place, somewhere between red and brown. She wasn't tall like Souriff but short like Hadley. It wasn't so much her shapely curves that drew my gaze down to her body but the many marks on her arms. I had never seen anything like them. It was like she had been painted, like she was a living work of art.

I let gravity take me to land as she came toward me. She seemed like she was as graceful as she was powerful as she slowed on her way to the ground, wind whooshing around her as if the natural elements of the world beckoned to her call.

She wasn't the most beautiful woman I had seen, but she might've been the most striking. She had smoldering eyes, cyan in color, accentuated by her dark eyebrows. Her jaw sloped down to a slightly pointed chin, giving her face a slender look of delicate beauty, which went along with her full lips, her mouth slightly agape as she looked at me with curiosity.

There wasn't much fabric covering her body, which I figured had to do with the immense amount of wind required to keep her in the air. Her short white dress fitted over her shoulders with straps and pinched around her waist with a wide belt. She wore close-fitting leggings beneath the dress, an outfit for a warmer day, not this cold winter one. And yet she didn't look the least bit cold.

"Failina?" I asked.

"Yes, and you are?"

"Jon Oklar."

"So it is you. Souriff has spoken about you, but she did not mention you could fly."

"It's a recent development."

She looked at me as if she didn't believe me. "It wasn't long ago that you required Souriff to take you into the forest on her back, but now you fly like you've been doing it for years. Have you kept this skill from Souriff?"

I didn't understand the point of her question, but it sounded like she was getting at something.

"I've probably been able to fly for some time, but I've never really tried until today." I was hesitant to show her the Induct stone, fearful she might take it away from me as I still had no idea what her intentions were.

I did think of something, though, that might ease the tension I was feeling.

"I want to thank you on behalf of everyone for keeping up the snowstorm as long as you did. We would be in much worse trouble if you hadn't."

She didn't crack a smile, only nodded. "I would like to speak to you about something, Jon Oklar. I was looking for someone of your group and happened to see you in the sky."

"The rest of my group is just a little ways back in the forest," I said with a glance over my shoulder, feeling a little uneasy about this without them here.

She was shaking her head by the time I glanced back at her. "This must be quick. I don't want Souriff to see us."

Had she meant to say Valinox? No, she wasn't correcting herself.

She continued, "It was wise of you to refuse Souriff's demands to meet me in the mountains. You would have died there. She has been responsible for the deaths of many humans, even men and women whose goals were aligned with hers at the time. You must remain cautious around her. Warn your king and the other sorcerers, but do not speak about this to Souriff.

She is as selfish as Valinox."

I knew Souriff was intense in her goals, but to hear from the sister who had been helping her that she was as selfish as Valinox came as a shock.

"When you say she's been responsible for the deaths of many humans, do you mean she's even murdered some?"

"She will not murder any more."

"Any more?" I asked with a rising pitch to my voice. "Who did she murder?"

Failina opened her mouth but did not speak. "That's not relevant right now. She could be returning from Rohaer soon. Tell me of your immediate plans so that we may strategize together while she is away."

"We could go see the king right now. We could be there in less than a minute."

She shook her head. "I have been alive a long time, Jon. I have spoken with many kings as well as many of the soldiers and sorcerers they have overseen. The decisions that kings make are always for their kingdoms, *their* kingdoms," she repeated. "These decisions are not made for the men, women, and children who live in their kingdoms. They are not made for the water and fire mages who allow their people to thrive, or the healers who bring prosperity through good health. Instead, these decisions usually pertain to their generals and soldiers, their witches and warlocks. There is a time to discuss war with kings. I will speak with Nykal Lennox. I will strategize with him while in my sister's company, but I came here to speak to you, healer, you and your kin. You must be protected from not only Rohaer but from my own brother and sister." She reached out and touched the underside of my chin. "Are you beginning to understand?"

I nodded as graciously as I could. "Thank you, goddess."

"Call me Failina."

"Before I tell you of my plan, I want to know if Souriff is truly as dangerous as Valinox."

"Not to Lycast. She is your strongest soldier, besides myself."

You're stronger than Souriff? But there was a more important question. "Does that mean you will kill for us?"

"I will not. Neither will Souriff, and that is the reason I am more valuable. With my power over the elements, I can do a lot more against your enemies than she can. That is not important right now. The only thing you need to know in this moment is that Souriff wants to be involved in human affairs as much as Valinox does. It is the reason they have waged war against each other."

"I thought it was Valinox who started this and Souriff just wanted to help us fight against him."

"She would have you believe that, but it's not the case."

"Then why are you helping Souriff and not Valinox if they seem to be equally responsible for the destruction they're causing?"

"Because of dteria, Jon," she said in a tone as if that should be obvious.

"I figured that, but you were starting to confuse me."

She let out a frustrated breath. "I'm only making matters worse by trying to explain. You will have to trust me for now. Be as wary of Souriff as you are vigilant of Valinox. That is all. Now tell me of the king's goals and the steps he is taking to accomplish them."

"I can, but help me understand something first. Why am I supposed to trust you implicitly?"

She seemed taken aback as her eyebrows lifted in apparent surprise.

"It is what you're asking, isn't it?" I confirmed. "To trust you more than I do Souriff?"

"Yes, because I spent months holed up in the mountains, suffering through the cold as I maintained an endless snowstorm. I did it for the benefit of Lycast, our mutual interest in this war."

"But I don't know for a fact that was you. I heard about it from Souriff, but I never saw you with my own eyes. I trusted you to be Failina, at first, but now I'm not so sure. You could be deceiving me, turning me against Souriff."

Her gaze became fiery.

I put up my hands in a gesture of appeasement. "I'm just hoping for a little proof before I choose to start distrusting Souriff, who I thought was one of our greatest allies. I don't mean to offend, goddess. You are the one teaching me to exercise more caution. I figured I'd start now before divulging our plans."

"Witnessing my power could very well summon my sister, and then we will no longer be able to speak in confidence."

"That's a risk I'm going to have to take."

"Very well, healer. If Souriff arrives, you are to follow my lie about how we came to meet. Are you skilled at twisting untruths to sound truthful?"

"Not at all."

"Then you will be completely quiet and let me do it.

Now brace yourself. You might've thought that you've been cold before, but nothing you have felt will have prepared you for this."

Oh shit, I grumbled inwardly as she lifted herself, hovered in the sky, and extended her arms.

The clouds darkened above as a shadow fell upon me. A great wind picked up as I pulled my coat up around my face. It howled, and soon I couldn't hear anything above it. I crouched and huddled in hopes of protecting myself.

The temperature dropped so drastically that it felt as if I had been thrown into an icy lake. I shivered as snow began to fall. It came down lightly as first, wetting my hair and ears, but then it poured down in buckets.

I couldn't see anything but white as my boots became buried in it. It grew denser still, and I couldn't see farther than a few feet in front of me.

"All right!" I yelled at the top of my lungs, my tiny voice barely piercing the sound of the wind. "I believe you!"

There was no way she could hear me. I wanted to yell again, but I felt like I might pass out if I opened my mouth once more. The cold penetrated my lungs like icy daggers. I tried to get smaller and huddle in on myself, but I didn't have enough fabric to stop the onslaught of wind and snow. I wanted to carry myself out of the snowstorm with dvinia, but the freezing cold broke my concentration.

There was panic in my heart, my instincts telling me I soon would die if I didn't get out of this. I wanted to make a run for it, but I felt like my joints couldn't move. My fingertips and toes had frozen.

I keeled over and gave in, shutting my eyes and feeling internal warmth that I knew couldn't be right.

It felt like I had just blinked my eyes when I woke up in a completely different place. Failina had her arm over me as she embraced me for warmth. She felt like a lit fire against my cold body, sending immense pain but even better pleasure across my skin.

I tried to talk, but I was shivering too much to get any words out.

"Breathe slow and deep," she said as she nestled me against her. I felt nurtured, like a small boy being warmed by his mother after staying too long in the snow. I had never gotten to know my mother. My father had only said good things about her before departing from this world.

"I'm putting my faith in you," Failina murmured into my ear. "You, healer, will bring victory to Lycast, but only if we properly take care of you."

I didn't know if it was the physical ordeal I had been through over the last few months, or if I just missed my loving family, but I felt overwhelmed by emotion as Failina's warmth spread through my body. I held back tears as I realized that this was the goddess we had all hoped Souriff would be, a mother to us all.

With a shaky voice, I said, "Thank you, Failina. I trust you." A single tear escaped before I composed myself.

She stood up and held out her hand. I reached up and took it.

She pulled me up. Though, to my surprise, she showed a little strain as she did so. It seemed clear to me that she didn't have the same physical strength as Souriff and Valinox, but I wouldn't worry about that. Not after what she had just displayed.

I felt a gust of air as I heard someone land behind me. I turned around to see Souriff, displeasure on her unblemished face.

"What's happening here?" she demanded.

"I witnessed the human flying," Failina answered, her hand protectively holding my shoulder. "He fell and injured himself. I came to check on him, but that's when I found out he was the healer you spoke of, Jon Oklar."

"He can fly now?"

"He started just today."

Failina took her hand off my shoulder as Souriff approached me. "I sense an Induct stone."

"Yes, I felt that too," Failina said.

I reluctantly took it out of my pocket and showed it to Souriff, fearful she might take it. But she didn't seem too interested as the gaze of her sharp blue eyes drifted over to Failina.

"I felt you use a great amount of power. Why?" She looked around at the snow covering the grass around us.

"The human wanted a demonstration to prove I was who I said I was."

Souriff, eyes narrowing, seemed overly skeptical, as if she had caught Failina lying to her in the past. If I had to choose one of them to trust over the other, however, it would be Failina even though I had just met her. Souriff had always rubbed me the wrong way, her pride and selfishness often palpable. Failina, on the other hand, made me feel like I was cared for in a way I hadn't felt since my father died.

Souriff looked me up and down, then narrowed in on the Induct stone in my hand. I wanted to get it away from her, to hide it where she would never be able to find it.

Was it the power this stone gave me that made me want to protect it at all costs, or was there something else to the Induct stone…something sinister that made me cling to it? The demigods would say so if that was the case, wouldn't they?

"I thought you were out looking for 'C,' " Souriff said.

I didn't know who "C" could refer to besides Cason, but he was dead.

"I couldn't find him," Failina answered, clearly knowing who Souriff was referring to. "What news do you have from Rohaer?"

"They're coming, as we figured."

"How many?" Failina asked.

My ears perked up. This was the army of my enemies, a large brigade of sorcerers and soldiers who would need to be defeated before we could ever reach peace with Rohaer. I didn't know what "defeated" entailed exactly. I knew they all didn't have to die, but something had to happen for them to give up. I couldn't imagine anything besides mass extinction of everyone who followed Valinox, but I did hope there was another way.

"I estimate five thousand fighting men among a much larger army marching with them for support."

Five thousand. I wondered how many we had. It had to be less than that, probably by a large amount.

"Did Valinox see you spying?"

"With his constant spell of invisibility, I cannot say for certain, but I didn't feel him. These are matters to discuss with Nykal Lennox. I'm headed there now." It seemed as if Souriff was imploring Failina to go with her, considering the look she gave her sister.

Failina glanced at me. I could almost feel in her gaze that she was trying to come up with some way to stay here and plot behind her sister's back.

"What are you not telling me?" Souriff accused. "Did this human tell you lies about me?"

I was certain my face showed how innocent I was, for there was no way I could feign as much shock as I felt come through my expression. I couldn't even fathom what lies Souriff might be referring to.

"Of course not," Failina said. "I was just considering if we should invite the healer with us to speak with the king. We both agree he is important to our cause. He should be involved in the decisions we make from now on."

"You have made that mistake before," Souriff lectured, sounding more like the older sister, if I had to guess. "I do not want to suffer the same consequences when you make it again."

"Fine," Failina said dutifully. "Jon, we will meet again."

It surprised me that Failina was so quick to let Souriff tell her what to do. Perhaps Souriff didn't know just how much Failina was willing to work against her, and Failina needed to keep it that way.

"Wait," I said as it looked like they were about to take off. "The other sorcerers and I have a plan that we just came up with. The king hasn't heard it yet. It involves the two of you."

I would've preferred to speak only to Failina about this, but that window had closed. I wasn't about to let them both disappear for an unknown amount of time, because there was no way to do this without their help.

"There's a simple way of getting rid of the gem Valinox has," I continued. "Nijja's gem."

"Unless you plan to take the gem from Valinox, then only Nijja herself can destroy it," Souriff said.

"We know," I replied. "That's why we want to fetch Nijja from Fyrren. We believe we just need to bring her into our realm for a moment for her to dissolve the enchantment."

"It can't be done," Souriff said. "Gourfist sleeps near the portal."

"We are considering killing him, with your help," I replied.

The sisters glanced at each other. It seemed clear to me that they hadn't thought of this, but I didn't know the reason. Gourfist had been their brother, but now he was a threat to their lives. Shouldn't it be an easy decision to eliminate him, even if he was once family? The answer would also tell me if Souriff and Failina would ever be capable of killing Valinox.

"He's long gone," Souriff told Failina.

"You can't be certain," Failina replied. "He could still be in that beast."

"So what if he is?" Souriff said. "He created dteria. He deserves death."

Although Failina looked like she disagreed, she didn't speak up.

"I wish you two would be less concerned about slaying your brother and more concerned about the future of Lycast," I said. "Getting rid of Gourfist is the only way to Nijja. We have to get rid of Valinox's invisibility. If not, there is a good chance Valinox will kill me. He brought a skilled mage into the castle last night. They were waiting for me to be alone. They would've killed me if it wasn't for our ranger and our wit…" I stopped myself from speaking about Hadley in that way to these demigods who did not know her very well. "And everyone else who came to my aid when I was under attack."

A silence passed before I added the words I was certain were on everyone's mind: "Neither of you showed up to save me."

"We didn't know—" Souriff began.

"I know neither of you were aware," I interrupted, "and that's my point. The other sorcerers and I have to be able to defend ourselves from Valinox, and the only way we can do that is if we can *see* him. Nijja has to help us, which means Gourfist has to die. Removing Gourfist *will* mean that Valinox can kill us without fear of him, but you have already mentioned, Souriff, that Valinox would no longer be afraid of Gourfist if he knew how weak the beast has become. Right now Gourfist is hindering us more than helping, and Valinox is sure to find out the truth about him soon enough."

The sisters glanced at each other. "He has a point," Failina said.

"And if Airinold is still alive, but trapped in the body of the beast?" Souriff questioned.

"The human convinced me that it needs to be done no matter what."

I was glad I didn't need to mention the other benefit —access to Induct stones. "Sooner is better," I said. "I can go with the two of you, but I'm not sure I can carry someone that far yet. You can take someone, though Souriff. And what about you, Failina?"

"I lack the physical strength of my sister. I don't believe I could carry someone far enough to reach the portal to Fyrren."

"But is there a chance you might be able to?" I asked.

She looked to be in thought. Remembering the harness idea that Jennava mentioned, I brought up another thought.

"What if we strap them to you, and you carry both you and them with wind?"

"I have never tried something like that. I fear it might go wrong."

"We don't need the extra human," Souriff said. "The three of us can defeat Gourfist alone, but we cannot open the portal to Fyrren. The human I bring must be able to do that."

"Eden can do that," I realized aloud. "She's done it before." But I feared what might happen with Eden. She was unpredictable these days, especially because she would have access to more Induct stones while there.

"It is a long distance to the center of the forest," Souriff said, addressing me. "If you injured yourself attempting to fly today, then it is unlikely you can make it there."

Failina's lie was coming back to bite us.

"I'm improving quickly. How far is it exactly?"

"About two hundred miles," Souriff said.

"Oh god." Maybe I couldn't make it after all, even with rest breaks. I had only gone as far as Koluk, about forty miles there and back. I was able to make it to Koluk without a break, but I was pretty tired once I landed.

"You can't do it?" Souriff asked.

"I can," I assured her. "I will just need to land in the forest several times to rest. Can the two of you stay with me all the way there to keep me safe when I land?"

"It's better if he stays," Failina told Souriff.

"I want to go," I said. I didn't trust Eden to be alone

with the demigods. Even with Failina present, there was a good chance they would let Eden die rather than risk injury to themselves to protect her, especially if she showed signs of dteria corruption.

"We need his help," Souriff said. "You have not met Eden. She is not a fighter like he is. Additionally, Valinox might show up if he senses what we are doing. He could bring someone to disrupt us."

"I'm going with you no matter what," I told them decidedly. "I suggest we go to the castle and equip the two of you with whatever weapons you need."

"Our weapons are our magic," Failina said, but she received a look from Souriff that seemed to sap her enthusiasm.

"We will take weapons and armor from Nykal Lennox," Souriff spoke for the both of them.

Failina didn't object.

I felt a surge of adrenaline. I did not know this would be so soon. "Are we heading to Gourfist right after?"

"It is unwise to go today," Failina said, easing my nerves. "It could be night by the time we start the return journey, and that would make the trip dangerous for you. We should leave tomorrow morning. Can you sleep somewhere where you will be protected tonight in case Valinox tries to have you killed again?"

"Yes, measures are being taken."

"Then we will meet with your king now before we meet again at the castle tomorrow morning," Failina said. "My sister and I have things to discuss in the time between."

I figured part of that discussion had to do with how they were going to convince Nijja to leave Fyrren and how they would keep her safe after.

"Let's go," Souriff said as she took off into the sky.

Failina gave me a worried look. "This is a good plan, but you must be careful of anything Souriff asks you to do during or after the battle. I can't stay to chat, or it will look suspicious."

Wind nearly blew me off my feet as it swept her into the air. Soon she was soaring off toward the castle with Souriff.

I chewed my lip as I watched them shrink away in the sky.

Just like that, I had agreed to fly hundreds of miles and slay a demigod beast. Yet neither of those things scared me as much as Failina's warning.

CHAPTER SIX

I didn't know if I would ever be able to fly as fast as the demigods, but I was happy with my speed for now. I couldn't imagine going much faster through the air anyway, not without some protection for my face and ears. Hell, what would I do if it rained? I needed a *lot* more protection.

It turned out to be much harder than I thought to land inside the castle, where I planned to set myself down in the courtyard. I flew too fast to reach ground before I would strike one of the curtain walls, deciding at the last moment to lift myself up and soar past the wall. My momentum took me out over the city low enough for me to hear the gasps of people looking up and finding a human in the sky. Perhaps some were already looking my way after they had seen the demigods fly into the castle.

I wanted to have a glimpse of their expressions, but it was difficult enough to control myself at this speed. I pulled up with my dvinia and felt my body lurch.

With the cold wind blowing the sweat off my forehead, I circled back in the air. It was more than a little difficult to change my momentum this way, making me desperate to land as I headed toward the castle again, this time slower and with more control.

Feeling the hold of my mind starting to slip off my spell of dvinia, I came down harder than I wanted and frightened a castle worker. She screamed as I landed in front of her and rolled across the dirt.

"I'm sorry," I said as I picked myself up.

"Oh, it's fine," she said as she continued on her way, not without a look back. I'd seen the matronly middle-aged woman around the castle, so she had seen me as well, but she had no idea I could fly until now. I figured word would spread.

"Jon, are you all right?" I heard Callie call to me from somewhere high in the keep.

I looked up to see her leaning out of a window. I was tired, a bit sweaty and dirty from my tumble, but I couldn't help but show off my new talent.

I tossed myself straight up, catching myself in the air in front of her window so that we were just a few feet apart. She gasped with her hand over her mouth.

"I'm fine, princess. Just practicing something new."

"Come here!" She reached out and grabbed my hands, pulling me into the keep through the large window. She laughed with excitement as I came down in front of her. "You can fly now?"

"I'm still getting the hang of it." I was painfully aware that she was not letting go of my hands.

"Does that mean you can take me on your back like the demigods can?"

"I don't think your father would ever allow that, no matter how safe it might be."

"He doesn't have to know," she said with a sly smile.

I made my hands heavy, forcing her to let go, though I immediately felt bad and put one on her shoulder for the briefest moment. "Did you see two demigods come by? I need to join the meeting between them and your father."

"No, I just heard they had arrived. I wanted to see Failina! There's so much I want to talk about with you. When will you be free?"

"I'm afraid not for a while. There's something I have to do starting tomorrow morning, and today I have to prepare. Where are they meeting?"

"What are you doing tomorrow?"

I couldn't possibly tell her before confirming it with her father, but I didn't know how else to get out of this conversation.

There were a few features I noticed about Callie whenever I looked at her. One was that her brown hair was very long, falling all the way to her waist. The other was the expression she often had when she looked at me with her large hazel eyes. I wished I could catch Hadley glancing at me that way every now and again, but it hadn't happened once, and I didn't know how I might make it so.

There was nothing specific I had done to earn the favor of the princess. I knew it probably had to do with the way I looked, which was the reason she'd taken an interest in me right away. She had helped me, though, and I did feel as if I hadn't taken advantage of her. I would continue to not take advantage of her by refusing to use her feelings, even if a marriage into the Lennox family might be best for my future.

Then again, I might be saving Callie from an even worse predicament if she was to marry Trevor Chespar.

There were too many people and politics to take into consideration. I found it easier just to follow my heart, not my brain, and my heart was set on Hadley. The only problem was that I was starting to doubt she felt the same about me.

"I haven't spoken with your father about what needs to happen tomorrow. Let me—"

"Please tell me, Jon. No one tells me anything. I have no idea what's happening. I'm trapped in my quarters day and night!"

I looked past her at the couple of armored guards standing a little ways down the hall. The window into the keep did not lead into the princess's room, for her safety. Until Valinox's invisibility was taken care of, she had to spend most of her time locked away so that she could not be captured and used as ransom.

There was a bit of good news I could share with her, even if I couldn't tell her everything just yet. "I don't think you're going to have to be trapped in your room much longer, if everything goes to plan. That's all I feel comfortable telling you right now. Please direct me to your father and the demigods."

"Yes, let me take you to see my father." She took my hand and rushed off down the hall. She led me deep through the keep, up a short, twisting staircase of stone that didn't end up taking us much higher. Her guards stayed some distance behind.

She ran down another hall with me in tow, glancing frantically at the rooms we passed.

"You don't know where he is?" I asked.

"I'll find him soon."

Her intentions were as clear as day, but how could I deny the princess a glimpse at a demigod?

We ventured down a couple more hallways before we came to a room with many guards stationed outside. The door was shut, but it was fairly obvious who was behind it. I went in front of the princess and knocked on the door. "It's Jon. May I come in?"

"Enter," the king announced.

I opened the door wide enough to make sure Callie had a good view of the two demigods standing in front of her father. I moved slightly to the side and bowed as Souriff and Failina faced me. I made sure my bow was slow and deep before finally straightening again and turning to close the door.

"Thank you," Callie mouthed silently.

I gave a nod.

"If it took you this long to get here," Souriff complained, "it will take too long for you to reach Gourfist tomorrow. We will go without you."

"You can try, but I will follow."

Souriff seemed shocked before her expression turned to anger.

"You will want me there, even if it takes a little longer," I added. "Remember that I distracted Gourfist the last time he came awake. I fought him for a while before you showed up."

I still never found out why Gourfist flew right to the capital, but a theory sometimes kept me awake at night. If he was searching for the demigods, then Souriff might've been in the capital already. He might've sensed her here, which meant that Souriff had taken her sweet time before helping me with him. She had probably heard the screams and knew the destruction her brother was capable of, and she still didn't arrive until she had gathered her courage.

Failina glared at Souriff. "You did not tell me that Jon fought Gourfist."

"It doesn't matter," Souriff said, a look of impatient annoyance crossing her face. "It was by chance that Jon wasn't killed before I showed up." Turning to me, she said, "If you do manage to make it all the way there, you will stay back and let us fight. Only if I call for your aid will you give it. And if you can't make it there, you will turn and head back. We can't hold your hand the whole way, or the day will go to waste."

"Listen to them, Jon," the king said. "I can't send anyone else with you for protection. It will just be you and Eden with these demigods."

"Have you considered sending Barrett instead of Eden?" I asked. "I'm sure he can open the portal as well."

"Eden will be going," the king said without explanation. I figured he didn't want to risk losing Barrett when he could put Eden's life on the line instead.

"We will return tomorrow at sunrise." Souriff started toward the door.

Failina followed a distance behind. She gave me a look of warning. I didn't know if she was telling me to be generally cautious or if there was something specific I was to watch out for, but I figured I already had enough to worry about given the difficulty of the trip and the battle to come soon after.

"Jon, stay a moment," the king said as the sisters left.

After a guardsman shut the door behind Failina, the king gestured at a chair. I sat in it, a desk between us, but he walked around and pulled up another chair to sit right beside me. He leaned forward.

"Are you sure you want to do this? Wait." He put up his hand. "Are you sure you are capable of doing this without getting yourself killed?"

"Capable, sure, but I can't guarantee I will live."

"You have faced Gourfist before, but this time you will have much more help. What do you believe your chances are?"

"I hardly think there's any chance of death. I saw a sample of what Failina can do. I bet she alone should be able to stand up to Gourfist. I'm more concerned about the trip there and back, but I do believe Failina will ensure my safety, even if Souriff says they won't."

"That's what I was hoping to hear, but I have something for you just in case." He gave a look to one of the servants standing by, and the man left the room in a hurry.

"Is it armor, sire?" I asked.

The king grew a smile. "Exactly. I've had some prepared for you, Leon, and Jennava. I plan to equip the rest of my sorcerers with the same armor. It's made from Valaer steel. You know how light the material is."

"I do, sire. How much will you have left after the armor is made?"

"Just enough for a few more swords. No helmets yet, I'm afraid. I'm waiting for word back from the krepps. I might need Souriff to visit them."

"About her, sire, Failina warned me before coming here that her selfishness could prove dangerous for me and the others."

The king leaned back. "How did she warn you, exactly?"

I tried to tell the king about the experience, though I couldn't be very clear considering how confusing it had been.

None of it seemed to surprise the king very much. He folded his hands over his lap and seemed saddened by the news.

"I knew I couldn't trust Souriff completely," he said. "But to actually receive a warning about her from her sister is alarming." He stood up and paced. He stopped a few feet away and let out a sigh. "I'm considering keeping you here. It will be safer that way."

"I can handle myself fine. I will be safe."

He turned around. "What if Valinox intercepts you on your way there and the demigods are too far ahead to even notice?"

"I will make sure they stay with me."

"You must, otherwise you are to head back. In fact, I don't want you leaving the castle again without a demigod with you."

I stood up. "Sire, I'm going to need to practice my new skill. It is far too valuable to be ignored, and we both know the demigods are not going to escort me during all the time I need to practice."

"I realize that, but I need time to plan."

It was silent for a little while.

"There is much happening that you are unaware of," the king said. "There are even some things I am still waiting to confirm. For example, I can only guess the reason why I haven't received a request about you from the Yorns or Chespars."

"About me?" I asked.

"For your healing," he specified. "They are training an army. There must be some injured and sick, but there has been no request. I would consider sending you there if you had a way of cloaking yourself, like Valinox can. I spoke to the demigods about this, but there seems to be little to no chance of Nijja creating a stone for you. And even if she did, it might not be able to hold an ordia spell cast by someone else. Have you practiced your illusion spell?"

"I've temporarily given up on that," I sadly informed him. "I'm not sure if I ever will be able to learn it. I don't seem to have any natural talent with ordia."

"In that case, I will most likely be sending Kataleya to check on this army. Her family name will keep her protected, no matter what the rest of her family might be planning."

I wasn't sure why his majesty was telling me this, but he seemed to be studying my expression for something. Then I figured out what it was. He wanted to know if Kat and I were together in a romantic sense. He was the only one, after all, who had found out about us. I hoped he and Kataleya had kept it that way.

"Kataleya and I are just friends, but like the rest of my friends, I would worry about her staying in the care of nobles who might mean to betray you."

"Of course, Jon. It is a decision to which she would have to agree."

He looked at me for a while. It seemed like something else was on his mind.

Finally he asked, "Do you believe Kataleya would put my daughter's safety as her highest priority if I sent Callie with her?"

"She would, sire." I supposed that meant the king had decided he wanted his daughter to meet Trevor Chespar, unless he was already a step ahead and this was the marriage proposal.

There was a knock at the door. "Come in," the king said.

The servant who had left earlier now returned with a small chest piece of armor that glistened from the reflection of the room's lamplight. The armor itself was just large enough to protect my heart and surrounding chest. With four straps, it was easy enough to get on over my head. I was glad to feel that it fit snugly and didn't seem to impede my movement at all.

"My armorer designed it small to weigh you down as little as possible," Nykal said. "Because you can heal any injury, I figured only your heart and head need protection. Unfortunately, we couldn't come up with a novel design for a helmet that protected you completely without limiting your visibility. Come battle, you will have a typical headpiece like everyone else, but I can't guarantee it will be made with Valaer steel unless the krepps bring more of the material. The same goes for the chainmail you are to wear."

"Thank you, sire."

"You can thank Charlie as well. He's returned from Koluk and should be in his quarters in the apartments."

I figured that meant the king was dismissing me. I bowed and left, eager to see Charlie.

I hopped out of the keep through the closest window I could find and, with a little aid from dvinia, landed safely in front of the apartments. I walked in and headed up the stairs, eventually arriving at the door to Charlie's room. I knocked.

"Who is it?" he asked with a gravelly voice.

"It's Jon."

I could hear him shuffling around. Eventually he unlocked the door and pulled it open. It was clear he had been sleeping, his darkish blond hair a messy mop on his head. His bedsheets were peeled open across his mattress.

"How are you?" I asked.

"Tired. Where is everyone?"

"They should be coming back from the forest soon." I gestured at the armor across my chest. I had worn it out of the king's chambers, but he might've been too tired to notice it. "I want to thank you for this."

He smiled proudly. "I was working on that just yesterday. Did you know that the only other metal mages are much older than me, but their skill is worse than mine?"

Coming from anyone else's mouth, it might've sounded like bragging, but Charlie genuinely seemed amused and curious.

"I didn't know, but it doesn't surprise me. I knew you were very talented."

"I asked the king why there aren't other metal mages better than me," he continued. "There are reports of one, but he's in Rohaer. The king has been trying to find others to help me. There are two more in Koluk right now. One is old enough to be my father, and he's the worst out of the three of us." Charlie chuckled. "I have to give him advice sometimes. Isn't that funny?"

I imagined Charlie wishing he had a friend in Koluk to share this with. He was probably eager to tell us as soon as he came back. I didn't find it too amusing. Like I had told Charlie, I had always considered him to be an exceptional metal mage, even if I hadn't met any others. I figured that there weren't many people who were better with mtalia, or I would've heard about them. It was the same with Aliana's tracking skill.

I had seen Charlie melt a metal axe head quickly enough to stop a krepp, Grufaeragar, from taking a blade in his chest. So it was pretty much Charlie who had prevented a war between us and the krepps, because we wouldn't have been able to explain Grufaeragar's death to his fellow creatures in a way that proved our innocence.

It felt like it had been a long time since the dark mages loyal to Rohaer had tried to pull a trick on us. Valinox was no doubt plotting against us all this time, and although he was frightening, it seemed like Cason had been the better strategist, at least while Aliana's father was at large and assisting him.

We had come a long way since then. Something to be proud of, I figured, though I couldn't really feel it knowing an army of thousands was on its way here.

"I'm glad you're back," I told Charlie. "I hope they won't be sending you to Koluk again anytime soon. I'll let you get back to sleep."

But the sound of the portcullis opening across the courtyard turned us toward Charlie's window. We both walked over to see our group returning from the forest.

"I can sleep later," Charlie said as I watched him go over to his mirror and start brushing his wild hair. "I want to see Remi."

I tried to hide my smile.

*****

I didn't spend much time with my friends the rest of the day. After informing them that our plan to take out Gourfist would be fulfilled tomorrow, I spent the rest of the afternoon practicing my new skill. I agreed with Jennava and the king that I should not stray too far from the castle, so I picked myself up and threw myself from one end of the city to the other.

The king said that Byron Lawson, the head guard and an old friend of my father's, would spread word to the city guards that I would be training in this way. They should not be alarmed, and they should offer support if Valinox, by chance, spotted me and attempted to intercept me. I didn't imagine it would be the case.

With my armor on, and with the speed at which I traveled, it seemed impossible for him to kill me in the air. First, he'd have to take me down to the ground, where many people would be. Guards or not, I'm sure they would do something to aid me. Attacking me was a risk for Valinox, especially with Souriff and Failina around, and he wasn't known for putting himself at risk by choice.

I was certain the people of Newhaven could see me, but I was too high up to hear anything they might've said about a young man flying through the sky faster than a bird. With cloths around my ears, nose, and mouth, it was only my eyes that suffered from the intense wind. But a small healing spell took away the pain every time I wanted to break.

I had only just begun training today, but I was already getting used to the feeling. The blood-pumping thrill that emanated out from my chest and put a smile on my lips was still there after hours of practice, but the idea that I soon must kill Gourfist dampened my spirit somewhat.

I kept wondering if there was another way. I would be with people I didn't trust. Souriff and Eden worried me for different reasons. I wanted to believe in Failina wholeheartedly, but I had just met her. All the demigods seemed a little off to me. She was probably no exception. I just hadn't gotten to know her well enough to figure out what made her odd, yet.

It was getting late when I decided to return to the castle. I had lost track of time and found out that I had missed eating supper with everyone else. A plate had been saved for me. I was given permission by the castle staff to take it to my room as they cleaned the dining hall. I would have to leave my plate against the wall outside my door when I was done, covered by my napkin. It reminded me of earlier times, when I had first come to the castle and the princess had personally delivered dinner to me while I was holed up in my room and trying to learn my first spell so I wouldn't be thrown out the next morning.

I now ate alone in my room, but something didn't seem right. It felt like time was moving slowly now that I wasn't outdoors flying. I was aware of every little sound, my fork clinking, my teeth grinding my food into paste, the lump of it going down my throat as I swallowed. Eating this meal didn't feel good. In fact, nothing seemed like it would again, nothing but flying.

This new skill was changing me in some drastic way, but I didn't know how. All I did know was that I felt like I should still be out there, practicing, like there was nothing more important, not even eating.

I cherished the Induct stone I had taken from Eden. Without it, this probably wouldn't have been possible without months more of practice.

There was a knock at my door. I wanted to be alone. Seeing one of my friends might pull me out of this state, and there was part of me that wanted to stay here and was ready to fight for it. I didn't budge from my seat.

They knocked again.

I grumbled. I wished I didn't have people looking out for me because then I could continue to ignore the insistent knocking. If I did that now, however, whoever it was would probably get guards to break down my door.

I opened the door to see Hadley. She had two empty vials in her hands. "Hello, Jon," she said with a grin as if happy to see me. "I came to wish you a safe trip tomorrow and request that you fill these vials with the blood of Gourfist if it's possible. Also, could you bring back as many feathers as you can? I'm not sure if you're planning to carry a bag on your back, or if Eden will carry food for the two of you." She seemed to stop in the middle of what she was saying. With a furrowed brow, she looked at me closely. "Are you all right?"

"Yeah, I'm fine," I said, eerily indifferent to not only the situation tomorrow but to the appearance of Hadley. I knew she was beautiful, but this time it didn't stir anything in me.

"Are you sure?" I didn't know what she saw in my eyes, but it had to be something. "May I come in?"

"I'd rather be alone."

I could hear voices in the hall. Some of my friends were probably outside their rooms, chatting. There were a couple of guards standing stoically, pretending to ignore it all. I remembered that it wouldn't be long before Michael would be sharing my room to keep me protected, while Eden would be spending the night in Aliana's room next door.

Dammit. I wasn't going to be alone no matter what I said.

I walked back to my plate. I should finish my supper. Then I could get to bed quickly so Michael wouldn't want to talk to me.

Earlier, when my friends had returned from the forest, I had informed them of my plans tomorrow and of my interaction with Failina, including her warning about Souriff. I hadn't been able to stick around and listen to all their concerns, as I had been too eager to spend as much time as I could practicing. If I couldn't keep up with the demigods tomorrow, they would leave me behind. Something told me I *had* to be with them when they faced Gourfist, not just to protect Eden, but to make sure everything went smoothly. Normally I took some semblance of pride in this, but now it felt like a chore.

I went back to my desk, sat down, picked up my fork, and continued the arduous task of shoveling food into my mouth. I couldn't remember the last time I had this little interest in eating.

It took me a moment before I realized that Hadley was sitting on the edge of my bed and staring at me with concern.

"What are you doing?" I asked.

"You spent all this time flying?"

"Yes."

"And now you have little interest in anything else?"

I felt my defenses go up. It wasn't so much that the question itself was incisive; it was the way she spoke it, as if she knew exactly what was wrong with me.

I didn't want anyone to know.

"Everything's as it should be," I tried to tell her casually, though I heard some anger come out through my tone.

She looked at me in silence for a long while. I ignored her until I finished the last of my food. There hadn't been much left.

Hadley calmly got up off my bed and walked over to my hearth. Only then did I realize that there was no fire. No one had come into my room to start one like they usually did. That's why it was so cold in here. Hadley knelt down in front of my hearth and stuck out her hand. A thin jet of fire came out and lit the wood.

She hissed as she backed away, holding her burned hand. She looked up at me a few times, silently beckoning for me to heal her. I walked over begrudgingly.

She didn't hold up her hand for me, so I took her arm to lift her hand on my own. I healed away her minor burns.

To my shock, she snatched her hand back and slapped me.

"What the hell?" I yelled.

She motioned to slap me again, but I grabbed her arm.

"What are you doing?" I said.

"Jon, you're in a lackadaze!" She tried to slap me with her other hand, but I grabbed that wrist as well. "Let go. I need to snap you out of it." She kicked me in the shin with what looked to be all of her strength.

"Ow!"

I hopped away from her as I grabbed my shin.

One of the guards threw open my door. "Is everything all right?" the man asked.

I looked back to see Hadley putting up her hands passively. "Everything's fine."

"Jon?" asked the guard.

"It's fine," I agreed.

He seemed a bit confused, but he closed the door as he left.

"Are you done hitting me?" I asked before I healed my stinging cheek and cut shin. "Damn, that was quite a kick. You drew blood." I showed her, rolling up my pants.

"I'm sorry. I was trying to get you out of your lackadaze, and it looks like it worked. Are you feeling more like yourself?"

"I suppose I am. That's the second time you've used that phrase. Are you saying lack a daze?"

"Yes, but it's one word that means something else from what you're thinking. It comes from the word lackadaisical, which is an adjective for lethargic and without interest. A lackadaze is a common occurrence in Rohaer when someone first uses great power with dteria. I saw it all the time. Afterward, it's as if nothing else matters to them. I didn't think it was possible with dvinia, but it seems to have happened to you." She looked up at me with her large dark eyes. "I'm worried for you."

"I am feeling much better," I said. The fog of my mind was gone. "My god, it was bad for a while. Thank you."

Hadley stepped close and opened her arms. I was a little confused, but I welcomed the embrace. But just as I was starting to hold her, she stole the Induct stone from my pocket and made for the door.

I was about to scream in fury for her to stop, but then I realized this was a test. I held my tongue, as difficult as it was. She got her hand on the door handle before she looked back.

I folded my arms and breathed out my frustration as calmly as I could.

She put on a sheepish grin. "I thought one more test was in order." She came back and placed the Induct stone in my hand. "It looks like there is quite a difference between a lackadaze caused by dteria and one caused by dvinia. You really do seem completely out of it now. It takes much longer to draw someone out of one caused by dteria."

"Hey," I said, just realizing something. "You cast a fire spell earlier."

"I was wondering if you'd noticed in your state. I learned it recently, but it's difficult to use without burning myself. I'm far from casting fire as a means of defending myself in battle."

"That's your intention with it?"

"Yes, I can't solely rely on curses if I plan to fight alongside the rest of the sorcerers."

"I didn't know you planned that."

"It's a recent plan."

We held each other's gazes for a moment.

"Could this happen to me again?" I asked. "Another lackadaze?"

"I don't think so. From what I know about them, they start off strong and only get worse if they are not stopped. But if the caster is pulled out of one, he or she is much less likely to fall into another."

"So this must've happened to Eden recently."

"I'm not sure. I don't know her that well."

"She's usually very different, funny in her own way."

"It sounds like she has, then. I thought that might be the case. I told the other girls about lackadazes already. They are working Eden out of hers, and I do believe they will be successful in a few days. Yours was much easier to disable, but it could've been worse had it gone on longer. I'm glad I came to see you now. I feared you might've fallen into one and wanted to check."

"Well, I am feeling much better," I said. "I owe you."

She gestured at the empty vials I didn't remember her putting on my bed. "You can pay me back by filling them."

A silence passed. I felt like she was about to go.

"You might need to check me for a lackadaze a few more times," I said facetiously. "Just to be sure. Maybe there is a less painful way of doing so."

She grinned for a moment but then lost her smile.

"I want to ask you something personal," she said. "Now you don't have to answer. In fact, it's probably not any of my business."

I had a feeling what this was about. "Go ahead," I said.

"Everyone seems to think that you are going to marry Callie Lennox one day. I heard what you said in the forest. You seem to be strongly against that idea. May I ask why?"

There was one benefit to my inability to hide my feelings, and it was in times like these. *Because of you,* I told her with my eyes as I answered. "I think you know."

"Oh." She looked down. "So there is something between us," she murmured, a blush coloring her cheeks. "I don't know what it is." Carefully, she glanced up from the tops of her eyes.

"We can find out right now," I told her, hoping this was the answer she wanted to hear.

But she didn't seem pleased as she studied me. "Are you only saying that because...?" She glanced away. "I'm not sure I can say it."

It was difficult for me to figure out what she was thinking, especially when my heart was pounding. I knew what I wanted, and I was about to show her. I put my hand on her shoulder to turn her toward me. I started to lean down toward her lips.

She didn't glance up to meet mine but turned away

instead—a dagger in my heart.

Oh god, I was wrong.

I was too embarrassed to look at her as I stepped back. "I'm sorry," I said. "I thought you felt the same way as I do."

"That's what I'm trying to figure out. There's much I still don't know about you. I don't know what you want with me."

I'd already thrown myself out there. I didn't see how I could make it worse. I was about to tell her.

Wait, it could be worse. This might end up like it had with Kataleya. After we had been together, I had practically pleaded with her to see me again. I was embarrassed every time I thought of it. The last thing I wanted was to go through that again.

"What do you want with me?" I asked.

"I don't know, but I can't stop thinking about you. When we are near, it's difficult to take my eyes off you. When we're not, I find myself hoping to see you soon. I've never felt this way before. I can't say it makes much sense because I haven't known you for that long. What's even more confusing is that there are beautiful girls in this castle who were here before me, and I don't know if you've had relations with them. If so, then why aren't you together? Would the same thing happen to me? Maybe you're planning to marry the princess after all and you just want to bed me. I don't know. Sometimes I think you feel the same way as I do, and other times I have no idea anymore."

Hadley looked down and away. "Listen to me. I sound like a fool. I don't know why I let all of this out. I couldn't stop once I started. I feared I might divulge my feelings one of these times I spoke to you. I knew I should've just checked on you and left. Why am I still talking? By the devil's tail, Jon, please say something!"

"Hadley."

She seemed frightened as she finally looked back at me. Her breathing was ragged, her face bright red.

"I did consider marriage into the Lennox family, but just for a moment," I explained. "Do you know what made me decide to stop considering it?"

She shook her head.

"Because then I would never have a future with you. The only reason I can function each and every day is because I suppress the feelings I have for you. That's why sometimes it seems like I'm not interested. It's the only way I can get through my day. You make me absolutely insane. In fact, I'm really worried about what's going to happen."

"What do you mean?"

"I mean, I'm going to kiss you now, and I don't know how I'm going to be able to let you go after."

She rushed to me. I was surprised by the enthusiasm of her lips, at first. But as the realization dawned on me that I was finally kissing Hadley and she showed no inclination of holding back, I let out the fire within my body. I forgot that there was anything else besides Hadley as our passion grew.

There was a knock at my door. "Jon, you decent?"

Dammit! Michael was of course coming to sleep in my room. I had blissfully forgotten.

Hadley and I separated, and only then did I realize that her hands were fisted in my hair and shirt.

Before I could think of something to tell Michael, he was opening my door and catching us tied up in each other's arms. I didn't know why my instinct was to pretend as if nothing had happened, but it seemed like Hadley's instincts were the same. Both of us jumped away from each other.

It didn't help.

"Whoa, uh, I'm sorry," Michael said with his hands up. "I'll come back later." He quickly shut the door.

Hadley started laughing. I did as well. She nestled up close to me, putting her head against my chest.

Our laughter died down. Then she glanced up, her eyes on my lips.

I kissed her softly this time. Nothing meant more to me in that moment than her. Michael was a distant memory. Even Gourfist seemed like someone else's problem.

Hadley felt small and delicate to me, wrapped in my arms. We seemed to fit together like a glove made for a hand, like a sheath for a sword, and she was a hot fire in a cold night.

Something ignited in her as we kissed, as she pressed herself against me and opened her mouth to have more of mine. I pulled her closer. I couldn't imagine letting go.

Hadley's warmth was not just heat but something else. It was intoxicating, reaching every corner of my limbs as we kissed.

Eventually we simply stood close, huddled together as she leaned her head against my chest. She let out a satisfied sigh.

"I should go," she said with glistening eyes.

"You don't have to. You could stay with me."

"I do have to. I can't stay with you. You need better protection than I can offer."

Unfortunately, it was true. Michael was my best bet

against an ambush by Valinox.

"I'll be thinking of you all night," I said as I gently fixed her twisted up shirt with soft pats and tugs across her shoulders and collar.

She put her hand over mine as it rested just below her collar. "But I want you thinking about what you have to do tomorrow. You have to make sure you come back safely."

"I will," I said.

She slowly peeled away from me. I took her hand and walked with her toward the door.

"Bye," she said, then went to her toes to give me a peck.

"Bye." I kissed her back.

"Bye," she said again, giving me a longer kiss this time.

"Goodbye," I said, returning with one of my own.

"Goodnight," she said, then devoured my mouth as she pushed herself up against me and vigorously fisted my hair.

I couldn't help but think it was a glimpse of what could soon be to come, her hot passion igniting a flame throughout my body. It left me tingling after she parted with a sultry look in her eyes.

I couldn't utter a word as I could only think about picking her up and carrying her to my bed.

"Goodnight," she said again as she opened the door just enough to slip out.

I was suddenly alone, the sound of my breath sharp. The fire in my hearth crackled. I could barely feel its heat, my insides already burning.

I didn't care that I would have to share a bed with Michael in case Valinox attacked. I didn't care that the next day I would have to kill Gourfist. I was too happy to worry about any of it.

CHAPTER SEVEN

Centuries ago

When Airinold turned thirteen, his father told him that the other demigods before him had spent their teen years designing their contribution to mankind. His father pressured him to do the same, but Airinold was different. He spent his teen years watching his siblings and learning from their mistakes.

At first, Airinold wanted to be more like his father, Basael, who had created something that others could build upon—mana. Basael had given meaning to notes and birthed sorcery by doing so. Soon after, Basael took a human as his wife and impregnated her. He gave up a little piece of himself with each child he brought to life within her, more so after seeing the good that they brought into the world.

He had sacrificed more power for Airinold than he had for any other demigod. For a while, Airinold was the strongest of them all, especially because he hadn't given up any of his own strength to create a school of magic like his siblings had. Then Basael gave life to Airinold's younger brother, Caarda.

Airinold's jealousy of his father's favorite son was short-lived. Caarda soon became his closest friend.

Airinold and Caarda both wanted to do something more than create a school of magic. They liked the idea of one day bringing life into the world, as their father had done. However, none of the demigods could procreate and were told by their father not to take wives or husbands. Continuously, Basael pressured both Airinold and Caarda into creating something on their own by giving up much of the power bestowed onto them. However, both could not decide what they wanted to make.

The rest of their siblings had finished their creations long before and had moved on to other goals. Failina, the sister closest to Airinold in age, had impressed their father the most of all, managing to find some way to turn mana into fire and water, the building blocks of life. She didn't stop there, giving sorcerers the ability to make wind and even ice.

Although awestruck by Failina, Airinold looked up to his oldest sister, Souriff, even more. She could fly faster than a falcon. Airinold wanted this ability for himself, but he also wanted to do more. Souriff seemed quite limited by her one school of dvinia. Airinold liked how their sister Nijja had created order from mana. Even if it wasn't as fun to use as Souriff's dvinia, it was much more useful. His creation would certainly be inspired by the two of them.

Meanwhile, Caarda took a very different interest in mana. Although he was pressured by their father, like Airinold was, Caarda said his creation would take the longest and eventually convinced Basael to give him more time.

Airinold enjoyed his days with Caarda as they walked aimlessly through Curdith Forest and ruminated about their potential creations. Although Caarda was the youngest demigod, at thirteen to Airinold's fifteen, Caarda was exceptionally wise. He felt things from the earth and the air that Airinold couldn't feel. He seemed to know how everything fit together and frequently commented on how beautiful it was. He tried many times to describe these unseen elements that made up their world to Airinold, but Airinold could never quite understand them like Caarda did.

Caarda wanted to make a school of magic that would help him further explore the mysteries of their world and the infinities of the universe. It didn't take him long to figure out exactly what he wanted to create, but he spent even more time contemplating whether he should do it. When pressured by their father, Caarda explained that he feared the outcome would not assist mankind as the other schools of magic had but might very well lead to the decimation of all life.

Basael was not so worried. He did not believe any of his children could create something so detrimental and pushed Caarda to make it so.

Nonetheless, Caarda withheld his creation for years on end, which came as a great disappointment to their father. Meanwhile, Airinold remained lost about what he should do. It wasn't like he could create something and then change his mind after. He had asked his siblings if they could destroy their creations and start over. None said it was possible, but Airinold believed they were keeping something from him. It was only Failina who admitted the truth.

"Yes," she had told him. "I think all of us can destroy what we've made, but it is likely to destroy us as well."

It was no wonder that Valinox, Souriff, and Nijja had refused to admit this. By then, Airinold had learned that the three of them were much more selfish than the humans and elves they held their noses over.

His realization about what kind of beings his siblings really were started when he noticed how there were always trifles and affairs between them. Valinox and Nijja found romantic interest in each other, as did Airinold and Failina eventually, but it was not at all like the relationship between their older siblings. Meanwhile, Souriff fawned after Caarda as he got older and grew even wiser, often offering guidance to the rest of their siblings. Souriff agreed with their father that Caarda could create something truly remarkable and that he could never make something detrimental to the precious life of the world. So she, too, pressured him to make his creation and be done with it already.

Things turned sour when Caarda started showing less interest in his siblings. He spent increasingly more time among the humans, dressing and acting like them to better understand mankind and to pass as one of them.

Airinold believed that Caarda never did so with intentions of falling in love, but he did eventually, with a human woman.

Their older siblings—the ones more loyal to Basael's will—were angry at Caarda when they found out, but no one's rage compared to Souriff's. There was no doubt in Airinold's mind that she had plans for a future with Caarda, only for them to be snuffed out in favor of a human woman. Of course, Souriff was deeply insulted.

"How could a human woman ever be as desirable as a demigod?" Airinold heard her complaining to their father.

"He will see the way eventually," Basael soothed. "Give him time."

Airinold eventually had the pleasure of meeting this human woman. She was one of the most beautiful beings Airinold had ever encountered, from inside to out.

Airinold, now in his twenties, still couldn't finalize a decision about his creation. By then, however, his father mostly left him alone. Basael was too focused on Caarda to care about Airinold. Caarda had been brought into this world to create a school of magic better than anyone else's, and he *would* obey his father's wish.

It was then that Basael decreed that no demigods should be involved in love affairs with humans, even though he still had a human wife at the time. Only Souriff was willing to look past Basael's hypocrisy and follow this rule without question. She was also the only one who had expressed no interest in mortals.

Airinold had spent many nights with Failina by then, but they had also, separately, explored the bedrooms of many mortals. There was no grudge between them, like the one festering between Valinox and Nijja. Airinold and Failina enjoyed each other's company, with no jealousy when they were apart. Caarda remained Airinold's closest friend, even if Airinold didn't see him nearly as often as before.

Caarda would return to the forest sometimes, however, and he always brought his human wife with him. He was displeased with Basael's rule, refusing to follow it, and the other demigods didn't fret much about it, either.

Failina's affairs with mortals caused one man to kill another out of jealousy. Then Basael killed the remaining one as a punishment to Failina. She drew away for a while after that. Valinox and Nijja fought with each other constantly, both using the hearts and bodies of mortals in order to twist each other's emotions. No deaths had occurred yet, but everyone knew it was only a matter of time. Meanwhile, Souriff remained loyal. Frustrated, but loyal.

Airinold grew angry with their father and wanted to stop invading the lives of mortals, so it was only by chance that he followed Basael's decree. Airinold took many strolls with Caarda through the forest, just like before, only with the human woman there, as well as a new bitterness against their father hanging in the air. That's when Airinold learned what it meant to be human.

This human woman did not struggle with the same things that demigods did. None of her kin did, either. Their problems did not arise out of arrogance and spite but out of a need to survive. Feeding their children and getting them through freezing winters and outbreaks of disease was enough of a struggle on its own. They didn't have time to worry about whose bed seemed more inviting. There seemed to be a bond between mortals that the demigods often broke when they interjected themselves into human affairs.

After that, Airinold appreciated even more what Failina had created for mortals and less what Souriff did. There were many humans who had learned to manipulate the elements, enhancing their lives with fire and water especially. Even Valinox's creation of mtalia, as simple as it was, did much more for human and elfkind than Souriff's dvinia.

"It was on purpose that Souriff has made it difficult for others to reach the necessary notes for dvinia," Caarda explained to Airinold one day. "She doesn't want anyone else to use it but her."

Airinold had found this hard to believe for a long time, but it was Souriff's later actions that confirmed it in his mind.

Eventually the demigods stopped meddling in human affairs and everything seemed to calm down. Failina had returned and reunited with Airinold. He was still far from deciding what he wanted to make, but Basael didn't pressure him as much. It was Caarda who their father had his eye on, though something had changed. Basael often spoke to Caarda as if there was something specific he expected Caarda to make, and it seemed to be different than the school of magic Caarda had already come up with yet feared to bring into the world.

Basael continued to warn Caarda that he would be better off if he separated from his wife. By then, Basael had returned his own wife to the human town he had plucked her out of and never spoke of her again.

"Time is not a merciful god, Airi," Caarda would often say, more so after his discussions with their father.

Airinold always figured this meant that time would take away his brother's wife, but he found out later that there was more to it than that.

"There's a door that, once I open it, it might never be shut," Caarda would sometimes say.

There was often a heaviness to his speech, as if he knew his time in this world might soon come to an end.

Eventually, things went back to how they were. Valinox and Nijja fought. Failina found company with more mortal men. And Souriff tried to turn Caarda against his wife by speaking ill of her and convincing him his choices were made in poor judgment.

Basael scolded his children and dished out punishments by entrapping them in cages of sorcery, but when he let them out later, all it seemed to do was teach them how to hide their illicit affairs better. These were beings who had never been admonished and had become spoiled, but their father wasn't any better. He was a hypocrite who did not care much about what his children wanted, only what they might be able to create. He constantly pressured Caarda and even threatened him at times, which only drove Caarda further away.

All of it disgusted Airinold to watch. He had grown too different from his oldest siblings to enjoy their company anymore and could only ever spend his days with Failina and Caarda. But soon, that too would be ruined by their oldest kin.

Caarda's wife was murdered.

Airinold accused Souriff of paying someone to kill Caarda's wife. Or perhaps she did it with her own hands. Souriff denied all of it, vehemently. Caarda didn't seem to care who did it. He didn't care about much anymore. He was not capable of anger, which frustrated Airinold, especially because Caarda seemed to feel despair stronger than anyone else could.

It wasn't the first time that a mortal lover had been murdered. Nijja was very promiscuous, and many of her lovers were found dead, most likely murdered by Valinox. However, because this was happening in Fyrren, it didn't come to Airinold's attention until later.

He was too heartbroken for Caarda to express any passion anymore, and so was Failina. They each saw this as the beginning of dark times. Failina changed. She marked her body in permanent ways, displaying symbols on her arms that seemed to mean something to her, though she never shared that meaning with anyone else. When their father expressed his displeasure in her appearance and punished her for it, she responded by cutting off most of her long hair. Basael locked her in a cage for a week after that.

It was only Souriff and Valinox who continued to seek favor from their father. The two of them held onto the belief that demigods should not lay with mortals and contemplated punishment for those who did. Meanwhile, no punishment came to Souriff for what she had most likely done to Caarda's wife, nor did any reach Valinox for the mortals he lay with earlier. As far as Airinold knew, Basael didn't even scold Valinox for the men he had killed in Fyrren because it had been in response to Nijja's promiscuity.

Airinold still hadn't created anything. He was physically more powerful than all his siblings except Caarda, though he was prepared to sacrifice that and become as weak as a mortal man if he could just make something that would fix all of this. Souriff and Valinox were still strong because neither of them had given up much of their power for their creations. Nijja and Failina had been different. Their power lay solely in the magical arts, a power easily accessible by all mortals, while mtalia and dvinia were almost impossible to reach.

Eventually Caarda convinced Airinold to confront their father with him. Caarda told Basael that his other children were out of control. They needed supervision so that more innocent people wouldn't die. Basael would hear none of it until Caarda and Airinold made the same sacrifice the rest of their siblings had made. They had to give up their power to create. It was their purpose. After that, Basael would have some say in the matter.

"One of you must create the most powerful form of sorcery seen yet," Basael had told them. "I know it is within one of you to do this. Don't disappoint me any longer."

It was clear to Airinold that their father was using their "purpose" as leverage. That did it for Airinold. He no longer respected Basael, no longer believed Basael was all-powerful and all-knowing.

Caarda withdrew from everyone afterward, even Airinold, claiming he needed some time to figure out things. Souriff said Caarda probably went far away to meet some other woman he would marry, but Airinold knew Caarda would not do that. After weeks, Airinold went looking for his brother, all the while reshaping his idea of what his creation would be.

Months went by without anyone hearing anything from Caarda. He and Airinold were the only two demigods who hadn't created something, but Airinold was close. He just wanted to find his brother and speak with him one more time before he unleashed his creation on the world. It was Caarda's opinion he trusted on the matter.

Caarda had been right. The demigods needed more supervision from their father. A war between humans and elves had broken out during this time. While the elves lived in Curdith Forest, humans had migrated there from the cold north. From before Airinold was born to the present day, humans had been forming towns around the forest. There had been no fighting until now.

The humans wanted resources from the forest that

the elves thought belonged to them. Failina had taken an elven lover recently and sided with the elves. Valinox took the humans' side after convincing them to choose him to be their leader. Nijja didn't get involved. Souriff joined Failina because she didn't think Valinox had good intentions, and soon Souriff was claiming to be the leader of the elves.

Valinox was powerful with mtalia, capable of melting the weapons of nearly every elven defender as he marched his humans into the forest looking for blood. But Souriff was even stronger, her weapon of dvinia a force that Valinox could not stop.

It wasn't long after the war began that Failina wanted Airinold's help in pacifying the situation. Many mortals were dying on both sides.

"It's Father's responsibility, not mine," Airinold said, hoping this would finally be the time when Basael did the right thing.

Failina went to their father for help, and Basael summoned all the demigods to the outskirts of the forest to meet between the human towns and the elven villages. Thousands of mortals gathered to watch and listen. Even Nijja responded to the summons, with great displeasure, but Caarda did not show up.

"Shouldn't Caarda be here?" Souriff complained as the meeting was beginning.

"He doesn't need to be," Basael replied sharply. "He is not the problem."

Basael looked as powerful as he was, a massive being ten feet tall with unmatched strength. His features resembled that of a human man, with long, gray hair and diamond gray eyes.

"All of you are here to swear an oath," Basael announced, addressing his children before the mortals. "You are not to interfere between the love and war of mortals, and your actions will not directly lead to the death of any mortal. Your purpose is to better the lives of everyone in this world, not just yourselves. You will start acting like it, or you will be punished more severely than ever before."

One by one, the demigods swore to the oath in front of their father and all the mortals who had come from afar to watch.

The war changed after that when the humans quickly took the advantage. Valinox still involved himself with them, though he didn't fight directly. With his mtalia, he was able to help them create a mass of weapons.

Souriff, no doubt regretting that she couldn't do more with her gift to mankind, gave up more of her power to bless the forest with dvinia. The mortals who trained in the magical arts in the elven territory found themselves with a gift of learning. It might've been the only good thing Souriff did in all of her existence. This weakened her for a while, but the elves prospered and kept themselves from being decimated without Failina, who had removed herself after taking the oath.

Watching everything unfold made Airinold furious. He and Failina wanted to put an end to the war, but there was little they could do on their own. So they went to their father for help, but Basael trusted that the demigods would work it out.

"And if not, Airinold," Basael said, "this will implore you or Caarda to finally create something that will prevent further death. If you still refuse to fulfill your purpose, Airinold, then you must find your brother. You will bring him back here to see what has happened in his absence."

Airinold tried to convince Basael that he needed to be the one to stop this before more mortals died, but Basael refused. Basael took himself away from it all, residing deep in the forest where he said he would not be disturbed until Airinold or Caarda fulfilled their purpose.

Airinold left to look for his brother, but it wasn't long after that the Day of Death occurred. There was a great fiery explosion that spread all across the forest when a massive rock fell from the sky and crashed into the forest center. Airinold returned as quickly as he could and found out that his siblings had survived, having been near the outskirts of the forest, but no one knew about Basael. No one could feel his presence anymore or locate him.

The fighting became worse as Valinox did everything he could, short of fighting, to help his humans destroy the elves. Souriff wanted to push back after many of her elves were killed, but she feared going against the oath. She expected repercussions to fall on Valinox, but they did not.

Eventually the elves gave in and left the forest for good. This didn't stop the humans from fighting amongst each other, however, as battles continued to rage. Souriff and Valinox continued to pick sides against each other, each vying for leadership of the most powerful group of humans. Airinold knew that with Caarda and their father gone, he had to be the one to stop all of this before the mortals destroyed everything they had built.

He let anger guide him as he thought through the

last nuances of his creation. He was just about to bring it to fruition when a mortal delivered a message to Airinold.

"Hold off on your creation for now. Meet me in the eastern mountains. Climb high. You will feel my presence when you are close."

It was signed by Caarda.

Airinold was reluctant at first, but he did decide he would see his brother. The journey took several days, but eventually he felt his brother's powerful presence near the peaks. The wind was strong here, whipping at Caarda's ragged cloak where he stood on the precipice of the mountains overlooking the sea. Airinold had never seen him this grim, his face caked with dirt and dark circles under his eyes as if he hadn't slept for days.

"I finished my creation," Caarda intoned. There was something sinister at play. Airinold kept his distance, for he felt that it wasn't his brother standing before him. This Caarda had been hurt beyond repair, and Airinold didn't know what he sought.

"Are you of sound mind?" Airinold asked nervously.

"I'm not sure I can answer that with certainty. What I can say is that I can't keep going on with this pain I carry, or I will not survive. I must leave this world."

It brought tears to Airinold's eyes. "You might feel better if you come back with me and take revenge against Souriff."

"Revenge would do no good for my wife and the other mortals who have been killed."

"Then do it for the rest of the people who are still alive. Souriff and Valinox will destroy every last mortal if they are not destroyed themselves."

"That is not true. I have determined what is going to happen, and there's only one role I can play without making everything worse."

"What do you mean you determined what is going to happen?"

"Because of my creation," Caarda said. "I now see glimpses of the past, present, and future."

Airinold feared his brother had gone mad. "Caarda, you call me to the summit of this mountain, where it seems you have dwelled without sleep. Then you spout nonsense about the future as if you've witnessed it come to pass. Don't you see that you are not making sense and need help?"

"I don't need any help. You do. I know what you've been working on." Caarda spoke as if catching Airinold misbehaving. "I've felt it for a long time."

Airinold took a few steps away from his brother.

"I did not bring you here to stop you," Caarda said. "I brought you here so we could help each other. My creation is done, Airi. It is active."

"Since when?"

"Since right before I sent for you."

"But I didn't feel anything. No one did." If they had, someone would've mentioned something.

"They won't for a long time. Neither will the mortals. I was selfish. I made it for myself."

"What does it do?" Airinold asked.

"I provided a way to physically and mentally connect to the world in ways that—I thought—were not possible before."

"You thought?" Airinold asked.

Caarda looked him up and down, tilting his head from one side to the other. He didn't answer Airinold's question but instead said, “Heed my warning: You must prepare for your own suffering if you truly mean to put an end to everyone else’s.”

“I am prepared for that, but I’m not prepared for you to leave. Why don’t you stay and help me?”

“I am in too much pain. I would rather die. The future I’ve chosen for myself is a compromise.”

If there was one thing that remained consistent about Caarda it was that once he made up his mind, no one could change it.

“You are weaker than I thought!” Airinold snapped. “You run from problems that you have the power to fix, and you abandon me in the process!”

Caarda frowned. “I never claimed to be strong, only wise. I ask that you trust me. If I got involved with the war, it would only make matters worse. Now that father is no longer here, you are the strongest of our family. You always have been. You will see this through, and then you will come back for me.”

Caarda walked over to a nearby cave with Airinold close behind. There was a loose slab of rock that was so large that even Caarda with his full strength probably could not move it.

“I’m going to kill Souriff for what she did,” Airinold said. “I will kill her and Valinox if that’s the only way to bring peace to the world.”

“I know that’s what you intend,” Caarda said without any semblance of surprise. “But you are going to be blamed for the misery caused by others. You must prepare for that.”

“I am prepared.”

“You will make peace for a time,” Caarda said. “But I believe you must rely on the mortals to put an end to our siblings' fighting for good."

"You believe?" Airinold questioned. "You claimed you can see what will happen."

"Time is mysterious in that way. I can't see all of it at once."

"Then your reasons for leaving us could be wrong," Airinold said. "Please. I have never asked you for anything. Stay with me and help."

Caarda shook his head. "No, I am certain. When I'm gone, don't look to me for guidance. Don't look to your mana, either. Only time can heal our wounds." He stepped into the nearby cave. "I'm going to tell you one last thing. When I am done, you must promise not to say anything. You will cover this cave to protect me from nature or any beast that might come across me while I am vulnerable...if that is what you wish." Caarda gestured at the massive rock nearby.

"I can't possibly move that."

"You can."

Airinold looked at the huge slab of mountain again. He had never tried to move something so large.

"You will know when I am gone," Caarda said. "Nothing I can say will stop you from checking on me afterward. Just try not to let what you see shape your choices, and make sure to cover my cave when you are done. Leave only enough space for air."

Besides the specific instructions to cover the cave, Airinold didn't quite know what any of this meant.

"Let's say our goodbyes now," Caarda said, "because you will not want to trust me after I tell you what I have to say."

Confused, Airinold didn't know what else to do besides give a slow nod. He did trust that Caarda knew best. Caarda squeezed his shoulder.

"You will come back for me when all of this is over. I see it. Only then can we move past what happened and start again."

"I promise I will."

They shared an embrace.

Caarda stepped away and told Airinold something that was too difficult for him to believe at first. When Caarda was done, Airinold was too shocked to move. Caarda merely sat in his cave with his head slumped as if he'd fallen into a deep sleep.

When Airinold's wits returned, he tried to ask his brother questions, but Caarda did not reply.

Eventually Airinold realized he had no choice but to try to protect his brother with the slab of rock. To his amazement, he found that he could move the stone if he gave it everything he had. He never knew himself to be this strong, but apparently Caarda did.

Time suddenly seemed to stop as Airinold felt that Caarda had finished whatever he was doing within the cave. Airinold could no longer feel the wind on his skin. The ocean below had gone quiet. The trees across the land did not sway. Not one loose pebble rolled down the mountain slopes. Everything was still.

Airinold knew that once he sacrificed his power to bring his creation to fruition, for a long time he would lack the physical strength that he needed to free his brother from this cave. He wasn't ready for that. He had to see his brother one last time.

He pushed the slab of rock back out of the way, just enough to squeeze into the cave. "Caarda?" he called as he stepped in.

He gasped at what he saw.

CHAPTER EIGHT

Airinold entered the cave. "What did you do to yourself?" he murmured, though he knew his brother couldn't hear him.

Caarda floated like a feather suspended by the wind. He was curled up into a ball, his hands around his knees and his head down on top of them. There was some sort of aura around him, a shimmering sphere that Airinold could barely make out in the dark cave.

Airinold cautiously moved his hand into the sphere surrounding his brother and took Caarda's arm. He could easily move Caarda through the air, but he stopped after a test, as he felt he was disrupting whatever it was Caarda had done to himself. So he just stood there and watched for a while.

Eventually, Airinold felt as though even his presence was disturbing Caarda's restful slumber. He walked out of the cave and pushed the slab of rock back to make sure Caarda would be safe.

He didn't know how long it would be until he would see Caarda again, but even when he did, it was unlikely he would see the version of his younger brother he had grown up with. That Caarda died when Souriff killed his human wife. He might never come back.

Grief took Airinold as he cried openly for a long while. Then anger came, and he realized it was time for him to act.

"Revenge might not make you feel better, brother, but it will me."

It took an entire day to bring dteria to light. Airinold was so exhausted by the time he finished that he slept for two days straight.

It was done. Now all he had to do was wait. He had been patient until now. He could be patient a little longer.

He didn't want to see his siblings while he was in this weakened state. He wasn't even sure he had the strength to descend the mountain if he tried. So he rested for months as he planned how he would use his power, realizing only later that Caarda must've seen this. He'd known that Airinold would need to be somewhere safe while he recovered.

Like the other demigods, Airinold would not perish without food, though he would without water. Caarda had collected enough rainwater, however, to see Airinold through this. Eventually the power given to him by dteria would make up for his lack of sustenance.

He created dteria as a way to kill his troublemaking siblings but also to target the weak-willed mortals who thirsted for power. He could feel sorcerers discovering it, experimenting, some already succumbing to the pleasure of its immediate strength as they craved more.

His dteria told him exactly where each person was whenever they used this sorcery. As it corrupted their soul, it empowered Airinold. However, nothing was permanent. As strong as Airinold was, even he couldn't bring a magical art to the mortal world that would permanently siphon power from these beings. They had to continue to use dteria for it to work.

When he was stronger than ever before, Airinold

descended the mountain and returned to the forest to check on the war between men and their demigods. It seemed like just about every capable fighter or sorcerer had joined the fray. Valinox and Souriff showed no regard for human life as they led battalions of men against one another.

When Airinold returned to society, he told people this new sorcery was named "dteria" to ensure the mortals who used it had no excuse. They had to know what it did to them and still choose it over any other form of mana. At first, Airinold joined Souriff's army and made it seem as if he had created dteria to vanquish Valinox and his followers. He warned Souriff's people about the effects of dteria and told them not to use it, ordering those who had already begun to stop immediately. Many heeded his warnings, but many more sought power no matter the consequences.

When it looked as if Valinox would soon surrender and no doubt flee for his own safety, Airinold switched to his side. He issued the same warning. They must not use dteria. Like Souriff's people, most didn't want to stop.

It wasn't long before everyone had at least heard of dteria, with many more picking up the sorcery every day.

"What have you done, Airi?" Failina accused her brother one night. "I thought you wanted to stop the fighting, but now you're feeding the flames."

"This is the only way it will stop. Give it time, sister. You will see."

And in the time that dteria spread across the land, Airinold grew so powerful that he eventually knew his siblings could not stop him.

He confronted Souriff first. He ordered her to make peace with Valinox and put an end to the fighting, or Airinold would kill her. She took the threat in the worst possible way and attacked Airinold, but it didn't take long for her to realize she was heavily outmatched by his dteria. She fled.

Airinold did not chase her but next confronted Valinox, who was using Souriff's absence to swiftly decimate his mortal enemies. Airinold issued the same ultimatum to his firstborn sibling. Valinox lied and said he would work toward peace, but he devised an ambush later in hopes that his mortal followers would kill Airinold in the night.

When that failed, Airinold went looking for Valinox to end his life, but he had gone deep into hiding and couldn't be found. With Souriff gone as well, and Nijja in her own world, only Failina was left. She was the only sibling who confronted Airinold rather than flee. No matter how hard he tried to explain his plan, she didn't agree that this would bring peace and at the same time get rid of everyone who would threaten that peace with their own greed.

The argument came to a head, and she fought him and lost. When she was at her weakest, on the ground as Airinold stood over her, she accepted what she figured was her imminent death.

"At least I tried," she said as she coughed out blood.

"You have been good, Lina. You always will be. Only Souriff and Valinox need to be stopped permanently. But first, I must destroy the humans who have succumbed to their greed."

"You took an oath not to kill them!" she said as he flew off.

Yes, he had taken an oath, but even if his father was still alive, Airinold would dare to break it. He swooped down and decimated every human who had given in to dteria. They had *still* been fighting against each other, even with their leaders in hiding, all of them ready to kill each other like beasts fighting over scraps of meat. There was plenty of land for everyone, but they thought it easier to take what already belonged to someone else.

That changed quickly. When it became clear to them what Airinold was doing, everyone finally stopped using dteria. The fighting between the humans came to a swift end. With everyone terrified of the "demigod who had gone mad from dteria," they banded together in hopes of eliminating him. It was exactly as Airinold had hoped.

There was only one problem. He hadn't been able to find Souriff and Valinox, and now—with no one using dteria anymore—he was weakening quickly.

He had prepared for this option. He put all of his last strength into a transformation spell, one that would turn him into a glorious winged beast he named Gourfist. With a heightened sense of mana, he would be able to tell whenever one of his siblings used a powerful spell of any kind. He knew them well. They wouldn't be able to stop casting forever. He would find and destroy them. Then he could finally rest.

He spent decades hunting down every trace of powerful mana he sensed. The humans saw him as a threat, often trying to fend him off with arrows or fire. But Gourfist's resistance was too strong for even the hellfire of Failina herself to catch his feathers aflame.

He did see his siblings many times, but most of the time they fled. There was only one instance when Failina and Souriff faced him in combat but soon found that their spells had little effect. Gourfist would've killed Souriff that day, but Failina ensured she escaped by throwing herself in front of Gourfist's talons, knowing Airinold would not kill her. He almost changed his mind that day, swearing to himself that the next time he would kill Failina if it came to that. Of course he couldn't warn Failina about this. His ability to speak was one of the first things to go after his transformation.

He felt nothing from Souriff or Valinox for quite some time, and the body of the beast he controlled eventually started to tire. When he finally let Gourfist rest, the beast did so for years at a time. Something unexpected happened when Airinold woke up. He found that his control over the beast's body had weakened. He considered destroying Gourfist while he still could, but then he would give up everything. Souriff would kill him because he would be too weak to defend himself. She and Valinox would start right where they left off, but now dteria would run rampant. The only way to keep this peace was to continue searching until he found and killed his siblings. It needed to happen before he lost complete control.

The beast exhausted itself searching, needing to rest more frequently. Airinold lost more and more control until eventually the beast began killing indiscriminately. First it targeted anyone who used mana, then anyone who got in its way. Without Airinold to give the beast any strength, however, even the beast started to weaken. It had to sleep for long periods to regain its strength. It would awaken and search, Airinold watching through its eyes like a prisoner in a cage of his making. He became completely stuck, powerless to do anything but screech in pain whenever the beast tried to let out a roar of anger. Part of him wished for death, but another part realized that it was Gourfist who kept the peace. What would happen after he was gone?

Decades went by, perhaps even centuries. How long had he been trapped in this body? It was difficult to tell because the seasons had always changed every time Gourfist awoke, but he had some sense by the growth of trees in Curdith Forest after most had been burned down from the Day of Death. His siblings still seemed to be in hiding, so at least there was that. They probably didn't know just how weak Gourfist had become.

One day, he came awake as Gourfist was disturbed out of its slumber by a young human woman opening the rift to Fyrren. Airinold wished no harm upon her, but Gourfist held nothing but anger. Thankfully, the young woman escaped into the portal. Airinold had no idea what she was doing. No one had gone into Fyrren that he was aware of, at least not after he started sleeping in front of the portal to keep Valinox and Souriff from escaping this realm.

The beast awoke groggy and weak, but enraged. It felt Souriff on the outskirts of the forest, a city, Airinold realized, as Gourfist flew there. It was a bigger city than he'd ever heard of. He really must've been asleep for decades.

He was powerless to stop Gourfist's aggression as the beast destroyed tall buildings and even tore through the flesh of a child. Gourfist was completely unhinged. Airinold wished he had the power to kill the beast, but he didn't even have the ability to stop witnessing all the death and destruction.

Then a young man landed near Gourfist, two spears in his hands, looking as if he had come to stop the beast on his own. Airinold couldn't believe it at first. Not even Valinox or Souriff had attempted to face Gourfist alone.

Airinold wanted to slow down Gourfist as much as he could during the fight, but there was absolutely nothing he could do but watch. He was dazzled by the bravery and physical prowess of this young man as he flew around Gourfist with *dvinia*, not dteria.

Gourfist chased him into a castle Airinold had not seen before, proving that at least a few decades must've passed since he was last awake, most likely more. Airinold screamed in frustration, his voice only heard when Gourfist decided to roar in anger. However, it was not a human sound but an animalistic screech. Only Airinold's pain got through in the message.

It was even more unbelievable to see Souriff land in front of the young man as if to protect him.

"Looking for me, brother?" she said, then took off across the sky.

Gourfist chased her until the beast was too tired to go on, returning to the crater at the center of the forest. Again, Gourfist lay down to rest. He didn't know what was happening in the world, but he could tell one thing. He no longer had any control over dteria. He couldn't even tell if it still existed. It was as if someone had usurped control from him.

How long had it been since he'd transformed into Gourfist? Had he stopped wars during all this time? Did that mean Caarda was ready to return?

Gourfist did not sleep for long. Airinold woke up with him as he felt his siblings approaching at high speed. The beast lifted its weary head.

A sudden cold wind assaulted Gourfist. Snow began to fall, hindering the beast's view. Gourfist beat its wings to rise off the ground, roaring in frustration. It did not need to see. Even Airinold, trapped within the beast, could feel Failina and Souriff just in front of it.

Surprise came when the same young man who had defended the city shot forward through the air. He weaved out of the way as Gourfist tried to snap its beak shut on him. Landing on Gourfist's back, the young man set the beast's feathers on fire as he had once before. The cold wind suddenly stopped, the snow clearing.

Airinold could feel Gourfist's pain, the agony, as if fire was spreading over his own body. But he welcomed it. This was it. He and Gourfist would finally perish. He hoped Failina, not Souriff, would one day find Caarda and wake him from his long slumber.

But Gourfist was not yet done. The beast swiped at the human, who swiftly flew out of the way. Failina sprinted at its head, a massive wall of fire growing in front of her. She cast the immensely powerful spell with a grunt, the fire blasting Gourfist in the face. It hurt, but it didn't do much to disable the beast as Gourfist slashed its claws across Failina's body, nearly splitting her in half.

She screamed and fell away, blood pouring out of her torso. Souriff scooped her up and flew back, hiding her among the trees. There was one being left in front of Gourfist, the slender young woman who had awoken him and entered the rift some time ago. She fled for the nearest trees, but she seemed unable to fly and was quite slow on her feet. Gourfist was just about to give chase.

"Hey!" yelled the young man from behind.

Gourfist spun around and faced him. This mortal wielded a sword the likes of which Airinold had not seen before. Brightly reflecting the greenery of the forest, the metal was difficult to look at directly.

Gourfist's resistance, although greatly weakened, was still strong enough to put out the fire that had been slowly spreading over the feathers along its back. Gourfist swiped at the young man, but he leapt over the beast with help from dvinia. He kept rising, floating high and threatening to land on Gourfist's head. Gourfist snapped its beak at him, but he lurched away.

"Now, Souriff!" yelled the man.

There was a blast to one of Gourfist's back feet, knocking the beast forward and onto its stomach.

Airinold felt the man land on Gourfist's head and drive his sword deep through feather and flesh. Gourfist screeched in pain as it got up and shook the man off, but he simply rose higher into the air rather than fall to the ground.

There was another blast of dvinia from behind, knocking Gourfist over once more. Gourfist seemed to know what their plan was and flipped over as quickly as it could to face the man flying at him with the point of his sword out.

Gourfist slashed the man out of the air, knocking him away like an annoying fly. But without any trees in the vicinity to throw the moral into, he hardly seemed injured from the blow.

The young man landed calmly. He caught his breath as he stared at Gourfist and waited. The beast got back on its feet and looked behind it as Souriff backed away nervously. Airinold knew to look for Failina, because she was probably the only one who could actually finish off Gourfist, but the beast didn't seem to care that she was nowhere in sight as it roared, then flew after Souriff toward the trees.

Souriff attempted to defend herself with a massive force of dvinia, but it merely blew Gourfist back for a brief moment before the beast flew after her again.

Someone landed on Gourfist's back. Airinold recognized Failina's voice.

"If you're still in there, Airi, then I'm sorry for this."

Fire felt like it was tearing into Gourfist from its head down to its back. The beast did not try to fight but roared in fear as it took off toward where it knew the nearest lake to be. The fire spread quickly across its feathers, too many flames for resistance alone to stop. The torment was unbearable to Airinold. He needed for this agony to be over, for Gourfist to finally fall dead even if it meant Airinold would likewise never draw breath again.

Neither he nor Gourfist realized until then that the human had attached himself to one of the ankles of the beast. Gourfist was too busy landing upside down on the water in hopes of putting out the fire to care about the human climbing on the underside of his belly.

The fire was just about out when the human must've driven his sword deep into the belly of the beast. The metal tore through the soft flesh like a knife through paper.

It wouldn't be long now. Gourfist, gushing blood, crawled out of the water after the young man. The beast thrashed at him a few times, but there was little fight left. The young man backed away and waited.

It went on for a long while, Gourfist stumbling and then picking itself back up as it spent its last moments seeking revenge, but the young man kept a safe distance while the demigods came over to watch.

Something changed within Gourfist. With the beast about to perish, Airinold finally felt like he had control over Gourfist again. He could die with the beast, or he could do something about it.

He wasn't done yet.

CHAPTER NINE

As I watched Gourfist bleed out, I did not fear that Valinox might now be coming for us. The three of us could handle him, I was pretty sure. I only worried that Eden was using this opportunity to stash Induct stones because I didn't know where she was.

I would have to deal with her later. For now, I would watch to make sure Gourfist died.

The creature let out one last shriek before a chunk of its body became detached, as if sliced off by an invisible guillotine. Another chunk came off on the other side of Gourfist's body. Then a third. The creature was coming apart like he had been physically put together in some sort of ungodly experiment.

I might've been disgusted by the sight of so much blood and innards if I wasn't so intrigued as to what the hell was happening. The two demigod sisters stared in silence beside me as more pieces of Gourfist separated off.

Soon there wasn't much of him still attached. The last piece was his long neck, the head at the end still moving about with a horrified look in those massive eagle eyes. I was relieved when I heard Eden's voice behind me.

"Disgusting! What the fuck is happening?"

She was just in time to see Gourfist's neck detach from what little was left of his body.

"Oh, I can't look!" she yelled, but I wouldn't look away.

The last remaining chunk of Gourfist was indistinguishable. There was too much blood to see what it was. But this thing morphed into something else, sucking up the blood into it like a bundled cloth dropped into liquid. It took shape, sprouting the head of a man, then four limbs. The red color of its body went pale as skin suddenly covered it from head to toe.

Fully formed and completely naked, the man collapsed into the pool of Gourfist's blood and did not move.

Souriff jammed the hilt of her dagger into my hand. "Kill him quickly," she ordered.

I took the weapon and started toward what looked like a human man, but I knew who it had to be.

"This is Airinold?" I asked with a look back.

"It is," Souriff confirmed. "Get rid of him now."

Failina had her hand up as if she was about to stop me, but she didn't. I held her gaze for a long while as she seemed to be undecided.

"Do it!" Souriff told me. "Before he wakes up and becomes a threat."

"Failina?" I asked.

Souriff's eyes practically bulged out of her head. "What reason do I have to lie, Jon? He created dteria. Isn't that enough for you? Kill him now!"

I agreed that Airinold should die, but I was still going to wait for the demigod I trusted to give the order. Failina chewed on her lip, however, looking between me and Airinold.

"I've seen him kill innocent people in the form of Gourfist," she said. "He could kill many others if we let him live."

I knew Souriff wanted me to do her dirty work because she was scared of violating the oath. I could do it; I had it in me, though I was still undecided as I walked through the blood, feathers, and innards of Gourfist, trying to ignore the wretched smell. I walked through it all until I was standing over the naked demigod.

Airinold looked frail as he lay with his eyes closed. He seemed...mortal, with his plain blond hair. It was only his size that tipped me off to his true nature, for he looked taller than any man I had ever seen.

His eyes fluttered open, and I recognized the same strange and otherworldly color of his irises that all demigods seemed to share, though the hue varied between them. His were bright green like emeralds catching the light. That's when I realized a sunbeam had broken through the forest canopy and struck him, and it was I who cast a shadow over the rest of his body. I had never felt so sinister, as I stood over him prepared to drive this dagger into his heart.

"Wait," he muttered weakly, barely with the strength to put up his hand in defense. "Souriff is a murderer. I was only trying to kill her and Valinox."

I halted and looked over my shoulder. The demigods stood too far away to hear his soft voice.

"I saw everything through the eyes of Gourfist," Airinold whispered. "I even saw you stand up to the beast outside that castle. You are a good man, whoever you are. If you want to do what's right, you will kill Souriff and not me."

"Stop hesitating and do it!" Souriff yelled.

I figured the demigods couldn't see that Airinold was moving, given the tall piles of disgusting flesh all around him.

"You created dteria," I whispered to him. "You killed innocent people."

"Only after I lost control of Gourfist. While I had control, I eliminated those who refused to stop using dteria and no one else." He seemed to be regaining strength as he spoke. "Dteria was used for peace."

If I was going to do this, it had to be now.

I hesitated.

"You can't possibly be trying to convince me that you created dteria for good."

"How is that not obvious?" But then he seemed to realize as he gasped. "My siblings. They must've spread lies to the mortals."

"Even Failina?"

"She misunderstood my purpose. Let me live, and I will explain everything to you. I don't—" he coughed violently. I stepped back as he spat up some blood. "I don't know what's happening these days between mortals, but I'm sure Souriff and Valinox are to blame if there is any strife."

I was surprised to hear him mention Souriff first. To my understanding, Valinox had started this war while Souriff was only trying to end it.

It sounded like there might be more history to their rivalry than I had been told.

Souriff landed beside me and grabbed Airinold by his hair. She took the dagger from my hand and held it up to his neck. Airinold grabbed her hands and tried to free himself, but he looked about as weak as a small child.

"What lies is he telling you?" she asked me. "Did he say that dteria was made by someone else?"

"No," I said.

"I gave him the truth, Souriff! I told him that I don't know what's happening in the world right now, but I'm sure you and Valinox are to blame. You always have been. I was just trying to stop the two of you from bringing about the complete destruction of every mortal."

"Valinox has taken control of your dteria and is using it to wipe out every human who doesn't bow down to him! Now tell me I'm to blame for that?"

"What? Let go of me!"

Souriff threw him into the puddle of blood.

My clothes were already pretty much ruined. I took off my coat and gave it to Airinold to cover himself. Failina had landed near us by the time he was done.

"It's true," Failina said, clearly overhearing the conversation. "Valinox has taken your dteria. Is there any way you can regain control?"

"Failina!" Souriff snapped. "It wouldn't be any better under Airinold's control. For the sake of all that is good, he must to die right now. Jon, I'm ordering you to kill him. Later we are going to destroy Valinox. That's the only way."

She pushed the flat end of the dagger against me until I took hold of it again.

"Don't let Airinold poison you with his lies," she said. "You've seen what dteria has done to this world. Kill him."

Airinold looked into my eyes. "You seem like the kind of mortal who wants the truth. Let me explain it, then you can decide who to kill."

Is he implying that Souriff should be the one to die?

"He created dteria, Jon. He created it!" Souriff repeated, then grabbed me by the back of my neck and shoved me a step toward Airinold. "Kill him!"

I looked back at Failina. She still seemed undecided.

"Lina," Airinold said. "You must remember what I was like, even after all these years."

"I do." Failina nodded. "I'm sure you have your reasons, but what you did was wrong—"

"I'll do it myself!" Souriff interrupted. She wrapped dvinia around Airinold's neck and made a squeezing motion with her hands. "I'm sure Father will understand."

Airinold couldn't make a sound as he tried to pry off the dvinia, his face quickly turning red.

"Souriff, let him go," Failina said.

She didn't.

"You have to at least hear him out."

"You're only saying that because you were in love with him."

What the hell? Aren't they siblings?

"He is not a threat to us anymore! Look at him!" Failina yelled. "He doesn't even have the power to stop you right now!"

It was true. Airinold's face was turning blue as he thrashed hopelessly. He didn't cast a single spell of dteria, of anything. I didn't see the harm of letting him live, especially if his words might be true.

I looked at the dagger in my hands. I could kill Souriff right now. I could stab her in the heart.

I would give anything to know the right answer. The only thing that remained clear was that Valinox needed to die. I couldn't tell about the rest of them.

"Let him go!" Failina screamed as she grabbed Souriff's arm.

Souriff shoved her sister back. "You're letting your

emotions get in the way!"

"I said let him go now!" Failina's eyes seemed to catch fire as she held up her palms in front of Souriff. The demigod of dvinia's face fell as she noticed Failina's expression.

"You wouldn't," Souriff said.

"Don't test me!"

Souriff groaned as she released Airinold.

He coughed as he grabbed his throat. "You haven't changed at all, Souriff," he said in a raspy voice.

"She was the first one to stand against Valinox when he took control of your dteria," Failina told him with subdued rage. "Then she convinced me to join. Souriff is doing everything she can to ensure that he is stopped."

"Because she wants control, like she always has," Airinold said.

But Failina shook her head. "You have been Gourfist for centuries, Airi. You couldn't possibly know everything that's happened."

"The world couldn't be worse off now compared to before I transformed." To me, he said, "I made dteria accessible because it was the only way to stop the constant fighting." He glared at Souriff. "I was going to kill Valinox, then Souriff, and then every corrupt mortal who had sought power through dteria. When all was done, I would destroy it. But my siblings were cowards. They ran from me. I hunted them for years, but I couldn't find them. That's when I became Gourfist. I should've transformed back to myself when I began to lose power over the beast, but I had already stopped everyone from using dteria by then and would no longer be strong without Gourfist. Without the beast's form to keep me safe, I knew I would be killed by my siblings. I was *going* to get rid of dteria as soon as I put a permanent end to Souriff and Valinox, but I just couldn't find them. That is the truth."

"What were Souriff and Valinox doing before you created dteria?" I asked as I noticed Eden trying to make her way toward us with her pants rolled up above her knees.

"I was just trying to stop Valinox!" Souriff said.

"What about before that?" Airinold asked with a hinting tone.

"What are you talking about?"

"I'm talking about what you did to destroy Caarda's soul."

I had never heard the name Caarda before. I looked at Eden. She shrugged.

"You don't honestly believe I murdered his wife."

"Listen to you, still lying! I can't take it!"

I was too surprised to act as he grabbed the knife out of my hand and jabbed it into Souriff's chest. He fell onto her as he stabbed her several more times before Failina and I finally pulled him off. Souriff groaned as she put her hands over her puncture wounds and healed them.

She was huffing in a rage when she got back up.

"Souriff, wait," Failina said, but it was no use.

Souriff took out the sword from her sheath and charged Airinold. Failina and I got in the way, but god Souriff was strong. She threw Failina maybe twenty yards away with one hand. She was about to grab me, but I fell back and let her have Airinold. At least that's what she thought.

She was about to impale him with her sword when

I blasted her with dvinia. She flew farther than she had tossed Failina, but she caught herself in the air and started hurtling toward us at startling speed.

"Enough!" I yelled as I put myself in front of Airinold.

I cringed as Souriff showed no signs of stopping. She would impale both of us, but I refused to move.

She stopped with her sword inches away from my chest.

"Move!"

"If you kill him," I said, "then I'm going to tell everyone not to trust you from now on. You will become as much of an enemy as Valinox is." I stepped aside. "If that's what you are prepared for, then go ahead."

She looked at Airinold as if she was actually contemplating it, but then she grunted in anger as she put her sword away.

The rest of us shared a collective breath of relief, except Airinold. He glared at his sister.

"You know he's still alive," Airinold told Souriff.

"You lie."

"When have you ever known me to lie? Caarda *is* alive."

Souriff's face softened. "Where did he go? I haven't felt him for centuries."

"He did that on purpose. I could bring you to him so you can see him for yourself, but only if you admit to what you did. Let the truth come out, finally. Haven't you wanted to all this time? How many centuries has it been that you've lived with this guilt?"

Souriff's shoulders slumped. I was surprised to see her break down, tears falling freely as she wept.

"Three," Failina said, glancing over at Souriff nervously. "Is it true, sister? It really was you who killed Caarda's wife?"

Souriff rubbed her eyes, but another tear fell right after. "It was the worst thing I've ever done," she admitted.

Eden and I shared a scared look. It felt like we were watching Leon cry.

"I regretted it as soon as I did it," Souriff said. "I did do it. I admit it. I never killed any other mortal who didn't deserve it, but she didn't deserve it at all. I killed Caarda's wife because I was jealous."

"Souriff..." Failina whispered in shock.

Even Airinold appeared surprised. "Maybe you have changed," he said, looking to Failina.

She nodded. "The world is not as it used to be. Valinox has corrupted a kingdom with dteria. They are marching toward this kingdom, Lycast, as the two of you stand here and argue. Thousands of them are blinded by the power of dteria and are prepared to kill anyone who stands in the way of their desires. What you made is horrid, Airinold. It is probably worse than anything Souriff has done."

Airinold scoffed. "Did my dteria not stop war until now?" he asked.

Souriff had stopped crying by then, though her eyes still glistened. "Yes, but..." She took a few breaths. "We are looking at the worst war in the history of Dorrinthal."

There had really been no war since the creation of dteria?

Airinold ignored this. "But it served its purpose. It stopped war. Only now things have changed because I've lost control."

"Yes, but it's—"

"Yes, it is horrid," Airinold interrupted. "But it was designed to be that way. It sounds as if this war between the mortals is worse than it's ever been, and I will take some responsibility for that, but it also sounds like Valinox is the one who deserves to be killed for this. Not me, Souriff."

I couldn't believe what I was hearing, but even more unbelievable was that I was starting to change my mind. I *did* see how dteria could have been made to keep peace, which meant Airinold was not the evil demigod we thought he was. Eden and I shared a look of amazement.

"Can you regain control?" Failina asked him.

"I don't think I can until Valinox is dead."

I asked, "Will you help us kill him?"

"Of course. It's what I've wanted to do for centuries. My firstborn brother has never known anything but selfishness, and it sounds like he hasn't changed, even if Souriff might've."

"Speaking of," Failina said. "We need Nijja's help. That's why we came here." She gestured at Eden. "I will take the enchanter to open the rift now so I can fetch Nijja. Souriff can explain our plans while I'm gone. Come on, enchanter. I must be quick in case Valinox shows up." She and Eden headed toward the rift.

"Is Caarda close?" Souriff asked excitedly, lovingly, like a wife wanting to reunite with her husband.

"You are the last being he wants to see," Airinold said. "Fortunately for you, he can't see anyone right now. I will take you to him after you tell me what's going on, but first I want to explain myself better to this mortal. It's time that people know the truth about dteria, especially if I'm going to be involved with these mortals who stand against Valinox. Otherwise, they'll never accept my help."

"Start from the beginning," I said. "Who is Caarda?"

"The most powerful demigod of all of us."

CHAPTER TEN

It was a relief when I finally separated from the demigods. Their presence grated on me. Although I was beginning to trust Airinold, and I had gratitude for Failina's dedication, I thought all of us "mortals" would be better off if there were no demigods involved in this war.

The trip back took hours, as it had on the way there. It was night long before I reached the castle. I was hungry, tired, and my clothes were stained by the blood and innards of Gourfist. Still, the thrill of flying was not lost on me. The only issue was the cold. I had given my coat to Airinold so he could cover himself and was now regretting it.

Eden was probably back by now. She had gone with Failina, who had been nervous about dropping a mortal by accident, but this was the only way Eden could return. I didn't think I had the strength to carry Eden such a distance, otherwise I would've. Airinold was much heavier than Eden, so Souriff took him, begrudgingly.

Before we left the center of Curdith Forest, Eden had opened the portal to Fyrren, and Failina had gone inside. Apparently, Nijja had invited Failina into Fyrren centuries ago with the purpose of Failina teaching erto to the fae so they could better defend themselves against the vicious creatures that inhabited that realm. I figured the sisters should still be on good terms even though it had been a long time since they had seen each other.

It didn't take Failina long before she returned with Nijja. The demigod of ordia looked different than her siblings, mostly because of her revealing attire. She did not have on clothes like those a human might wear but intricate weaves of grass and other elements of nature I couldn't quite identify.

Failina had already convinced her to destroy the enchantment of her gem that Valinox kept in his possession. The only reason Nijja hadn't gone into our realm and done this already was because she feared Valinox would come back and kill more of her fae until she made another stone for him. The way around this was simple.

Souriff and Failina were capable of hardening their mana in a spell I had actually cast as an experiment for Charlie. It involved using the three frequencies of D: lD, D, and uD. However, when the sisters cast this spell, the amount of mana they created was ten times what I could ever hope to make. After Nijja disabled the enchantment of her gem, telling us Valinox had it a hundred miles away and it wouldn't work from now on, she didn't stick around long to chat.

She asked me something that amused Eden and then left shortly after. After she went back into Fyrren, Souriff and Failina spent hours forming a dense barrier around the rift. It was grayish blue in color, the same hue made by my mana when I had cast the same spell. The barrier was about as thick as a barrel and as hard as metal. It surrounded the portal to Fyrren in the shape of a box.

Souriff and Failina had made it about ten feet taller than it needed to be. When it was done, Souriff and I hovered above it and pummeled the barrier from above with dvinia, driving it deep into the dirt so that no one could dig underneath it to get through.

The sun had already begun to set by the time we finished, and that was before I'd started my long journey back. I'd wished I'd brought more food.

As I arrived at the castle, I saw that someone had lit a beacon on the ramparts. It was a warm welcome and exactly what I needed to guide me home.

It felt like ages ago that I had trouble guiding myself into the castle without slamming into one of the walls, but that was just yesterday, wasn't it? Now I landed easily in the courtyard.

I had no doubt that Eden had arrived with Failina long before me, though I doubted that Failina was still here. Eden had probably eaten supper with our friends and told them, as well as the king and our instructors, about Airinold. I was eager to find out what everyone thought. He'd shared his story with us when Failina had left to retrieve Nijja. I was convinced by him, but I was a bit more trusting than most. I very much wanted to find out what Leon thought. He was the most cynical person I knew, and he was more aware of the demigod's history than the rest of us. If there was doubt to find in Airinold's tale, Leon would be the one to do it.

Although Airinold was most likely an ally, it didn't seem as if he would be a very powerful one. He had completely lost his hold on not only dteria but all mana. He couldn't cast a single spell. I wasn't sure if that would change soon enough for it to matter for us, but he wasn't very strong physically. Last I saw him, he was on Souriff's back and guiding her to the mountains somewhere south of here, where apparently Caarda was somehow frozen in time.

I looked forward to one day finding out more about this demigod, Caarda. Airinold had made it sound as if he had created something that had not been discovered yet, but I'd had hours to think about that statement during my trip back. There was one thing Caarda made that we already used, and that was Aliana and Reuben's tracking through the spell Earth. It made me wonder what else Caarda had created that awaited our discovery.

Airinold had made it quite clear to us that he didn't care about the oath he and the other demigods agreed to in front of their father. In the form of Gourfist, he'd already killed many mortals, and he was willing to kill many more who had given in to their worst desires and let dteria empower them. He would also gladly destroy Valinox if given the chance.

I wondered if he might go so far as to attempt to kill Souriff when this was all over. As curious as I was about everything, I didn't want to be involved in their drama. I was tired of them. "Just let us humans fight," I wanted to tell them. "Let us resolve this on our own." But there was no stopping Valinox, so we needed the others to face him.

I was even more convinced now that Valinox was the one who'd started this war. For us to end it, he had to be stopped, even if that meant dealing with Souriff and the drama surrounding her.

I had expected Valinox to show up either during or after our slaying of Gourfist, especially when we were fetching Nijja and building a barrier around the rift, but there were no signs of him. We assumed he was just too far away to reach us before we left the forest. He had probably given up attempting to kill me or anyone else here, for we had almost ended his life the last time. It brought some comfort to know he was probably afraid of the curse Hadley had used, but it also terrified me. What if she had become as much of a target as I was?

Valinox could no longer maintain a spell of invisibility, but he could still cast the spell as he had before. Therefore, he could still cloak himself temporarily. That meant that he couldn't hide in waiting in my room without anyone seeing him because, even for a demigod, the invisibility spell was too difficult to maintain for long. Michael wouldn't have to spend any more nights sharing my bed in order to keep me safe.

I went to the dining hall before the bathing quarters, finding some dried food on a plate with a metal lid. I ate quickly, as I always did, hoping I might see Michael wander into the dining hall like I had long ago when I had missed supper before. This time, however, all was quiet.

I went to the bathing quarters to find a bath had been drawn for me, the water barely still warm. The castle was eerily quiet. I didn't know how late it was exactly, though I figured it was closer to daybreak than nightfall. I heated the water by casting the Fire spell with my hand submerged, then took my bath with drooping eyelids. When I was done, I dried off, put on my robe, and returned to the upstairs apartments.

There were still guards standing in the hall. Both of them nodded to me when I walked past them.

"Thank you," I told them.

"Of course, Jon," one replied.

"Take care," said the other.

I was quite tired, but something was really beginning to bother me. I had seen these guards many times, both men in their mid-to-late twenties. I trusted them, and I still didn't know their names.

I turned around and stopped in front of them. They were murmuring to each other casually as if to pass the time but stopped to face me as if I were their lord. I didn't like the feeling.

"I should've introduced myself long ago," I said. "You already know my name, but I don't know yours."

They grinned warmly.

It turned out that Rick and Randy Wepper were cousins. Rick was older by a year and had spent much of his life acting as a guard to Nykal long before the nobleman became king. Rick convinced Randy to join him during the rebellion against Oquin Calloum. They fought together against dark mages but knew it wasn't the end of dteria. They had both pledged service to the kingdom since then.

"Do you mind standing guard for so many hours straight?" I asked.

Rick was the chattier one, usually answering my questions so quickly that it was as if he didn't need a second to think. "Guarding makes fighting appealing, and fighting does the same for guarding. I reckon we've done enough fighting for at least a few years of guarding."

"Except we aren't going to be so lucky," Randy added.

"Aye," Rick agreed. "We're ready to fight but not eager."

I nodded. I couldn't truly empathize because, even after all the fighting I had done, I would grow terribly bored standing guard, but I was glad they didn't mind.

"You should get some sleep, healer," Randy said.

"I will soon. There's something I have to do first." I bowed. They returned the gesture.

I decided to try the door of Michael's room. It was open. I wondered if that meant he might have expected me to come by.

"Eden?" he asked as I walked in, his tone hopeful.

"It's Jon," I said.

"Oh," he said with disappointment, at first. "Oh," he repeated with a bit more enthusiasm. He sat up in his bed. I had gotten used to the coif he wore on his head, but it still put a smile on my face to see it.

"I'm sorry to wake you," I said as I stood at the side of his bed. "I really needed to thank you while I could speak with you alone."

"Even after I walked in on you and Hadley?" he asked in a gravelly voice.

"Yes," I said with a light laugh. "Even after that. Thank you for keeping me safe these nights. I take it Eden told you that it's not necessary anymore?"

"She did, and you're welcome. By the way, did she mention anything about me?"

"Oh sure," I said sarcastically. "Between killing Gourfist and flying back against a freezing wind, she was gushing about how much she misses you."

It wasn't funny at all. I didn't even know why I tried. I was about to apologize when Michael spoke.

"Jon, can I give you some advice?"

"Yes."

"Leave the jokes to me."

"You're right. I'm sorry. You're the best friend I could ask for, Michael. Forgive me for my poor attempt at a joke."

"I forgive you."

"I'll let you get back to sleep."

I started to walk out, but I turned around. "Michael, Eden is lucky to have you, whether she accepts it or not."

"Thank you."

I was about to open the door to my room, but I started to think through the next day. I wasn't going to have any time alone with Hadley. I just wanted to see her, maybe touch her for just a moment. I figured she might want the same thing. I would find out in a moment.

I tried her door and found it to be open. I took it as a sign that she had hoped I would come see her before I laid my weary head to rest.

She didn't wake up as I walked in past her hearth and came up to the side of her bed. Now standing there awkwardly, I wasn't sure what to do. I didn't feel right waking her up. She was bundled up tightly under her covers, but there seemed to be a look of anguish on her face. I felt like I might be violating her privacy by watching her, but I was concerned she might be having a nightmare.

I heard her groan in fear, my suspicions confirmed.

I knelt by her bed and put my hand on her shoulder. "Hadley, everything's fine. You're just having a dream."

Her face unclenched.

I watched her for a while. She looked so cute and peaceful. I couldn't possibly wake her. I started toward her door.

"Jon?" She sat up.

"I'm sorry to wake you."

"I left the door unlocked hoping you would." She

pushed open the covers in invitation, blessing me with quite a sight of her beauty. The fire in her hearth provided just enough light for me to make out the soft edges of her body, from her supple shoulders down to her bare knees. She wore a nightgown of silk, the rounded curve of her bosom peeking out with a deep line of cleavage. She pulled back her lush dark hair that had fallen in front of one eye, smiling at me tiredly.

I had lost my exhaustion. I didn't know where it had gone. It was like I had misplaced it somewhere and I wasn't going to bother looking for it. I took off my robe, leaving me in just my undershorts, and started to maneuver into her bed to lie facing her, but she whispered, "Turn the other way."

I was disappointed that I wouldn't be able to see her or explore her body with my lips. "How come?" I asked as I obliged, showing her my back.

"Because otherwise you're going to make me want to do things that I'm not ready to do. Come closer. You must be cold. Let me warm you."

She slipped her small but warm hand over my cold torso as I nestled in. Pulling herself to me, she closed the last little gaps between us. There she held me in a way I hadn't been held by anyone before. I was so comfortable that a quiver ran through my body.

"Thank you waking me from my nightmare," she whispered, then pecked the side of my neck.

"Are you still having a lot of them?"

"Yes, unfortunately."

"Was it the same one I witnessed?" I asked.

"No, this was about you. I'd rather not remember it."

She pulled the covers past my shoulder and up to

my chin, then kissed me softly on my cheek. As warmth spread through my body, I accidentally found my exhaustion again. My eyes fluttered shut as she ran her hand through my hair. I let a moan of pleasure slip. I hadn't known how much I liked to be touched this way.

"Eden told us everything that happened," she said. "So Nijja invited you to be her pet?"

I sighed. "Eden said she wasn't going to mention that."

"Apparently she lied to you."

Before Nijja had gone back through the rift to Fyrren, she had asked me if I wanted to go with her. I hadn't understood her request, at first, but she soon made it clear that she wanted me to be her lover. I'd asked Eden not to mention it to anyone, but apparently that was too much to ask of her.

"If things were different, would you have gone with her?" Hadley asked me. "If there was no war and you had never met me?"

"No," I told her.

"It's all right, you can be honest."

"I am being honest. I'm guessing Eden didn't mention what Failina told me after I denied Nijja's request."

"No, what did she say?"

"That I should not be flattered because the doorman at the town's oldest brothel has seen fewer men come and go than Nijja has."

Hadley laughed.

"I did wish we had more time with Nijja, though. We could've gathered the necessary ingredients for her to enchant my weapon and armor to make them even more durable. She was eager to leave our realm, though."

"Yes, I heard that from Eden."

"What did Leon say about everything that happened?" I asked. "I was hoping to hear his take."

"Let's see if I can remember exactly." She paused for a moment. "Oh, right." In a deep voice of imitation, she said, "If the demigods want to kill each other, let the bastards do it. Meanwhile I'm not making any plans that involve their trust."

"I think that sums up my thoughts," I said. "You do Leon pretty well."

"Thank you. Personally, I would love to speak to Airinold about curses. Perhaps he remembers powerful ones he made that I have not discovered."

"So that means you trust him?"

"No, I'm with you and Leon. I'd rather avoid having to decide whether to trust him, and I believe the king feels the same way after hearing how Souriff murdered a human woman out of jealousy. You actually saw her cry?"

"A few tears."

"I can't picture it."

"It was like watching Leon cry."

"Yes," Hadley said. "That would be hard to imagine as well."

A moment passed. As tired as I was, I found myself wanting to know everything I possibly could about Hadley.

"Have you heard anything about your family back in Rohaer?"

"I haven't, but I've imagined many times that my father probably spearheaded a group to go looking for me. Anything to please King Frederick."

"That's terrible. And your mother?" I asked.

"Anything to please Father," she mumbled.

"I'm sorry."

"The only reason I got involved with the king was because I wanted to make them proud of me, for once. I should've given up on that notion long ago. I only regret not taking more of their coin before leaving, but I didn't want to be caught. Do you recall me telling you that they are very rich?"

"I remember."

"Does that mean you remember the other thing you promised me...regarding my parents and the king?"

"I do, but I'm not sure if I can keep that promise anymore." She had asked me to kill her if it was the only way to keep her from getting captured.

She didn't respond. Her hand stopped moving through my hair.

I turned around in her arms to face her. Worry was evident in her eyes. I put my hand on her cheek.

"I'm not going to let anyone take you away from me."

She smiled. "Somehow, I believe you." She kissed my lips, then stroked my hair as she looked into my eyes again. "Why do I feel like I've known you for years?"

"I feel the same way."

I kissed her this time.

As our passion built, and a yearning set my body on fire, she pulled away.

"I could kiss you all night, but I think you should return to your room. I don't know what the king has in store for you tomorrow, but I'm sure you'll need rest for it."

"You're right." I was so very tired.

I was glad she was being responsible, because I was

powerless to do so. I kissed her one last time, then got up and put on my robe.

She blew me a kiss before I left.

I returned to my room, completely and hopelessly obsessed with her.

CHAPTER ELEVEN

I was becoming increasingly aware that I didn't need as much sleep as everyone else. It probably had to do with my affinity toward uF, the life-giving note of mana that happened to be my natural frequency. I felt pretty tired when I made my way to the dining hall for a late breakfast, but with only a few hours of sleep in me, I should have felt worse. My peers seemed to be just finishing up as I arrived, but the king stopped those who were leaving.

"Gather here. Sit and face me," he said as he stood in front of one side of our table. Everyone moved to sit on the other, many still with their breakfast bowl in front of them, but all had stopped eating. Just behind him stood a middle-aged man with graying hair who I had not seen before.

"You may finish your breakfast as you listen," he said. "You will all be leaving the castle shortly."

I could feel nervous energy in the air in the silence that followed.

The king gave a breath, then continued, "You are to meet Byron Lawson at our wooden fortress. It's located near the road to Rohaer that runs between the eastern mountains and the western forest. Leon and Jennava will lead most of you there. I have no doubt that Rohaer's scouts have seen our fortress and reported its existence to King Frederick Garlin, but it will still serve its purpose, which I will get to in a moment."

I looked around the dining hall and saw that the princess and the queen were not here. I wondered if Callie had been sent off to meet Trevor yesterday, but Kataleya was still around. Clearly, she not gone with the princess to keep her safe, or perhaps Callie was elsewhere.

Although the king had permitted us to eat, I seemed to be the only one who was still working on my bowl of oats. Knowing we were leaving had taken away my hunger, but I always found that I could still eat.

"Rohaer has five thousand fighting men, observed by Souriff," King Nykal continued. "They used to have more, but Garlin must not have enough coin to pay for them all. That means only the best of them are left. Most if not all of these five thousand troops probably have some capability with sorcery. Many more are marching with them to ensure they reach Lycast safe and healthy. It might not feel this way, but all of the people who do not plan to fight against us but are merely there in support of the others are as much our enemies as the soldiers who will try to end your lives on the battlefield. In the near future, some of you may have to do things that you will not be proud of, but it is to ensure that Lycast is not taken over. This is not a time for mercy. Do all of you understand?"

We nodded.

"Recruitment has finished, on our side," the king said. I took that to mean that, like the king of Rohaer, our king had already employed all the men that he could afford. "We have three thousand soldiers, many of whom are amateurs to combat like all of you once were. However, we also have some veterans, like men who fought to overthrow Oquin Calloum. We have three hundred sorcerers, but only a few are as powerful as most of you. The rest specialize in one spell and have made a living from casting it, without taking much time to empower said spell. I tell you this because you need to know what kind of people your allies are. There are a wide range of them, and some are more valuable than others but not because of their skill. Let me explain."

Seeing as how it didn't seem like he was going to introduce the man standing behind him, I whispered to Michael sitting next to me, "Who is that?"

"A fire mage who will protect the king in our absence."

He must be the man Nykal mentioned earlier. I expected someone younger. I took it as a sign that most of the people we would meet in our army were older than us.

"Thanks to nobles I trust, we have five hundred archers," the king said. "Most of them are not novices to the bow. They are to be protected by all of you because they are paramount to stopping Rohaer before the pillagers and rapists reach my kingdom."

I audibly heard Michael swallow, though he had stopped eating a while ago.

"Rohaer must be stopped before they pass the defile south of here," Nykal continued.

"What's a defile?" I asked Michael quietly.

"No idea."

"The defile..." the king said, possibly hearing my whisper, "is an area of road near our fortress. It cuts between the mountains on one side and forested hills on the other. It is narrow, forcing soldiers to march in tight rows. Right now, Harold Chespar is leading the majority of our foot soldiers south. They will arrive at the defile before Rohaer does. My trusted archers will stand behind them as they face our enemies there, head on. If Rohaer tries to go through the forest to get around the defile, they will march into view of the fortress I mentioned earlier. They could take a wider route in hopes of avoiding the fortress, but that would put them deep into Curdith Forest where there are no paths. They would have to make their own through the dense forest while dealing with aggressive beasts. Their only other option is to stop before they reach the defile and hold out there, and we welcome that. We can hold the defile and the fortress and attack their supply chain until they can no longer support their army."

"Oh, that's smart," Charlie said.

The king didn't appear ready for this interruption, his stern expression softening a bit. "Yes, thank you, Charlie. The fate of this war will most likely depend not on one single battle but on the overall health of each army through hygiene, and the abundance of food and clean water. It is crucial that we establish our own supply chain and that it is kept safe from ambush. For that reason, Kataleya will be staying with the Chespar-led battalion. She will provide them with clean water and also act as my eyes and ears."

Kataleya did not appear surprised but nodded dutifully. She must've already agreed to this earlier.

"Jon," the king said, "with your ability to travel quickly, you will go ahead of everyone and arrive at the fort a day or two early. You will inform Byron Lawson of everyone's whereabouts and intentions. If possible, you will bring Charlie on your back because he's going to have a lot of work to do there."

"I'm going to fly there with Jon?" Charlie asked worriedly.

"After we are done here, Jon will perform a test flight with you in the new harness I had constructed with Jennava's help. If Jon feels that he cannot make the seventy-mile trip safely, then you can ride to the fort on horseback with the others, Charlie."

It seemed like all of this had been thought out. I trusted that the king knew what he was doing. I just wasn't sure Charlie did.

The metal mage looked at me with gaping eyes, as if we were about to take off right now. "You won't let me fall, will you Jon?"

That's what we need to find out with a test flight. But I thought better about saying those words aloud.

"I promise," I told him instead, and it was true. I wouldn't let him fall no matter what. If there was a chance of it happening, I wouldn't take him.

Charlie asked the king, "What metal will I be working on?"

"Most likely a missile weapon, but there could be other work for you there. Byron will oversee it."

With enthusiasm, Michael asked, "What kind of missile weapon? A ballista?"

The king seemed a little surprised. "Yes, actually."

"I've always wanted to shoot a ballista!" Michael said, looking around as if expecting everyone to agree.

"You're not getting anywhere near that thing," Leon told Michael. "Not if I can help it. We need a calm hand to aim such a weapon, not one like yours."

Michael looked at his lap and grumbled, unaware of Eden smirking at him.

Reuben said, "Sire, will you be safe here with all of us gone?"

"I will stay where Valinox cannot reach me easily, and I will have plenty of guards as well as this sorcerer by my side." He gestured at the older man, who gave a nod toward us. "My safety should not be of concern. Now all of you will prepare to leave. You might be gone a long while. It is up to Byron, Jennava, and Leon to instruct you after you leave this castle, though I will be in communication with them. Jon, you may need to act as a messenger at times. I don't want you flying off anywhere without permission from Byron or Leon. Not even one time. It is too risky."

He waited for my reply.

"Yes, sire," I said, though I was glad he wasn't making me promise. I had no idea what we were going to find once we crossed into Rohaer territory. I glanced at Hadley. I probably shouldn't be concerned about this right now, but I wondered if the previous night was the last time I would be able to share a bed with her for a long time. She met my glance. I could feel from her longing expression that we were on the same page about this.

The king dismissed us. We headed to the apartments to pack. I wished I could take a bow, but there would be no room for it on my person. I would wear the same armor I had yesterday while facing Gourfist, my new chestpiece of Valaer steel. I would bring my sword made from the same material. Besides a small bag for my necessities, anything else I needed would come later with the supply train.

I met Charlie in his room and convinced him to bring a large enough bag to fit mine inside. He was still figuring out what to bring when I noticed all the girls grouped and chatting in the hall. I had a number of questions for Kataleya that I didn't think she would mind, so I left Charlie to join them.

As I approached, I could hear Aliana already expressing the same concerns I had for Kataleya. "Are you sure it will be safe?"

"It will be. Don't worry about me."

"Mind if I join?" I asked as I noticed them glancing at me.

"Of course not," Kataleya said. "How is Charlie?"

"Deciding which books are worth weighing me down," I joked, though it was true.

Hadley asked me, "Do you really think you'll be able to fly seventy miles with him strapped to your back?"

"I think so. I'll know better after the test flight, though don't tell him I have any doubts. He's nervous."

I noticed Hadley's look. She was, too.

"What about the princess?" Aliana asked Kataleya. I was glad someone else had asked about her, so I wouldn't have to. "I thought she was going to marry Trevor Chespar."

Kataleya shook her head. "The Chespars postponed the meeting because now is not a good time. At least that's what they said as an excuse."

"What does the king think?" I asked.

"He and I both agree that it could very well be a sign they might commit treason."

A tense silence passed between everyone.

"Fuck," Eden said.

"What can we do about it?" I asked Kataleya.

"Do about what?" Michael asked as he and Reuben joined us. Charlie came out of his room as well.

I was certain I wasn't the only one who didn't like the fact that Kataleya would be separating from us.

"The Chespars refused the king's invitation for Callie and Trevor to meet," Kataleya explained. "It might be a sign of a rebellion to come, but there's nothing we can do about it right now. We need them, and they are not currently a threat to our king."

"Unless they join our enemies," Michael said.

"They wouldn't," Reuben retorted.

"Why not?" Michael asked.

"It's true," Kataleya said. "They wouldn't. Before my father was killed, he worked closely with Harold Chespar." I was surprised to hear her get the words out without any emotion. "As corrupt as my father might've been, there's no way he would ever condone the spread of dteria, and neither would the soldiers loyal to my family or the Chespars. It doesn't matter how much they are being paid. I'm sure they mean to win the war against Rohaer. Only then might they turn on our king."

Eden asked, "Are many troops still loyal to your family?"

"Some are, to my brother now. The rest are loyal to the Chespars."

"Are there many other noble families with soldiers?" Eden asked.

"They've probably been bought," Hadley said, and Kataleya nodded.

"Bought? What does that mean exactly?" Eden asked.

Kataleya answered, "Other noble families are most likely assisting the larger army with resources and troops. Their loyalty has been purchased by the Chespars and my brother with my family's coin, or perhaps with a betrothal in the future."

"Why didn't the king purchase them?" Charlie asked.

"He can't afford anyone else," Michael explained. "So he went with ranged combat, mostly archers from families he trusts. Like Reuben's family, and maybe Ali's?" he asked.

"Yes," Aliana said. "My father has contributed."

"Yet he's still in prison?" I asked her.

"For now. He still has a lot to prove, to undo his treason charge."

My head was swimming. It reminded me of all the drama surrounding the demigods. I wanted all of this to be simpler, but wishing it so was not an effective approach. I could only take care of the things I could possibly change.

"Why the hell are all of you standing around?" Leon yelled, quickly stirring everyone into action as we fetched our bags. "You're gossiping like old ladies when we have to get going!"

"We're trying to figure out if there's going to be treason!" Charlie was the only one to stand in the hall and speak back.

"Leave that to me and the other officers while you focus on the tasks you're given."

"You and Jennava are officially officers now?" Charlie asked.

"Yes, now get your things together."

I hated to agree with Leon, but he was right. As much as I trusted my friends, I better trusted the king and the people he'd reached out to for help to handle this matter. He would lean on us when it was time, as he had before.

*****

The harness was less than comfortable for both me and Charlie. It held him to me with loops of leather around my hips and shoulders. I still had to hold Charlie's legs as if he had jumped onto my back without a harness, but with the help of the straps, there wasn't much weight on my arms.

The king had people watching our test flight with spyglasses as I took Charlie up over the castle walls and high into the sky. Charlie gripped my chest so tightly that it was difficult for me to maintain focus. I told him to loosen his hold several times during the flight, but he never did. I wasn't sure he even heard me while he was whimpering with his head down on my shoulder, clearly unable to see.

"Charlie, relax," I told him while we were soaring. "I have us. Enjoy it."

"How much longer?" he asked without taking his forehand off my shoulder.

"I'm not bringing us back until you relax."

"Jon!"

"I can't have you squeezing the air out of my chest the whole way to Rohaer. Pick your head up and take a few breaths. Here, I'll slow down." *At first.*

Rather than holding myself suspended, which still drained my stamina quickly, I continued to fly by tossing the dvinia gripping my body, only now I didn't throw the energy with my mind quite as hard.

Charlie looked down over the trees of Curdith Forest. He dug his nails into me as he gasped in fear. "We are too high!"

"It's safe. You have to start telling yourself that. Don't you trust me?"

"I do."

"You're not going to fall. Believe me."

"Are you certain?"

"Yes."

"All right. I believe you."

I picked up speed with the next push of dvinia, the wind screaming past our ears. Charlie screamed with it and squeezed his arm tighter, threatening to choke the base of my neck.

"Charlie," I wheezed out.

"Sorry!"

It went on like that for some time as I circled around the forest near the capital. I didn't know if it was one of the many things I said in hopes of calming him down, or if it was because enough time had passed without incident, but eventually Charlie came to realize that he wasn't going to fall. He relaxed his grip and started hooting with joy when I picked up speed.

I needed a long break by the time I took us back and landed in the courtyard.

"When will we go again?" Charlie was asking excitedly as he took off the cloth wrapped around his ears and over his eyelids.

Meanwhile, I was peeling the sweaty bandanna off my face as I huffed for breath. "Not for a little while."

We looked around for our peers. I caught sight of them on horses ready to go near the open drawbridge beyond the portcullis. Leon had dismounted and was walking toward us. He had on a breastplate of Valaer steel, like the one protecting my heart. In fact, all of my peers behind him had one as well. Most of them carried

Induct stones with them now—not Eden for obvious reasons—but I hadn't seen them in armor before now. It filled me with pride.

"Is Charlie coming with us or not?" Leon yelled across the courtyard.

"Not," he replied. "I'm going with Jon."

"We'll see you in a couple of days, then," Leon said, turning to join the others.

They waved as they left the castle through the open drawbridge. We returned the gesture. Hadley blew me a kiss.

"I was hoping we would get to say goodbye," Charlie told me.

I was, too, especially to Hadley. "Like Leon said, we'll see them soon. Hey Charlie, do you know anything about how Eden is doing now?"

"Remi says she's doing much better."

"I was hoping that was the case."

"Jon, Charlie," the king said from the great hall, gesturing for us to come to him.

I was still dabbing my sweat with the dry parts of my bandanna as we headed over.

The king was tall, leaning a bit to meet our eyes. "Here's a callring, Jon. Leon has the other. You might be too far away to feel a distress shake through the ring depending on when Leon might signal for you, but if you do, look for them north along the road. That's where they will be traveling."

"I understand." I slid the ring onto my middle finger.

"I'm proud of you two," the king told us to my surprise. "You've both improved in ways none of us expected. There are troubling times ahead of us, but I have my best people looking out for you and the other young sorcerers. I told you a long time ago that I would not have all of you trained just to send you into battle like a common soldier, and I'm keeping my promise, Charlie."

"Thank you, sire."

"Jon, I know you are different. You want to fight, and you have certainly proven that you can. But anything can happen in war, especially where sorcery is involved. I know I touched on this earlier, but now I need a promise. With your new ability to travel quickly, you might be tempted to take certain matters into your own hands."

"I won't, sire, not without consent from my immediate officer."

"I'm asking for a promise."

"I promise."

"Good, then say goodbye to Callie and you can be on your way. She's in her quarters in the keep and could use some cheering up."

"Oh," I said. "Yes, sire."

"Hurry, Jon, I want to fly again," Charlie said as I picked myself up with dvinia and soared toward one of the high windows of the keep.

I knocked on it. Rick, standing guard inside, opened it for me.

"Are you headed off soon?" he asked.

"Yes, after I say goodbye to the princess."

"I'll take you there."

We walked through the keep. Rick looked as if he disapproved of something.

"You know, Jon, the king asked us if we've seen any cohorting around between the boys and girls in the apartments."

"What does cohorting mean exactly?"

"It means what you think it does. Probably what happened when you went to visit Hadley last night."

I felt my cheeks turn red. I knew I should be more discreet, but visiting her room with the guards standing there was the only way I could see her. "What did you tell the king?"

"The truth. Randy and I are not being paid to withhold things. I think it's fair to let you know."

Then I wondered why the king was still pushing me toward Callie. Perhaps he didn't know how strong my feelings were for Hadley.

The king was right that I should say goodbye to Callie because she was my friend, but it still felt uncomfortable the way he'd turned it into a duty. With her betrothal to the Chespars just about nonexistent, it seemed obvious that the king now had me in mind. My world was getting messier as this went on. I almost missed the days I first came to the castle, when all I had to do was learn dvinia.

I knocked on the door to the princess's chambers and announced myself. Callie's mother, the queen, answered the door. I hadn't spoken one word to her and figured I should change that. I bowed.

"I apologize that we haven't met formally before," I said. "I'm Jon Oklar."

"I'm Esma Lennox, Jon. It's my pleasure. I already feel like I know you well. Have you come to tell the princess goodbye before you leave?"

"I have, um." I didn't know how to address the queen, but I noticed Callie smiling behind her as she cupped her hands around her mouth and silently told me the answer. "My queen," I continued.

"I will leave you two alone," Esma said as she walked out.

Now there was no doubt in my mind that the whole Lennox family looked at me like a suitor for Callie.

I made my way over to Callie and bowed, but I noticed her eyes were red and puffy. She did smile at me, but her lips looked as if weights were attached to the corners.

I made a guess as to the cause. "I heard the Chespars would not meet with you yet."

She nodded solemnly. "I very much wanted to meet Trevor." I was a little surprised but glad to hear that. "Mother says it's better that they have delayed. It gives us time to test their loyalty, but father is unhappy. I think he's worried about a rebellion."

"I think so, too."

She seemed nervous as she looked at me. "You know?"

"I've heard things."

"Like what?"

I felt like I was overstepping. It was one thing to speak about dangerous nobles among my friends, but to possibly poison the mind of the princess who looked forward to meeting the son of one of these nobles…that was too much.

"It's not my place to speak about things I have no way of knowing, and I don't have the luxury of time, either. I must be going very soon. I just wanted to wish you goodbye."

"How long will you be gone?"

I have absolutely no idea. "Not long," I lied. "With my new ability to fly, it's likely I will bring news back to the castle when necessary. I could see you then." That part was true.

"I want to fly with you at least one time. Can you promise me that we will?"

"You'll have to speak your father about that." I was pretty sure he wouldn't allow it.

"Please, Jon. I can tell him that I demanded you do it."

I was hesitant, but it was the least I could do after everything she had done for me.

"All right, I promise I will at some point in the near future."

"Wonderful!"

"Have you learned any spells yet?" I asked, remembering how she had been training with sorcery. It would be good to know if the princess could protect herself while we were gone.

"I have actually." She stepped back and made a ball of light.

"Holy hell," I muttered in shock.

She snickered. "Jon, you just swore in front of a princess."

"What, 'hell'?"

"Yes!" she said in mock annoyance with a laugh.

"I'm sorry. I was surprised. With how fast you're learning, your father soon isn't going to need the help of another fire mage to keep him safe."

"Thank you, Jon. That means a lot coming from you."

I bowed. "I have to go."

She squeezed me and held on tightly. "Be careful," she whispered. "You are everyone's hope. You must not let anything happen to you."

"I won't."

CHAPTER TWELVE

Although I was given a map with the location of the wooden fortress, it still took most of the day for us to find it. Charlie went from whooping in excitement to complaining about how long this was taking and how abrasive the wind was to his eyes. It was a relief to both of us when we finally found the fortress, until we realized that the word "fortress" was a stretch.

"This is it?" Charlie asked dubiously.

"It must be," I said.

The walls of the fort were not very tall, maybe ten feet from where the logs were embedded in the dirt to their spiked tops. At least there were a few large turrets built into the walls. Covered with wooden roofs, they stood twice as tall as the walls and provided a good place for lookouts, sorcerers, or even officers to better survey the fort during the battle. There were ramparts as well, I saw as I walked closer with Charlie, and a tower standing at the center of the fort.

In its entirety, the fort was quite large, but it seemed very susceptible to fire. I supposed this was the best our king could put together in the short time he was given.

Not wanting to alarm the archers observing us silently from the ramparts, we walked toward the gate where we were stopped only for a moment before I recognized Byron's voice. He showed himself in one of the turrets nearby.

"That's our bladedancer and metal mage. Open the gate."

Byron came down to meet us within the fort. He looked to be similar to the age my father would be if he were still alive. Although unlike my father—who'd had a beard and a general rugged look about him—Byron didn't seem like he belonged out in the forest. It might've had to do with his neatly trimmed speckled beard, or perhaps it was the kind, soft look in his eyes. I just couldn't imagine him giving orders during a battle if the fort was to come under attack. It seemed more like he belonged beside the king, safe from harm.

It was good to see him, nonetheless. We hadn't spoken more than a few times, but it felt like I'd known him for years as he shook my hand and greeted me with a warm smile.

"I've heard wondrous things about your recent developments with sorcery, Jon. And you as well, Charlie. We are happy to have you here."

"We're happy to be here," I said.

"Do I have to work all day?" was the first thing Charlie said to the nice man.

"I'm sure you'll have some leisure time eventually, but we need you for as long as you can manage. We have plenty of iron that needs shaping. Did the king tell you we're building a ballista?"

"I've never built anything like that before."

"You'll have direction." Byron gestured for someone.

An older man with a long beard introduced himself as the designer. With no grace period after introductions were done, the designer led Charlie toward the eastern wall where heaps of iron sat in piles.

"What will I be doing?" I asked Byron.

"A number of men need healing."

It didn't take long before I was standing before a line of men, none with grievous injuries. Most had simple aches and pains that would've gone away with a day of rest, but I had a feeling that there wasn't much time for that. Much of the trees had been cleared around the fort, and from the bits of conversation I heard between healings, there seemed to be a plan in place to chop down all the rest that blocked our view of the road a mile east. There didn't seem to be anywhere to sleep, though I did see a number of tents that had been folded and collapsed, sitting in one corner of the fort. It might be difficult to get used to these conditions considering I was used to a pampered life at the castle.

Soon after I finished healing, I heard a lookout near the gate asking someone approaching to identify himself. I was close enough to hear the man's reply.

"My name is Ray Burner. I'm coming to you because we need your help," said the voice. I couldn't see who was speaking.

"Who is we?" asked the lookout.

"The good people of Drayer. Please, may I come in and speak to whoever's in charge?"

"Drayer—your town is in Rohaer." It sounded like he was about to turn Ray away.

"Let him in," Byron told the inquisitor. "Open the gate."

The gate began to open, but the inquisitor voiced his complaints to Byron, nonetheless. "Sir, his town is under the jurisdiction of King Frederick. Why would he come to us for help unless he plans to deceive us?"

"I can think of a number of reasons," Byron said.

"Let's hear him out."

I had my first view of the man as he walked through the open gate, and he wasn't a man at all. He was younger than I'd thought, perhaps fifteen or sixteen. He had the voice of someone much older. His clothes were dirty, and he wore an expression of anguish as if uncomfortable from a difficult journey. He was checked for weapons, a dagger taken out of the holster on his belt. Nothing else was found.

"I'm Byron Lawson."

"Ray Burner," said the teen.

"How far is Drayer from here?"

"About five miles. I made the trek through the forest to get to you as quickly as I could. I came be… because," he stammered a bit, "a man showed up this morning. He…" The young man's face took on a dark look. He shook his head and continued. "He seems to be an officer of Rohaer's army, his name's Davon Rimner. He brought a bunch of his men, and they…they raped some of the girls in our town and killed the men who tried to stop them." Tears fell as he spoke, the teen unable to look up from the ground. "One of them was my father." He broke down for the briefest of moments, crying openly before he sucked up his breath and composed himself. "They said they're going to come back tomorrow morning. They expect us to supply them with grains every week from now on, or they'll continue to…"

"That's fine, I think we understand," Byron interrupted.

Ray seemed relieved that he didn't have to keep on going, but his relief only lasted a moment as he looked up at Byron with worry in his eyes. "Can you help us?

We don't have the means to provide them with what they're asking for. Drayer is a farming town, but the winter has been dry. We're mostly surviving on what we stored before winter, but they took most of it yesterday. Many of us will starve if this goes on."

The interrogator from earlier listened to everything with his arms folded. He said, "How do we know this isn't a trap?"

I believed Ray, but just in case I was wrong, I wasn't going to reveal my quickly forming plan in front of the teen. I would wait until he was finished.

"It is the truth, I swear. We thought about going to the other towns and recruiting men to stand up against Davon's bunch, but no one would be willing to help us because he has the king's support. Our only hope is with you, the enemies of the king."

"How did you know about our fort here?" Byron asked.

"Everyone in Drayer knows. Someone heard you chopping down trees a while ago, and word got around. We have a couple sorcerers who don't mind taking a stroll through the forest when they want to work on their skills. It was probably one of them, if I had to guess. I never asked."

That sounded good enough for me to trust him.

"Thank you for bringing this to us," I said to the young man. "Allow us some time."

He looked at Byron, who seemed a little surprised by my initiative before nodding in agreement. "A moment, Ray."

He walked off to give us some time. Byron took a moment to gather a couple other men I had not met. He quickly informed them of the situation. When he was done, I had a question that needed asking before I got to my plan.

"Is it a shock to you, sir, that this town knows of the existence of our fort?"

"No, we expected it," Byron answered. "Our purpose isn't to surprise but to eliminate our enemy's options."

"I would like to tell you what I would like to do about this, if you don't mind, sir."

"I think I already know," he said with a fatherly wrinkle of concern across his forehead. "Am I right to assume that you are eager to fly there and scope out this town?"

"I am," I admitted.

I noticed the four other men looking at me curiously. The interrogator asked me, "How fast can you get there and back?"

"In less than an hour, but that's if I go alone. I'm not planning on doing that."

"Why are we talking about helping them at all?" The interrogator looked at Byron. "We gain nothing by throwing away the life of our healer. He's much too valuable to defend these people."

"I'm inclined to agree, Jon," Byron told me. "I empathize for the people of Drayer, but I'm not going to allow you to endanger yourself or anyone else if this doesn't benefit us."

"The king told us that this war might be won not by battle but by attacking supply chains," I argued. "Isn't that true?"

"Yes, but stopping them from stealing food from one town isn't going to make a difference," Byron replied.

"It's a start." I couldn't imagine letting all these innocent people fend for themselves, even if their town did reside in Rohaer.

Ray called to us, "I forgot to tell you something."

Byron gestured for Ray to join us.

The young man walked over and said, "The officer, Davon, he melted our swords when we tried to defend our women. We've been hearing legends about a powerful metal mage. I think he's it. Wouldn't all of you like to get rid of him? He could take out the armor and weapons from all of your troops come battle."

Byron asked, "How far away was he when he melted them?"

"We can't take his answer as reliable," the interrogator interrupted.

"I would not lie!" Ray said. "He wasn't very far when he melted our swords. I'd say five yards. It was still far enough for none of us to get close enough, and that's all that matters."

"Did anyone try to put an arrow through him?" Byron asked.

"One man, but no one else did after that. Not after what Davon did to him once they caught him." It didn't seem like Ray wanted to speak about it, and I certainly didn't want to hear it. I had already made up my mind, anyway.

"How many were there?" I asked.

"Just ten. All were dteria mages, some with bows and others with swords and shields. All had on thick armor."

I had another important question, "How many will they bring tomorrow?"

"He didn't say."

Byron excused Ray again so we could finalize a decision.

This time I was adamant. "This is a chance to take out someone who could be detrimental to us. I'm going, and I'm going to take one of my friends with me. He has a sword like this one." I pulled out my blade of Valaer steel. "Not even the strongest metal mage in Lycast could melt it. I doubt this Davon could, either. We'll kill him tomorrow morning, and then I'll report back to you, sir," I told Byron.

"I'll give you permission to go, but you're not fighting. You'll wait until the metal mage is headed there tomorrow. See how many are coming before they enter the town. Then you will come here and notify me, and I can send bows and arrows for the people of Drayer to defend themselves if it seems like they may be able to take out this officer. He is probably stationed somewhere nearby with a small army, most likely in a camp that has been set up far ahead of King Garlin's larger group. I'm sure they've branched out and imposed their will on many more towns than Drayer."

"I could find out where they're located and how many there are."

"That is too much of a risk with Valinox watching out for you. Besides, we don't have the means to do much right now except kill that metal mage. We can deal with whatever happens after. However, if you have even the smallest sense that Valinox might be nearby or this is all some elaborate setup, you will get out of there. We cannot lose you over this."

It was true. I had to start thinking in bigger terms than wanting to defend the innocent people of a small farming village. As much as it pained me to allow this injustice to continue, I wasn't going to risk my life over it.

“I agree,” I said. “Now I should get going if I’m going to grab my friend. He’s quite a ways north.”

“Why do you need him?”

“He’s the only one I trust to help me deal with the unexpected.”

CHAPTER THIRTEEN

I flew north quickly, as there wasn't much time. I didn't have to search the road for long before I found my peers on horseback, led by Leon and Jennava. The sun was beginning to set by then, most of the day lost to my earlier travels. I landed in front of them, visibly startling all of them including their horses.

"Hey, I, oh shit, sorry!"

Hadley's horse darted off into the forest while a few others went down the road. Knowing she was probably the least skilled rider of our group, I took off through the air after her and her animal. I landed in front of the horse. The mare knew me. I had ridden her several times. I was sure she was just startled from my sudden appearance but would calm soon.

"It's just me," I told the mare as Hadley pulled on the reins.

The horse reared up. Hadley fell off and struck the ground with an "*oof*."

"Are you all right?" I asked as I helped her up.

"Fine, can you get my horse?"

I flew after the animal and landed in front. It reared up again. I took the reins.

"It's all right," I said as. "Easy, there."

I could see her recognizing me and slowing her movements. I brought her back to Hadley. She had dusted herself off by then.

"Do you need healing?" I asked.

"That depends on what kind, handsome."

I matched her grin.

"It's good to see you," she said as we came close and put our hands on each other. She kissed me but then pulled back. "Hold on, is something wrong?"

"Jon, what the hell is going on?" Leon was yelling from the road a little ways back.

"Nothing's wrong," I told Hadley quietly, "but time is against me. I'll explain everything to you with the others." I gave her hand a quick squeeze before I took off to rejoin them on the road, knowing she would bring her horse back to us soon enough.

I started attaching the flying harness to my body as I spoke. "I need Michael to come with me."

"What's the matter?" he asked.

"They have a metal mage, one who seems to be even stronger than Charlie."

"Who does, Rohaer?" Michael asked.

"Yes, he's an officer in their army. He led a group of men to a town not far from the fort, which is more of a palisade I would say, but that's not important right now. He's probably going to return to that town tomorrow morning."

"Slow down." Leon said. "What town?"

"Drayer, it's a farming town in Rohaer. The metal mage—his name is Davon—and his men raped and killed and took much of the food Drayer had stored for the winter. That was this morning. One young man made the five-mile trek through the forest to our fort to beg us for help. The metal mage melted the swords of the men who tried to stand up for the others. He's most likely coming back tomorrow morning, like I said, which means he can only be stopped with sorcery and Valaer steel. It's probably our only chance to kill him so we don't have to face him at the defile, where he is likely to disable all the armor and weapons of our front line."

"And you want me to go?" Michael asked dubiously.

"I need someone to help me meet with these people tonight and formulate a plan. I might've asked Leon, but I don't feel right taking him away from the rest of you in case there's an ambush. Reuben's another choice, but his sorcery isn't suited for this kind of encounter."

"What about Remi?" Michael asked.

"Yeah," Remi said.

"See, she *wants* to go, unlike me."

"I have a plan that's better suited for you, but if you're too much of a coward..."

"Hey, wait a minute."

We argued back and forth for a while as they tried to get more information out of me about my plan. Eventually, I realized that it would be faster if I told them everything, because I wasn't going to convince them to help otherwise. Only then did my peers stop voicing complaints and realize that Michael really was the best for this. He would leave his horse behind, but I was certain my peers would be able to get the extra animal to the fort without much issue. That's when I finally noticed that Kataleya wasn't here. I had forgotten she would split off to join with the Yorns and the Chespars. She was probably with her brother now, as well as Trevor Chespar. She should be safe, no matter what they had planned. It was Michael and I who would be at risk.

Michael was a lot heavier than Charlie. Getting him into the harness involved a lot of jokes and uncomfortable proximity, and after a few laughs from the others, I soon took off with him in tow.

We soared, the wind whipping our clothes. "Good god, Jon, do you have to go so fast?"

"We don't have many hours of daylight left."

"This is all happening too quickly."

"I know, but there's nothing I can do about that."

"You could've let this metal mage have one more day of food grabbing and...uh."

"Raping and killing?"

"All right, I see what you mean."

We should be able to return to the fort, collect the swords we needed, and land in Drayer before Ray returned there. It might make things difficult to arrive before Ray, but we didn't have the luxury of time. I had been given a little direction from Ray before leaving, but I didn't know these parts very well. It was easy to get lost. We might even land in a different village without realizing it. It was best to go as quickly as we could.

*****

When we finally found the town, there weren't many people in sight. The red sun, barely visible on the horizon, colored the sky crimson. I was careful not to lift us too high because I didn't want anyone in Drayer to see what I could do, just in case this was a trap. That meant Michael and I had to walk into the town from the surrounding forest. Even Ray didn't know the extent of my abilities.

Drayer was a large town, possibly bigger than the

capital in Newhaven, but that was because of the farms. There had to be fewer people here. Straw seemed to be in abundance, covering thatch roofs of nearly every home except the small mansion of the lord of the manor on the northern side of town. Each home had its own fence, a few neighbors close enough to share a side.

There were a few connecting roads between the homes, with a village church enclosed by a stone wall and an apple tree in its field. A river ran underneath a small bridge around the edge of the city, passing by the mill where a waterwheel turned. Smoke billowed out of the chimney of the blacksmith's quarters nearby.

We didn't see a single person until we took the road uphill and got a closer view of the lord's manor. What looked to be a hundred people were gathered in the courtyard through the open gate.

Michael and I walked there briskly. There was just one man with a sword visible. He stood near the person I assumed to be the lord of Drayer, an older gentleman with his back to the closed door of his mansion, his wife standing beside him. A boy, perhaps twelve, stood on the other side of his father, their layered and bright robes marking their rank above everyone else.

I recognized Ray at the head of the group of townspeople, as he stood between them and the lord. He seemed to be saying something to the lord but stopped when he realized that everyone was turning to face us.

"Look," he announced. "Lycast has already sent two capable sorcerers to help us. I told you they would."

Ray ran through the crowd to get to us. His forehead glistened with sweat.

"I just told them of the plan," he said mostly to me. "I think you should say something to convince them."

Most of the crowd was turned my way, but they turned back to face their lord when the older man addressed us.

"I'm in charge of this city," he intoned. "I did not allow you, sorcerers of our enemies, to come here, and I certainly didn't allow you, Ray, to invite these sorcerers —"

"You are only in charge of the city because you kiss the ass of the noble who put you here!" Ray interrupted. It shocked me, and clearly Michael as well as he let out a sound of "uh oh." But it didn't seem to surprise the rest of the townspeople. Perhaps they were used to Ray speaking like this.

Ray continued, addressing the crowd this time, "After Rohaer's soldiers came here, Hamel said it's best to let them come back without opposition! Is that still what you believe, Hamel?"

"We have to support the army," the lord explained.

"Even when they kill and rape and will cause us to starve?" Ray asked incredulously.

"They only killed because some people tried to stop them," Hamel replied.

"And what they did to our girls? Our daughters and sisters? Our mothers?"

"I will speak to them and try to ensure it doesn't happen again."

"You are nothing but a stooge!" Ray yelled. "You are useless to the people you are supposed to watch over."

"You can't talk to my father that way!" screamed the lord's son. "You are just a farmer, and he is lord!"

Hamel put his hand on his son's shoulder and said something. Although the boy had balled fists, he stepped back and didn't look like he would speak again.

Michael whispered to me, "I don't know about this, Jon."

I was having my doubts as well. I had expected everyone in the city to rally behind Ray's cause, but I was starting to get the idea that he had left for our fort on his own. He seemed to have a bit of a temper, or was that just because his father was recently killed? Either way, he was clearly unstable.

The lord calmly explained, "The king will always send more, no matter how many stand in his way. His soldiers will take what food the army needs, and it is their right to kill anyone who tries to interfere. If you go against the orders, you are breaking the law. There is nothing I can do about that right now. I advise you not to interfere."

"Is it their right to rape and rob the personal valuables from our rooms?" Ray replied.

"I said I would speak to them about that."

"And I say you can't do shit even if you wanted to! We are done listening to you. The only way to stop them is by doing something ourselves. Isn't that right?" he asked the crowd.

Murmurs of agreement sprang out but were quickly silenced by the lord. "You will listen to me, Ray, or I will have the army take you. Then they will do what they want with you!"

I could hear Ray's breathing as a tense moment passed in near silence.

He drew his knife and darted through the crowd too fast for me to figure out what I should do. The lord ran to his guard, but the guard just stepped out of Ray's path.

Over the screams of the crowd, Ray drove his dagger

into the leg of the lord. Michael and I watched, frozen in horror, as Ray yanked out the dagger, blood glistening on the blade. Thankfully he did not drive it into the chest of the lord but stepped away as the older man fell with a gasp and clutched his leg.

The lord shot a look of betrayal at his guard as Ray, too, watched the armored man fail to draw his sword and observe with folded arms below a scowl at the lord.

"Even your own guardsman knows you are wrong!" Ray accused.

"That's right, I do," said the guard. "I can't stomach it any longer. I don't understand how any man can choose not to act after he saw what our own soldiers did to our people. Let me be the first to volunteer. I will never again choose my sworn duties over what I know to be right."

"You are dead, both of you," the lord brazenly announced from the stoop of his mansion. "Whoever else does not cooperate will be killed as well."

His wife was trying to silence him, but the lord seemed to think he wasn't in danger of further attack. His confidence abated, however, as Ray glared at him while clutching the dagger with the lord's blood still dripping from it.

The wife got the door open and practically dragged her husband in as she called for their child to come. No one pursued them as they retreated into their mansion and audibly locked the door from the inside.

The boy showed up behind the nearby window. He pointed at Ray with a sniveling face. "You're only doing this because you were a coward before, and now your father's dead because of it."

I was certain Ray heard, but he pretended not to

as he looked over the crowd with a spark of fury in his eyes. "We need more people to volunteer, otherwise they won't turn back when they see us."

That was the plan Ray and I had discussed before I left to retrieve Michael. The soldiers who came here tomorrow would have to be afraid to engage us without their officer and leave to fetch him. That's when I would get word to Byron. We should have time to set up a trap of archers to take down the powerful metal mage.

A man with graying hair stood up. "I want to say two things. I will fight, even though I have never used a sword in my life. The other thing is, Lesla." He looked pointedly at a woman in her forties who showed a pained expression throughout most of the ordeal. "I must thank you publicly for what you did for my daughter. She was being accosted by two men before you stepped in. Now it's up to me to do something, me and the rest of us. If all we have to do is hold a sword to scare them off, then I don't see why more of us aren't volunteering. We should all be more like Lesla."

I heard mutterings—people asking what Lesla could possibly do to stop two soldiers. Then an answer buzzed around that she had volunteered herself. I distinctly heard a woman's voice say, "The whore probably enjoyed it."

Lesla grabbed the older woman by her hair and started thrashing. The woman screamed as she was dragged around, people in the crowd falling over as some tried to interfere while others wanted to get out of the way.

"Stop!" Ray announced. "Lesla, even though we all know Connie's a bitch, you have to let her go. There isn't much daylight left."

Lesla pushed the woman's head away. "Enjoyed it?" She spat on the woman. "You think I enjoyed it? Next time I'll send them to your house and see how much you enjoy it. Better you than an innocent girl. The lord knows you aren't."

"Everyone calm down," Ray said. "We need more volunteers, and those who don't step forward need to promise that they will not inform the army of our plans. I'll kill you myself if I find out any of you betrayed us. Now who's with me?"

Michael and I shared another look. This group was sorely in need of a leader, and although Ray had the enthusiasm, I didn't think he was the right person. Unfortunately, Michael and I weren't either. Half of these people still looked at us like we might be enemy soldiers here for selfish reasons.

I supposed we were. As much as I wanted to help these people, our priority was killing the metal mage. I didn't know how this was going to end, but it wasn't like we were going to stay here and protect these people until the end of the war. Perhaps many were realizing that and that's why no one volunteered, the silence drawing on.

"Come on!" Ray said with a crack of his voice. "We need volunteers or I'm going to choose some of you myself!"

"Ray," I said in hopes of pacifying him. "We can't make anyone volunteer, or it's not going to work." I sure wasn't going to risk my neck standing beside people who were only there because of a threat.

"Then come on, volunteer!" Ray pleaded.

The crowd seemed uneasy as they glanced at each other. I could see there was hope, but no one wanted to take up the responsibility.

Michael cleared his throat. "Listen, all of you. We know you're afraid. In this moment, it might seem easier to let Rohaer's soldiers do whatever they want with your town. You might think that your fear will go away if you cooperate with them. Let me explain what's really going to happen. As they take more of your crops, you're going to start fighting each other to ensure your neighbor starves before you do. Then the soldiers are going to snatch up a couple of your girls and take them off with them. They might come back for others, or they might not. They might leave you with just enough food for you to survive, or they might let you die. You won't know, and you will be terrified waiting to find out. You will want to stand against them then, but you will be too weak and divided. Now, Jon and I can turn around and leave you all to fend for yourselves, but this terror will only get worse after we go. I'm talking about *months* of suffering. The lucky ones will make it through this war, but even they will have lost nearly everything. You only have one chance to save yourselves from this fate. This is it, with Jon and me. Stand up to these people now or cower in fear as you hope they don't destroy your lives."

Slowly, men started to volunteer. Most of them were older, many winters past their prime, but then some of the younger men joined in. It didn't take long before we had fifteen people volunteering, and that was more than enough for all the swords I had brought.

"Good," I said. "I will pass out a sword to each of you. Now we need someone who can ride well to act as a scout. We need to know when they're coming so we can organize."

One of the men who volunteered earlier was looking around. "I could do that if no one else will."

"He's a good rider," Ray told me.

"Then it's settled," I announced.

"What about the lord and his family?" Ray asked, many of us turning to the window where the boy was still watching. "I say we rope them for the night."

"I can watch them," said the guard. "I'll make sure they don't leave or send any messengers."

"Are you sure you can do that?" I asked. It was a large mansion with seemingly many ways one might be able to get out.

"The lord's not going anywhere, and his wife is too much of a coward. I'm sure I can convince the rest of the lord's staff to cooperate and keep an eye on the boy."

"Then there's just one other matter," Michael said a little shyly. "We need a place to sleep and hopefully some supper."

Most of the crowd was dispersing, but a large woman seemed to overhear as she approached us. Not only did she have the girth of a barrel, she was as tall as I was. She seemed to have a son with her, a giant of a young man. He was the kind of large that could defeat most opponents just by falling on them. With his clean-shaven face, it was difficult to place his age. I figured he was only a couple years older than I was.

"You've come all this way to help us," said the lady. "I'd be happy to take you in."

"I'm sorry to trouble you, Bertha," Ray said with a bowed head. "But could I—?"

"Of course you'll eat with us," she interrupted. "I wouldn't have it any other way."

"Thank you."

CHAPTER FOURTEEN

Michael and I, with a bag of swords, walked with the large lady and her huge son to their house near the river. Ray looked as though the day had caught up to him, as he dragged his feet behind us. Or perhaps the death of his father was finally overwhelming his thoughts.

"Do you two know each other?" Michael asked as he gestured at the two young men.

"Graham and I used to wrestle before he got so big," Ray said. "Now I wouldn't stand a chance."

I wondered if Ray was hinting at how Graham had not volunteered to fight with the others.

"I'm very sorry about your father," Bertha said.

Ray looked at the ground. "Thank you."

Bertha told us, "Many people came to Ray's father for help. He was kind through and through. Drayer will feel his loss."

"I appreciate those words, ma'am."

"Take off your shoes," she said as we arrived at her house. "There's still some soup and bread. I assume all of you are too hungry to mind the taste."

"I'm sure it will be fine," I said. "Thank you."

Michael and Ray echoed my gratitude. Soon the three of us were seated around an old table. Graham stood near the large pot of soup as his mother filled three bowls. He glanced inside when she was done.

"I could have another serving, mother."

"Then I'll have one, too, just to make our company feel better about eating."

Although these people were kind, I could tell Michael felt the same awkwardness that I did as we ate in silence. These were people of Rohaer, and we were from Lycast. I couldn't imagine anywhere else between the two kingdoms where soldiers in one country were dining with the denizens of the other.

"You really were a good wrestler," Ray told Graham. "Do you remember? Even when I was bigger than you I had a tough time."

"I remember."

"I'm sure you'd be good with a sword, too."

Bertha stopped eating for a moment and looked as if she would say something, but her son spoke up first.

"I've been thinking about it."

"You have?" she asked worriedly.

"I'm bigger than most men," said Graham. "I should take advantage of that. Isn't that what father's doing?"

"Well, yes, but—"

"They're paying him well in the army even though he's never had training before." The young man's voice was picking up.

I didn't like the thought of having to face Graham's father in combat. Not only must he be huge, but I couldn't imagine killing the family of these kind people who'd invited us into their home.

Bertha's face had lost some color. "You can't mean to fight, Graham."

"I'm almost as big as father, so why shouldn't I?"

"Because you're only thirteen!"

Michael spat out his drink and started coughing. I gave his back a few slaps, but I was in shock as well.

"I'm sorry," Michael wheezed out. "I thought he was at least twenty."

But the two members of possibly the largest family I had ever met hardly noticed Michael as they argued.

"You may be big, but there's a reason boys your age are never recruited to the army."

"I'm going to fight. I've decided," Graham told his mother. "Father would do the same if he hadn't already been roped into joining Rohaer."

"I will not allow it!"

"There might not be any fighting," Ray said. "Not by us, anyway. Remember the plan, ma'am?"

"Anyone who stands in the way of the army will have a bounty on their heads," Bertha said. "There will be fighting at some point, I'm sure of it."

"Then I will be part of it." Her son crossed his arms and sat with a mulish expression.

"Graham—"

"Mother, didn't you hear the screams of the girls?"

"I..."

"Didn't you see what they did to Ray's father and the others who were brave enough to try to stop them?"

Bertha seemed to be speechless as she stared at her son in surprise.

"And didn't you hear the speech of this sorcerer? Forgive me, sir, but I don't know your name."

"Michael."

"This sorcerer, Michael. He said we are going to have to live with this fear unless we do something about it. But he left out one thing. We are also going to have to live with our guilt. Is that really what you want for me, Mother?"

She had her hand over her chest. Slowly, a smile grew on her lips. "Oh, my boy. You are right." But a tear fell from her eyes. "I can't force you to stay out of the fight. Just please be careful. And you, Michael, and Jon, is it? Please protect my boy."

"He will be safe with us," I said, and I would do everything in my power to make it true.

*****

I felt bad when later we had to lie to these kind people. They had asked what kind of sorcerers Michael and I were, and we had both said that we knew some fire but we were mostly here for our skill with sword. To turn attention away from ourselves while we were helping Bertha and Graham Craw clean up supper, I asked about the two sorcerers Ray had mentioned earlier at the fort.

"One's a wind mage," Ray said. "I don't think she can do much with it. The other's a fire mage who sounds a lot like the two of you. She doesn't have good control over the fire, so she doesn't like to use it. She's the only woman who volunteered to stand with us tomorrow."

"Is her name Lesla?" I asked.

"That's the one. When the army men were on the prowl, she took the attention of two of them by saying she wouldn't fight their advances. You saw the kind of thanks she got for it." Ray clicked his tongue and shook his head. "Some of the people in this town. Fuck 'em. It's only the good ones who are dying and getting...well, you know."

"There isn't going to be any more of that," I said.

"I should've stabbed the lord's boy as well," Ray muttered as he glanced at me sideways. "It's not too late. He's a risk, you know."

"I know," I agreed, "but someone's more likely to wind up dead if you try to break in there and get to that boy."

"No one's stabbing anyone else," Bertha lectured as if reproaching young boys. "That's enough talk for tonight. I have a bed made up for you two soldiers. It should be big enough so you're not bumping knees. I hope you don't mind sharing."

"I'm sure it will be fine," I answered for us.

"I'll come by early in the morning," Ray said, "to help you distribute those swords."

His assistance wasn't necessary because everyone should be gathered before Rohaer's soldiers showed up, but I nodded. There was no harm in letting him help.

As Michael and I were preparing to sleep later, I noticed that he had been much quieter than usual. I couldn't tell if he was nervous about tomorrow or if something else was on his mind.

He sat on the other side of the bed and put on his coif. "Never thought I would get used to sharing a bed with another man," he said with a chuckle.

"Hey, can I ask you something?"

He looked at me over his shoulder. "What about?"

"It sounded like you were speaking from experience when you were talking about fear."

"I was." He lay on his back, looking up at the ceiling. I lay beside him and did the same.

"I was worried you would ask about that."

"You don't have to tell me," I said.

"No, it's fine. It was after my father died."

"Oh."

"Yeah," he grumbled. "Something happened to me. You see, Jon, I wasn't always this brave man lying here in his heroic coif."

"My father's death also did something to me."

"I'm sure it did, but I can't imagine your experience was the same as mine. Yours died from a sickness, right?"

"Yes. I remember you told me your father was killed by a thief at night."

"Yeah, on the street. They never found who did it or even why it happened. It wasn't as if my father had a lot of money on him." Michael paused. "Afterward, I could barely leave my house."

"Why not?"

"I wish I could say I had a good reason, but I didn't. Often when I walked alone, I would find myself starting to panic when it seemed like someone was headed toward me. I guess I thought they could be the person who killed my father and now they were after me. My father and I looked a lot alike. I thought maybe there was something about the murder that was going to fall onto my lap."

He fell silent for a little while.

"I know it's an odd thing to be afraid of," he continued. "But the truth is, I was a coward for a long time, and it was the most difficult period of my life. I had to avoid certain streets that spooked me. I couldn't stay out when it started to get dark. I lived with this fear for months until I eventually told myself that I couldn't spend the rest of my life like that. It took a while of forcing myself to be brave, but I eventually got over it."

"I know how you feel. I had a different kind of fear,

but I understand yours."

"What was yours like?"

"I was terrified I was going to spend my whole life in Bhode, lonely and hurting. I had to get out of there, even if it killed me."

He turned to me. "Let's not let that happen."

"I will get us out of here if this all goes wrong."

"Even if it means abandoning the people here?"

"Yes, as difficult as that would be."

"I'm glad to hear that." He sighed as if tired.

"But you're ready to fight if needed?"

"I'm ready, Jon. If needed," he added reluctantly.

CHAPTER FIFTEEN

As Michael and I ate breakfast with Graham and Bertha, Ray opened the door to the house and stepped right into the kitchen. "Seymour's back, and he says thirty of them are coming."

"Who's Seymour?" Michael asked.

Having just woken up, I was also a little confused. Thirty sounded like a lot, but Ray didn't appear too alarmed. His blond hair was combed back. His blue eyes were sharp, attentive. He seemed to be waiting for something, but I didn't know what.

"Seymour's the rider who's acting as our scout. He's come back, and there's thirty of them. Jon, the officer is with them, and so is the lord's son. We were betrayed."

Michael and I jumped up from our chairs. "Why the hell didn't you say so earlier?" Michael yelled.

"How far away are they?" I asked.

"Seymour says they'll be here in half an hour."

I suddenly realized what emotion I saw behind Ray's stoic expression. Sometimes a man can become so afraid that he blocks out everything in the world, even the danger that threatens his life. But this fear would not last. Instincts would kick in. I could see him starting to panic as he ran to the window for a look.

I hurried into the other room to grab the bag of swords. "Here," I said as I handed them to Michael. "Gather everyone."

"What good will these do?" Michael asked. "The officer is the metal mage, Jon. He melts *metal*, if that wasn't clear already! Wait, where the hell are you going without me?" He followed me back through the kitchen.

"I'm not running away. I'm getting Leon and coming back."

I blocked out Graham and his mother speaking to each other fearfully. I also ignored Ray's question of, "How far away is this Leon person?" Instead, I looked directly at Michael.

"I will be back in time," I said. "Gather as many as you can to fight."

"Jon, you promised we'd leave if this went wrong," he whispered as I was headed toward the door.

"I promise you it hasn't yet. We can do this, but you need to believe. Otherwise, there's no convincing the others. Now do you believe me?"

Michael looked into my eyes. His expression hardened. "I believe you."

"Gather them. I will be back in time."

"How can he get someone that quickly?" I heard Ray asking as I was running out from the house.

I didn't mind if Ray now found out the truth about me. It was the soldiers of Rohaer possibly seeing me fly off that I needed to prevent. Surprise was the only way this was going to work out in our favor.

I sprinted out of the town and into the nearby forest. I wasn't sure if anyone in Drayer had noticed me. If so, they might've assumed I was fleeing. It would be up to Michael to calm them and convince them I would be back with help.

As soon as I was deep enough in the woods, I took flight. I navigated through the trees as I picked up speed.

I wasn't sure if Leon and the others were still traveling or if they had made it to the fort. It was only five miles away. I would head there first.

I pulled up on my dvinia, my body lurching higher. At this speed, I risked a blow from a branch. I put my arm up as I threw myself still higher, flying through leaves and thin branches high up in the trees. I felt cuts on my arms as the wood cracked. It didn't matter.

The pain brought out my anger. Damn that boy who'd betrayed us, the lord's son. I didn't even know his name, and yet I was so enraged I might order his death when this was over. People were probably going to die now, and it was his fault. What had happened to the guard who claimed he could watch over the lord's family? Was *he* the one who had betrayed us?

Soon I was flying over the forest in the open air. I had never gone this speed before. If I wasn't so panicked, I might've been proud at how quickly I was improving.

I found the fort and landed in the middle of it.

"Leon!" I yelled. "Are you here?"

I was relieved when I saw him jogging to me, especially because he still had on his armor and his sheathed sword.

"What the hell is it now?"

"We were betrayed by the lord's son, but this kid doesn't know what we're capable of." I saw I was attracting a crowd, with a few of my peers joining. "There are *thirty* of Rohaer's soldiers coming. I'm sure the kid told them there would only be two of us there trying to rally the people to stand with us. Rohaer thinks we're just buying time, scaring them, to set up a trap for their officer and take him out with arrows. I have no doubt they believe they have us trapped now because their officer will melt our swords. That's why I've come to get you, Leon. We're going to fight them right now. They'll never expect it, especially with our swords of Valaer steel. We're turning the trap around on them, but we can only do it with your help right now. There isn't much time before they get to Drayer."

"Then let's go," he said.

I was a little surprised that he didn't put up an argument, but I got over it pretty quickly. I turned around for him, and he hopped on my back.

He was about as heavy as Michael, but I hadn't had time to get the harness ready.

"Don't drop me," Leon growled in my ear as I got my hands under his legs.

"Hold on tight and don't choke me."

I jumped as I hoisted up the dvinia around my torso. There were no trees to block us as I hurled us up and out of the forest.

"Airinold's taint!" Leon said as the wind screamed.

"Hold on!" I hurled us again, straining my mind to throw us as fast as I could.

Leon cursed in my ear as he clutched my chest.

I didn't have to guess how far the town was from our location. I would see it soon. What I was more worried about was Valinox spotting us, or perhaps someone else would and tell him we were on our way. I wouldn't be able to land in Drayer without spoiling everything.

Soon, we could see the town from high up. There were few good places to descend into the forest, so I picked one at random where the leaves didn't seem as dense.

I came down fast. We crashed through light twigs

and leaves. Leon seemingly held in a scream of terror as he groaned. I felt more cuts on my arms.

We crashed down near the edge of the forest, the town in front of us. I was wildly out of breath. The strain of carrying another person with no harness might be something I never got used to.

I healed the cuts on my arms and asked Leon if he needed any healing.

"No. Now what, Jon?"

"It doesn't sound like they're here yet." I panted. "There's no screaming. We can't let them see that I can fly. Do you see that house there, near the river? That's where I left Michael."

"I see it. Let's go."

We bustled out from the trees. The town seemed too quiet. I didn't see anyone out of their homes.

I looked south to find the soldiers of Rohaer on horseback as they entered Drayer through its only road. They were too far away for me to tell their speed or what kind of armor they wore, but there looked like a lot of them.

We made our way to the Craw house. I was sweating and still regaining my stamina as I opened the door for Leon. Michael and the two Craws were in their kitchen, Michael using the window there to look out with a spyglass.

"Where's Ray?" I asked.

"He's been trying to round up the volunteers, but no one wants to leave their house."

"Do they at least have the swords we brought?"

"I made sure everyone got one," Michael said.

"How many are there exactly?" Leon peered out the window with a squint.

"Thirty, probably all sorcerers."

"Any archers?"

"A few."

"How many exactly?"

"Two."

"That's not a few. Be specific!"

"All right, *two* archers. What do you want to do?"

Leon stared out the window a while longer before looking back at the Craws. They stood on the other side of the room, Bertha beside her son.

"Any others like *him* ready to help us?" Leon asked us while pointing with his thumb at the massive lad.

"No others like him," Michael answered.

"Then maybe it's best we handle this ourselves, but tell me something first. What happens if we leave?"

I spoke up. "This town will be drained of its harvest. People might be killed, and girls will surely be raped. It's happened already."

"And what does winning look like?" he asked.

"Rohaer won't be able to take any food or use this town to bolster their supply chain," I said. "Not only do they have a healthy harvest here in Drayer, but there's a blacksmith." I wasn't sure about the healthy harvest, but I wasn't about to let Leon leave these people unless we determined it was absolutely necessary to our survival.

"A skilled blacksmith?" Leon turned toward the Craws.

"Very," Bertha said. "I'm sure the good people of Drayer would be in your debt, sir, if you defended us."

"The fort's only five miles from here," I muttered quietly. "Having the town in our favor would be very beneficial. Plus, we might get to kill that metal mage who seems strong enough to turn the tide against us in battle."

Leon stared out the window again. "I'm not seeing anyone coming out to help us."

"They're probably waiting to make sure it's a fight we can win," Michael said. "Once we start, they might join in."

A silence passed as we watched Leon observe our enemies with the spyglass. Then he stepped away from the window and eyed Michael and me. "Are you both ready to give this your all?"

"That depends," Michael said. "Are you convinced the three of us can take on thirty armored sorcerers?"

"Hell yes we can with the right battle plan."

I got my armor into place as he spoke, knowing we were going to fight. Michael was already dressed in his.

Leon looked out the window again. "The two of you are lucky. There's only one thing I like better than killing dark mages, and that's killing rapists."

"You're kind of sick," Michael said with a grin. "And I kind of like it."

"Oy, big boy," Leon told Graham. "Point out the metal mage to us."

Graham moved up to take Leon's spot in front of the open window. "He's there in the front, with the best armor." He quickly moved back.

"That ugly fucker with the nose?"

"Yes."

"Got it. All right boys, here's the plan."

*****

The soldiers of Rohaer waited until they were deep in

the town before they dismounted. The officer, a pale skinned man with a long nose, took off his helmet and handed it to one of his people. He brushed his hand through his blond hair and seemed happy to be here, a little smile on his face.

"For those who didn't catch my name the last time I was here, I'm Davon Rimner." He had a deep voice that carried across the town. "Your lord reports to me, and you report to him. Therefore, you would be wise to think of me as your superior. I can see all of you are hiding in your homes because you are afraid. There is no need to be. As long as someone tells me where the two sorcerers of Lycast are currently hiding, then we will leave with some of your crops. I promise you peace so long as you cooperate."

"He promised peace the last time, and we did cooperate," Graham told us as we watched from the kitchen window.

All remained quiet in the town. Davon spoke again, anger coloring his voice. "If no one comes forward right now with the information we want, then the last time we were here will look like a mere warning compared to what we are about to do!"

I could see my enemies well from here. There were a few who looked to be close to my age, but most were older, seasoned. I figured they had seen combat before.

I gripped the Induct stone in my pocket. Even I wasn't aware of what I could do in battle with my new power. My pulse was rapid with my nerves tingling, excitement coursing through my veins. I could see by the looks on the faces of my enemies that these men felt like gods. They thought this town and all the people in it already belonged to them. Perhaps that would be true except for one thing. Us.

"We go now," Leon said to Michael, who gave a nervous nod. "That's good," Leon said, "keep pretending you're scared."

"Yeah, pretending, right."

Leon opened the door and walked out toward the large group of armored sorcerers. "We're the sorcerers you're looking for."

Michael looked reluctant as he remained a step behind Leon most of the way there. I wondered if Leon could feign fear, because he seemed confident even now as he marched up to the soldiers and stopped in front of them.

"What do you want with us?" Leon asked.

"That's some armor you're wearing," Davon said. "It would be a shame for me to ruin it with mtalia, but I assure you I can even melt the swords resting in your sheaths before you draw them. Take off that armor and drop your weapons. You will be kept alive as my prisoners, I promise you."

Another empty promise.

"You're a man of honor?" Leon asked. "You'll stick to your word?"

Davon put his hand over his chest. "I swear."

"Then we submit," Leon said. He put his hands up and looked at Michael.

But Michael seemed too busy waiting for an archer to loose an arrow or possibly for one of the sorcerers to shoot a fireball. Leon kicked him with the side of his foot.

"Ow, oh." Michael put up his hands.

"You can take the armor off yourself," Leon said as he and Michael approached the officer standing in front of his men.

That was the signal.

The last I saw before I crept out of the Craw house was Davon shrugging and gesturing at Leon and Michael as he gave a nod to his soldiers. Even if he figured Leon and Michael were powerful sorcerers, there was no way he thought the two of them could defeat thirty of his men.

With the Valaer steel protecting my heart and my sword ready near my hip, I took to the air, my eyes on the soldiers. One man saw me and gaped, but he seemed too surprised to know what to do.

I was quick, coming down over the officer as his soldiers started to lift ropes in place to tie up my comrades.

"Watch out!" yelled the man who had seen me earlier. "Above!"

The soldiers stopped looking around and glanced up as I readied my blade to drive it through Davon's skull.

A sheet of clear energy stopped me dead in the air as my feet hit first and then the rest of me tumbled into it. It remained between me and the officer as I tried to break through with stabs of my sword. I expected it to break any second, but whoever held me was more powerful than I had anticipated.

The energy hooked and tossed me away from Davon. I caught myself in the air with dvinia and soared right back toward my target, who stared up at me in shock.

Leon had tossed away all of Rohaer's troops on one side, while Michael had blown back those on his side. Together, they charged Davon with their swords drawn as I came in from the air, the sun glinting off our reflective weapons and breastplates.

Leon was first to Davon, swinging to take off his unprotected head. Davon ducked and moved forward past Leon. Michael swung at him next, but this officer was faster than he looked. He jumped out of the way of that attack as well.

Turning back with his hand out as if casting a spell, Davon's face contorted, he said, "I can't melt that metal!"

"Above!" said someone else.

I was just about to land on Davon sword first, but I was hit with dteria. Gravity took me the rest of the way into the ground before I could catch myself. Vulnerable, I shot a look toward the two archers standing away from the fray. Both had arrows lined up at me.

I made a wall of dvinia that caught the arrows. It bought me a moment as they loaded more. Davon scurried into town, away from Leon and Michael. They fought back-to-back while most of the thirty men tried to get in their licks with their blades, only to be blown away.

My comrades were doing their part of the plan. It was up to me to get Davon. As I picked myself up, I noticed Graham charging toward Davon from his house as Ray charged in from the other direction. There were many more watching from their doorways, including some of the people who had volunteered to stand with us. All had swords, but none looked ready to use them.

Davon stopped short of running into Graham, then turned to see Ray coming toward him. He lifted up two hands, and their swords melted off their hilts from ten yards away.

Graham and Ray stopped short as Davon took out his own sword. I landed near the two teens.

"Get out of here," I told them as three dark mages flew toward Davon and landed beside him. Each of them stumbled upon landing, as if this was a skill they weren't used to using. I took it to mean their power was far from my level.

I put up dvinia to block several blasts of dteria. As soon as the onslaught was over, I hurled a dense cluster of dvinia at one of the armored sorcerers. It punched the man in his chest so hard that it rolled him back several yards. I wondered if it might've been strong enough to break bone if he hadn't been wearing armor.

The spell had brought out looks of shock from the other two mages. It gave me a moment to take them out in the same fashion.

When I was done, and only Davon stood in front of me, I noticed someone from the corner of my eye. He rushed toward me as he formed a ball of fire in front of him. He performed a throwing motion with his whole body, his fireball spiraling toward me at shocking speed. I put up another wall of dvinia. There was an explosion of flames too bright for me to see anything, forcing me to keep up my wall until I could figure out where the next attack was coming from.

It was the fire mage again—closer to me now. He let out a jet of fire into my wall of dvinia. The painful heat caused me to grit my teeth as I blocked all of it, though I felt my dvinia burning away. It reminded me of the time I had held Remi's fireball to see how fast we could launch it, but I had grown much stronger since then.

I pushed my wall of dvinia hard against the jet of fire, unable to see past it, but that didn't matter. I felt it connect with something solid, the sorcerer. His fire spell came to an end as I flung the mage away from me like an annoying bug.

Davon shot a look over his shoulder as if thinking about fleeing. It gave me time to check on Leon and Michael. I didn't know how, but they had killed two men among the dozens of sorcerers trying to get through to them, and neither of my allies seemed to show any fatigue.

I could feel the tide shifting, our enemies looking to retreat as the aggression drained from their faces. They glanced at one another, waiting for an order. I was horrified to see Davon flicking a ring on his finger because I knew it meant he was calling for aid. There wasn't much time.

Davon sprinted away, but there weren't many routes for him to choose from. Ray jumped in his way, forcing him to veer off toward Graham. The boy was slow, and Davon seemed to take his chances to get around him, but Graham reached out with a meaty arm and hooked his fingers over the top of Davon's armor. He yanked Davon to a stop and fell on top of him.

Now with victory certain, there wasn't a single one of Davon's sorcerers who wasn't running away from the fray. I had just landed in front of Davon as he tried to squirm out from underneath Graham when I heard something crash down behind me.

I knew it had to be Valinox. I could see it in the scared look on Graham's face. I tried to drive my sword through Davon's head before Valinox could get to me, but I was too late. Dteria struck me in the back and sent me hurtling over Graham and toward the many onlookers.

I caught myself in the air, adding shock to their expressions, and turned around before landing. With a hurl, I threw myself back toward Davon as Valinox tossed Graham off him with one hand as if the huge boy weighed nothing.

Ray was just about there, but Valinox threw him back with a spell of dteria. He laid his heavy gaze on me next as he lifted a hand. I produced as thick a wall as I could manage as the demigod made a clawing motion in the air.

I could almost feel his clear energy trying to grab me, but my dvinia not only kept it at bay, it pushed it back toward him as I continued my sprint. His surprise lasted just a moment. He punched the air and a dense cluster of dteria broke through my wall and slammed into my armor. I never would've guessed that the cushiony energy could create such a loud thud, as if it were as hard as a rock, as it struck my Valaer steel.

The force of the blow slid me across the dirt on my back. Michael and Leon charged at the demigod's back. He looked over his shoulder before turning fully around. Leon made a dense wall of water that stopped one blast of dteria. I was taking off again as I figured Valinox would try another spell, but he took out his extraordinarily long blade instead.

Michael seemed to be faster than Leon, taking the lead. He showed no fear as he was about to engage with Valinox, but then Valinox clutched his hand in the air and Michael stopped with whiplash. Valinox hoisted him up and squeezed his fingers. Michael dropped his weapon as he screamed in agony and tried to pry the energy away from his body where it crushed him below his short chestpiece.

Leon ignored Michael for the moment, making another cube of water to block a second blast of dteria. He burst through his own disintegrating wall of water and looked ready to chop off Valinox's head. As the demigod got his sword up to block the blow, Leon revealed his trick, stopping to scorch Valinox with a jet of fire.

Valinox screamed as he backed away and hurried to form a barrier of dteria, the fire threatening to wrap around it. But the demigod extended the energy until it protected him completely. Then, smoking and charred, he pushed the dteria into Leon, who rolled over himself.

Michael was back on his feet, doubled over in pain. His eyes seemed to meet Valinox's.

"Oh shit," he wheezed, then put up a wall of wind.

It did little good as Valinox's cluster of dteria broke through and punched Michael hard enough to flip him several times before he crashed into the ground.

As Valinox turned toward me, I let gravity take me down. I didn't have the wherewithal to hold myself up with dvinia and make a wall, and I knew I needed the wall more. Valinox, with his metal mage standing by awkwardly, scowled at me with a mouth missing half its lips.

He cast. My thick barrier of dvinia couldn't stop his spell, a piece of the dteria breaking through and colliding with my mouth. It disoriented me a moment as Valinox got ready for a more powerful version.

I tried to strike first. Maybe I could knock him out. I tried to aim at his head as my mana condensed into the hardest cluster of dvinia I could make. I threw with all my strength.

Unfortunately, aiming at a small target was not something I had practiced very much. It seemed to strike him in the chest just as he was casting at me, and his spell hit me in the same place.

Both of us flew backward away from each other, and both of us caught ourselves midair.

I soared toward Valinox, my weapon still in hand. I could see his hair regrowing even though Cason's hadn't when Leon had scorched him. Valinox's face also repaired itself, his scowl reforming as his lips regenerated. I trusted my armor as I prepared to meet the demigod sword to sword in the air.

He dipped below me as we were about to collide, perhaps unsure of himself or reluctant to kill me because of his oath. I landed and turned around in hopes of facing him again, but he took himself high into the air. Arcing, he came down toward my head feet-first.

I jumped out of the way to avoid being crushed. *He doesn't seem too worried about the oath.*

I didn't know what I was thinking. I wasn't going to be able to kill this demigod without the help of another demigod.

But I might be able to kill his metal mage.

I tossed myself away from Valinox and toward Davon as fast as I could. The officer turned and fled from me, but I was much faster.

Unfortunately, Valinox was even faster than I was. He cut in front of me and scooped up Davon in his arms. It barely slowed the demigod, and soon both were far gone.

I could've chased after them. I did think about it, but what could I hope to do alone? Valinox would eventually find some way to kill me without Leon and Michael there to help, especially if neither Failina nor Souriff showed up.

Anger forced a few expletives out of my mouth as I barely managed not to throw my sword. "This is why we need a callring—!" But I stopped as I saw how much pain Michael was in. He clutched his sides as Leon dragged him to me by his arms.

"I think he's got a few ribs cracked," Leon said.

Most everyone else in the town slowly gathered around. All of Rohaer's soldiers had fled, and none looked as if they had any wish of returning. Two of them lay dead.

Michael was wheezing uncomfortably. I let my mana course through him. There was more damage than just to his ribs, but it wasn't anything my healing spell couldn't handle. There was no point in trying to hide anything any longer from the people of Drayer. I healed Michael in front of many of them. I heard many gasp and others claim that I must be Lycast's healer they had heard about. I ignored them for now.

"Thanks, Jon," Michael muttered when I was done. "I'm sorry we couldn't get that bastard before his daddy showed up."

"Me, too."

A silence fell over the crowd as what looked to be the entire town of Drayer now stared at me in shock.

CHAPTER SIXTEEN

The more time that passed, the less we looked to the skies for Valinox to return. Although we probably wouldn't be able to kill him if he tried to take us on by himself, he must know there was a slim chance we could. He was a coward. He wasn't going to risk his life when he felt that his victory in this war was certain.

It took about an hour after the short battle ended before we could investigate the lord's manor and find out what had happened. First we had to explain things to the people of Drayer. Yes, it was Valinox the demigod who had come to rescue the metal mage after Davon had signaled for help using his callring. Yes, I'm not just any sorcerer but one who can fly and heal. Yes, I'm that healer you've heard of. Yes, there is something special about Leon and Michael, which is why I brought them here over other sorcerers.

The explaining part was actually quite brief. It was offering my healing services to the entire town that took the rest of the hour. Fortunately, not many people needed treatment.

No one had checked on the lord and the guard who had claimed he would stand beside us. Most everyone was too afraid to enter without a sorcerer nearby. I headed there with Leon and Michael as I complained to them about *our* demigods who had not come to our aid.

"I don't care what Souriff or Failina says. The next

time we speak to them, I'm going to demand that at least one of them has a callring so we can signal to them when their brother shows up again."

The last time we had brought it up to Souriff, she had arrogantly replied that she was not our pet that we could call upon whenever we wanted her help.

"At least Failina should agree," I continued. "She doesn't seem as proud as Souriff."

"I don't care who agrees as long as one of them does it," Leon said. "It's in their best interest. I don't see why they won't after this."

Michael was oddly silent. He looked to be in thought as he kept his head down.

"What's on your mind, Michael?" I asked.

"That maybe Reuben would've been better for you to choose."

"What do you mean?"

"Instead of me," he said. "Because Reuben could've disabled the enchantment of the callring."

Leon said, "But what would Reuben have done against all those dark mages? He doesn't have any defensive magic that could block their spells or arrows. He would've been killed, then I would've been soon after. You kept both of us safe. That's exactly what we needed here. The plan was to hold the rest of them off as Jon took out the metal mage, and it would've worked had Valinox not shown up."

"If he'd arrived just a few seconds later, I would've had that mage," I said.

"Well, then Eden could've done just as good a job," Michael said.

"Eden wouldn't have been the right person for the first part of the plan," I explained. "I needed someone who could speak to these people the way you could. Yes, I suppose if we had predicted that we would be betrayed and the metal mage would use a callring to signal for Valinox, Eden might've been better in your spot then. But we couldn't have expected it."

"I just hope next time we'll have more with us." Michael's voice quieted as he checked on the dozens of denizens following behind us. "We're not staying here, right?"

"No," Leon answered softly. "I'll tell you what's going to happen after we figure out the situation with the lord."

We crossed through the gate and into the courtyard of the lord's manor. The mansion looked just as I remembered it from yesterday. There were no broken windows, and the door was perfectly intact and most likely locked. I had little idea what had transpired. I thought at first that the boy might've snuck out, but then the guard would've informed us. The other thought that crossed my mind was that the guard remained loyal to this lord and Rohaer's army, and he let the boy inform our enemies of our plan.

I was surprised when Leon twisted the doorknob and pushed the door open freely. He entered cautiously with Michael and me on our guard behind him.

We walked into the antechamber. Out of an opening along the wall stepped a serving woman with blood on her apron.

"We didn't know what to do," she said in a soft voice, her face stuck in a sad expression. "He said we would be tried for treason if we told."

"Who said that?" Leon asked.

"The young lord, sir."

Leon impatiently walked up to the woman and turned for a look into the room behind her. "Airinold's taint," he muttered in shock.

"We tried to save them," said the serving woman as Michael and I followed Leon for a look.

"Save who?" Leon asked. "All of them?"

"Yes."

In the sitting room lay three bodies in pools of blood: the lord, his wife, and the guardsman who'd claimed to be on our side. A few servants stood around the outskirts of the room, most with blood on their shoes.

The lord and his wife had been stabbed multiple times in their torsos and had most likely bled out. A great number of red-soaked towels lay near them. The guardsman lay on his stomach, his head turned to the side. There seemed to be only one wound in his back, but I couldn't see if there were any on the other side of his body.

"What the hell happened?" Leon asked. "And don't bother me with any names. I don't know any of these people. What happened to him, the lord's guard?"

"He was stabbed in the back by the lord's son," said the woman meekly. "The guard then grabbed the lord's wife and threatened to kill her if the lord's son fled the mansion."

"He did this with a knife in his back?"

"He did, but the young lord ran anyway. The guard cut the throat of the lord's wife as the lord took the knife from the guard's back and tried to use it against him. They stabbed each other several times as the lady of the house bled out."

"Good god," Michael uttered. "The little shit

must've known the guard might follow through with his threat, and he still ran off. Where is he now?"

"He never returned," said the serving woman.

"He probably fled with Rohaer's soldiers," I suggested. "He might not know the guard actually went through with it."

The townspeople slowly filed into the mansion. One by one they saw the scene in the sitting room and reacted with shock and disgust. They tried to warn the others behind them not to look, but it seemed like everyone wanted to see for themselves.

No one seemed to mourn the loss of the lord, which did not surprise me. As Leon and Michael discussed what to do now, Ray asked if he could speak with me. He brought me outside the mansion, to a far corner of the courtyard where Graham was waiting.

"We want to join your army," Ray said.

"I'm glad to hear it," I replied without hesitation. "But what about your mother, Graham?"

"I reckon she'll try to talk me out of it, but she can't force me."

"Well, I don't think either of you will have to leave Drayer. We're going to need people here who we can trust to keep the town safe. With the lord dead, I'm sure we'll send someone who will keep in mind the best interests of the people here, as well as provide aid to our cause." It was what Leon and Michael were discussing before Ray asked to speak with me.

"Does that mean we won't be fighting?" Ray asked dubiously.

"You want to see more combat?" I asked in return.

"I do."

"So do I," Graham added.

"What about your father?" I asked Graham. "He fights for Rohaer."

"I hope to see him. I can convince him to join us."

"That might be hard in the middle of a bout."

"I have to try."

"That's very brave of you, but it could be impossible."

They looked at me imploringly.

"I'll have to bring it up with my officer," I said, thinking of Byron Lawson. He would know what to do, if Leon didn't figure it out beforehand. "First, I have a favor to ask of you, Ray. Meanwhile, Graham, you should explain the situation to your mother."

The large boy nodded and headed off.

I checked to make sure there was no one listening before I leaned in. "Can you keep this between us, Ray?"

"Sure, what is it?"

"There are two bodies where we fought Rohaer's sorcerers. I need you to get their papers and bring them to me. Try not to get any blood on them if you can. If someone sees you and asks, tell them you're just curious."

"Why do you want the papers?"

"That's not something I can share right now, not even with my friends. Trust that it's for the greater good. You'll keep this request between us?"

"I will." He hurried off.

When I went back into the mansion, it looked like Leon was giving directions to the small crowd of townspeople crammed in the antechamber.

"Lycast is going to send people here. They're going to work with you fine people, but they will require supplies. It won't be anything like what Rohaer would've taken from you had we not intervened." Leon paused. "All of you know why we're fighting, don't you?"

There were a few murmurs about dteria, but no one seemed certain.

"We're only trying to stop them," he said. "That's it. There is no conquest into Rohaer, no desire for land. As soon as the war's over, we're gone. We'll try to keep your town in the good shape it is now; I promise you that."

There were more murmurs. The people sounded nervous.

"I'm not demanding," Leon said, and they quieted once again. "You can send us away now or later, and we'll leave peacefully without taking anything. But know that you'll be on your own as soon as we're gone. I don't know which Rohaer noble looks after these lands, but he's not going to be too happy after hearing what happened. He'll send men, lots of them. If you want to deal with them yourselves, just say so. We never wanted to come here, but we were asked for help and thought it might be a mutually beneficial situation. We'll just need some food and supplies for our fort in the forest. It's up to you."

The fire mage who had volunteered yesterday before she had been insulted for her heroic efforts stepped out of the crowd. "I'm sure we'll find a way for all of us to help each other." She looked back at the crowd.

There seemed to be no hesitation as people nodded and murmured in agreement.

"I'm glad," Leon said. "Then all that's left to do now is rummage through this mansion and take what we feel like we're owed. Now there's a civil way to go about this. The three of us from Lycast are going to spread out, and a few of you can join us to keep us honest.

We're going to collect all the valuables we find and bring everything here, and I mean everything. No one is to pocket anything until everything of value has been collected and sorted. Once that's done, my sorcerers and I are going to take some valuables to help pay for our army, then you all can distribute the rest fairly. I imagine this lord has a pretty penny stashed away, so all of us can leave happy today. Now how does that sound?"

Applause followed.

CHAPTER SEVENTEEN

I brought Leon back to the fortress. After dropping him off, I returned to Drayer for Michael. It was a quick trip, but I could already feel a difference in the town in the short time since I'd left. It was the quiet after the storm. I was used to it at the end of every battle, small or large. I looked forward to this feeling when the war was good and over.

As I came down into the fortress with Michael on my back, he gasped in what I thought to be alarm, startling me.

"What is it?" I asked as I looked around for a threat.

"They finished the ballista! Look." He pointed at the eastern-facing wall where the massive weapon peeked over the pointed wooden ends

"Oh, that's it?"

"It's a ballista, Jon! I'm going to fire it. Put us down there."

"I don't know if that's a good idea."

"Ah, you're no fun."

I landed instead near the center of the camp, beside Leon and Byron. I could hear Leon updating Byron as to what had happened. Michael hurried off to the ballista. I decided that worrying about him wasn't my problem as

I greeted Byron with a slight bow.

He had concern wrinkled across his face. “I never would’ve sent you over there if I knew this would happen,” he said apologetically, as if the danger was his fault somehow.

“It was for the best,” Leon spoke for us. “Drayer will serve us well, as we them. I suggest choosing Jennava to be the one you send over as we wait for someone more suited to act as lord of the town. I’ll do just fine without her here in the meantime, seeing as how most of these men are archers picked out of villages with little experience of a real fight. Just make sure she has a callring.”

I looked closer at the men here who I would most likely be fighting beside. None of them looked particularly strong in combat, or perhaps that was just because none held a weapon. Most everyone busied themselves by hauling tree trunks into the encampment and breaking them down. Others cooked, some cleaned their garbs, and a few more tended to the small farm stationed in one corner. There were no women here, which came as a bit of a surprise. Even the female sorcerers of my group were not within view, except for Remi, I soon realized.

She approached me while holding her bloody hand. I took my leave to tend to her.

“What happened?” I asked.

“I hurt myself trying to chop down a sapling. It was much stronger than it looked. Can you heal me?”

“Sure.” I put my hands around her gash and closed it up in a matter of seconds.

She gritted her teeth during the short process but smiled when it was done. “So that’s what it feels like. Thank you, Jon. I take it everything went well in the nearby town?"

I noticed Michael near the ballista. He was attempting to load a huge bolt onto the device, but a man put himself in front of Michael and gestured for him to stop.

"All is well," I said. "Though it would be better if we had managed to kill the metal mage."

"What happened?"

I briefly went through the events. When I was done, I said, "We need a way to call Souriff or Failina like our enemies called Valinox."

She nodded silently. Her eyes fell to the ground. "So you're available right now?"

"I believe so. What is it?"

"Jon," Byron called to me.

"Perhaps not," I told Remi and headed over to Byron with Remi close behind. Leon seemed to be on his way out of the fortress, most likely to fetch Jennava.

Byron told me, "We need to send word to the king of what transpired. Better than sending a messenger, I think it's best if you go yourself. There's only the small matter of Valinox possibly seeing you."

"He can't do much to me on his own now that he's no longer invisible," I interrupted. "I should always be able to flee."

"That's what Leon and I discussed. The king may wish to discuss the situation with you while you're there and might even ask you to pick up the new lord of Drayer to bring with you on your way back. It's best if you leave now so you can return before dark."

I was hoping to see Hadley first, even for just a moment, but there was something even more pressing. "I can after I have a bite to eat, sir."

"Yes, of course."

*****

Remi and Michael ate with me. Michael and I asked her about their trip here, but it turned out to be uneventful. I was burning to see Hadley and share the events of Drayer with her. She always had an interesting perspective on these sorts of things, but it didn't seem as if there would be time.

I suddenly remembered that Remi wanted to ask me something. I hoped she wouldn't be too shy to tell me in front of Michael.

"Remi, earlier you made it seem like I could help you with something."

She looked down once more. "I'm hoping you might be able to take me to Granlo. Maybe you can set me down there on your way to the castle?"

Michael asked, "Granlo…is that the place where you're from?"

She nodded.

I wasn't sure if Michael was aware of what had transpired there. It was the last town I'd visited before arriving in Kataleya's hometown of Livea, where I met her father and then watched his cousin murder him with the help of Valinox.

"Remi…" Michael said with a sly smile. "What exactly are you going to do there? Maybe pay a visit to your ex-husband and make him regret his actions?"

Her pale cheeks blushed. "I would like to make sure he is not hurting his new wife."

"How do you know he married again?"

"Because of Jon."

"I met Gerald when I went there," I told Michael.

Michael seemed shocked. "And…?"

"And I told him to stop abusing his new wife. He didn't take kindly to it, so I tossed him into the air and broke his leg in front of most of the town. That was after he drove his mining pick into my shoulder, by the way. He promised he would behave after I was done with him. I think I might've scared him so badly that his promise was real."

"Good god, Jon."

"What would you do, Remi, if he's gone against his word?" I asked.

"I don't know," she said. "I feel like it's my responsibility to figure that out. I was the one who asked you to see him in the first place. It would be wrong for me to ask you to finish what I started."

"I don't mind being there with you so long as I have time."

She looked right into my eyes. "No, I want to do it alone. Because…I also want to speak to my parents, alone."

"I see."

"Are you sure it's safe to ride on your back over such a long distance? Even with a harness, I'm a bit worried."

"Charlie did it," I said.

"Yeah, but Charlie can be a little wild in his decision-making."

Michael smirked. "Wild, eh, Remi? Jon and I weren't aware."

"Oh, quiet." She pinched his arm and twisted.

"Ow!" Michael yelped as he leaned away from her.

"It is safe so long as Valinox doesn't intercept us in the air," I answered her.

"I will burn him if he does."

"Good."

"Sounds like you two are going to have a lot of fun," Michael commented as he rubbed his arm. He leaned away nervously as Remi looked at him. "Please don't pinch me again."

"You had your fun this morning," Remi said with a little smile.

Michael scoffed. "If that's your idea of fun, I'm nervous for the people of Granlo."

"It might be right to be a little nervous for them," she said in a quiet, dark tone. "They knew Veronica. They haven't met Remi."

Michael laughed nervously. "Holy hell, Remi, I was joking before, but now I'm really scared."

I had to agree with Michael. The petite fire mage looked a little sinister as she glanced at him with the sides of her eyes. But then she laughed and seemed about as threatening as a puppy dog.

"You should see your faces!" she said. "There's nothing to worry about. I swear."

I wasn't so sure, especially later when I noticed her equipping her sword while Michael helped strap the harness to my body.

"I didn't know you had helped Remi with this earlier," he said. "It seems like you're involved in just about everyone's life."

"I wouldn't say that's accurate. I still don't feel like I know Remi very well."

"You know her a lot better than I do. And it's not just Remi. You were the one who got most involved with Eden and her Induct stone. Also, it seems like you and Aliana had something when all of us first met. Oh, and how could I forget Reuben? The two of you were caught up in each other's business like begrudging siblings. And let's not leave out Kataleya. I know you told me nothing happened between the two of you, but I'm still not so sure."

"First of all, nothing ever happened with Ali. I've gotten to know her pretty well, but I still know next to nothing about her father. Is he still imprisoned in the castle?"

"Last I heard."

"About Kataleya, we're just friends. We went through a lot together when I visited her in Livea. As for Eden, you know her a lot better than I do, and it might be the same with Remi."

"All right, there's no need to get defensive." Michael put his hand over the back of his neck. "I'm only trying to give you a compliment. We've all relied on you, Jon." He paused for a breath. "I suppose what I'm trying to say is that I'm glad I had the chance to help you today, and that, um, I'm here if you need me for anything else." He glanced down. "You don't have to wait for something to become life or death before you come to me again."

"Oh."

"Yeah, oh look, Remi's ready," he said with some relief.

She approached us.

"Are you ready?" she asked.

"Yes."

It was always difficult to get someone situated in the harness their first time, but Michael helped make the process as smooth as possible. By the time Remi was strapped to my back, I still hadn't figured out how to thank Michael.

"This morning in Drayer," I said. "You, um…"

"I know, Jon. Be safe out there. You too, Remi." He put his palm on my shoulder and squeezed her hand with his other.

"We'll be back tonight," I said. "Will you tell Hadley that, um."

"I know, Jon," he repeated. "Go on."

I trusted Michael did.

With a lurch I was still getting used to, I propelled my body, with Remi attached, out of the fort and all the way above the forest. She gripped me tightly but did not scream.

I felt her hold loosening a bit as the flight became steady high above the trees. I did not fear Valinox, especially with Remi here. I took us toward the road between the kingdoms.

"Why are you going that way?" Remi asked.

"I'm curious if we might be able to see them. Yes, there they are…do you see?" I pointed south as I slowed to a near stop.

"Rohaer," Remi grumbled.

Thousands of troops marched north. I could see their kingdom far behind, a tall castle poking out from the middle of a grand city surrounded by walls. It reminded me of our capital, Newhaven, except that everything seemed to be bigger. My eyes traced the road from Rohaer to the army and then beyond. There were a few turns, but it was mostly straight even as it passed along the mountains and the forest.

"It won't be long now before they reach the defile," I said, gesturing at the stretch of land where the road dipped into a valley.

"That's where we attack?" Remi asked.

"That's my understanding, so long as Rohaer

doesn't retreat into the forest to try to get around us. If they do that, we can strike them from the fort. But the rest of our troops need to get here before any plan can work."

I twisted us around to face north. An army that looked about half the size of Rohaer's seemed to be just a couple days away from the fort…or perhaps longer? They traveled so slowly that I couldn't see them moving from here.

"I'm still a little lost about whose army that is," Remi said.

"It's our king's by right, but it's my understanding that they are commanded by Harold Chespar. What he will decide to do with them is a mystery to me, but Kataleya's somewhere among them providing clean water. If a sickness does come that the abundance of clean water cannot prevent, I'm sure they will send for me. Hold on." I hurled us north toward them.

Remi laughed with excitement. "The feeling never gets old, does it?"

A smile grew on my face. "Not yet, at least."

It was mere minutes before we flew over our army on the road. We saw many heads tilt back as we zoomed over them. I would've liked to stop and greet Kataleya, but the number of people was in the thousands. It might take over an hour to find her, and we didn't have the time.

"So, you and Hadley?" Remi asked near my ear after it was empty road beneath us again.

"Yes," I answered definitively.

"That's good. She's been gushing about you ever since you brought her to the castle, and I always thought she was far too beautiful for the young men making passes at her while she was a grocer in the capital."

"This happened a lot?"

"I wasn't around her all the time, but I did see it. Girls blessed like her are usually mean to me, so I was surprised to find out she was not only nice but smart as a whip."

Remi fell silent. I found myself smiling as I listened to things about Hadley. I wanted to know more.

"So that's how you two became friends?"

"Yeah, she taught me many things. First was how to have a good time in the city. We would drink and dance. I'd only known her for a short while, but…then something happened." Remi paused for a moment. "Afterward, we knew we could trust each other."

"What was it?"

"We had some fun in a tavern, drinking with a couple young men. They seemed nice. They wanted us to go home with them, which we politely declined. Things took a turn after we left. I hadn't realized they were following us, but Hadley realized right away and had been prepared. She'd rustled their hair a few times in jest and must've snagged a couple hairs. I thought it was a little weird for her to touch both of their heads, but it just seemed like one of her quirks. I mean, she was always fairly touchy with people I thought she should keep more distance from. Only later that night, when I found out she was a witch, did it make more sense."

"What did she do?"

"While they were following us, she turned around and told them to stop. They said they would, but they stayed even closer behind us. Eventually she took my hand and told me to run and not look back. But I wasn't prepared to run from any man ever again after I fled from my ex-husband. Hadley didn't know I had some skill with fire. Even if it was difficult to control back then, I was prepared to hurt myself if it meant hurting these boys as well. It turned out I didn't need to. They both suddenly looked like they were having trouble standing straight. They staggered around for a bit before they fell and looked like they would retch. We took off after that. When we were a few streets away, she told me we should be safe now. I wasn't going to leave it at that, though. I knew she had cursed them. Even though I had never met a witch before, I just knew, and I wasn't going to let her get away with not admitting it to me. That's when she took me to her home and explained that she was a good witch, not one who had lost her mind to dteria. She showed me some of the ingredients she had while we stayed up all night and spoke about sorcery and shared secrets. I told her things of my past I had never told anyone else. Everyone knows now that I was abused by Josef Webb, don't they, Jon?"

"I think we all assumed it after the way you spoke about him in the forest a while ago. I hope you don't have any shame about it."

"I don't anymore, but I did when I told Hadley about it. She said I could come to her with one of his hairs if I ever got one. She would make sure he couldn't do the same thing to another girl. I didn't know the curse would be temporary, though. She told me later that she had left out that part because she wanted me to feel better, and that might ruin it."

"But then how come you paid her when you left one of his hairs at her place? I thought you were close friends."

"Hadley was more of a mentor than a friend to me. She instructed me to leave a payment with one of his hairs to show me how serious I was about the curse. I'm sure she planned to return the payment when the curse was done. She only used it as a way to ensure I was certain. I left her a gold coin to show how much I wanted it to happen. Josef got what he deserved, though. He's been removed from the life he cultivated in the capital, which I know meant everything to him. It's Hadley who has had it rough since all this began, not me. But she's strong, you know. I don't think she's ever had to rely on anyone but herself. Kind of like me. I guess that's why we learned to trust each other. Hey, you're the same way, aren't you?"

"Actually, I'm not. I relied on my father for everything. We were each other's world. Sometimes I still can't believe he's gone for good." It pained me every time I thought about how I now had the power that would've saved his life.

"I didn't know," she said. "I'm sorry."

With her already wrapped up around my back, it just took a little squeeze and lean of her head on my shoulder for her to embrace me.

"There's too much pain in this world, even if there wasn't dteria," she said. "I'm very glad we're in a position to make it better."

I put my hand on her arm. "I couldn't agree more."

We chatted about lighter topics for a while, such as the castle food, Rick and Randy—who Remi had also met—and of course about our peers. Eventually, however, I became too tired from the long journey to keep up the conversation, and Remi fell quiet to let me concentrate.

I was sweaty and exhausted by the time we reached Granlo. Remi instructed me to set her down within the city. She wanted to turn as many heads as she could. Needless to say, there were dozens of people upon us before we could finish unstrapping her from the harness.

I recognized a few of them, namely the sheriff who had taken me in for the night and introduced me to his daughter. She was also with him, and she appeared very nervous to see Remi.

I could hear Veronica's name buzzing around the gathering crowd. Remi smiled confidently back at everyone.

"I'll return whenever my business is done with the king," I said. "It shouldn't take more than a few hours."

"I'll meet you here," she said as the sheriff approached.

"Jon?" he asked.

"Is anyone dying who needs immediate help?" I asked dutifully before I left.

"Uh, no, but—"

"Then Remi, or Veronica as you know her, will explain," I interrupted. "I have to be going. It is good to see all of you again. If anyone is in serious need of healing when I come back, have them wait here in a few hours."

I took off as I heard many utterings of shock.

Normally, I looked forward to returning to the castle, but without any of my peers there, I thought I would feel like a visitor. That feeling changed when I landed in the courtyard near the keep and Randy nodded to me as he opened the door. I thanked him and entered.

I encountered more guards on the first floor, most of whom I didn't recognize. I figured Nykal had brought in more men to keep the castle defended while his trusted sorcerers were gone. A couple of them escorted me up through the keep to the second floor, where a few more guards stood outside a closed door.

"I have urgent news for the king," I explained. Recognizing Rick in front of me, I figured more explanation would not be necessary.

He gave a nod and opened the door for me. The king sat at one end of the table with a number of parchments in front of him. On one side, sitting close by, was his councilman, Barrett. The man sitting close to the king's other side looked familiar, but I couldn't place him. With gray hair and a wrinkled face, he didn't appear too threatening, so I didn't know why my instincts were telling me not to trust him.

The king's glance appeared heavy, his eyelids drooping as if he'd been missing sleep. "What happened, Jon?"

I glanced at the other man, not sure if I should divulge this with him here.

"This is Luther Prigg," Nykal said. "Aliana's father."

That's how I recognized him. I had seen him once before. He had the same bronze skin as Aliana, though he was much older than her mother and not easy on the eyes, as she and her daughter were.

I didn't know how to ask politely, so I just let it out. "Wasn't he in prison for treason?"

"He was, but now he has, and continues to, make up for his crime." The king spoke mostly to the noble.

Luther nodded. I thought it was done with a little too much pride when it should've been with a lot more shame.

I figured the king enlisting Luther's help was a matter of need more than forgiveness. The king had to trust nobles if we were going to have any chance in this war.

Most were either his enemies or his allies. If he could turn one of his former enemies into his ally, then it was worth the minimal risk. I just wasn't sure how minimal the risk really was, but I had to trust that the king knew. Nykal couldn't have his subjects second-guessing him, especially now. And as powerful as I had become, I was still a subject of the king.

I explained how Ray from Drayer had come to our fortress and told us of the event that had transpired in his town earlier in the day. I then explained how I'd fetched Michael and taken him to the town after making a plan with Byron. I went into detail about how that plan didn't work out and we were forced to improvise. I relayed my frustration as I explained how Valinox had saved this metal mage of Rohaer who had the capability of making our army impotent one row of armored men at a time during even the most chaotic of battles. I concluded by explaining how Jennava was probably just now arriving in Drayer to act as lord regent until his majesty chose someone more suitable to replace her.

I had not discussed this last part with Byron, but I told the king bluntly: "We have to have a way to contact either Souriff or Failina in a timely fashion when we need their help, or Rohaer will always remain a step ahead of us."

"I have pushed Souriff to accept a callring," Nykal said. "However, my request has done nothing but irk her."

"I believe it would be best to speak to Failina about taking a callring, and without her sister there."

"I have tried to set up such a meeting, but without a way of contacting them. I must wait for them to show up in front of me. I understand your frustration, Jon, for

I feel it too."

"So you haven't heard anything from them since the events with Airinold?"

"That's correct."

I wondered what they were up to. It probably had something to do with this Caarda demigod they had been talking about.

"Regarding the new lord of Drayer," the king said, "I believe the best man for the task is right here in this room."

I was hoping he was talking about Barrett, but it was clear from his gaze that he referred to Luther.

"Yes, I think that would be best," Luther said. "I'm certain I can keep a town of farmers in line."

"They're good people," I said. "They want to cooperate with us already."

"You will see to their needs," the king stated.

"I will, sire, of course, but the priority is your archers and the fortress. Their needs far outweigh the needs of civilians, especially those in Rohaer. I would like to take five good men who I trust. They can stay with me in the lord's manor to help ensure our will is followed."

"Make a list of their names, and I will send them by carriage, but I want you there immediately. Jon will take you to the fortress where you will speak with Byron. You should be able to arrive there by this evening and speak with Byron. It will then be up to Byron when you will be escorted to Drayer, or if Jon is to take you there immediately after your meeting is finished. I leave Drayer up to the two of you. Ensure that the people there are happy enough that they would never even think of rebelling. However, if the town cannot be defended without losing many of our men, then you'll retreat to safety."

"I will, sire," Luther said. "Considering what Rohaer's army has done to their own people, they will be counting their blessings every day I watch over them." He glanced at me and rubbed his nose, then looked back at the king. "My only concern is traveling all the way there on this boy's back."

"It has been tested," the king said. "Travel is safe through the air."

It was safe, yes, but that didn't mean it would be enjoyable for either of us. I knew I couldn't ease Luther's worries with a charming smile. I just didn't have it in me, so I didn't even try when he glanced at me again.

I was concerned about three things. One, I didn't trust him nearly as much as the king did. Two, I wasn't sure I would be able to get him to the fortress and then retrieve Remi before nightfall. And three, the most important thing, it looked like I was going to miss supper.

CHAPTER EIGHTEEN

"There must be some other way for you to carry me," Luther insisted in the courtyard as I tried to show him how to get in the harness. "A method that doesn't involve me clutching your body."

"There isn't. Just get on."

There was something strange that happened to me when I knew I wouldn't be eating for a long time. It wasn't that I was hungry yet, but because I knew that I would be soon, my body had the opposite reaction than I wanted. With the idea of food tantalizing me, I was already salivating.

I wished I had time to convince the king's chef to make me a dish before I left. He would, I was certain, which was why it was even more difficult to fly out of here without eating while this arrogant noble was practically wrapped around my back.

"This can't possibly be safe," he complained. "I have not heard of any mortal flying like a demigod. Even Cason could not sustain himself in the air for such a distance."

It was a reminder that Luther's traitorous actions had helped Cason and his loyal dark mages, probably through coin and shelter.

"Were you in contact with anyone from Rohaer?" I asked.

"No, but Cason was." Luther finished strapping himself in with the harness. "Like this?"

I tested a few of the straps. "There's one way to find out for sure."

I wrapped dvinia around my torso, hoisted us a few feet into the air, and suspended us there.

"Shit, you little runt! Put me down, I'm not ready!" He squirmed wildly.

I ignored him. "The harness holds fine. Look."

I hurled us much higher this time. He screamed and wrapped his arms around my neck, probably without realizing he was choking me.

"If I can't breathe, I will drop us," I warned him.

"Let me down. Let me *down*!"

"Relax! Look, the king is watching. Do you want him to see you acting like this?" I turned so we would face the top of the keep, where the king looked at Luther disapprovingly through a closed window.

I didn't know what face Luther made, but I could feel him relaxing as he loosened his hold. Then I noticed Callie looking from another window on the second floor of the keep. She waved to me. I waved back, then gestured at Luther with a roll of my eyes. I could see Callie laugh.

"You're going to drop me and make it look like an accident!" he whined.

"I promise you're not going to fall," I assured Luther. "Unless you choke me."

He lowered his arm across my chest.

"Here we go," I warned him.

He screamed again as I hurled us over the castle

wall. I wasn't done yet. We picked up more speed as I hurled us farther and higher. He wrapped his limbs around me as he pushed his head against the top of my shoulder.

"Slow down, sorcerer!" he yelled in my ear.

"This is the speed we need to go," I yelled back with a turn of my head.

He lifted his head up. "We're starting to sink!"

"That's normal." I propelled us again. He screamed once more.

"You're enjoying this, aren't you?" he accused.

"What is there to enjoy? A man I hardly trust is clutched around my back and screaming in my ear."

"You *are* enjoying this! I bet you've dreamed of embarrassing someone of my class since you were young."

I rolled my eyes. "Yes, all the hours I spent training with dvinia was just so I could frighten an arrogant noble. I'm practically giddy with enjoyment."

"How much longer will this take?"

"A long time, especially if you constantly distract me."

The next few minutes passed in blissful silence. Luther no longer expressed fear when we started to slow and sink, or when I would jolt us higher with another heave of my mind. Eventually we passed over the army marching to meet our enemies. I could feel Luther shifting to look down at them.

"What can you tell me of them?" I asked.

"What do you mean, sorcerer?"

"My name is Jon. I'm sure you know that. And I mean, should we be worried about them turning against us?"

"Nothing that concerns you."

"You do realize that I'm going to be the one who has to fight, don't you?"

He waited a moment before he spoke. "That's a fair point," he said to my shock. "I imagine you are very useful on the battlefield if you can take us this far through the air without a break. That must be why you are so arrogant."

"*I'm* arrogant? Ugh, never mind." I didn't want to argue. I only cared about convincing him to share valuable information with me. "If you really are on the side of the king, then I'm your greatest ally."

"You question my loyalty?"

"Of course I do."

He sucked in air as if insulted. I expected something else to come out of his mouth, but nothing did for some time. Eventually the Chespar army was far behind us.

"Are you loyal or not?" I asked.

"I am, and it is not your place to question me."

"I'll question you if I want and tell the king if I don't think you can be trusted. If you don't care about that, you can choose not to answer, but you might as well make this easier for everyone and cooperate. Now why were you helping Cason?"

"That should be obvious. Because I thought Lycast stood no chance in this war. I still would believe that if Cason were alive, but now that he's dead there is a chance to defeat Rohaer."

"So you admit to making a mistake."

"I have done much more than admit to it. I have been punished."

"And with Aliana?" I asked.

"What about her?" He spoke defensively. "That's none of your business, anyway."

He didn't say anything else. I decided to let it go because I trusted that it's what Aliana would've preferred.

We were silent for the better part of an hour. Eventually I took us off the road and flew over the forest. I felt safer away from the main route between the kingdoms, where I could descend into the trees if I saw something dangerous approaching, like a flying demigod.

"Have there been sightings of the helpful elf?" Luther asked.

"I haven't heard from Eslenda in a long time. The king hasn't, either?"

"No, we believe she has left the area."

"What does his majesty take that to mean?"

"Just that she has nothing left to gain."

I didn't think that was the right reason, though. What had Eslenda gained by sticking around so far? She cared about stopping the spread of dteria, though she seemed more interested in the rivalry between the demigods than in the war between the kingdoms. I wondered if she had somehow figured out that we had destroyed Gourfist and brought Airinold back. Perhaps she didn't approve. Perhaps it was the last straw after we had recruited a witch—Hadley—and now we had shown mercy to the creator of dteria. She had probably gone back to live with the other elves in Evesfer.

"We may not like each other," I said, "but I will fulfill your requests so long as they come from a good place. If they don't, if they come from greed, I won't hesitate to throw you back in the dungeons myself. And you can imagine what will happen if you try to fight me on that. I don't care if you're the father of my friend. I can deal with Ali hating me as well. What I can't deal with is letting you ruin the lives of innocent people."

"You speak as if you're above me, but you're not. You are simply lucky you've had the good fortune of obtaining such powerful sorcery. Would things be different, I'd have you cleaning my privy when this is done."

"And you're lucky you were born into wealth. The difference between us is what we do with our power. Are you going to behave in Drayer, or am I going to have to personally do something about your greed?"

"Greed? You do not know me at all. I am not greedy."

"Then what are you? *Honorable*?"

"I'm smart."

"Yes, you seem absolutely brilliant. And who does this brilliance benefit besides yourself?"

"Lycast, you impudent hog. I have paid my dues, so you will speak to me with respect or you will regret it later."

"I will give you respect when you've earned it. I have friends in Drayer. I plan to speak with them as this war goes on. I recommend you make sure they have nothing bad to say about their new lord, or *you* will regret it later."

A silence stretched on. "What are the names of these so-called friends of yours?" he asked.

"Find out yourself after you get to know the people."

*****

I dropped Luther off in the fort and directed him to Byron. Having gone the whole way without a break, I needed some time before I headed all the way back for Remi. Even the cold settling in for the evening hadn't managed to prevent me from sweating. I figured I had just enough time for a bit of bread during my break before I went for Remi. I didn't see any of my friends during that time. They were probably busy in the forest.

I felt my skill with dvinia growing stronger each time I carried someone a long distance. Unlike muscle pains in my body after heavy use, the ache of sorcery was fleeting. So long as I ate and slept, I felt as though I could keep up my spells throughout the whole day with minimal breaks because the exhaustion was purely mental. Although I was certain a lot of this extra power had to do with the Induct stone I kept in my pocket, which seemed to feed me mana in the form of dvinia, I knew a larger part had to do with all the time I had spent casting in the forest.

I was quite pleased with my progress. Perhaps I would even have the time to learn a new spell soon. I wondered if there was one I had not discovered yet in the school of dvinia. I needed Charlie and Leon's help to figure out what notes to try, but we hadn't been able to conduct the necessary experiments.

Souriff should know, shouldn't she? I mean, she created the school of magic. Knowing how she was, however, she might prefer to keep the secrets of dvinia to herself. Everything I'd heard about her from Airinold made complete sense to me. Souriff had purposefully made dvinia difficult for others to reach because that's the kind of demigod she was. I imagined Valinox had done the same with mtalia. The two schools were on opposite ends of the spectrum of mana, one requiring extremely high frequency and the other extremely low. The other schools required frequencies more in the middle of the spectrum, which made them more accessible to anyone who had a decent grasp on their mana.

I wondered about this demigod Caarda. I felt my thoughts going toward him for the first time since meeting Airinold in person. The only thing I had figured out about him before now was that Caarda had probably made Earth—the single note that represented an entire school of magic the same way that the note of mtalia did. Or was that wrong? What if Caarda had created a more complex school of magic and the single note of Earth, llB, was just one part of it?

I spent the rest of the trip wondering what else could be related to Earth—Aliana's tracking skill—that had not been discovered. Unfortunately, I couldn't come up with anything that seemed possible based on any of my experiences with mana.

I finished my bread. *Time to go.*

*****

It was difficult to find Granlo after sunset, but I knew I was close. I soared around the open land looking for lights, but there were none to find. It was so late that most people had gone to bed.

Then I noticed a beacon, a ray of yellow light like a column. *Remi*, I thought with a grin. She was maybe a mile away from me.

I reached her in less than a minute, though I was surprised when I came down to see that three young men stood around her. The town of Granlo seemed to be a short ways north. She must've walked out to make light so as not to disrupt the townspeople, but why were others here with her?

Remi said nothing about them to me as she started

getting into the harness. "What took so long?" she asked.

"The king made me take someone back to the fortress first."

The three young men varied in age. One looked to be about our age of eighteen, though I supposed Remi could still be seventeen as far as I knew. The other two seemed a bit older, perhaps in their early twenties.

Wait, has my birthday passed? I'd been so busy that I hadn't thought about it until now. The blasted thing was yesterday. *Oh well, I'm probably not the only one of our group who had a birthday pass without anyone knowing.* The king might know, I realized. He had looked at all of our papers, but he was even busier than I was. I didn't hold it against him.

"Are you going to tell us your decision?" the oldest asked Remi. I had no idea what he was talking about.

"I'm still not sure," she said as she finished getting in the harness and started wrapping the protective cloth around her face. "We have to go, Jon. It's late."

I was confused about these men, but I was eager to go. "Did anyone need healing?" I asked Remi first.

"A few had some minor injuries, but they gave up waiting. They'll heal on their own. We can go."

The men, all at the same time, bombarded Remi with farewells.

"Goodbye," she told them.

I took off with Remi and headed back the way I'd come.

"Who did you take back to the fortress?" Remi asked near my ear.

"Aliana's father," I shouted back over the wind. "He's going to be the new lord of Drayer, and I don't know if it's the best idea."

"Aliana says he can be trusted now."

"She does?"

"Yes, they have been in contact for a while."

"Do you know if he apologized for refusing to acknowledge her as his daughter?"

"He has," Remi replied.

I still didn't know if that meant he could be trusted. I wondered if Aliana might be too easily convinced because they shared blood, but it wasn't my job to worry. I was glad to let it out of my mind for now.

"Who were those boys?" I asked.

"One is an old friend from when I was young. The other two have never spoken to me before, but all three have expressed interest in marriage."

"I see."

"I thought you would be much more surprised."

"No, I'm not."

"Well, I was!"

I chuckled.

"Why are you not surprised?" she asked.

"Kataleya and I both received many marriage proposals as we traveled across Lycast and offered healing and water to the people."

"Yes, but you are handsome and Kataleya is beautiful."

"So are you, Remi."

She was silent for a time. "Thank you," she finally said.

"Let me tell you, Remi, I much prefer having you on my back over Luther Prigg, and not just because of the weight difference. It's probably best Aliana didn't have contact with him growing up. That man is obnoxious."

"I figured he is. I've tried to tell her that just because he's her father doesn't mean she owes him anything."

I took us another mile or so through the cold night sky, but she didn't continue. I had hoped Remi would tell me about her experience in her hometown. I felt a little bad for asking, but this was a *long* trip, and I was doing her a favor by bringing her there and back.

"Did you see your parents in Granlo?"

She gasped. "I forgot to tell you! It feels like it happened days ago. I saw them in the crowd after you left. They invited me to my old house where they practically begged me to forgive them. I didn't know why they were being nice to me when they never had before, until the end, when they asked if I had coin to spare. I was so angry I thought I might burn their house down. They had always wanted a son but gave up after my mother had a number of failed pregnancies. They haven't changed at all, so I told them to eat shit, and then I went to check on Gerald."

"Wow," I exclaimed. I had to assume Remi's parents were even worse than she described, or perhaps Remi had a worse temper than I'd thought.

"I'm not very proud of it," she said. "I might offer them an apology when I return, but it would take a lot for them to prove to me they've changed before I give them even a single copper bit. My father wanted me to at least pay for the dowry that he couldn't get back from Gerald's family after I left. They had *no* regret for forcing me into that marriage, even after they heard about why I ran away. That was just another disappointment to them."

"Now I'm starting to understand your reaction. Maybe you should be proud of it."

"Yeah, maybe I should. Most of us sorcerers of the king don't have parents we can rely on, and all of us turned out good."

"Well…my father…and Michael's…and Aliana's mother, and Kataleya, you know—"

"All right, all right, I misspoke. Do you want to know what happened with Gerald?"

"I'm not sure I do now, to be honest."

"You can relax, Jon." Remi chuckled. "Nothing happened. I found no bruises and sensed nothing amiss from his new wife. He even apologized to me in front of her. Either we really turned him around, or he knew how to put on a convincing act. I'm inclined to believe it's the former. I told him I would be back another time. He said goodbye, and that was it."

"He didn't threaten you or anything?"

"Well, you did break his leg when you were there before, and I'm sure he saw the size of the fireball I put on display in front of the crowd soon after you left. Just about everyone was nice to me after that." Her laugh sounded a little sinister.

"There's a difference between love and fear, you know," I teased.

She kept her thoughts to herself for a little while. "I have love from those who matter to me. So I'll gladly take fear from those who don't."

Remi had a way of declaring her opinion that put me in a strange state, somewhere between agreement and disagreement, though I often could do neither.

"So you spent the rest of the time flirting with these older boys?"

"I sure did," she said proudly. "Though I can't honestly say I was flirting. I don't know how. I told them everything I did since coming to the castle the first time. I'm sure they will be sharin' and flarin' my stories with the whole town, and eventually people will be speaking about me as if I killed Cason myself."

"Sharin' and flarin'?" I asked.

"Sharing and flaring," she spoke more clearly. "Adding heroic flair as they share. They like to exaggerate in Granlo, most likely because there's little else to do to pass the time. Bill Ushler once caught a fish as big as a man, but his line broke when he just about had it reeled in. Gary Green was attacked by a dark mage and barely got away to tell the tale. Even Gerald used to say that he went to the city with his father when he was a kid and they were attacked by two muggers, and his father fought them both off. Hell, Jon, I used to tell people that a raven came to my window one night and told me I would be a sorcerer of fire. I told the story so many times that even I began to believe it. I think it started as a dream, but it was so long ago that I can't remember." She gasped.

"What is it?"

"Richi often talked about his trip to Curdith Forest and how he saw a beautiful elf. His story was believed about as much as everyone else's, which is to say that it wasn't, but now I'm thinking he might've been the only one who was actually telling the truth. I should've told him that I believed him. That would've meant something. I will when I go back after we're done with Rohaer."

"You are? What does this mean about you and Charlie?"

"Charlie? Oh hell, Jon, he promised he wouldn't tell anyone."

Charlie had said nothing to me. The only thing that had been clear to me was that he was interested in Remi, but now I was wondering what exactly had happened between them, and when? I had seen them kiss, but they had done that right in front of me while crazy from a curse. Remi no doubt was referring to something else they had done.

"You know Charlie," I said. "He can't keep his mouth shut when he's excited about something."

"This was different. He really promised, and I believed him."

Her gloomy tone made me regret my method of deception.

"Remi, I lied. Charlie hasn't said anything to me. I was just trying to get you to talk."

"What? No, but you brought up Charlie as if you knew something."

"Just because I've seen the way he looks at you. I didn't know anything had happened besides the kissing while we were all cursed."

She slapped my cheek lightly. "Jon, I expected more out of you!"

"Maybe that's why it worked."

She laughed, then gave a sigh. "The truth is that I don't know what I'm doing with Charlie. I don't want either of us to be hurt. Sometimes I think he's the cutest boy I've ever met, and other times I have to keep myself from throttling him. I'm the first girl Charlie's ever kissed, and he's the first boy I ever did so willingly. I'm worried he thinks we're going to be married because he doesn't understand how these things work."

"How do these things work?" I asked.

She leaned over my shoulder for a close look at my

face. "You're being serious, aren't you?"

"Yes, unfortunately."

She leaned back again. "Are you concerned you might hurt Hadley?"

I wasn't, but I didn't know how much I wanted to reveal. Truthfully, I was more worried I would be the one who was hurt, like what had happened with Kataleya. Was that selfish? No, I just figured I couldn't possibly hurt Hadley, not when I was ready to be there for her.

"I wouldn't worry," Remi said. "I've never seen her this happy. She's always smiling as if she has a little secret, and now it's clear what it is. Just make sure nothing happens to you, all right?"

"The more I hear that the more I worry that something might actually happen."

"Because you keep putting yourself in dangerous situations."

"I don't see any way around it."

"That's what we all love about you." She rested her head on my shoulder and squeezed me in a light embrace. "Don't tell anyone about Charlie, please? It's not that I'm embarrassed. I just don't know what it is, and everyone else finding out could turn it into something it's not."

"I won't, but you should probably figure it out soon. Charlie's not very good with the unknown or keeping secrets."

"He's better than you think. Trust me." I could almost hear her winking from her tone.

For a long moment, I didn't know what to say.

"Remi, my imagination is going wild after hearing that. I bet the truth is much milder than what I'm thinking."

"Oh, you would be surprised." She laughed again.

CHAPTER NINETEEN

I had little idea of the time when I descended into the forest. The night was so dark beneath the trees that I feared Remi and I wouldn't be able to find the fortress until morning. I should've taken a tracker ring before leaving.

We searched for the better part of an hour. I was certain Remi was tired, but she couldn't have been as exhausted as I was after the long day I'd had. She made a beacon of light as we flew around shrubbery and between trees, hoping someone awake in the fortress would know it was us and give us a signal.

Eventually it came. A beam of yellow light broke through the darkness and swept across our faces. I took us toward it.

I brought us down in the fortress to find that Leon was the one who had made light. "It's about damn time!" he said. "What the hell took so long? Never mind, I'm tired. These are your tents. Yours, Jon, and yours, Remi." He pointed at them separately. "If you need fresh water, it's over here." He gestured at a covered basin near the two large tents."

"You stayed up for us?" Remi asked.

"With Jennava gone, I'm the one who has to look

after you. I don't like it any better than you do, but I will keep you safe and comfortable so long as I can. I'm in that tent near the wall. Don't bother me unless it's important. Now it's time to sleep, unless either of you are too hungry. Jon?"

"Yes, I am."

"I figured. There's some bread covered on that table." He directed a beam of light at it.

"Put out that light!" someone yelled from the many tents bunched together around us.

"Shut up, I'm trying to sleep!" said someone else.

There were a few other mutterings, but my attention was directed at movement nearby. The silhouette of a girl emerged out of one of the tents. She seemed to have something wrapped around her, possibly fur. It was too dark to tell who it was just by looking, but something told me it was Hadley.

"Jon?" she whispered sleepily.

"It's us," I said.

It looked like she was rubbing her eyes as she walked over.

"Is everything all right?" she whispered.

"Everything's fine," Leon answered for us. "Get back to sleep, Hadley."

"I'd like to stay up if Jon is."

"I bet you would, but I'm not going to allow that. The two of you need your rest just like everyone else. Go back to your tent, Hadley."

Remi approached Hadley. The two girls took each other's hands for a brief moment as they said good night.

"You all can sleep," I said. "I will as soon as I eat some bread on that table." I pointed.

"I see what you're doing." Leon spoke with a gravelly voice. "You're letting Hadley know where you're going to be. Fine. I give up. Stay up all night if you want to, but I'm not letting you sleep in tomorrow, Hadley. Jon needs the rest because he's been busy. You have no excuse."

"That's fine," Hadley said.

"Good night, Leon," I said happily.

Hadley walked past him as she took what I was now certain was a coat of fur and tossed one side around my shoulder. She gathered it as she huddled close to me, our arms touching.

"Hi," she said, her sweet tone warming my heart.

We wrapped our fingers around each other's hands as we walked to the table and maneuvered over the bench until we were seated on it close beside each other.

"I wanted to stay up and wait for you, but I fell asleep," she said. "I'm glad someone shouted and woke me up."

"I'm glad, too." We spoke in whispers.

"We shouldn't stay up long." She put her hand on my leg and kissed my cheek. "Eat, Jon."

"I think I lost my appetite. For food, anyway." I leaned close to her lips.

"Did you now?" She took hold of my shirt and pulled me in the rest of the way.

We didn't kiss for long before Hadley climbed on my lap to provide a better angle for our lips. She held the fur around us, but the night alone provided a blanket of darkness that was all the privacy we needed.

A heat spread through my chest. I didn't care about the bread anymore. I put my hands beneath her bottom and stood up with her. She wrapped her legs around me, our lips never parting.

I carefully walked us away from the table. "Where are you taking me, Jon?" she whispered playfully.

"To my tent."

"Your tent is filled with Charlie, Michael, and Reuben."

"Then to your tent. I thought we might fall asleep with each other." *Or maybe more.*

"I would like that, but I have even more people in mine."

I let out my breath.

"Jon..." She sounded to be smiling, but I could hear she was against this idea. "This is not our night."

"You're right." I hadn't been thinking clearly.

I let her down.

"I will keep you warm as you eat," she said. "Then we must sleep."

*****

When I emerged from the boys' tent in the morning, I had no recollection of anyone else getting up or even leaving the tent. It was well into the morning. Empty bowls of porridge still sat on the tables. I was starving and dirty. Leon's "parenting" had made me feel more like a young boy last night than I had in a long time. *A young boy who has to fight in a war.* It was a strange feeling.

But now as I looked around, I again felt like the young man I was. Although almost everyone in the camp who wasn't a sorcerer of the king seemed to be older than I was, I had duties and responsibilities to worry about. I fixed myself a bowl of porridge, glad for the time to be left alone as I gathered myself. However, as I started to eat, I became curious about what my peers seemed to be arguing about near Leon. I went over with my breakfast for a listen.

I was too groggy to realize until now that it was all the girls and none of the boys complaining here, and it was Leon who seemed to be the cause of their frustration, as all glared at him.

"There's plenty of bathing barrels. What's the problem?" Leon was asking defensively.

"There's no privacy," Aliana complained.

"There are sheets around them!" Leon replied as he gestured at the thick cloths hung around the bathing barrels.

"Anyone can just walk in!" Aliana said. "And the barrels don't even reach high enough to cover us completely."

"Then go to the river."

Most of the girls expressed their displeasure through groans.

"It's freezing!" Aliana said.

"The river can't be heated," Remi added.

Leon huffed. "What the hell do you want me to do?"

All went quiet as many of the girls looked down, appearing depressed. The sound of my spoon bumping against the wooden bowl as I ate turned a few heads in my direction.

"If there was somewhere close I could take you all, I would," was all I could offer.

"What about Drayer?" Aliana suggested.

"No way," Leon replied. "It's too far, and we aren't going to strain our early relationship with those people by forcing them to bathe you girls." He let out a frustrated breath. "I *suppose* you all can use my tent. I'll have empty barrels fetched and filled by our resident water mage."

"That water mage is weak," Eden said. "It'll take him until the afternoon to fill our barrels."

"Then fill them in the river yourself and roll them back."

"They're going to be too heavy," Aliana complained.

"We can help," Michael said as he came up from behind me and put his hand on my shoulder.

"Yeah," I agreed. "Just let me finish my breakfast."

The girls gave us their thanks.

I hadn't noticed last night how large Leon's tent was. Like Byron's toward the center of camp, it made the rest of our tents look like dog houses in comparison.

It took until midday for all of us to set up Leon's tent into a bathing quarters for the girls. The sun had come out by then, and the day was quite warm. I had worked up quite a sweat, so I actually found pleasure in bathing in the cold river. It wasn't the most private place, as a few of our archers came by here and there to gather water, but they politely kept their gazes down.

I felt refreshed by the time I finished and dried off. I had a late lunch with Hadley and Aliana, who were still eating when I joined them at their table. I felt a little bad that I hadn't noticed until then that I had no idea where Reuben and Charlie were. Michael stood near the ballista and seemed to be having an argument with the man in charge of guarding it, but I had not seen the other two boys in quite a while.

"Where are Reuben and Charlie?" I asked.

"They've gone out into the woods to work on multicasting," Aliana said.

"Multicasting?"

"Leon brought it up on the way here," Hadley answered. "He said some of us are ready to begin training it."

"Is it just casting two spells at the same time?" I asked.

"That's my understanding," she said.

I thought about what might happen if I combined two spells, like Grab and Fire. I wasn't sure I had it in me. There were too many notes involved, but what if I could? Would a successful spell mean I could grab someone with a ring of fire? It didn't seem right. Fire didn't have the ability to hold like dvinia did, and I couldn't imagine any combination of spells that would set my mana aflame yet still retain its strength to pick up a person.

The sudden sound of the ballista firing drew our attention to Michael, where he stood behind the device. He pumped his fist in excitement. "Yeah!" he hooted. "Did you see that?" he asked the very displeased man next to him.

"Michael!" Leon screamed.

Michael turned with absolute fear, putting his shoulders up in a defensive way as if expecting Leon to attack him.

"I hit the bush I was aiming at," Michael said, as if that would make it better.

"You fire that thing again, and I'm going to take off one of your fingers!"

Just about all the men in the camp seemed to be watching Leon yell at Michael while Michael slumped his shoulders and headed down from the ramparts. He perked up a bit when Leon stopped staring at him, then he smiled at us as he walked over.

I hadn't noticed until this morning, when the girls were complaining about the lack of privacy, that they were the only females here. It was a busy scene in the wooden fort, but some men did enjoy some leisure time as they played cards, fiddled with a lute, and sparred casually.

"I don't see how some spells can be combined," I admitted.

"I don't think all can," Aliana said. "Leon said combining works best with schools of magic that are single notes, like Earth or mtalia."

Hadley began to nod. "And I think he's right. I believe I could curse a piece of metal if I could reach the frequency of mtalia. I might even be able to curse a section of the earth if I could reach your note of llB, Aliana."

"Are you close?" she asked.

"No, my range is quite narrow. I believe only dteria, fire, and water will ever be available to me. Can you reach a high enough frequency for any other spells?" she asked Aliana.

"I don't think so. My range starts and ends too low."

"Did Leon say if anything could be done with vtalia?" I asked.

"No," Hadley said. "He mostly spoke to Reuben about it. He said that Reuben has the best chance of anyone because he can use ordia and Earth, and those are the only two combinations Leon has heard about before."

"What does combining them do?" I asked.

"It depends on how ordia is used," Hadley answered. "I imagine Reuben could identify and track enchantments that are set in things that came from the earth, like gemstones. He might even be able to disable one from a long distance."

I felt my face change in shock. "That's actually very useful."

"I might be wrong," Hadley was quick to tell me. "I only say that because of my loose understanding of how combinations work."

"Kataleya might know more," Aliana commented. "I hope she's well."

Hadley and I nodded. I had been worried about Kat, traveling all this way with men we could not completely rely on. I figured the king would've told me if something had happened, but he never mentioned Kataleya or the Chespar army.

I noticed Aliana and Hadley looking nervously at something behind me. I glanced over my shoulder to see two young men speaking with Eden and Remi. They seemed flirtatious as they stood close to the girls and held small smiles, but neither Eden nor Remi appeared uncomfortable as they grinned back. The two young men were older, probably in their twenties, but there was nothing about them that alarmed me.

"Is it strange to be the only females here?" I asked Aliana and Hadley.

They looked at each other and shrugged. "Not yet," Aliana said. "But we only just arrived."

"Yeah," Hadley agreed, her gaze drifting toward the group of archers practicing their aim against a set of targets. She watched them for a little while before commenting. "Ali, you shoot a lot better than they do."

Aliana and I watched. The three archers stood about twenty yards away from their round targets. More often than not, they missed completely.

"That is concerning," Aliana said.

The gate began to open, allowing in a man on a horse. He rode to Byron and Leon, then dismounted to speak with them.

"I'd wager that's a scout from Chespar's troops," Hadley said. "They could be close."

That reminded me of something. "Aliana, did you speak with your father after I dropped him off?"

She snickered. "Yes, he had a lot to say about you."

"I was meaning to ask you about that. Are you sure we can trust him?"

She frowned. "Not completely. He is selfish, but I don't think we have a choice. We need his help."

"Even if he could betray us?"

Her mouth flattened. "He's not going to betray us and side with Rohaer, but I have no doubt about him acting according to his own wishes."

"That sounds like he'll create problems in Drayer."

"I don't think so," she said without certainty. "He wants to make up for his mistakes."

"Are we talking about his mistake with Cason or his mistake with you?"

Aliana seemed a bit surprised as she leaned back. "Jon, it's not your responsibility to be angry for me."

I felt as though my words had come across too aggressively. I had to pause to gather my thoughts.

"I wasn't angry at him before, but that changed after I took him here, on my back, and he wouldn't stop speaking down to me the entire time."

She nodded solemnly. "Yeah, I know what he's like. Still, I'd rather you let me worry about the way he treats me."

"I'll back off," I said.

"Thank you."

I figured that would mean I'd go back to knowing nothing about how Aliana's father treated her, but if that's what Aliana preferred, then I would respect her wishes. My only fear was that she wanted no one to know because she knew that it wasn't right, and she didn't wish for any of us to attempt to help her. It was like she'd rather suffer, but have him in her life, than push him out.

I started to understand it better, though, as I finished my lunch and thought more on it. Perhaps it wasn't so much that she wanted him in her life but that she knew the king needed him. She could just be performing a duty. That, I respected.

"Jon," Hadley said, "might I convince you to keep a mana break stone with you?"

"I thought it would be best for the rest of you to have one." As far as I remembered, there weren't enough for everyone who had skill with ordia to keep one in their possession. "I'm confident I could escape if Valinox tried to kill me, now that he's no longer hidden by a cloaking spell."

"All right, but I'm going to keep one with me at all times. I might use it if he attacks, if I think we might be able to slay him."

"I trust your judgment," I told her.

Aliana blew out a loud breath. "I can't take it any longer," she said, staring at the archers missing their targets. "I have to show them how it's done. Excuse me."

With Hadley and me the last ones at the table, she came over to sit on my side. She took my hand under the table.

"Have you felt another lackadaze since that one

time?" she asked.

"No, I'm pretty sure you fixed me."

"I'm glad. Seeing you in that state has made me wonder if it's power in its own right that can alter a mind. Dteria provides the addiction, but without the power it provides, the mind may remain unaltered."

"I'll admit it feels unnatural for a man to fly like a bird."

"Still?"

"Yes. It's completely twisted the way I think about travel. Keeping my feet on the ground feels like crawling now. Even when I'm not traveling, like now, I want to take off into the forest. Remaining here against my wishes feels like I'm trapped in a cage."

"Even when you're with me?"

"I was thinking I'd take you with me."

She formed a wide smile. "That sounds quite fun. Do you think Leon might be upset?"

"I think I could get us out of here without him seeing. I'm willing to risk it."

"So am I."

"All right, but not for too long. I'm sure there are duties waiting for us." I took her hand and stood. "Be ready to jump on my back."

We got into position as we watched Leon and Byron, the two speaking leisurely. It was because I saw no concern on their faces that I figured Hadley and I could have a little tryst in the woods.

"Now," I said, and caught her legs as she jumped onto my back.

She gasped as I took us into the air and over the wall, behind the backs of our supervisors. I soared toward the thick trees, dipping under branches and weaving around trunks. Hadley laughed in delight.

I landed softly and set her down. She pulled my head down and kissed my lips with a growing hunger.

*****

We had found an enclosure where the bushes grew tall. We lay in the thick weeds, rolling around on top of each other and laughing as we talked about nothing important, every word out of her mouth a lovely tune to me. I had grown fond of her voice. She had a wise manner of speaking in just about every circumstance except moments like these, when her voice became low and raspy, and I could almost feel her passion behind every phrase.

"You seem uncomfortable," she whispered with a sly look. "Let me help you." She pulled up my shirt until I straightened out. Then she yanked it over my head. "That's much better, isn't it?"

"Much," I agreed.

She looked me over and seemed quite pleased. "Come here."

I eased down on top of her and kissed her neck. She moaned as she moved her hands out from my abs around to my back, where she dug her nails into me. She kissed my lips as she moved into a position that pushed all of the right parts together.

"Maybe you should be more comfortable as well," I whispered.

"Just *a little* more comfortable, but not *completely* comfortable," she said with a slight giggle. "Not where people might come upon us," she whispered into my ear, then nibbled on the lobe.

My heart raced as I sat up for a look as she peeled

down one strap of her tunic. Hadley was a slender girl, petite, with soft edges and a very shapely figure. She brushed her lush dark hair out of the way, her eyes boring into me. My gaze traveled down her slender neck and her prominent collarbone to the top of her generous bosom wanting to burst from her tunic.

"Hadley, my god."

She smiled seductively.

That's when my whole world crumbled to dust as I heard someone coming through the bushes.

Hadley gasped in horror as she quickly pulled up her tunic and I rolled off her.

Reuben clicked his tongue in disapproval as Charlie stood behind him with wide eyes. "Hadley, I'm disappointed in you. Out in public like this?"

"Watch it, Reuben," I said, deflated, as I slipped my shirt on and helped Hadley up.

"I might expect this from you, Jon, but she's highborn, and a lady!"

"Don't hold your nose above us," Hadley said. "You're the one intruding on our privacy."

"Privacy? Did the two of you hit your heads? Look around. You have the woodsmen within sight *right* over there, picking apart saplings, and hunters track big game past you this way. You can even see one of them right now. Look!" He pointed. It was true. One had his back to us about thirty yards away. "There's more privacy offered in a brothel than the two of you have here."

I was still angry, but when I noticed Hadley giving me a look as if Reuben was right, I realized our mistake.

Hadley spoke it for us. "We might've been a little too preoccupied to notice."

"It's my fault," I said. "It was my idea to come out

here."

"Were the two of you about to lie together?" Charlie asked. I could've whacked him.

"No, Charlie," Hadley said, then glanced at me. "We were just…looking for some time to ourselves and might've gotten carried away."

"Wait," I said. "How did the two of you know to look here? I highly doubt you could've seen us."

"Does one of you have one of those curse stones Hadley made?" Reuben asked.

Hadley took it out of her pocket.

"I knew it!" Reuben told Charlie victoriously. "Didn't I say?"

"You did," Charlie said with an equally proud smile.

"I felt it from nearly a mile away!" Reuben told Hadley. "I came all the way here to see if I was right, not expecting to find you and Jon with most of your clothes off." There was his aristocratic tone again.

"We get it, Reuben," I said, but Hadley spoke at the same time and didn't seem as bothered by his attitude.

"That's spectacular, Reuben! You did that by combining ordia and Earth?"

"I sure did."

Had I let go of my anger earlier, I would've realized what this meant, like Hadley clearly had already.

I asked, "So you can strengthen your tracking if someone has an enchantment on them?"

"By a lot."

Hadley asked, "Could you use the same multicasting to break the enchantment from a longer distance away?"

"I believe so, but not from a mile out. I have to train more and test. Charlie, my good friend, will you spend the rest of the day with me as you have the morning? I can re-enchant the items I disenchant from afar, but I need you to hold them and assist me in my training."

"Yes, but I'm hungry. Can we eat first?"

Reuben glanced up at the canopy. "What time is it? I completely forgot about eating!"

"You just missed lunch," I informed him, "but you might be able to grab something if you hurry."

"Come on!" Charlie yelled as he ran toward the fort. Reuben trailed after him.

"I've never seen Reuben so focused on something that he'd miss a meal," I commented.

Hadley seemed to be staring at me rather than at our friends. She gave a long sigh.

"What is it?" I asked.

"I think he's right. We shouldn't have tried to hide from everyone. It isn't going to work, and it's a little embarrassing when we're caught."

"I hope you're not saying that we should stop seeing each other in that way, because I don't think I'm capable."

"No." She grinned. "I'm not, either." She took my hand and leaned against my shoulder. "I'm not sure what to do. Soon the rest of the army will arrive and we will march with them to meet Rohaer at the defile. This was probably the last private time we'll have for a while, and it wasn't even as private as we thought." She gestured at a couple woodsmen not thirty yards away.

I wanted to argue with her, but I knew she was right. Although I'd rather spend the day with Hadley, I knew it was best to focus on my sorcery while I still could.

"I can feel you trying to think of a way around it,"

she said.

I nodded.

She went up to her toes and kissed my cheek. "I'm glad I can make you feel this way," she whispered in my ear, sending a chill down my back. She went back to her heels and looked into my eyes. "But I feel that it's selfish to take you away from everything and keep you for myself. You're special because of how quickly you improve. The rest of us aren't like that. It takes weeks before we notice the slightest difference. I think it's best if we stop trying to create moments for us, at least until things calm down."

"I know what you're saying is right," I said with a nod. "And I will accept it. Soon."

She let out a light laugh and leaned into me for an embrace. For a while, we held each other in silence, her head against my chest.

"I don't know where your sorcery will take you, but will you wait for me?" she asked.

"What do you mean?"

"I mean more temptations might present themselves to you." She seemed nervous as she looked at the ground.

"Hadley, if I would turn Nijja away for you, then there's certainly no one else for you to worry about."

She wore a half grin as she looked up. "So she really is that beautiful?"

"She is, but not as beautiful as you."

Hadley stepped close, and I knew this would be the last time in a while that we could let out our passion without causing a scene.

But again we were interrupted as I heard shouts of fear from the nearby woodsmen, who darted toward us and ultimately in the direction of the fort behind us. A massive cantar prowled in the distance, stalking between the trees as if looking for unsuspecting prey. Unfortunately, it seemed to think the men running away were its best chance for a meal as it suddenly darted toward one of them.

I sighed as I took out my sword.

CHAPTER TWENTY

I was sitting and cleaning cantar blood off my sword in the fortress when I noticed Reuben rushing toward Leon, a fork in one hand. I couldn't see his face as I stood with Hadley and Michael, the three of us gravitating toward Leon after we saw Reuben sprint away from Charlie and his meal.

"I've never seen Reuben move like that," Michael said.

We jogged over as Reuben looked around and found me. "Jon!" he called, as Leon gestured for me to hurry.

"What is it?" I asked as I tossed myself lightly with dvinia, landing in front of them in what was basically one massive leap.

"I felt an enchantment pass by faster than a man on horseback," Reuben said. "It had to be a demigod."

"Fly up and see what you can," Leon said as he handed me a spyglass.

"Which direction should I look?" I asked as I readied myself.

"That way, toward the road." Reuben pointed east.

I hoisted myself up into the sky. The forest extended for about a mile east before it met the road and came to an end. I looked southward to find someone soaring away from us. I put the spyglass to my eye.

I couldn't quite track the fast-moving demigod as I held myself up with dvinia, but I managed to get a few good glimpses. It looked to be Valinox, and he seemed to be carrying a girl with long brown hair.

I was about to descend and inform the others what I'd seen when I noticed another demigod coming from the north. I put the spyglass to my eye again and recognized Souriff by her silvery blond hair billowing behind her. Her whole body was covered in a glistening metallic material that I figured was a suit of Valaer steel armor. Far behind her was a third figure. Even with the spyglass, I couldn't discern any of her features, but I knew it had to be Failina simply because there was no one else who could fly like that. She looked like a beam of glowing light, no doubt covered in the same armor as Souriff.

I let myself freefall back into the fort, slowing at the last moment to avoid injury. I gave the spyglass back to Leon.

"Get my armor, Michael," I said.

"Just yours?"

"Yes."

As he ran off, I continued, "It was Valinox you felt, Reuben. He has someone with him, and he seems to be taking her to Rohaer. Souriff is chasing Valinox, and Failina is far behind. It looks like they are ready to fight. I should be able to catch up to Failina and find out what's going on, but depending on the circumstances I might not be able to return to inform the rest of you."

"Who did Valinox take?" Leon asked.

The obvious answer came to me. "Most likely the princess, but I can't be sure." I suppressed my horror and fear as I focused on my duty to get her back.

Men were quickly gathering around, Byron included. There was no time for me to stay and chat, or I'd miss Failina.

"I have to go now," I said as I noticed Michael returning with not just my breastplate but a wooden shield as well.

"I overheard," he said. "You might need this."

I lifted my arms as Michael and Leon helped me into the armor. Then I slid my left arm through the straps on the inside of the shield and took out my sword.

I soared out of the fortress and toward the road. I made it there as Failina was about to cross by. She spotted me and shifted in the air. Wind whipped her short hair as it carried her toward me.

"What happened?" I asked.

"Valinox broke into the castle and stole the princess while we were meeting with the king."

She spoke while out of breath. I held myself suspended with dvinia, something I still wasn't quite used to. The difference was like holding something heavy with my arms rather than tossing it and resting before another toss. However, Failina seemed even less comfortable remaining in one spot as her wind jittered her left and right, forward and back. She gestured for us to land. We went down onto the empty road.

"He was outfitting us with armor when we heard the screams," she continued. "We hoped to catch up before Valinox could bring the princess to his army, but even Souriff can't match his speed. We have to either steal her back or take someone else of equal value for a trade."

"There's an officer, a metal mage who seems as valuable to Valinox as Cason was."

"You will look for him when we arrive. Defend me from arrows with that shield, and I will create a blizzard. If the princess is guarded too heavily, then take the metal mage. Bundle up and meet us south. Souriff will provide a distraction. She should be able to keep herself alive and take all the attention off us until my blizzard sets in."

"All right," I replied with an uneasy tone, remembering how the cold of Failina's blizzard had nearly killed me the last time.

"I will inform my sister of the plan. We must hurry. I'm not sure if Valinox was aware we were in the castle. I don't believe he can sense us when we are not using sorcery, but he probably felt us following him. He will tell his army to set up a defense against us. Go now."

I rushed back through the air until I was over the fort, then I let gravity take me down, slowing at the last moment.

A few hundred archers had gathered by then, as well as all of my peers.

"Valinox took the king's daughter from the castle," I explained, "no doubt to use her as ransom. I'm going with Failina and Souriff to get her back, or at least to take Valinox's metal mage if we can't get her. Failina is going to make a blizzard. I need as much protection from the cold as possible, but I still need to be able to fight."

"I have furs," Hadley said.

"You can use my coif," Michael added.

A few others ran off as well, and soon I was bombarded with furs, coats, and hats. By then I had explained that the demigod sisters were in the castle when this happened.

"This sounds like it could be a trap," Byron said.

"I agree," said Leon. "They could have all their casters and archers ready. If you see a formation that you won't be able to get through, turn back. I don't care what Failina or Souriff try to make you do. Do you hear me?"

"I do."

During the time it took me to prepare for the cold, a few of the onlookers had asked if there was anything anyone could do, but Rohaer's army was too far away. We didn't have the means to surprise them except by air.

I was certain that Valinox planned to use Callie, but he might very well have her killed if he saw us about to rescue her. That gave me pause for just a moment, but it was all the time we had. If we waited too long, Souriff would lose sight of him, and we wouldn't be able to get her back.

"I have to go now."

"Go," Leon said.

I flew out of the fortress and headed south. The demigod sisters seemed to be about a mile ahead when I reached their altitude, and it looked like they were waiting for me. They started moving before I arrived, no doubt expecting me to catch up.

I was covered in fur and wool, my limbs less mobile, but I just had to grab Callie and get out of there. Failina's blizzard should take care of everyone trying to stop me.

"We're just about to lose him," Souriff called back to me and jutted forward.

Failina flew more smoothly, while I soared like Souriff, with sudden lurches from powerful tosses of my mind. It didn't take long before I surpassed Failina, but the distance between us and Souriff had increased.

The road ran out from under us between a long range of mountains to my left and the forest to my right. Rohaer was tucked far to the south, the nearby mountains blocking our view, but the camp of Rohaer's army soon came to be in plain sight.

I hurled myself one more time before I let my momentum slow, then I held myself up with dvinia and took the spyglass out of my pocket for a look.

White tents not too unlike ours sat in clustered rows and made up the bulk of their huge encampment. There seemed to be little order to their massive group of thousands, though just about everyone seemed to be looking up at Valinox as he landed near the largest tent in the center. He tossed Callie to the ground and pointed at her. A bunch of men with ropes in hand surrounded her.

"What do you see?" Souriff asked as Failina caught up. "Did he hand her off?"

"He did. She's there near the largest tent in the middle."

I watched as they tied her hands and ankles, then moved her into the tent. About ten men stood watch outside. Many others were pointing in our direction, some with spyglasses of their own. I grew tired as I held myself, but I stayed there a while longer as I described the scene to the demigods.

"They're giving Valinox a spyglass. He's looking our way. I haven't seen any signs of a trap. Men are running for their bows. It's only going to get harder the longer we wait."

"Then we go now," Souriff said.

"After I find Davon, the metal mage." I surveyed the encampment for a long while but couldn't locate him.

"Hurry up," Souriff said.

"You're not helping," I replied.

Many of the men seemed to be grouping around someone as if to protect him, like they did the large tent. However, I did not recognize the dark-haired man they'd gathered around. He must've been someone else of importance.

I noticed more groups forming as archers took their places at the front of the encampment. Priority targets, surely, but neither I nor the demigods knew our enemies well enough to tell who these people were and why exactly they were so important. It served to remind me just how disadvantaged we were.

I eventually found Davon toward the back. There had to be fifty men packed closely around him. Valinox stood nearby, in front of the large tent. I was content to ignore him if I could.

I described everything as I handed the spyglass to Souriff, who glanced quickly before passing it off to her sister.

"Keep Failina safe in the beginning," Souriff told me.

I waited for her to soar toward the waiting army, but she didn't move.

Souriff looked back at us. "It's not worth it."

"What?" I said.

"We might not get back alive. It's not worth it."

Was that fear in her voice?

"You have met the king of Lycast," Failina said. "He is soft for his daughter. He will order his men back from the defile if Valinox threatens the life of the princess."

"No, he won't. He knows not to do something so foolish."

"He is a father as much as a king."

"Then he should've kept her better guarded," Souriff said. "Or better yet, we can put someone else in charge who has the stomach to do the job."

I was about to speak up, but it seemed like Failina was doing it for me. "The people have love for their king, but not for us. That will not work. The longer we wait, the more prepared they will be for us."

Souriff stared at the army, unmoving.

"We discussed this even before the princess was captured," Failina said. "We were prepared to infiltrate their army and take a prized sorcerer. We were just about to leave to find the fortress and bring Jon with us. We agreed that now that Valinox has taken the princess, it's even more important."

I had no idea of this plan. They must've formed it recently with the king. I was surprised. It was a good plan that would've done a lot to help our cause in this war. Now it would only keep Callie safe, but that was enough.

"You don't need to remind me," Souriff said.

"It seems like I do!" Failina replied in anger. "Airinold is right about you, isn't he? You created dvinia in a way that only you could use it. You have sacrificed nothing, while Airinold and I sacrificed so much more. I have held my tongue all these years, but I can't any longer. You have seen what Caarda has become because of your actions. You even drove our other brother to attempt to kill you. That is on you, sister, you and Valinox. The rest of us are doing our part to put an end to this, and so must you. That means putting yourself at risk of death. It is the least you can do after all the trouble you've caused. *This* is when you decide what your legacy will be, this war and *this* moment. You and Valinox can live on in history as the instigators of war and the reason Airinold created dteria, or you can change that and make up for your selfishness!"

Souriff looked back at her sister. She gathered herself quickly with a few strong breaths, then wiped burgeoning tears from her eyes. A hardened look came across her face.

"I will go in first with a shield of dvinia and disrupt the archers. You will make the snowstorm, Failina, as Jon protects you. Unlike Lina, I cannot take the cold much longer than the mortals, Jon, so you must be quick. Once everyone's vision is impaired, it's up to you to retrieve the metal mage. I would help you, but it's unlikely I'll be able to find you during the chaos. My brother, however, I can sense. I will distract him so that you can escape back to the fortress. If I do not meet you there, then do not come back for me. Are you both ready?"

"I'm ready," I said, as Failina put her hand on her sister's shoulder and looked proud.

Souriff flew off at a blurring speed. We followed some distance behind as she descended over the archers. They took aim.

"Stay behind me until I say so, Jon," Failina said as she zipped in front of me with a powerful gust of wind.

"Fire!" ordered a man wearing a decorated uniform and standing among the hundreds of archers.

A swarm of arrows came at Souriff, but she did not slow. Many missed while a dozen others became embedded in her shield of dvinia. A few passed by Souriff, splitting the air with a screeching sound, but Failina's wall of wind deflected them away from us.

Souriff landed hard among the archers and pushed out her hands. A wave of dvinia knocked over hundreds and caused those farther from her to stumble away.

"Now," Failina said as she suspended herself in the air above the army.

I put myself beneath her and readied my lowly shield. Failina's wind whipped at my back as I hovered a few hundred feet off the ground. The sisters had put a lot of faith in my ability to protect Failina from not only arrows but fireballs as well, as I saw a couple forming above the many ranks of sorcerers below us. I could block almost anything with dvinia, but I had never tried to do so while suspending myself at the same time.

Souriff, however, had all the archers disabled for now. There were just a few others along the outskirts, disorganized, as they fired frantically.

Most of the arrows slowed on their way up to us, making it easy for me to see that none would hit their mark. The temperature of the air dropped suddenly. Snow fell, lightly at first, but quickly became dense.

I used my shield to block an arrow that I had not seen coming until the last instant. The force of it reverberated through my arm, but it didn't do much else. Then two large fireballs rose and fell beneath us. We were too far for any sorcerer or even most archers to reach us, and it looked like they were starting to realize this. Men in decorated uniforms yelled to kill Souriff first.

"Go now," Failina said. "My blizzard will soon be upon them."

I kept my eyes on the metal mage. There was no way to tell what kind of sorcerers protected him, just that dozens stayed close as if they knew I was coming for him.

I let go of myself with dvinia and formed a wall of it beneath my feet. Letting myself freefall while keeping the dvinia intact with my mind, I had effectively created a shield beneath me in case an archer or a fire mage got lucky.

The snow was so dense by then, the air so cold, that I felt as though I couldn't breathe as the frigid wind sapped my strength. I steeled my nerves as everything became white.

I could no longer see my enemies. I couldn't even see the ground. But I had seen where they were a moment ago. I slowed before coming down onto a group of them, landing on one man and rolling off him across the ground.

I took a note from Souriff's book and blasted out dvinia in every direction, knocking over too many to count. I couldn't see past my hands, the snow was so dense. Shouts of confusion rang out from every direction, too many orders at once for most to be understood.

I had lost Davon, but I knew he was close. I took out my sword as I saw a blade come for my head without seeing the hand attached to it. I ducked as a heavily bearded face burst through the white wall and growled at me. I took one step past him, and he sounded a mile away as he shouted that the bladedancer was here. I bumped into the shoulder of someone else who didn't seem to realize I was the enemy.

"Where is he?"

"Behind me, I think," I replied.

"It's you!" said the soldier as his eyes widened. "He's here!"

There was a scream of agony, then, "You stabbed me!"

"Goddammit, I thought you were him!"

I found no one for a breath. I figured I was about to

lose Davon for good. I couldn't stay here much longer. The cold felt like daggers in my lungs. My body urged me to get out as my joints became stiff and my eyes burned.

I made a wall of dvinia and threw it in front of me, clearing the snow for a breath. I knocked over two soldiers with it, both rolling back into the white and out of view.

I thought one of them had been Davon, but I couldn't be sure. I ran toward him, wondering how the hell I could possibly get him out of here alive. Killing him would be good for our cause, but not for Callie.

A large body fell on me, taking me to the ground and rolling over me. He grabbed my layers of fur, but I kicked him off as he yelled for the others that I was here.

I took to the air as I heard men collide beneath me, one screaming that he had been stabbed.

Suddenly, the wind stopped screaming, and the snow began to clear.

Failina, what are you doing? I wondered as I felt warmth run through my body, the sun reaching me again.

At least it allowed me to spot Davon.

"There," he announced as he trudge toward me confidently. "Surround him."

I looked around me to see dozens coming from every angle.

"I've got him," said a woman as she formed a fireball.

I threw myself into the air as she cast, the fireball hitting her own man square in the chest. He fell back into three others with a scream, and the sheer density of the crowd came to my field of view. There had to be hundreds within a stone's throw.

I had just enough time to check on Failina in the sky above me. Where she had been earlier, Valinox now hovered. Failina's body spiraled away from him. I hoped she was still alive. Valinox, meanwhile, found Souriff somewhere beneath him and flew straight at her. She was maybe fifty yards from me and still looked to have all the archers distracted, but she wouldn't as soon as Valinox was upon her.

Davon was completely surrounded by his people, our plan to take or kill him obvious to everyone in the vicinity. There was no way I was getting to him now and escaping with my life.

With Valinox distracted, however, I might be able to get Callie out of here. I soared toward the large tent in the center of the encampment.

Two heavily armored soldiers positioned themselves in front of the flap of the tent, but I didn't bother to deal with them. I flew above it and cut a slit in the roof, toward the back of the tent where I suspected Callie to be held.

I fell through and landed on someone's back, giving me just a moment to look around. Soldiers and sorcerers packed the tent, with Callie just a few steps away from me. Her hands and ankles were tied, while two men held her arms and dragged her away from me. An archer had an arrow ready, firing across the interior of the tent.

I caught it with my shield in front of my face. I made a wall of dvinia to block a fireball. I tossed the shield into the mouth of someone rushing at me with a sword. He fell back with a curse as I weaved around the attack of another swordsman and had just enough time to stick the tip of my blade into his side, where his armor was open.

My dvinia blocked a jet of fire. I kicked a table into the path of someone rushing me and ducked under a swipe at my head. A flash of light turned my head toward Callie. Flames exploded from her hands. The two men holding her arms fell away as she hollered, "Jon!"

She hopped toward me as someone called out, "Kill her before he gets away with her."

I noticed the archer taking aim again, shifting to fire at the princess. I grabbed her with dvinia and pulled her the rest of the way to me, catching her in the air with my hands and putting myself between her and the bowman as I ducked my head down.

It felt like a pinch against my back as the arrow failed to break through my armor. Men came at us from every angle, a vicious look in their eyes as they steeled themselves to kill this innocent girl. I tossed her high into the air with dvinia, through the opening in the tent. I tried to hurl myself out after her in the same fashion, but someone grabbed my legs as I was taking off.

The extra weight pulled me down, ruining my aim and causing my head to brush against the top of the tent as my body flew into the side wall. I felt the man's hold come loose from my legs as we hit the ground. I got up and cut a hole in the tent as I felt someone strike my armor with his blade and someone else grab my ankle.

I looked back and thought about using the hilt of my sword to bash in the head of the man grabbing me, but three more were just about upon me. I had to get out of here *now*. Callie must be on the way down in a fall that would kill her. With one still clutching my ankle, I hurled myself out of the fresh opening in the tent and into the sky.

I kicked and spun, flinging off the large man previously attached to me. Then I spotted the princess falling not far from my trajectory. I tossed myself in her direction and stopped underneath her in the air. I made a blanket of dvinia far above my head to catch and slow her, though she broke through it and still came at me fast! I opened my arms and hoped for the best.

She collided into me, but I somehow managed to get my arms around her. She screamed as we tumbled wildly, arcing quickly toward the ground. I was unable to tell just how I was holding the princess, as my focus was poured into getting dvinia around my waist while the ground came at us.

I lurched with a great pull of my mind, the strain coming out through a grunt behind gritted teeth. Only then did I realize that I had Callie over my shoulder and she was about to slip off.

"Jon!" she screamed.

"I got you!"

"No, the arrows!"

Only she could see what I hoped to be two or three archers aiming at us, but then a dozen arrows flew by.

One struck me in the armor and didn't stick, but another got me in the leg and stayed there. Surprisingly, it didn't hurt one bit, though it did throw me off my trajectory and nearly caused the princess to tumble off my shoulder as she shrieked in fear.

She ended up pulling me upside down as I held her legs with both hands. "Hold on!" I yelled over her screams. "I won't drop you!"

I flew out of the encampment, both of us upside down, as arrows missed us at greater and greater distances, and soon the archers had given up.

Callie never stopped screaming as she hung with

my hands around her ankles. Blood rushed to my head as I took her another mile away from the encampment, my hands starting to ache. I didn't know how I was supposed to land like this, but I had to set her down before she slipped.

She suddenly stopped screaming, and I looked down to see that she had passed out, her arms dangling. It was probably a good thing, I figured, as I took her over the forest. I carefully navigated the two of us down through the canopy of trees and on to the forest floor, where I slowed to gently ease Callie down on her back.

I took a moment for myself, as I sat and put my hand on my head and waited for the dizziness to abate.

Callie woke up suddenly, screaming and thrashing on the ground.

I held her shoulders. "Calm down. You're safe."

"Jon?" she asked as she looked around.

I was breathless as I pulled out the arrow in my leg and healed my wound. "I'll be back soon."

"Where are you going?" she asked as I took off again.

There wasn't enough time to answer.

I flew high into the sky and suspended myself as I checked each direction for my demigod allies. I noticed Failina soaring toward me from far away. Valinox seemed to have driven her a couple miles north. I didn't see any sign of him, though.

She arrived promptly. Out of breath and with her tunic partially ripped, she asked me, "Where's the metal mage?"

"He was too well-defended, but I did manage to get back the princess."

"Good, very good! Where's Souriff?" Failina asked.

"I don't know," I said. "I haven't seen her since I went down."

We held in the air. The only sound was Failina's constantly moving wind as she jittered back and forth.

"Oh," Failina said in a small voice.

CHAPTER TWENTY-ONE

We waited for Souriff. And then we waited some more. We couldn't see within the encampment from here, even with the spyglass. We edged closer. Failina watched through the far-seeing lens as I listened to her creak and moan with worry. I was prepared to go back for her sister, but only if Failina gave the word.

"She must need our help if she's still alive," Failina said.

"Wait, look." I thought I saw someone fly out from the encampment.

Failina gasped and put the spyglass to her eye. "It's her. Go."

We soared toward her. Someone else flew out soon after Souriff. As we came closer, two things became clear. One, Valinox was quickly gaining on Souriff. Two, she had a tremendous number of arrows stuck in her limbs, where her armor didn't reach.

We closed the distance quickly. "Move away from me," Failina warned me as she formed a fireball that soon grew to be bigger than I was. A few moments later, it was twice that size. We hovered in the air as Souriff barreled toward us with a trail of blood falling from the sky behind her. Failina's fireball continued to grow, the heat unbearable even as I waited twenty yards from her. I wasn't sure even Valinox could stop such power at this point.

"I will kill you!" Failina yelled when he seemed close enough to hear.

It looked like he believed her as he stopped in the air, scowled for a moment, then turned and flew back toward the encampment.

"I need these arrows out of me now so I can heal myself," Souriff groaned and pulled one from her thigh, blood spurting out. "Where's the metal mage?" she asked me.

"I'll explain when we get back to the fort," Failina said as she lowered the spyglass. "This fight is over. Jon, meet us there with the princess."

"You got her?" Souriff asked.

"I did."

"Fine." She seemed pissed off, not relieved. I didn't quite understand it.

The three of us headed in the same direction at first, but I veered away from them to return to the spot where I had dropped Callie off in the forest.

I landed near her. She held a face of pain, and I noticed then the tears in her dress and the speckles of soot all over her. She had clearly burned herself when she had blown away the two men holding her captive.

"What happened?" she asked.

"I went back to check on Souriff and Failina. They're both fine. They'll meet us in the fortress." I approached her. "Can I heal your wounds?"

She nodded as she held out her arms, showing painful burns streaking the back of her hands.

I repaired the damage her spell had done, then

asked, "Did they hurt you in any way?"

"No, but some of them discussed making a mockery of me by publicly disrobing me for the entertainment of their soldiers, and others suggested even worse things I'd rather not say. These men are pigs, Jon. They *deserve* to die."

I nodded. "I'm sorry you had to go through that."

"Why did you land so far from me? I thought at first you weren't coming to rescue me."

"I'll be honest, princess. We didn't think we would be able to get you back right away because Valinox seemed to be guarding you. We were going to take someone valuable to him and set up a trade for you after. But as soon as I saw Valinox leaving, I went for you. I hope you are not offended."

"Oh no, I understand. I'm very glad it worked out this way." She slowly formed a smile. "You were marvelous, Jon! I've never seen that side of you before, but I had heard stories. I'm glad I finally got to witness why my father has put so much trust in you. I do wish, however, that you were able to get me here a little safer. I was so terrified you were about to drop me! I believe I passed out."

"You did, but I wouldn't drop you," I assured her. "We should get to the fortress. You can ride on my back this time. It should be a tad more comfortable for you than upside down by your ankles."

She chuckled. "Yes, it will be. If I had to choose between flying upside down or never flying again, I would never fly again."

I turned so she could hop on my back.

Like most of my passengers, she gasped and clutched tightly as we took off from the ground. I brought her up through the canopy of the forest.

"God above," she uttered. "How far to the fortress?"

"Far by foot, but we will get there quickly. Why?"

"Oh," she said in disappointment. "Because I don't want this to end. I could not enjoy it when Valinox took me all the way here because I was too afraid of what was going to happen."

"Then hold on, and I'll take you faster."

She squealed in delight as I tossed us eastward. For a short time, Callie made it clear how much she enjoyed the feeling with hollers here and whoops there, but then she had a serious question.

"My father must be worried sick. Will you be taking me back later?"

"I think instead I should bring your father to the fortress, as it is now clear that the castle is not safe for any of you."

"I suppose you're right. Valinox did break into my quarters even with the door locked. He's too powerful, Jon. He's even stronger than the last time he was there. Not even a demigod should have the ability to break down a locked door of the castle keep."

"His power comes from everyone's increasing use of dteria. We might not be able to kill him right now, but we should be able to sometime after this is over and we have gotten rid of most of his dark mages."

"You sound like you really have hope that we are going to win this war."

"Don't you?"

"I do now that I know you do," she said as she rested her chin on my shoulder and hugged me.

It taught me something about hope that I might've always known but had never thought about until then.

It could be just as contagious as despair.

*****

By the time I brought Callie to the fortress, Souriff appeared to have recovered from her injuries. She still had the same pissed off expression now as she did before, and I was starting to make sense of it. It was as if she thought the trouble she'd gone through had not been worth the result. Perhaps she saw little to no value in the princess and was frustrated she had taken such a risk. Or perhaps Souriff was angry with me for giving up on the metal mage and going for Callie.

I wasn't going to start a quarrel with her. There was no point. The demigods and our commanding officers, Byron and Leon, seemed to be in the midst of a conversation similar to the one I'd just had with Callie.

It sounded as if everyone was in agreement that the king should be here now. It wouldn't be long before we faced off with Rohaer's army. Nykal had remained in the castle because that's where we all believed he would be the safest, not just from Valinox but from possible traitors who would look for an opportunity to take him out and put a Chespar in charge. Now that Valinox had proven that he could take the princess from within the walls of the castle, the entire royal family should be here with the rest of the army loyal to his majesty.

The only part of the topic that still seemed to be up for discussion was whether the demigods and I should strike our enemies again before the battle. I voiced my opinion then.

"It's not worth it," I said. "There is a much greater chance that one of us will be killed before we would be able to take out someone like their metal mage. If Valinox wasn't around, it would be different, but he's always with them, as I believe the two of you should be with us," I told the demigod sisters. "It's time to give you call-rings like we have seen the metal mage use to summon Valinox when he needed help."

"We already decided that with your king," Souriff snapped. "But don't think that we're going to fight this war for you. When it's time for the armies to engage, we will draw Valinox away—and that is it. The whole purpose of our assistance is to stop his influence. We will not do more."

I looked at Failina to make sure this was true. She nodded at me. "We have done enough fighting in the past and agreed that it only results in the massacre of humans. The loss of life will be too great if we focus our efforts on Rohaer and Valinox does the same to your people. It will take the two of us to distract him, anyway."

I asked, "What if he stays back with his army in the fight? He could offer protection in the form of walls of dteria while showing no aggression."

"Then we will do the same," Failina answered. "However, that is unlikely of our brother. He wishes to use the power he has obtained from Airinold and will not be content to sit back and watch. Now we must leave to fetch your king before Valinox decides to make another play at him or his family."

The sisters took off abruptly, leaving the rest of us in surprised silence as we watched them go.

At least I didn't have to be the one who went for the king and queen.

I remembered Failina expressing concern about

carrying a mortal on her back. Perhaps she had gotten over that fear, though I doubted the same could be said of Souriff's fear to face our enemies again.

"It's probably best that the demigods aren't involved in this fight," Leon said. "They just create chaos." He slapped my back. "Good work getting back the princess. It doesn't look like it was easy." He lifted a flap of fur that stuck out from my Valaer steel chest plate. Flakes of snow fell off, revealing a hole.

With the help of a few others, I took off my armor, as well as my helmet and Michael's coif underneath. It looked as if much of the fur had been damaged where it had been exposed, snow baked in around the gashes.

"I'm sorry," I told Hadley as I unwrapped the fur from my torso and handed it to her.

"Don't you worry about it," she said as she brushed off the snow with her gaze on me. "As long as you're okay?"

"I'm fine," I said as I handed Michael his coif.

"I couldn't believe my eyes when I saw Jon fight," I overheard Callie telling the rest of the group. "He took on more than a dozen men just to get to me, many of them sorcerers."

"What happened exactly?" Charlie asked. "Tell me every detail."

I didn't feel very comfortable hearing it. Fortunately, distraction came as Jennava arrived. I met her gaze, and she gestured for me. She had a worried expression as I left everyone behind to approach her. Leon and Byron followed me to speak with Jennava. I assumed this was the first time she had returned from Drayer. Now with Aliana's father there to act as lord, she could be more useful here.

"I heard from..." Her eyes widened as she gaped at me. "Jon, what happened? There's a tear in your shirt and some snow on your shoulders."

Leon answered, "The princess was captured by Valinox. Jon got her back with the help of Failina's snowstorm and Souriff's dvinia. The demigods are going back for the king and queen now. You didn't see the snow?"

"I've been walking through the forest all morning to get here. Is the princess all right?"

"Fine," Leon said. "She doesn't even seem spooked by the event. She's either stronger or stupider than she looks." He gave a quick glance over his shoulder after uttering the words.

"You have news from Drayer?" Byron asked.

Jennava took a breath. "There's a sickness running rampant through Rohaer."

"What kind of sickness?" Byron asked.

"A bad one. I don't have many details. A traveler spoke about it upon visiting Drayer, and I believe some of the people there are showing early signs of the illness. We haven't heard anything from our spy?"

"No," Byron answered. "He can't give us news until he's ready to leave their army for good. That will most likely be before battle."

"Will you check me for illness, Jon?" Jennava asked.

"You don't feel well?"

"I feel fine, but I've heard infection starts long before we turn unwell. I don't want to spread it if I have it."

I gave her body a quick perusal. "Where should I look?"

"In my chest, I'd wager."

I put one hand beneath her collarbone and the other

on the back of her shoulders. Then I closed my eyes and let my mana run through her as I listened.

I found nothing in her chest, but I thought it wise to check the rest of her body. It took several long minutes.

"You're healthy," I said.

"Can you be completely sure?"

"I am."

Byron asked, "How many people in Drayer are sick?"

"Just a few feel unwell, but there could be more. I think Jon should examine every person there. The sooner the better."

"The king's going to want to hear about this," Leon said. "We might be able to use it to our advantage. How long until the rest of our army arrives?" he asked Byron.

"Some will start setting up camp around the fort today. I expect the army to trickle in tomorrow and the day after. There's time for Jon to heal the people of Drayer."

"After I eat," I said, remembering to take time for myself when I needed it.

CHAPTER TWENTY-TWO

The rest of the day went by slowly. It was good to see Ray and Graham again when I went to Drayer to investigate this sickness Jennava had reported, though I made Graham disappointed when I told him I had not seen or heard anything about his father. They had nothing to say about Luther Prigg, their new lord. He hadn't left much of an impression on anyone, apparently. I took that to mean things could be much worse.

There were a total of seven people with an infection that I got rid of, but only a few of them had felt weakened by the illness. It had taken the better part of the day to examine everyone, though much of that time had been spent ensuring that everyone came to see me in the courtyard of the lord's manor. Actually investigating their bodies with mana was quick.

When I returned to the fort, the place looked very different. Hundreds, if not thousands of tents crowded the fort and took up all the space around the outside. Some tents even breached the dense forest that had not been cleared around us.

I had a late supper, missing Hadley and the rest of my peers, and went to sleep in the boys' tent. The next day brought rain and cold wind, but at least the king and queen didn't have to soar through that cold air because they had arrived the night before. I found out when I was summoned to his majesty's tent.

It was a surprise to see Rick standing guard. "I didn't know you would be here," I said as I shook his hand.

"Souriff brought me here this morning."

"In the rain?" I asked.

"Yes, it was as unpleasant as you could imagine." His expression remained indifferent and dutiful. I figured it was the approaching battle on his mind more than the recent flight.

"Did the demigods bring anyone else from the castle?"

"Just the queen. The king's fire mage is still back there with Randy and the councilman. Some have to guard the castle, just in case something happens while the rest of us are gone."

It sounded like a good idea to me.

"Jon, come in," called the king.

I had not seen his majesty until then. I figured he had bunked with his family here, but the queen and princess were out when I entered.

"Sire," I said with a bow.

"Greetings Jon, come and sit."

There was a large table within the tent, but it was not the one the king directed me to. Instead, he sat at a small round table and had me take the seat next to him. He leaned toward me and lowered his voice.

"I need to thank you for rescuing my daughter. Now I'm telling you not to do it again."

Had I heard that correctly?

"I mean what I say." Nykal leaned closer. "If someone else is captured—and that includes my daughter or my wife—you are not to put yourself at that kind of risk again. I would include myself in that list, but the contract you signed to protect me would implore you to help me no matter what I tell you now."

"But sire—?"

"But nothing. Do I make myself clear?"

"Yes, but I don't understand."

He leaned back a bit. "I do not know the chances we have of winning this war," Nykal said, "but they are probably not great. If something was to happen to you, Souriff, or Failina, our slim chance is going to diminish to almost nothing. And there's even more to consider than just the outcome of the war. If we do lose to Rohaer, you might be able to escape when our loss is imminent. I think you may be able to bring some semblance of peace to an unstable world that will be rife with dteria and sickness. My family and I cannot. If we lose this, we will be put to the noose. Do you understand now?"

I did, and unfortunately, it was starting to make me lose hope. I gave a nod.

"I don't believe it's necessary for me to say the following, but I'm going to anyway just to be sure," the king uttered. "You are not to repeat what I told you to anyone. Not Michael, not Leon, not anyone. You will demonstrate hope and tell people I brought you here to thank you for bringing Callie back safely."

"I will, sire."

"Good, now I don't believe it's necessary to have you investigate thousands of our soldiers and supporters for sickness because it will take everyone away from their duties for more than a day. We'll wait to see if an infection begins to spread, then we will do what we must. In the meantime, I want you to be at my side when I speak to Harold Chespar and Alecott Yorn."

"Is Alecott Kataleya's brother?"

"Yes, but that alone does not give us reason to trust him, which was the advice of Kataleya herself after spending time with him recently."

"She's here?" I hadn't seen her, but as the king said, there were thousands of people buzzing around the fort now.

"She is. I spoke with her before calling you here. She feels confident that her brother and the Chespars will do what they can to stop Rohaer's army and keep dteria out of our land, but they might make a play for the crown depending on how the dust settles." He lowered his eyebrows. "We have looked at this at every angle and are taking measures to prepare for a rebellion at the end of the war, but forcing Rohaer to give up and draw back is our priority."

"You don't expect us to...?" I realized then that I didn't know exactly what I had anticipated would happen in a victory. There were so many enemy troops. Had I really thought that we could decimate them all?

"Don't expect us to what?" Nykal asked.

"To slay enough of them that they give up?"

"That is unlikely," the king said. "Our means of victory is through starvation, sickness, or causing distrust and rebellion. We are working on all three."

"What can I do?"

"Not much. Everything you might be able to accomplish right now puts you at great risk of death. Be calm and patient. There will be a battle soon at the defile. There's no way around that. Depending on what happens there, we will discuss the next step."

Kataleya stepped into the tent. She smiled at me briefly. "Jon," she said with a slight bow of her head, which I reciprocated as she turned to the king. "Harold and my brother are here if you are ready to meet them, sire."

"Yes, bring them here, then fetch Leon and Byron for me."

Kataleya gave a quick bow and left.

While those people filed in, I found myself wondering about each of their ranks and how the king would address them. When comparing our army to Rohaer's, it felt like ours was functioning without a clear hierarchy, but I didn't know how long that would last, especially if one officer was to fall.

Kataleya's brother had the same shade of blond hair as she did, but his beauty, or lack thereof, seemed to come from their father's side. There was nothing particularly odd about his features. There just wasn't any harmony to his spread-apart eyes, thin nose, and pointed chin.

Harold Chespar entered with his son, Trevor, who I recognized. While Trevor was tall with kind features, his father's excess weight engorged his similar features to the point of little resemblance.

I felt a surge of mana outside the tent. Soon after, the demigod sisters entered. I hadn't noticed the king summon them with his callring, but I figured that must've been the case.

I recognized Airinold immediately as he walked in behind Failina. He made Trevor look short as he towered over his already tall sisters. He seemed much less thin and frail than the last time I had seen him, when he lay naked in the pool of Gourfist's blood, which I often wondered if it was the same as his own blood. There was added girth to his body, no doubt toned muscles beneath his simple shirt. His blond hair appeared longer as well, wavy and draped down around his ears or eyes.

I hadn't heard anything about Airinold since I'd last seen him. I had no idea of his capability with sorcery, but I had little doubt that he was physically stronger than anyone here, except perhaps Souriff.

Alecott and the Chespars were sharply dressed in uniforms, with gold tassels hanging from their shoulders and large, silver buttons abundant down their midsections. They both wore white underneath their uniform, big collars on display. They made most of the rest of us appear underdressed, including the demigods.

I faintly heard Michael's voice outside the tent as plainly dressed people brought in chairs and set them around the large table. "What's going on in there?"

Someone replied, though I couldn't tell who it was or discern what they said.

"They are? Well, who's the fat one?" Michael asked, and a few of us gazed at Harold, his cheeks reddening as he took on a look of anger.

The king gestured with a turn of his head for me to take care of this. "Have someone secure a perimeter around the tent," he added as I was on my way out.

I walked out briskly and found Michael speaking with Reuben. I put my hand on Michael's back and led him away from the tent as I whispered, "We can hear you *quite* clearly."

His face went white. "Does that mean everyone heard?"

"Yes, no one is speaking yet, and the walls of the tent do nothing to dampen sound."

"Why is no one talking?" Reuben asked as he walked with us.

"I don't know. It's tense."

"I should be in there, and so should my father," Reuben proclaimed. "He's paying for many of the soldiers who were here before the rest arrived."

I shrugged. "You can take that up with the king afterward. I'd best get back. Reuben, will you take responsibility for keeping people away from the tent where they might overhear?"

"Yes, I can do that," he said dutifully.

"Thank you."

As I returned to the tent, I seemed to be stepping into the middle of an argument.

"...you would still be in your castle," Harold was telling the king. Everyone was seated, but close to the edges of their chairs. "I have been with my troops for months. I know what they can do and what they cannot do, and they cannot hold back thousands of dark mages attempting to cross the defile. If you managed to capture or kill this metal mage, perhaps there would be a chance of avoiding slaughter, but as it is now I cannot condone the destruction of my men."

"So you propose we allow Rohaer onto our land?" the king asked incredulously. "After coming this far, you'd simply let them pass through the defile? No, that is not an option. They must be held back as their supply line is weakened. That is the easiest means of victory. If you go against this order, you are dooming your nation and defying your king."

Harold looked as if he'd bitten into a lemon and was

trying not to give a reaction. "Your majesty, I am merely attempting to discuss tactics with you. This should not be a time to order us to your will but to discuss strategy openly."

"Then I suggest you change your tone, and I may do the same."

A silence held in the air like a string about to break.

"How many sorcerers do you have?" Leon asked Harold.

"None who can use their magic as a shield, as I've heard you can," Harold replied. "We have a number of fire mages who pose as great a risk to the men around them as they do to their targets. Everyone will be clustered in the defile. Our shield wall will be blown apart, and our weapons will be melted by the army with the superior sorcery. I would agree that normally stopping the larger army in a narrow pathway would be the right choice, but because of the current circumstances it is not the case. It was a good plan months ago, but it has not come to fruition as we all had hoped. Our sorcerers are too weak and too few."

Nykal glanced at the demigods. "We just have to keep them from progressing," he told the sisters. "The two of you should be able to hold the line on your own, and yet I'll have my strongest sorcerers with you, Jon and Leon."

Souriff scowled and shook her head. "Absolutely not. Valinox will break through if we are there. The only hope is for us to take him out of the fight by creating a snowstorm and forcing him away from the defile. I must stay with Failina to keep her alive when Valinox attacks. Even then, it might not be enough to distract Valinox during the entire battle if it is expected to go on most of the day."

Most of the day? I'd certainly had a different idea about this battle. I had assumed it would be like the others I'd experienced, quick and bloody. Now it sounded as if the battle would entail a lot of casting against magical and physical barriers, almost like a tug-of-war match with magic.

Reuben suddenly ran into the tent. "It's Valinox," he said as a commotion broke out outside. "He approaches the fort."

"With how many others?" Nykal asked as everyone stood.

"It's just him."

I ran out past Reuben. I didn't have on my armor, but I always kept my sword with me. I noticed everyone standing on the ramparts facing east, so that's where I flew. I landed beside Michael as he stood at the ballista, which was already aimed at Valinox.

The demigod walked around the tents outside our wall, approaching us with his arms in the air. "I came to discuss peace."

"Let me shoot him. I can do it," Michael muttered to Aliana as she tried to gently pull him away from the weapon.

"You will not unless the king gives the order," she said.

"Come on, let me do it."

"There's a reason Byron put me in charge of you. Now listen!"

Michael didn't back off. Valinox pointed at him as he lowered his eyebrows. "I recognize you, wind mage. If you fire that thing at me, I will block it. Then I will twist your head off your body."

"I'd like to see you try to stop one of these bolts," Michael muttered too quietly, thankfully, for the demigod to hear.

Souriff landed behind Michael and grabbed him by his shirt. She tossed him off the ramparts as he squealed like a thrown piglet.

"Finally, you show some sense, sister," Valinox said as he continued to approach. "I'm here to make peace."

"Why the hell would you do that?" Souriff asked.

"You'll find out," he said. "Let's talk." He continued through dense clusters of soldiers as they watched him with their weapons ready.

"Fine. No one is to attack Valinox."

"Little good it would do anyway." Valinox took to the air, soaring over our heads and landing near the king's tent, where our leaders were gathered among dozens of soldiers just a sword's-length away from him.

Airinold came toward Valinox from around the back of the group. They shared no words as Valinox froze and appeared shocked. Then Airinold walked forward to meet his brother.

While Valinox was tall and strong, Airinold was bigger in every sense of the word. Airinold did not speak, just held his older brother in his gaze as he waited.

"It's been a long time," Valinox said, with a tinge of apprehension in his tone I had not heard from him before.

"It hasn't been that long," Airinold said with a mean glare. "I saw you while I was stuck in Gourfist's body."

"You mean when you tried to kill me," Valinox replied defensively.

"I wish I had succeeded. Look what you have done

with your life. You have given power to the mortals who crave it the most, and at the same time taken it away from the good people who don't desire to lord over their friends and family. By doing so you have fomented a world in which the worst of mankind is rewarded. It is the exact opposite of what dteria was created to do. Don't you have shame? Or is it so overshadowed by your deep need for validation that you no longer feel it?"

There sounded to be genuine curiosity behind Airinold's words, but Valinox took on a hardened look.

"I did what I had to survive you, brother. It doesn't matter. I don't need to explain myself. I am too powerful for you or anyone to stop, and I can finally reveal the change I am making to the mortal world." He seemed now to be addressing the gathering crowd. "I have only ever wanted one thing. Mankind is troubled. You fight each other over such trifles, from the differences in your beliefs to your supplies of food. Laws will never fully protect you from one another. You require direction, or you will destroy each other. Under my guidance you will worship my father, and there will finally be order and lasting peace."

"You can't truly believe any of that," Airinold said. Thousands had now come close to listen, but neither brother stole a glance away from the other. "Our father will never return."

"He will. I can feel him watching. He will approve of everything I've done once he sees the order I've established. That's when he will return and see that he was wrong to cast me aside."

"And what is to happen to dteria and the thousands who use it in this *paradise* you describe?"

"Strict sanctions, oaths, and laws will turn the disorderly obedient," Valinox replied. "Those with power will be rewarded with roles of enforcement and land to oversee. If they abuse that power, their punishment will be swift and severe."

Failina spoke, "You mean to bring Nijja out of Fyrren to rule with you?"

"She might need some convincing, but she will see the right path eventually." I had not seen this side of Valinox. It was almost as if he spoke sweetly about Nijja.

"This is not at all the right path," Airinold said. "Peace through the destruction of dteria is the only way."

Valinox lifted an eyebrow. "Who are you lying to? Is it our sisters, specifically, or is it everyone here listening?"

"What do you mean?" Airinold asked.

"Don't you think I have learned enough about dteria by now to tell that it cannot be destroyed?"

"What?" Souriff said in anger.

"So you told them you could destroy it, I see," Valinox said. "I may be many things, Airinold, but I'm not a liar like you."

"You said you could undo it," Failina accused Airinold. "Was that really a lie?"

Airinold's shoulders drooped as he looked at Failina. "I wanted to create dteria in a way where I could destroy it, but it was impossible."

Failina seemed weak in the knees as she looked away, while Souriff cursed her brother.

"What else is a lie?" Souriff asked. "Did you really make dteria to stop all the fighting, or did you do it for yourself?"

"Everything else I told you is true," Airinold retorted. "Something had to be done to stop you and Valinox from destroying mankind. I knew I wouldn't be able to completely undo dteria, but I trusted I would be able to control it. And it was working. Too well, in fact. There were so few people using dteria after I started hunting them down that I quickly became weak. I feared the two of you," he told Souriff, "would band together and destroy me. Then everything would go back to how it was before. That is why I became Gourfist. I needed to maintain my power while continuing to threaten those who used dteria. I did not anticipate losing control to Gourfist. If I had managed to keep it, there would be no dteria today.

"It doesn't need to be destroyed so long as it is managed. It is Valinox's fault that it has gotten so out of hand. You told me yourselves. He has empowered a king in Rohaer who strives to spread dteria across not only his kingdom but Lycast as well. If Valinox used his power to stop the use of dteria, we would be looking at a peaceful world right now. You can't blame the maker of the sword for war."

"Everything I've done is for a good cause," Valinox argued. "I wish to begin a new world."

"In which you rule over everyone through fear," Airinold said. "It would never work. There will be revolts. The people aren't going to allow dark mages to govern them because dark mages behave like drunken men with bad morals who indulge their worst impulses. Even if there is no war, people will suffer more than they do now. You are not all-seeing. You cannot stop all forms of power abuse. You can only hope to prevent it through giving power to good people who will not abuse it. It is not too late to give up this notion and join the rest of your family, Valinox. Don't you see that we all stand against you for good reason? You have become corrupted."

"You do not have my vision," Valinox said. "In the end you will see that I know what's best, if you are still alive. Now these are my demands." He glanced around, keeping a calm demeanor as he surveyed the crowd. When his eyes passed over the queen next to her daughter, the queen put her hand across Callie protectively. Valinox ignored them and met the king's gaze as Nykal stood near the demigods.

"You will concede Lycast to me, king," Valinox said. "You will do so by dismissing your army. My men will then spread across Lycast and take rule over each town. I have chosen my rulers wisely. They have good hearts and have not become corrupted by Airinold's creation. They will rule without causing suffering. There will be enough crops so that mankind will live prosperously. So will you and your family, king. You will be given land like the other nobles who will report to me. So long as you obey my orders, you and the people you lord over will be happy. My orders will include ensuring that your people worship Basael, that no crimes are committed, and that enough food is made to feed everyone. Hard work and beneficial inventions will be rewarded, while crime will be punished. It has been too long since such a time existed."

There were many of us surrounding Valinox, but I could feel a layer of dteria all around his head, while his chest was protected with armor. There was probably no way to get through with a surprise attack, but Hadley had come to stand beside me and we were sharing looks as she showed me the mana break stone she had cautiously taken from her pocket.

Before I could figure out whether Souriff or the other demigods would let us kill Valinox so dishonorably, he glowered at Hadley in a way that stilled my heart.

"What do you have there, witch?" he asked.

Everyone turned to Hadley. Her face reddened as she looked around nervously and pocketed the stone.

"You had better not be thinking about using one of those curses that disables mana," he warned her. I wasn't sure if he could feel it or if he'd just guessed it was what she had in mind. He continued, "Even if you are so dishonorable as to curse this area when I came to discuss peace, it won't work. I will kill hundreds of you before I escape, and Basael will not punish me for it. Then I will never again give your king another chance for peace."

The king gestured for Hadley not to do anything.

"Too risky," I whispered.

She nodded and took her hand out of her pocket, leaving the stone there. Without a real plan in motion, and with so many people around, I was worried Valinox might be right. I didn't think it would go as we hoped if all sorcery was disabled, even with all of us against him.

"Valinox," Nykal said to regain the demigod's attention. "In this plan of yours, what is to happen to the thousands of dark mages who will surely be upset when they are not rewarded for fighting in the war you instigated?"

"Some will be rewarded. The strongest and most trusted will be given nobility. Like you and the other nobles here, they will follow my strict rules and perform their duties. The others who have become too corrupted will be killed if they cannot show change. Some of these people exhibit the worst qualities of mankind I have ever had the displeasure of encountering. Airinold's creation has done well to bring them to light. I will destroy them myself, if need be, but only after I have victory."

"Knowing you," Airinold said, "this could all be a trick used to push our army back."

Valinox appeared insulted. "I have only ever wanted peace," he claimed. "It is why I've strived to rule over mankind. This is not a trick. Your defeat is inevitable, King Nykal. You must see that you cannot hope to stop my army. This is your only chance to avoid the slaughter of your people. Let them live so they can help you help me. Together, we will bring peace to the kingdoms. We will unify and become so powerful that this peace can spread across the whole world. All I ask is that you move back your army and send Jon Oklar with me. I'm sure you've heard by now that there is a sickness spreading. He, along with Souriff, will put an end to it before it gets out of hand. When the dust settles, I will replace Frederick Garlin with a new king who will better help me bring peace to Rohaer."

I was starting to see how Valinox had convinced so many people to fight for him. Even though I had wanted to kill him with my own hands just a moment ago, I felt that I could believe in him if I let myself.

Of course I wouldn't. The only thing I couldn't figure out was whether he was telling the truth and really thought he could change the world as he described, or if he was lying to all of us, and this new world would be even worse than the one left behind. Either way, I wasn't going to stand around and let it happen, and I was sure the others here wouldn't as well.

"You look at me as if I lie," Valinox told his siblings. "Fine. It is your right to mistrust me. But you will see by the end of the battle that I came here with the truth. I wanted to spare the lives of people. After you retreat and lose many of your valuable sorcerers, I will *still* allow Souriff to come to me and give up on behalf of Lycast. That is because I am generous. However, the longer this goes on, the less generous I will be feeling. Keep that in mind as your people die and the end draws near."

He gathered dteria around him as if to take off.

"Do you want to hear the truth that Caarda told me about our father?" Airinold asked, stopping him.

Valinox had turned away, but he looked back over his shoulder. "What are you talking about?"

"It was something he said before he locked himself away for centuries."

Valinox appeared confused. "Caarda is gone."

"No one told you that he's still alive?" Airinold asked, looking at his sisters.

"We haven't had the chance," Souriff said.

"It's true," Failina told Valinox. "Caarda is alive. We've seen him."

Valinox looked as if he was torn between believing them or cussing them out for toying with him.

"He couldn't bear his grief," Airinold explained, "so he removed himself from our world in his own way. I don't know when he will return, but I believe that he will."

"What do you mean removed himself?" Valinox asked. "Where is he?"

"He trapped himself in a pocket of time and is inaccessible to us. He had visions of the future and knew this was the only way he could survive all these years without killing himself. He told me something right before he shut himself out. I didn't want to believe it at first, but I see now that it's the truth. It's something I think everyone has the right to know, especially you, Valinox. I warn you, though. It changes everything. You will never believe it unless you are open to it. If you can't manage that, you might as well leave right now."

I was surprised to see Valinox listening with rapt attention. I didn't know what it was about Caarda that seemed to bring out a different side of these demigods. I could only hope to find out one day.

"Go on," Valinox said.

"Caarda told me that mana is part of the world, part of our life, of our existence," Airinold said. "Which means it wasn't created by our father."

Valinox scoffed. "You lie. Caarda wouldn't speak blasphemously about our father."

"I swear that Caarda spoke these words to me. He said there are other forms of sorcery besides mana and that Basael did something to accentuate mana in our world: He created a bubble, a dome of some kind, which keeps mana from leaving, intensifying it over the years. This same dome keeps out other forms of sorcery that would normally be in the air and are also part of our existence. There are likely other places in the world where sorcery is very different from here. The people there probably don't have the same access to mana as we do but find these other forms of sorcery more readily available. There are likely other beings like Basael who have toyed with these forms of sorcery. I'm sure you see what this means. You cannot live in dedication to our father, a false idol. He is not even a god. He's just a powerful being with a long life, as are his children."

Anger twisted Valinox's face. "I should kill you right now for speaking like that against Basael."

"I'm trying to open your mind," Airinold replied, seemingly unafraid.

I was surprised to see Failina and Souriff appear shocked as well.

"You didn't tell us any of this," Failina told her brother.

"There's *much* more." There was something in Airinold's tone that made me inclined to believe him—a certain desperation, as if he knew they couldn't possibly take his word for it but hoped against all odds they just might trust him.

"What you say doesn't make sense," Souriff glared at her brother. "How could we create schools of magic if mana already existed in its current form as you imply?"

"I know it has been a long time since you think you 'created' something, but if it was fresher in your mind you might realize that you didn't create it. You shaped mana into what you wanted and you held it there." Airinold made a fist. "You held it and held it. You've held it for so long that it is a part of you, but without you, your 'creation' would slowly stop existing."

"You're not making any sense," Souriff said.

"No, I think he is. Keep going," Failina said.

"Mana is complicated beyond comprehension, but we are able to grasp pieces of understanding," Airinold continued. "What we know is that mana can be altered in nearly permanent ways. Think of mana like a clear mind that has no knowledge. It has the capability of learning just about anything, given the right instruction. As beings like us grow from children to adults, we become connected to mana in such a way that we can teach it to work differently. Doing so requires a huge amount of force, and this force has to come from somewhere. In our case, it comes from us and leaves us through our connection to mana. We use this force to change how mana works. It doesn't necessarily weaken us in the same sense that age or an illness will weaken a mortal.

"We are feeding some of our power into mana, and this transition of power remains nearly permanent, connecting us to the specific changes we made. If we were able to take back what we put into mana, we should regain the power we lost, and mana will be changed back to how it was. That is why we are not creating a school of magic but taking mana and twisting it so some of its properties become more accessible than others. In the process, we are making it nearly impossible for sorcerers to access forms of mana that once would've been accessible to them, but we are making other forms of mana easier to reach."

Leon lifted his finger at Airinold. "Holy shit."

I suddenly remembered something Jennava had said about Leon. She had never met anyone else who understood mana better. So to see him have this reaction, like this epiphany was about to cause his eyes to bulge out of his head, turned me around completely. I no longer wondered whether Airinold was telling the truth. All I could think about was what this meant going forward.

Failina said, "But that would mean that our father lied to us…about everything."

"Yes, and even after a hundred more centuries, Lina,

I think you're too good to ever see why that is. So allow me to explain it and tell you how Caarda figured it out. Our father wanted all of us to be weak compared to him. He pushed the strongest of us to give up the most power. It is why he was so demanding about Caarda following in all of your footsteps. Basael was threatened by his lastborn because he knew that Caarda might eventually figure out our father's plans before it was too late to stop them. He was the ruler over dteria. He expected one of us to find it and spread it across mankind so that he could always lord over us."

"That can't be true," Souriff said, but her stricken expression indicated she feared it was.

"It explains why Father never showed love toward us, toward mankind, or ever 'created' any schools of magic of his own," Airinold continued. "He had already given up much of his power to prevent us from accessing other forms of sorcery. The rest of his power went into maintaining a connection to all of us through the use of mana so that he would have control over however we used it. He then pushed one of us to create something like dteria, which would take power from mortals and feed it to us, but more would transfer to him.

"We haven't felt this dome around our world that Basael made, but Caarda has. He also realized that Basael did not anticipate his own death. Now that he is gone, his dome weakens with each passing year. That is why all of us are not as powerful as we used to be, not because of age, but because the mana we are connected to and depend upon for our strength is not as potent as it once was. Caarda told me all of this, and like you, my kin, I did not want to believe it at first. But why would Caarda lie? He's never had any reason to, and I don't either. You can believe what you want, Valinox, but you should at least hear the truth. Going to war in order to force mankind to worship Basael is probably exactly what Basael wanted, but is it right? That's what you should be asking yourself."

A man I did not know suddenly thrust a dagger at the back of Valinox's head. It got stuck in the dteria the man obviously did not know was there. Valinox spun around and grabbed the man's arm and broke it with a quick twist as he howled in pain. The demigod kicked the man as he fell, flipping him into the dense crowd.

"Enough of this," Valinox said with a bit of a snarl. "You've always been poisonous with your words, Airinold. You and Caarda both. You both rebelled against a father who did nothing but care for us. I refuse to let you speak about him this way. *You* are the false idol, and you will be stopped."

Valinox's scowl turned darker as he fixed his gaze on Souriff. "Surrender today and hand over Airinold, or prepare for your followers to be slaughtered."

Then he took off out of the fort. He was gone but a second before Airinold addressed everyone, as I quickly healed the broken arm and damaged torso of the man who Valinox had injured.

"Do not even think about giving up," the demigod cautioned. "I may not have the power of sorcery that I once did, but I will hold them back from the front line with the strongest of you by my side. With a shield in my hand and my resistance ready, they will not get through me while I can stand on two feet. So long as a few good sorcerers can promise the same, Rohaer will not pass."

"I will stand with you," Leon said.

"So will I," I said.

"I will be at your side, Jon," Michael added.

But Leon put his hand on Michael's shoulder. "We need water. Wind is too flammable, and they will have fire."

"Then I will be there," Kataleya said.

"I can be just behind," Hadley added. "My curses will weaken the strongest foes."

"And I will burn them," Remi said.

I noticed Jennava and Eden sharing a glance before Jennava spoke. "Eden and I will be ready to step in if someone must fall back."

"What sorcery do you cast?" Airinold asked Jennava.

"We use dteria," she answered, then lifted an eyebrow and waited for his reaction.

"I thought I felt that coming from you." Then to the king, he asked, "How many dark mages and witches do you have here?"

"Just the two dark mages and one witch." The king gestured at them. "They are not corrupted by the magic."

Airinold looked over Jennava and Hadley. Then his gaze slowly traveled up and down Eden. She fidgeted with her feet.

"Are you sure they can be trusted?" Airinold asked the king.

"Don't you recognize the witch?" Nykal retorted. "She was the one who blinded Gourfist when Jon was defending the capital against him."

"Ah yes, that is right," he said. Hadley formed a tiny smile aimed at me. "But I also remember that this is the one who opened the rift to Fyrren," Airinold said as he pointed at Eden. "She might be a spy for Valinox."

Failina walked up to Airinold and put her hand on his back. He eased up at her touch.

"She was," Failina said. "And she wasn't the only one. But these people have been rescued from corruption by the mortals who just volunteered to stand next to you. They now trust one another with their lives, so you can, too."

Apparently, the king had updated Failina on recent events.

"I understand, Lina," Airinold said in a gentle voice he seemed to reserve for her. "That is what I will do. Now it's my understanding that Rohaer marches toward the defile with each passing moment. That means that it is time to work out the intricacies of our defense."

"I know you are a demigod," Harold Chespar stated somewhat dismissively. "But that does not make you in charge. There is still a lot we have to discuss with you and the king."

"I will be leading the men into battle," Airinold replied. "Unless you wish to do that, then yes, I am now in charge."

"Whose coin do you to think pays for the service of all these people?" Harold challenged.

"If it is yours as you claim, then you have done well to bring them here. Now let me show them the way to victory, or you will have wasted your coin on a great loss."

Harold stared at the demigod, his gaze unwavering.

"Challenge me, if you dare," Airinold said. "Have me imprisoned if it fills you with pride. I won't fight your soldiers. You will, however, regret that decision later when Valinox decimates your army and spreads a pox across the land. They are too large of a force to stop except here and now, where they are vulnerable."

Everyone's gaze fell on Harold. He glanced over at Alecott, who stood back and lowered his head ever so slightly.

"You can take command for this battle only," Harold told the demigod. My low opinion of the man sank even lower at this display of impudence.

I still wondered how much the other demigods believed what Airinold had said about mana and Basael, but from the way Leon had reacted, I figured most of my peers believed him and had a dozen questions buzzing around their heads as I did. I wondered if it was true that Basael was not a god but just a powerful being with a long life. Or was that what had made him a god to the rest of us?

For now, I would think of these beings as demigods, because there were more pressing matters. We had to figure out how to keep Rohaer from getting past us, or this might be the beginning of the end.

CHAPTER TWENTY-THREE

It took just one day for us to set up our defense at the narrowest point at the defile. There we waited for Rohaer's army to come around the bend, where the mountains pushed the twisting road west, close to the edge of Curdith Forest on the other side. Having walked down this road, I could tell that one day the forest might envelop the whole area. In fact, there were already a few trees seeming to defy nature as they grew out of the rock at the foot of the mountains.

A large group of people, probably over the course of years, had created this road between the kingdoms. I wondered if any of them had a clue that it would be a battleground one day.

Harold Chespar had given in to Airinold soon after the demigod had challenged him. After that, every leader seemed to be on the same page. We would stop Rohaer when they tried to get through the narrow pathway between the mountains and the forest. Kataleya's brother had expressed fears that Rohaer would attempt to go into the forest to get around us, but so long as we saw them in time, most everyone agreed that we should be able to shift our line to keep our advantageous position. We could drive them to the fort. Even though the walls were not tall and had potential to be set aflame, I imagined we would hold the fort and slay many of the soldiers who tried to get in.

I was a bit worried about Rohaer trying to get around our fort, but it seemed unlikely for them to attempt this. They would have to deviate two miles from the road to make it all the way around us, but that would leave them open to ambush. The forest was dense, with many hiding places for us. They would certainly lose many troops.

Their best bet seemed to be using their superior sorcery to force us to retreat. That meant they would have to get through me first.

Airinold had garnered a lot of attention after his various speeches in our fort. On the way to the defile, hundreds of people felt inclined to introduce themselves. Many asked him questions about his siblings, Gourfist, Basael, and other details of how he came to create dteria that he had already shared with me after I had freed him from the demise of his own making.

When it was just Hadley and me with him later, I asked him my own question, "If everything you said was true, could there be other types of magic we might be able to discover?"

"Other schools of magic within mana, yes, but other forms of sorcery might be too difficult to feel for mortals or demigods until more time passes," he said.

It was Hadley's questions that I soon became more interested in. After introducing herself and explaining her affinity for curses, she had asked Airinold to tell her of curses she might not be aware of, in particular any powerful ones.

Airinold had appeared uneasy at first, admitting

that he had never taken the time to speak to any dteria user after creating the school of magic.

"Swiftly and without remorse, I killed anyone who had used it long enough for me to sense them. I am now wondering if I took it too far. I might even say that perhaps I shouldn't have ever discovered it in the first place. I believe Basael had intentions to keep producing offspring until one of us did, but he was gone by then. Dteria probably wouldn't exist in its current form if it wasn't for me."

Hadley shared a look of concern with me as she walked between the demigod and me. But after a moment of what appeared to be silent thought, Airinold gave a more complete answer.

"I might've been able to provide you with more information when I first thought I created dteria, but that was centuries ago. Even then, I couldn't be aware of all possible curses. Think of it like the inventor of the lute. Could he be aware of every possible sound the instrument can make? A school of magic is the same, in some sense. I thought I created the rules and let mana do the rest. It is how all my siblings thought we created, by establishing rules. We thought we built upon Basael's creation of mana and made our own magic."

He sighed. "But mana is more complicated than even demigods can tell. Only Caarda seemed to truly understand it."

"Is there anything else he told you about it that you haven't shared yet?" I asked.

"Many things. He would be able to explain it better than I can, but basically he told me that mana has many more capabilities than we are aware of. What a demigod is doing through the process of 'creation' is actually altering a piece of mana. This is almost like making an essence. It is forming an attraction to mana, and that attraction changes how mana behaves. Ultimately what this does is make certain schools of magic much more accessible than they were before. However, when many schools of magic are created in this way, none of them can overlap, or they will not work well together. So demigods have chosen different frequencies of mana from each other and connected themselves to these frequencies in a way that alters themselves and the mana and allows this mana to be more accessible. The demigods feel like they have created something, but it would be like someone taking a rope and making a pulley out of it and thinking they had created the pulley."

I had been paying such close attention that I didn't realize until then that Failina had come to stand behind us, listening. "Airi, you're filling everyone's head with confusion," she complained.

"Perhaps," he replied. "But I find the confusion makes me sane, as it should everyone else. It's much better than blindly believing something they have no proof of. At least this way their mind is open."

"And this is what Caarda wanted?" Failina asked.

"I'm not sure. You know how he is, always mysterious."

Hadley asked Airinold, "Is there maybe one specialized curse which could help us that you can remember?"

"There is one I distinctly remember for which I thought I 'created' the rules for. I feared I might lose power and would have to rely on the crutch of curses to disempower my siblings once they turned against me."

Hadley wrinkled her nose at hearing curses referred to as crutches, but she didn't voice an objection.

"Unfortunately, the most powerful curses are indiscriminate," Airinold continued. "The targets they choose are out of control of the witch, but in this case it might not matter. There is a curse that targets souls darkened by corruption, but for the life of me I can't recall the necessary ingredients."

"Maybe you have a guess?" Hadley prodded.

"Give me a moment to think." He fell silent for a short while. "I don't believe it was a curse that targeted corruption, after all. It's more likely to have targeted dteria itself. It should involve two things: the blood of a sorcerer who has exceptional power over a school of magic, and a part of an animal that has been modified by mana."

Hadley gasped. "I have felt that something like that is possible, but I have been unable to test it. I have a small bit of Valinox's blood and some feathers of...well, Gourfist. His form was created through mana, wasn't it?"

"Not created. I grew Gourfist from my own body, and it was mana that decided what elements would be taken from me and what would be drawn from my surroundings. I had gathered many dead creatures before beginning. Mana started the process but had little to do with the transformation. The same occurs in many animals of the forest that have been permanently altered by dteria, such as their overgrown fangs or even the discoloration in their fur."

"I understand," Hadley said. "But that means a feather from Gourfist mixed with the blood of Valinox could still potentially create a curse that disrupts dteria?"

"I believe so, as would the blood of my brother

and an animal part from any other creature altered by mana. It's the power of the witch and the ingredient that determines the strength of the curse, but you have to take into consideration the resistance of the target."

Hadley nodded enthusiastically. "Yes, I know."

He seemed surprised as he looked down at her. "You seem to know a lot for someone who has not been corrupted by dteria."

"Because I have a gift yet no thirst for power."

The conversation that followed left little imprint on my memory, as Hadley and Airinold delved deeper into curses. I eventually went to chat with Leon so we could go through every possible scenario Rohaer could throw at us. From a line of shield-bearers, to a horde of dark mages, and even the possibility of a dozen fire mages all at the front and covered in armor, we discussed it all. There was a counter to everything, and most of the time that counter was a wall of dvinia or water. There was only one problem, and that was running out of stamina.

With so many potential dark mages attempting to get past us, our mana was likely to run dry before long. That was where Reuben—I was surprised to find out—was to balance out the scale. With Hadley weakening the front line of the enemies with curses, their ability to fight would not last for long. Meanwhile, Reuben had learned to disable enchantments from a safe distance, meaning that any imbued stone of dteria, fire, or even water—if Rohaer used water mages against us—could be disenchanted in the midst of battle. I knew how greatly I would be weakened if my Induct stone was taken away from me, especially considering how long it would take to re-enchant the stone afterward. It was such a viable strategy that the thought of Rohaer using it against us scared me more than it excited me.

There was a deep need for me to protect this Induct stone of dvinia that allowed me to fly great distances without rest. I still didn't know exactly where this need came from, just that it had nothing to do with dvinia itself. It was something within me, something corruptible. Perhaps it was in every man. This was not the time to worry about it, though I'd better make time eventually.

As afternoon turned into evening, we received word that Rohaer wasn't going to make it to us today. There was contemplation between the demigods, the king, and the officers about whether we should strike our enemies with a surprise ambush. Unfortunately, it became obvious this wasn't feasible when we saw Valinox circling the skies above. Any attack we planned would be spotted, and our enemies would be well-prepared. There were no worthwhile traps we could set, either. Rohaer would not charge through them. They would disarm them as they slowly passed by.

The only thing that might work to our advantage would be destroying the road in front of us with holes, but they were ready for this. Our spy told us so when he snuck out of their brigade and joined us. They had planks to cross over any holes and even the tools to rebuild the road, if that's what it took. They knew we wouldn't attempt to advance on them. We didn't have the means.

I didn't meet this spy, but I heard he had been living in Rohaer for nearly a year and had joined their army. He provided detailed information to our king about Rohaer's forces, but it didn't change our strategy. Holding them at the defile was still the best way to go about this.

Rohaer's army was falling sick. There were just a few infections in the beginning, but now this illness seemed to be spreading quickly. Stricter measures had been taken only recently to separate the sick from the healthy, but there was chaos within the encampment. While the dark mages were powerful, they lacked patience, so said the spy. We just had to hold them back. Time was on our side.

We decided to set up camp on and around the road. I was certain most of us would not sleep well tonight because we feared tomorrow. I wished I could say the same of our enemies, but I had faced the kind of men we would soon fight against—those corrupted by dteria. They did not feel fear like we did. They lived life as if every step was toward success and victory. I would've given up a lot for that feeling tonight.

One good thing did happen. I had the chance to share a small tent with Hadley now that our sleeping arrangements had lost order and supervision. I did not let my mind take me to a place of fantasy, as it surely would've had we truly been alone. I knew nothing was to happen tonight, for the privacy that tents created was a visual privacy, not an audible one. I was fine with that, nonetheless. It was her touch I craved, and any words she chose to spoke.

We cuddled close underneath her furs as owls hooted and the cold wind shook the thin walls. I was warm and cozy with her head on my chest, her arm draped across my body. I could think about her instead of tomorrow, providing some measure of peace before the coming chaos and uncertainty.

She told me sweet things, little appreciations about

my muscular chest or taut stomach that she discovered with her hand. She leaned her head back and pecked my cheek. I made sure to catch her lips with mine the next time I felt her moving.

Hadley's warmth was a blanket of comfort, like a bed in a safe place, or like knowing that tomorrow would bring better fortunes. It didn't matter if that wasn't true. She always made me feel it. She melted away all the tension in my muscles and brought out a wide smile when she playfully nibbled on my ear.

I didn't want to go to sleep, but eventually my eyes closed on their own.

*****

The king gathered us, his sorcerers, after breakfast. "A long time ago," he said, "I told all of you that you wouldn't ever need to face hordes of enemies. I said your talents would be used in other ways. Today, I admit I was wrong. I didn't plan this, I want all of you to know. I never thought it would come to this. However, I have been convinced that without some of you putting yourselves in the front line, Rohaer will get past us. I want to take this moment to recognize a few things about all of you."

Jennava handed the king a parchment that Nykal glanced over briefly before he looked at us again and spoke.

"It's been less than a year since all of you were invited to the castle. A number of you have had birthdays, some more recently than others." He glanced at me. Yes, I had turned nineteen recently, but it had meant nearly nothing. "You have given up a piece of your lives in your dedication to Lycast, and it will not go unnoticed. You will get each other through this battle. So long as no one does anything rash, you will all remain safe from harm. This will not at all be like the fights you've been through before. It will be slow and frustrating, and less dangerous so long as you stay focused. You will tire out. Listen to your bodies and fall back when you need to. You will be fighting alongside soldiers of an army that I have little control over, though I do know these men can hold a shield and certainly don't want to die. While I want you to protect them, it is each other you need to look out for the most. All of you are going to get through this; you will make sure of it. Let's hear an aye."

"Aye," we said in unison.

"Rohaer cannot get past you, no matter how hard they try. Let's hear an aye."

"Aye," we repeated.

"You will make them feel doubt deep in their hearts, a doubt we will feed on."

"Aye!"

"They will turn and flee, and you will pounce on them and kill as many as you can!"

"Aye!"

"This will be the turning point in the war. This will be the time when Rohaer sees that we are not a kingdom for the taking. We are Lycast, and we will destroy anyone who threatens our people!"

"Aye!"

A horn blew from the forest south of us—from where our scouts watched the road ahead.

"They are coming," Nykal said as we helped each other into our Valaer steel armor. "Show them you are unafraid. Show them what a true army looks like. Now let's hear a 'give them hell.' "

"Give them hell!" we boomed.

With my heart lifted, I felt like we were floating as we marched down the road toward the bend as the rest of our army filed into place behind us.

It didn't take long for us to see Rohaer come around the bend toward us. They wore black tabards over their metal armor. We had on blue over our boiled leather. While their swords, shields, and spears were made of steel, only those of us in the very front, with Valaer steel, were better equipped. Everyone else behind us had wooden shields and spears. It was unlikely that such a spear could penetrate metal armor, but anything that wasn't Valaer steel could be melted by Davon.

I recognized him in the second row, behind the most heavily armored men. The king had thought about putting Charlie behind us, but our metal mage didn't have the same kind of capabilities as theirs. Though he could melt metal, he could only do so when it was close to his touch. He would probably have to fight beside me for that to do any good. It was better that he stayed out of this, especially given that he wasn't as brave as the rest of us.

Airinold, meanwhile, might've been a little too brave. There wasn't a Valaer steel breastplate that fit him, forcing him to stand tall in leather armor instead. At least he had on a Valaer steel helmet, like all of us sorcerers of the king had recently received via a cart from Koluk.

Rohaer didn't seem interested in stopping in front of us as they continued closing the distance. We held our ground at the tightest turn of the road, where there were rocky slopes to our left and the steep hills of Curdith Forest to our right. If Rohaer became incredibly desperate, they could attempt to infiltrate our ranks by using these slopes, but they were just as likely to slip in their haste as they were to be stabbed by our wooden spears. Then, of course, there were those who held swords far behind us, out of range of Davon, just in case things did not go according to plan and we had to resort to old tactics. Many people would surely die in that scenario, most of them on our side.

Souriff took off with Failina right behind her. I saw the heads of Rohaer's army tilt upward to watch them soar overhead. Souriff landed high on the mountains, on a precipice. She stood on the edge, appearing as small as an insect. Failina came down behind her somewhere, out of my view. The blue sky turned white as snow began to fall over Rohaer's army.

"Archers!" yelled someone from within the midst of enemy soldiers. "Fire!"

A hail of arrows shot out over the heads of Rohaer's soldiers and mine, traveling far toward the deep ranks of our army before descending. I had little idea what kind of damage these arrows would do, but our army was prepared for this. Everyone knew to hold their shields overhead and protect each other as our own archers fired back.

Our arrows rained down onto Rohaer's army as they came around the turn a good distance ahead. I heard nothing except the patter of arrows against shields, not a scream or a single sound of worry.

"You're just going to waste arrows, like I said!" Leon yelled back. Of course he was too far away for any of the archers to hear him, but our highest-ranking officials were mixed in with the rest of us, including Kataleya's brother and Harold Chespar himself. Orders would be spread and heard by all.

There was a strange moment of silence as neither army fired another round of arrows, both probably realizing the same thing. It would be a waste.

That's when the fireballs began.

Unfortunately, all came from Rohaer's side toward my allies far behind. I heard the crash of burning mana against shields, and this time I did hear screams.

Remi fired back, but she took aim at the sorcerers not ten yards away from us. A woman waved her hand and caught Remi's massive fireball with a shell of dteria.

"Damn," Remi said.

"Wait until they're close," Leon said.

But Rohaer stopped there, ten yards away. The temperature had dropped severely. I had just noticed a couple of our enemies shivering when Valinox flew out from the middle of the army, toward the precipice where his sisters awaited him.

Dense snow fell onto Rohaer's army, and soon I could see them no longer.

"Now. While we still have time," Leon said.

We rushed toward them as quietly as we could. Soon the snow enveloped us, too, and I couldn't see past Airinold on my left and Leon on my right.

"Shields," Leon practically whispered, and we made barriers of dvinia and water.

I felt the blast of dteria against my wall, but it held firm.

"Hold here," Leon said, and I heard Airinold repeat the same thing down the line to my left.

We stopped. All was white, the air frigid cold. I figured our enemies were just a few feet in front of us, but

I could barely see my own hands.

I felt another dark mage cast, my shield absorbing the spell. Leon's wall of water cracked and froze from the outer edges in, but something unseen struck it. Shards of ice and freezing water splashed us, but we did not move. We couldn't possibly be as cold as the enemy sorcerers in front of us, in the heart of the snowstorm.

"They're right here!" yelled someone in front of us with a shaky voice, as if he couldn't speak clearly through his shivers.

Rohaer's front line let out a wild battle cry followed by an onslaught of dteria and fire, but we stopped it all.

"I'm going now, Leon," I said.

"Make it quick." His wall of quickly freezing water extended to cover Airinold.

I took off vertically, the cold air and dense snow forcing me to put my hand up over my eyes protectively. Above me, I could feel dense mana from where the demigods fought.

I had seen Valinox take off fully covered in a suit of armor. I had as much chance of killing him from behind with my sword as I did of blindly shooting an arrow at him through the snowstorm. But there was something else that would be better so long as he was too distracted to notice.

I heard Souriff and Failina grunting in pain as I reached the precipice of the mountains where I had last seen Souriff. The snow quickly began to clear as I landed quietly behind Valinox. He was taking out his longsword as he trudged toward a fallen Failina, Souriff standing in front of her protectively with blood running from a badly broken nose. I did not use mana but approached on foot as I took out a small wooden box from my pocket and opened it.

I felt Souriff put up a dense shield of dvinia as Valinox threw out his fist and struck her shield with dteria. There was just enough shape and visibility to Souriff's dvinia for me to see a ripple as Valinox struck it again, and again. Souriff strained to keep it up and even managed to counterattack with her own blast of dvinia, but Valinox blocked it and used the opening to strike her person this time, sending her tumbling through the air, over Failina's head.

Failina, back on her feet, cast a massive stream of fire at Valinox. She and Souriff figured they could not kill Valinox, but they knew their efforts would keep him distracted. I crept closer, the heat from Failina's spell melting the snow in my hair and causing me to break out in a sweat as Valinox blocked it all with dteria, though not so easily as he groaned and turned his head. I froze in fear as I thought he might see me, but he had his eyes shut from the intense heat.

The fire roared so loudly I thought about abandoning my plan and attempting to find a way in with my weapon through Valinox's full suit of armor, but if it failed, it would ruin everything we'd set up. Instead, I came up right behind him, slowly and quietly.

Within the wooden box that I put back in my pocket had been a cursed stone. We had adhered it to a small bit of metal, and Reuben had enchanted that metal into a powerful magnet. The wooden box served as protection against Rohaer's enchanters. Without it, one of them would be able to pull the curse out from the stone in the midst of our front line, and that could be the end of all of us. I did not fear they would feel the cursed stone or have the ability to remove the curse from such a distance now, while I was so high above them. Failina just had to make sure Valinox wasn't aware of it.

I stuck the magnetized metal, with a cursed stone attached, to the back of Valinox's armor.

He still didn't notice me as he pushed his dteria at Failina and forced her fire back on herself, his wall of dteria smacking her in the process and sending her tumbling off the back summit.

That's when I jammed my sword up under one of the flaps of metal covering his hips and felt my Valaer steel drive into his side. He screamed as he spun and tried to backhand me, but I ducked and pulled my sword out from his body. Hopefully, he would assume I had come here to stab him and wouldn't feel the curse trapped in the stone on his back.

This was not a fight I could win. I did not need to pretend as I showed fear and fled, forming a wall of dvinia behind me to protect my back. I was just about to hop off the precipice when I felt a spell of dteria break through my wall. The clear energy grabbed me and started to crush my ribs beneath my armor, but I stabbed my sword down through the right side of the ring of energy, breaking free and tumbling out.

I fell off the precipice, back first, as I looked up and saw Valinox lean over to watch me go.

Come on, Souriff. He had to remain distracted.

Valinox looked back over his shoulder and seemed surprised by something. I felt an immense amount of dvinia and dteria all at once as he disappeared from view.

Good.

I turned to get my feet underneath me as I made a ring of dvinia around my torso. I let gravity take me down as I pushed myself toward my allies, so as not to come down on the heads of Rohaer's army. All traces of Failina's blizzard were gone, the sun bright in the sky.

"Make way!" Leon called as he kept up a wall of water behind him and turned to clear a bit of space for me to land.

I tried to protect myself from Rohaer's archers and fire mages with a wall of dvinia, but I still wasn't very good at casting two spells at the same time, and I couldn't exactly let my Grab spell dissipate while I was still falling.

An arrow broke through my thin protective wall and stuck in my leg. I shrugged it off as I slowed and landed in the midst of my peers. Then I yanked out the arrow.

By the time I had healed myself, I noticed Failina and Souriff coming down to join us.

"Did you do it?" Souriff asked.

"Yes," I said.

"Really?" Failina made a massive wall of water as she spoke, giving us all a break as she covered the entire front line from mountain to forest. Airinold had to crouch slightly to get his tall self completely beneath it.

"I did, but I don't know if it's still there," I said. "Did you keep him distracted?"

"We did," Failina said. "He should be coming any second."

"Here he comes," Leon called as he pointed at the sky. "Reuben, do you feel it on him?"

Reuben stepped forward and stuck out his hand in the direction of the demigod. "I do."

Valinox might've been twenty yards ahead of us, descending down behind the first few rows of his men. He had an arrogant smirk on his face. Clearly, he thought victory would soon be in his grasp with Failina no longer able to continue her snowstorm.

"Get him, Reuben!" Michael yelled.

Reuben made a pulling motion through the air while Valinox was still a few stories high. "I got it!" he yelled in triumph.

Shock twisted Valinox's expression as he started to flail and turn in the air. He looked down and gasped. Never had I seen him look more mortal as he plummeted like a rock and screamed in absolute terror.

I couldn't see him crash, as Failina's wall of water blocked my view, but I heard the slam of metal and the yelps of several men.

Leon removed a wooden box from his pocket identical to the one in mine. He tossed the box and the stone over Failina's wall of water. I saw the box open and the stone come out in the air, but through Failina's water barrier, I couldn't see where it landed. Everything was a blur, black tabards twisting and wiggling.

"Can you get it, Reuben?" Leon asked.

"Hold on."

"Hurry up! We have to get to Valinox before he recovers," Leon urged.

"What's taking so long?" Airinold snarled at us. He looked more eager than the rest of us to get to the final step.

"I think I've got it." Reuben grunted as he pulled his hand through the air. "There! Go now!"

A moment later, I smelled the earthy scent of the curse as it disabled all mana in the vicinity. Failina's wall of water fell with a splash. We charged through it, boots sloshing as we gave a battle cry. Arrows flew out overhead and found new homes in many soldiers.

"Time to die!" Michael yelled.

I focused on the soldiers just in front of me, two men who did not even have weapons up as they tried to cast at me and failed, their expressions morphing from confusion to horror.

From the corner of my eye, I noticed Airinold pull ahead of me. He chose boot over sword as he kicked the shield of a man trying to keep him out, driving the man into the others crowding behind him.

The two in front of me barely got their shields up as I came at them. Their meek defense would not be good enough. I leapt and lifted my sword over the shield, driving it down into the neck of another man as the one trying to keep me out with his shield looked over in alarm.

A number of cries rang out from within the ranks of Rohaer:

"Melt them, Davon!"

"We need fire!"

"They've disabled sorcery here!"

"Move back. Move back!"

They didn't put up much of a fight as we pushed through them one rank at a time. I could feel Michael and Reuben close behind me, breathing down my neck in their eagerness to get around me and claim some kills for themselves. The road was too narrow between the slopes, and that was the whole point to engaging Rohaer here.

It didn't take long for Rohaer to fully turn and flee. I had probably fatally injured a dozen men by then. I noticed Michael making his way up the forest slope to my right and jumping at the fleeing sorcerers with an overhead slash.

"Michael!" I yelled, fearful he had gone too far ahead and would be overwhelmed.

"I'm with him Jon, *raaaaahh*!" screamed Reuben as he jumped through the air in a similar fashion.

Still in the midst of the curse, none of us could cast as we cut down Rohaer's troops, all showing us their backs as they tried to push through each other to safety. But where was the demigod of dteria? I had to slow to check the ground, thinking that this was where he had fallen. I did not see him.

"Where is Valinox?" I called out for anyone who might have eyes on him.

"They're carrying him off!" I heard Michael yell from ahead.

"Failina, hurry!" Souriff said from somewhere to my left.

"Everyone, stay on your feet," Failina warned us from the woods. She had climbed up the slope and run as far into the forest as was necessary to get away from the curse so that she could cast.

Intense wind kicked up the dust and dirt from the forest earth and blew it into our faces. Our tabards whipped, some breaking off as I heard cloth tearing. All of us halted, crouching and covering our eyes as we tried not to fall over.

It came to a sudden end, and I realized I could cast again. I picked myself up without caution and hurled myself toward the retreating enemies, who had gained quite a bit of distance from where we'd removed the curse from the air.

I realized my mistake too late as Rohaer's army had now turned around to face us, a number of archers ready at the bend in the road. Dark mages put up a barrier as a hail of arrows fired at me. I turned in the air and ducked my head. They pattered against my armor, many finding new homes in my legs and ass.

With the ring of dvinia around me now broken by arrows, I crashed down near my peers and rolled as the shafts of arrows splintered off. Pain like I've never felt tore through my legs and rear end. I finally came to a stop, but it felt even worse when I noticed the horror written on Reuben's face.

"Nox's blade."

I could barely see straight as I looked down to investigate the damage. I counted seven arrows stuck in my legs. I felt one in the back of my shoulder and at least two more in my ass. I must've tucked my arms in front of me because they were clear.

"Make sure Souriff and Failina don't go after them," I groaned out.

"They're not," Reuben said after a quick glance. "I think it's over."

"It is," Michael said as he walked up to us, out of breath. "Good god, Jon."

"Get these arrows out of me, will you?"

"Hold on. Ass first or last?"

"First!" I moaned.

"All right, but you're going to owe me for this."

Michael and Reuben crouched and painstakingly pulled out each shaft one by one. I could barely think through the pain, but I did notice that there were many bodies around me, all draped with the black tabards of Rohaer. A few still squirmed as they held onto life, but our soldiers were walking around and putting a swift end to that.

I began to heal my injuries before Michael and Reuben were finished pulling out all the arrows. Hadley came around and let out an audible gasp as she met my gaze. She rushed over to me and went to her knees.

"I'm all right," I said, but then I hissed as she put her hand on my shoulder.

"Oh, sorry!" She looked behind me and grimaced at the arrow near her fingertips.

"At least we won, thanks to your stones," I said.

Reuben spoke. "I'm incredulous that we did. Flawlessly, as well."

"Yeah, I don't think any of us expected it to go that well," Michael agreed. "It's too bad we didn't get to Valinox before they carried them off."

"He might be dead already," Reuben said. "He was falling fast before I lost sight of him."

I heard footsteps coming up behind me, and then Souriff's voice, "He's still alive. They got away with him."

I painfully craned my neck to see Airinold and Failina approaching as well. They smiled at each other as Failina touched Airinold's arm. I could see Souriff watching the same thing and letting out a breath of annoyance. Then Airinold put his arm around Failina and pulled her in for a kiss, surprising her for a moment before she became supple in his hold and kissed him back with a caress to his cheek. Souriff looked away, as did I.

"We're going to have a lot more stones after this," Hadley said as she surveyed the many bodies in our wake. "I don't believe they're going to try to get past us on the road again."

At the time of the chase, it didn't seem like we had covered a long distance, but there looked to be about eighty yards of bodies around us, some piled on top of each other. We must've slain hundreds of them.

"Did you or the other demigods kill any of these mortals?" I asked Souriff. My curiosity about the demigods' potentially broken oath was a good distraction to the terrible pain in my legs.

"Failina and I did not, but I saw Airinold slay many. I am concerned what Basael will think of this, but at least Valinox has never been this close to death before. He is not brave. He will be scared. His plans may change."

"All done, Jon," Michael said as he took the last arrow out of the back of my thigh. "You can heal yourself."

After I finished, I helped the others look over the bodies to see if we might've taken down Davon. Unfortunately, we didn't find him among the others. I did notice, however, some of the fire mages who had shown great strength with their sorcery, as well as the two men trying to stop us with shields when the curse had broken mana and the fight had turned in our favor.

Eventually, the king arrived, along with the rest of our peers.

"Well done! Very well done!" Nykal said, smiling more than I had ever seen him before as he opened his arms in a welcoming gesture. "This victory goes to my sorcerers and the demigods!"

There were many cheers as I walked over to his majesty.

"What's the next part of the plan?" I asked as the cheering died down.

"We have to wait for them to act again," the king replied, still smiling. "I'm sure we will be ready for anything they throw at us."

But waiting was always difficult for me, especially when I had an idea of how to turn this success into an even greater one. Unfortunately, I was pretty sure the king wasn't going to allow me to do it, which meant I might have to break my promise to him.

CHAPTER TWENTY-FOUR

We celebrated with music and food. I enjoyed the company of my friends, though without ale because we had to be ready for another possible attack the next day. The king still didn't know that I could and had cured drunkenness when the other of his sorcerers had taken their celebrations a little too far in the past, and I liked keeping it a secret. It was one of two things the king wouldn't know about until later.

I took Hadley by her hand and led her away from the group. "I have a favor to ask you," I said.

"What is it?"

"Do you remember when we first met and we were riding to the castle from Livea? You ran your hands through my hair and said you could give me a trim."

"I remember. I had stolen one of your hairs, but you realized what I was doing." She brushed her hands through my hair. "It has gotten long, but I like it this way."

"Then you're not going to like what I'm going to ask."

She frowned. "Don't tell me you want me to cut it *all* off."

"More than that."

"More? How can there be more?"

"I have a plan."

"What is it?" she asked.

"Not here. Can I take you to the river?"

"Sure."

"Do you happen to have shears you can bring?"

"No, but Eden does."

"I'd rather she doesn't know."

Hadley's dark eyebrows lowered. "What kind of plan is this?"

"One that only you're going to know about for now. There must be a barber in this place with some shears we can borrow."

"I know where Eden keeps hers. I'm sure I could snag them without her knowing, so long as we bring them back."

"Yes, we will."

"And then you'll explain the plan?"

"Once we get to the river."

"All right, wait here."

*****

I carried Hadley to the river on my back. Once there, I took out the mirror wrapped in cloth that I had stashed in a small bag. I then took out a small shaving blade.

"I want you to cut off as much of my hair as possible," I said as I sat on a flat rock near the river.

Hadley stood behind me and played with my hair. "But it's perfect as it is right now."

My light brown hair had gotten long enough to fall over my eyes if I didn't brush it back. My stubble had become a little shaggier as well in the recent days, as I had removed trimming from my routine. It covered the planes of my defined jaw and brought out the shapes of my lips. I was going to miss it, along with my hair, but probably not as much as Hadley would.

I looked back over my shoulder. "You're going shave my face as well."

Hadley clicked her tongue. "Why?" She pinched my cheeks as she made a kissing face. "You are so darn handsome right now."

I chuckled. "I'm going to have to look very different for this plan to work."

"Why…? Oh god, Jon, you're not suggesting what I think?"

"What are you thinking?" I couldn't imagine that she had figured it out this quickly.

"Those papers from Rohaer—I've been wondering about them. Now I understand."

"How did you see them?" I had thought I had kept them well-hidden in the pocket of my pants.

"One of the times we were…having some fun, I felt something in your pocket. I was curious, so I checked later when you had taken off those pants. I'm sorry. It's just that you're not a secretive person, so I wondered what you might be keeping to yourself. I thought you could've been up to something dangerous. Are you angry?"

"No, but you could've asked."

"I'm sorry. I will from now on. Will you forgive me?"

I took her hands. "Yes, of course, but you can see now I was going to tell you."

She nodded. "I know."

"You seem to have an idea of what I might be planning. Can I hear?"

Hadley laid out my plan with very specific details. It concerned me that she had figured it out so easily. The only way it would work would be if Rohaer couldn't peace it together as easily.

"But a trim to your hair and beard won't be enough," Hadley said when we were finished discussing the plan.

"I know, but let's worry about that later. It's probably going to take a while to cut off all my hair, and soon it might be cold out." I took off my shirt to keep hair off it.

Hadley let out a slow breath. "All right." She walked in front of me and crouched down, staring at my face and chest for a long while.

"What are you doing?"

"Memorizing you." She bit her lips seductively, then walked over and climbed onto my lap as she faced me. She leaned close to my lips but stopped short. Whispering, she said, "You promise me that you will not do this plan unless you are unrecognizable by those closest to you, because only then will you be safe in enemy territory."

"I promise."

She kissed me.

*****

When we were done, I asked Hadley that, if anyone was to inquire about me, to tell them I had gone to Drayer to check on the people there and that I might not be back until tomorrow. It was important that my peers, and especially the king, did not know the truth. With the time left in the day, I actually flew north all the way to the capital. I trusted a certain tailor there to provide me with everything I needed.

It was late in the evening by the time I arrived. I landed right on the street in front of many people who seemed shocked. I waved to them to show them I wasn't a threat. Then I walked quickly into the tailor's shop to demonstrate the rush I was in, as it seemed like a few of them wanted to come up and speak to me.

The tailor was an older gentleman named William. When I entered his shop, he was performing some measurements for a middle-aged man who held out his arms. The tailor straightened his back as he saw me heading toward him.

"Jon, it's good to see you again," William said. "This is Jon Oklar, the healer," he told the other man.

"I've heard of him." The man bowed to me.

I bowed back. "Pleased to meet you. I'm actually in a hurry. I have to get back south before Rohaer strikes again. We just held them back today and almost killed Valinox in the process."

"Good lord, then what are you doing here?" the tailor asked.

"I'm hoping we can discuss that alone." I addressed the man, "Would you mind coming back in an hour?" I handed over a gold coin.

"That's no problem, healer," he said, "but can I ask you for something instead of coin?"

"What hurts?"

He gave a nod and a half smile. "My shoulder. My horse kicked me when my back was turned, and I think my shoulder popped out. I believe I fixed it myself after, but it's still bothering me. The bloody nag has had it out for me since I bought her a week ago."

I put my hand on his shoulder and healed away the

damage in a matter of seconds. He groaned for a breath, then grinned when I told him it was done.

"It feels just perfect!" he said.

His smile widened even more when I handed him the gold coin. "Save it toward a horse that likes you better."

"Will do. Thank you, young man, for the healing and for your service. I'll be back in an hour," he told William and headed out.

"What can I do for you, or is it for the king?" William asked me.

"You're going to help me win this war."

"From right here in my shop?"

"That's right. I'm actually disappointed that you recognized me because I've come here to make myself unrecognizable."

"Considering I'm the one who made your shirt and your pants, and a man's clothes are what I look at the moment he enters, you shouldn't be so disappointed after all. From the shoulders up, I hardly see the old Jon. Hey, wait. How come you need to be unrecognizable?"

"Because I'm going to pose as a soldier from Rohaer, and there are several of them who would recognize me, including Valinox himself. I want you to put together a tunic for me. Black seems to be the style in Rohaer." I thought this mostly from Rohaer's black tabard but also from some of the clothes under the armor of the soldiers we fought. I usually preferred shirts and pants instead of tunics, and I didn't own any in black.

"Medium quality is best," I continued, "and the tunic doesn't need to fit perfectly. I'm also going to need an eyepatch made by tomorrow morning, one that will cover as much of my head without looking suspicious."

"I'll need to measure your head then."

I took out three gold coins from my pouch and handed them to him as he came close with his measuring tape.

"I have to say," he spoke in a dubious tone, "that I don't think even an eyepatch is going to make you unrecognizable. You have a very distinct face."

"Leave that to me."

"All right, I will, but which eye do you want covered?" he asked as I started to leave, making me realize that I hadn't thought of it yet.

A chill ran down my spine. If I hadn't thought of that yet, could there be something else that might surprise me? My plan suddenly seemed very fragile, so much so that I started to wonder if I should just head back now.

No, it was just my nerves looking for a way out of this. The plan was solid. I had been considering it ever since Ray had fetched me the papers of two of Rohaer's soldiers. One identified a man as thirty-three and the other as twenty-two. Depending on how I looked when I was done altering my face, I could choose the papers of the older or the younger.

"Cover my left eye." Being right-handed, it seemed like the better choice.

*****

I retired at an inn that served supper. The day had been long. It felt like a week ago that I had fought against Rohaer at the defile, but it was just earlier that morning. The last items I had to purchase were a couple of cloths that I knew I would ruin soon. I requested a few extra candles in my room, as well. I needed as much light as I could safely procure.

I had chosen this room specifically because of the large mirror hanging on the wall. It cost me more, but it was necessary. I pulled over the two bedside tables, positioning them on either side of me. I put two candles on each of them. Then I shut the curtains to the room. With it now being dark outside, only the bright flames on the candles gave me sight.

I picked up my knife from the table to my right and had a few breaths as I leaned close to the mirror and positioned it over my cheek. I was going to start with the easy cuts and work up to the worst one.

It took me well into the night to finish warping my face. It was a learning process that dragged on for many painful hours. I ran the knife down the smile wrinkles on my cheeks and across the concern lines on my forehead. It took just the right amount of strength with my knife, and later with my healing spell, to make the scars resemble wrinkles from age. When I was finally satisfied, it was time to really ugly myself up and distract people from the rest of what might be familiar about my face.

I hissed in pain as I slid the tip of the knife down from above my right eyebrow to the top of my eye. That's when I halted and healed it just enough to stop the bleeding. I wiped my blood off and had a look.

That's quite gruesome, all right. I didn't want it to look so fresh, however, as it appeared too red and open. I healed little by little, watching the open wound close before my eyes as the pain brought on tears and blurred my vision. Eventually the wound closed completely and turned pinkish. It was still not easy to look at, but that was the point. I was satisfied with it.

It hurt even worse to continue the wound beneath my eye, down across my cheek. I wiped off the blood and repeated the same process, wiping my tears on my sleeve throughout.

Finally, I was done. It was surprisingly disheartening to look at myself. I appeared many years older, and I was ugly. The large scar traveling down my face and across my eye brought out embarrassment at the thought of others staring at it.

This was absurd. Why did I feel this way when I had done this to myself on purpose? Perhaps I was vainer than I thought. I had better get over it quickly. The soldier I was soon to become was not supposed to be embarrassed by his scar.

I used the water basin to wash my face. Then I blew out the candles and immediately fell sleep.

CHAPTER TWENTY-FIVE

I visited the castle before the long trip back. In our haste to get the king and his family to safety, no one had been able to grab the king's councilman. I wanted to check on him to see if he wished to go back with me, but I also wanted to test out my new disguise.

I landed in the courtyard with my black tabard and matching black eye patch. William had made it out of leather, and it was uncomfortable. I hoped I would get used to the feeling soon. The worst part was not the strap around my head but being forced to look out of only one eye.

Randy stood outside the closed door to the keep as castle workers bustled about. All stopped to look at me shortly after I landed, fear evident in their eyes. It was a good sign, as I had seen all of these people before and they surely would've recognized me without my disguise.

"It's Jon Oklar," I said as I lifted up the eyepatch. "I've changed my appearance."

There was a collective breath of relief as they must've recognized my voice.

"Any news?" Randy asked as I stopped in front of him.

"We're winning, and the king and his family are safe."

"That is good to hear. Looking for the councilman?"

"I am."

"He's in the great hall."

"Thank you."

I glanced the other way, at the apartments, before turning toward the great hall. I missed my room, my bed, and my friends living comfortably all around me. But as I entered the great hall, I realized that I missed the meals almost as much. I wandered into the dining area to find a number of the castle workers eating. I had never seen them eat before. They must usually do so before us, early in the morning as it was now. Or perhaps they normally ate elsewhere while we stayed at the castle. They all stopped and looked over in alarm.

"It's just me, Jon Oklar," I said, lifting the eyepatch again and giving a friendly wave. "I'm testing out a disguise and looking for Barrett."

His voice came from the corner of the room, a little behind me. "Jon?"

I put the eyepatch back down and turned.

He gasped. "Some disguise. What happened after the demigods took the king and queen?"

"Many things. I can tell you on the way, if you would like to go there. I'm headed back now."

"Did the king send you?"

"No, he doesn't know I'm here. I need to test out the disguise on him before I can convince him to let me use it."

"Oh." The councilman hummed in thought. "I have never flown before." He hummed again. "No, someone must manage the castle in the king's absence. Unless

Nykal sends for me, I'm staying put."

"I should head back, then. I'm sure news is on the way."

"Wait, at least tell me something. Is everyone safe?"

"They are, and we are winning. I believe it won't be much longer now."

"Very good," he said with a smile.

I packed my eyepatch in my bag so as not to lose it during my trip back. "Goodbye for now," I said.

"Goodbye and good luck."

*****

This time upon returning, I figured I wouldn't have trouble finding our fort in the forest. First of all, it was light out. Second, I knew it to be near the defile, which I could now recognize from the air when I was close. I had followed the road between the kingdoms the whole way here, now coming down to land in the forest before anyone in the fort could spot me. I took off the wraps of cloth, healed my wind-burned eyes, and flew carefully through the trees toward my destination.

With our entire army packed around the fort, I spotted the tents first. I figured I wouldn't cause alarm walking toward them from beyond the outskirts. There were so many soldiers and support workers in our army that most people probably saw many faces every day they hadn't before, but what about a man with an eyepatch? He might arouse suspicion, but I didn't want to skulk around the trees while looking for my peers, either.

I decided to walk confidently through the fort. When I noticed a few heads turning toward me, I felt blood rush to my cheeks.

It's fine, I told myself. *If at any point while in Rohaer you are in danger, you can always escape.*

No one tried to stop me as I made my way around the tents and toward the fort. I noticed a small fireball floating in the air. I headed over to find Remi beneath it, contorting her hands as she looked up at it with a squint. The princess stood by, with a couple of guards watching. Kataleya stood near Reuben as they gazed at the fireball. They seemed to be chatting comfortably. Kataleya even gave a laugh as she said something, which brought out a smile from Reuben.

"Let me try now," Callie said.

"Be careful," Remi said. "I haven't heard that Jon is back yet."

"I'm sure I won't need healing."

I tried to get a little closer, but one of the guards extended his arm to keep me from entering the small circle.

"Go find somewhere else to be," he recommended.

I moved back a step and watched.

The princess moved her hands about. A cluster of fire, loosely connected and about the size of her small fist, swirled around above her hands.

"You need more control," Remi said. "Think of enclosing the fire with your mind."

"I know that," Callie said with a bit of irritation. "It just takes me longer, but I can do it. Watch."

But the fire extended down toward her hand, licking her wrist as she screamed and jumped away. The fire fell to the dirt. Kataleya stepped toward it, but it quickly died down to embers before water was needed.

I took this as my opportunity for theatrics and

rushed toward Callie. "Are you all right, princess?" I asked in my altered voice, speaking more with a frown and from the top of my throat as I had practiced on the way here.

"Step away," said one of her guards as he and another man got between me and Callie.

I put up my hands and backed away, making eye contact with Callie between the large men. "It's all right, we're friends, aren't we Callie?"

She looked confused as she stared at me. "No, I don't know you."

It was hard to hold back my smile. "We are. And you, Remi. I know you as well."

Remi tilted her head as she stared at me. "What's your name?"

"Jon," I said, knowing it was a somewhat common name I could get away with.

"Jon what?"

I glanced over at Kataleya and Reuben looking at me with the same quizzical expression. I wondered if there was something about me that was familiar, or if they really felt as though they had never seen me before.

"You are Remi Ryler, from Granlo," I said, dropping my hands and gesturing at her casually. "One of the king's sorcerers, along with Kataleya Yorn over there, who comes from Livea. Reuben, meanwhile, hails from the capital."

"Excuse me, but who are you?" Kataleya said, approaching with Reuben defensively at her side.

"You and Remi haven't known each other a full year, and yet you're close friends, along with Eden and Aliana. The newest sorcerer who took an oath to the king is Hadley, and I'd say you are warming up to her as well, Kataleya. However, you didn't get along with her one bit in the beginning. In fact, I'd go so far as to say that you hated her."

I realized I had overplayed my hand when Kataleya started to form a grin. "God above! Jon?"

Callie gasped as Remi cursed.

"It is you, isn't it?" Callie asked.

I took off my eyepatch. "Surprise," I said in my normal voice.

"Nox's blade!" Reuben exclaimed as he leaned forward and squinted at me. "It is you; I can feel your Induct stone!"

"What did you do to yourself?" Callie asked as she came up and touched my face. She gasped again. "It's not paint!"

"I wouldn't trust paint to do this kind of job."

Remi and Kataleya came close as well. "Egad, Jon," Remi said. "You've done a marvelous job with the light wrinkles on your cheeks and forehead. I can barely tell that you cut yourself to make them."

Kataleya ran her finger down the scar. "God above," she repeated. "Let me see again with the eyepatch."

She stepped back as I put it on. Then she turned to Remi, "I can barely tell it's him."

"Same."

"Now I must speak with the king," I said and took off suddenly. I had made quite an entrance, so I figured a theatrical exit would be appropriate.

His majesty had to be where he was most secure. If he was not near Remi and his daughter, he was most likely in the fort, probably in his tent or nearby.

Rather than fly there directly, I took myself out of the large encampment to the northern outskirts and walked toward the fort that way. I didn't want many people to see me in the air. It was highly unlikely that a spy of Rohaer would find out about me and warn my enemies, but it was better to be safe and limit my exposure. Also, I wanted to surprise my peers if I came across more of them on the way to the king.

I did not see anyone else I knew as I came to the fort and went through the open gate, but there I did pass by Michael and Eden, who seemed to be enjoying each other's company as they stood a tiny bit closer to each other than friends tended to stand. I walked right by them.

"Good morning," I said in my altered voice.

They each glanced at me for a moment, told me good morning, then seemed to forget I existed. I spotted more of my friends soon after.

Three of them sat at a table where they looked to be having a late breakfast. Hadley sat beside Aliana, with Charlie on the bench on the other side of the table. I thought for sure I would be recognized by one of them, most likely Hadley because she knew what I was doing.

I sat next to Charlie, halting everyone's conversation as they stared at me. I noticed Hadley leaning toward me with a stare. I met her gaze. She opened her mouth in surprise, but closed it with a smile.

"Good morning, Charlie, Aliana, Hadley," I said. "How are all of you today?"

"Um, fine," Charlie answered with a puzzled expression.

Hadley put her hand over her mouth as she seemed to be holding in a laugh.

"What's going on, here?" Aliana asked, clearly noticing Hadley smiling while attempting to cover her mouth. "Who are you?" she asked me.

"You know me very well," I said in my altered voice.

She and Charlie looked at my face closely. Suddenly, Aliana gasped. "Jon?"

"Yes." I took off the eyepatch.

"Wow, Jon?" Charlie laughed with delight. "It is you!"

Hadley came around the table and took my face in her hands. "The devil's tail, Jon, this is truly extreme."

"It has to be if it's going to work." I stood and put on the eyepatch, then leaned toward her as I altered my voice. "Now how about a kiss, young lady. Mmm, you're looking rather delicious today."

She let out a half-scream, half-laugh as she recoiled. "It's really like a different person." She smiled at me again and looked closely into my eyes.

Then her smile faded as she let out a breath. "So this means you're really going to do it."

"I am. I just have to convince the king." *And leave behind my Induct stone.*

"Do what?" Charlie asked.

"I'm going into Rohaer. Hadley can explain. I have to see the king now."

"You will see us again before you leave, right?" Hadley asked.

"I will." I kissed her forehead and headed off to the large tent at the center of the fort.

I removed my eyepatch on the way there and addressed Rick at the tent in a whisper. "It's Jon Oklar. I need to speak with the king immediately." I showed my papers just in case. "I have to test out this disguise on him to convince him it will work."

Rick seemed confused, or perhaps concerned. He

glanced at my papers. Then he looked at me again, nodded, and moved aside without question. I put on my eye patch before passing through the tent flap. Within the tent, our various leaders seemed to be in good spirits. Cheery tones were shared between the king, Byron, and even Leon. That changed, however, when they looked over and noticed me.

Leon took a defensive stance in front of the others. "Who are you? How did you get in here?"

"I'm an old friend of yours and the king's," I announced mysteriously. "I've come to bring victory."

"Rick?" the king called dubiously.

Rick walked in behind me. "Sire?" he asked.

"You let this man in?"

I figured my point had been proven, but I was still having fun.

"He did because he knows me well," I said. "As do you, sire. You trust me."

I came closer to give him a better look at my face. Leon remained standing in front of Nykal, scowling at me as if he was restraining himself from casting a spell.

"I am one of your *most* trusted sorcerers," I hinted.

I stared at the king as he looked back at me, waiting for him to recognize my eyes.

He didn't.

"I do not know this man," he said as he backed away nervously.

Perhaps he had never taken the time to really look at me before.

"Leon?" I tried, this time in my normal voice.

"It's Jon," Rick said, probably too nervous to let this go on.

"Jon who?" the king asked.

"Oh shit, it is!" Leon said and gave my shoulder a good shake as he let out a laugh.

"Jon Oklar?" Nykal took an uneasy step toward me.

"Yes, it's me."

"What have you done to yourself? What is all this?"

"He means to put himself behind enemy lines," Leon said. "Don't you?"

Byron came forward. "Jon, this is true?"

"Yes." I showed the papers I had obtained from one of Rohaer's soldiers. I had Ray fetch them from the bodies after we first tried to take down Davon. "This belonged to one of the men who came to Drayer. He would be thirty-three if he was still alive, according to his birthday. I'm sure I could pass as him. And if I'm wrong, I'll get myself out of there safely."

"What do you intend to do while you're there?" the king asked.

"Yesterday we took a major step toward winning this war. I plan to take another."

CHAPTER TWENTY-SIX

I kept my goodbyes short, with promises to return soon. I left behind my Valaer steel armor and sword and instead brought with me a normal blade of steel like the kind our enemies had. I wore no armor, just my black tunic and black tabard of Rohaer over it. The hardest part was giving my Induct stone to Hadley to hold on to.

After the king had agreed to my plan, the demigods were informed. Failina went with me. We flew south through the forest without going above the canopy. Even though I only flew for a minute without my stone with me, I could feel the difference. A voice told me to give up this entire plan and go back so I wouldn't have to part with it. I couldn't get rid of the voice completely, but I could ignore it. Hopefully it would go away soon, because it was rather distracting.

With Souriff, Failina had performed much of our scouting and knew just how far to lead me through the woods before I might encounter one of our enemies. We did not speak on the way there.

I was a little nervous, mostly because of the injury Failina was going to inflict on my body. Such an injury would make things difficult if I was discovered and needed to evacuate myself quickly.

Eventually Failina landed in the middle of the woods in front of me. To my untrained eyes, there was nothing different about this area from the rest.

"Here is close enough," she said as I came down near her. "Their camp is about a mile east."

"Are you sure you know where to shoot me?"

"We went over this, Jon. I remember. I will embed the arrow between your spine and shoulder, not too deep."

I nodded as I showed her my back and looked over my shoulder. She loaded an arrow onto the bow she had brought with her.

"Look forward and take a deep breath in," she advised.

I straightened my neck and took a breath.

She loosed.

I groaned as I staggered away from her. I would've thought it would help that I had an arrow embedded in almost the same place just yesterday, but it didn't. The pain only got worse as I tried to come to terms with the idea that I would be running a mile with this blasted thing sticking out of my shoulder.

"Are you sure you can make it?" Failina asked.

"I am."

"Then good luck. This is very brave of you, but don't let pride keep you from fleeing. If your life is in danger, get out."

"I will."

She took off back the way we came. Soon she was out of sight.

I screamed, "Help! One of them shot me in the back!"

I heard nothing.

I ran east frantically as if fearful for my life. I screamed a few more times for help, but it seemed like I was putting on a show for no one.

I did not let discouragement stop me. I ran and screamed until eventually someone called back.

"Over here!"

I rushed toward the voice and eventually caught sight of two men displaying the same black tabard of Rohaer on their bodies as I did. One had a bow, while the other carried his sword openly.

"Someone shot me," I said in my practiced voice.

"Did you see who?" asked the bowman.

"No, I was too busy running away so they wouldn't kill me!"

"What were you doing out there alone?" asked the other.

"I went out to forage, just a mile." Souriff and Failina had reported that foraging among Rohaer's soldiers was common. Sometimes they were even found going it alone.

We watched the forest silently for a long while.

"It doesn't look like they followed you," the bowman said.

"Maybe it's a trap," I replied. "They could expect us to go after them."

The one with his sword ready headed east with confidence. "Come and get us cowards!" he called. "I challenge you to fight me!" He cast dteria one way, then another. The whoosh of his energy picked up leaves and dirt and rustled nearby bushes.

The archer soon joined him in taunting absolutely no one. "Fight us, cowards!"

"I'm going to the healer," I said as I turned away

from them. They continued to shout into the forest, barely aware of me leaving.

It didn't take long for me to see the enemy camp ahead. I found it difficult to be nervous with pain radiating through my back, as I was just too eager to get this blasted arrow out of my body.

The camp was located near the river that ran alongside the road between kingdoms. I crossed over the water by a short bridge as a couple of men with empty wheelbarrows went past me the other way. They seemed more interested in the arrow sticking out of my back than in my face. I wanted to ask them to point me in the direction of the healer, but I figured most of the soldiers should know.

It was easy to keep up a contorted expression that showed my pain. If someone caught me going the wrong direction, I was certain the arrow in my back would be a good enough excuse for my confusion.

I saw many leaving the camp on my way in, some on horseback with wagons in tow. Most of the tents ahead of me were circular and large, clearly meant for sharing. Almost all were plain white. Only the large tent near the middle had a bit of decoration, black lines down its sides. I stayed clear of it.

Entering Rohaer's camp felt like entering a small city. Defined paths, almost wide enough to be called roads, divided the entire encampment. And on every path, at least one horse could be found pulling a wagon. There were huts where smelters worked, the smell of burning wood in the air. Corralled livestock took up a massive corner toward the back end, deeper south. On the other side, to the north, a large group of men seemed intent on building up a palisade as if expecting an attack.

Are they really planning to stay here for a while? Hopefully what I was going to accomplish here would change that.

At the far corner from where I was awaited the siege weapons. I counted three catapults and two trebuchets. There might've been others. I couldn't see well from here. The demigods had already taken note of these siege weapons during their scouting. What we couldn't tell was when they planned to use them. Now that we had shown that many more of them were likely to die if they tried to get past us on the road, would they hit our fortress with everything they had? If so, the demigods and I would probably be able to take out their siege weapons if Valinox attempted to use them without much of a distraction at the same time.

They might opt for a siege, instead, and attempt to block us from receiving food, but I welcomed that, as I was sure many of my allies did. I was confident we could break through their lines in that scenario. It was the all-out attack to our fort that worried me the most, but at least then they wouldn't be able to utilize their siege weapons without risk of destroying their own troops.

I noticed the area for the sick before I found the healer. Hundreds of beds sat in rows, stretching even past the siege weapons and almost out of the camp entirely. Not every bed was occupied, as if Valinox anticipated more would fall ill soon.

Many people stared at the arrow jutting out of my shoulder, some stopping as if to help, but I trudged past them. There was nothing they could do for me, and I think they realized this. The arrow shouldn't be pulled out until someone was ready to patch me up. Some asked who shot me.

I told the same thing to each one who asked: "Someone from Lycast. I didn't see who."

I needed someone to direct me to the healer, but asking where he or she was would be too suspicious. As time went on, however, I became impatient.

I figured I was used to pain more than most men. I could probably walk a while longer before the arrow embedded in my shoulder did anything to my mind, but I was now very tired of looking for the other injured, where I expected the healer to be. I made my way to one of the busier walkways between the tents. I collapsed to my knees and let out a groan.

A small group of soldiers came to my aid. One helped me up as he asked what happened.

"I was shot in the back while foraging a mile west," I said. "I didn't see who did it. Will you help me to the healer? I've got to get this arrow out of me."

"Do you have any idea who shot you?" The man led me off the busy path while the other two soldiers went with us.

"It has to be someone from Lycast. I thought it might be a trap when they didn't chase me. There could be a group of them waiting."

"Sounds like it," agreed the soldier.

He led me toward the infected people. As I got closer, I saw that there were injured here, but they were separated from the bedridden sick by a wide berth. There weren't many injured lying in beds. Most sat with wrapped limbs or their torsos partially covered by bandages, as I was sure mine would be soon. I would probably also soon have the same bored look on my face.

The soldiers left me on my own there. A blonde

woman in her thirties seemed to be the only healer. I watched her cast a spell of water, forming a tiny sphere of the clear liquid that she stuck a cloth into and used to clean a gash on a man's arm.

I staggered over to the both of them. "I've been shot in the back," I said with some alarm.

"Mercy, come with me."

She led me to a table covered by a cloth, where she instructed me to lie on my stomach.

I turned toward the sick. The first row of their beds seemed about ten yards from here. I couldn't see anything on their bodies, like a pox or any other visible infection. I thought about projecting my mana to see if it could reach one of them and tell me something, but I feared a powerful spell like that might be sensed by this water mage or someone else in the vicinity.

She pulled the arrow from my shoulder as I squirmed in pain. "I'm sorry," she told me a few times during the process and then once more when it was done.

"It's fine," I said as I turned toward her.

She suddenly stood and walked away from me as she took out a handkerchief and coughed into it, all the while gesturing for me to turn away. I did so to keep up appearances.

"Are you sick?" I asked when she returned.

She stuffed her handkerchief back in her pocket "I am. They've sent for another water mage, but it's up to me to take care of the injured until then." Her voice verged on breaking as she spoke, tears welling in her eyes. "I'll take care of your wound as quickly as I can and step away if I need to cough," she said apologetically. "Take off your tunic and lie back down."

"I'm not worried about being sick," I told her as I took off my tunic. "No one in my family ever falls ill. You can take your time."

"You shouldn't think like that. This sickness is not like any other. I've seen it kill a man as strong as an ox who was completely fine just three days before he died."

"How do you know you have the sickness going around and not something else?"

She pulled down the collar of her shirt to reveal white pox making their way up toward her neck. She blinked away tears as she put her collar back in place.

This woman clearly thought she was going to die, and that might be true.

I pitied her.

I would heal her. I just didn't know how yet. This was a kind woman, not one warped by dteria. In addition to her good heart was a skill with water, a rarity among sorcerers because most opted for fire, which required the same range as water.

There were probably two hundred others just in my field of view who were sick and dying, and who I could save. Not all of them were kindhearted like this woman, but at least some of them had to be. It was depressing to think that they would die. We didn't have to fight each other. If Rohaer gave up and turned around, they would survive.

I had to push the thought out of my mind. Such was war. At least I could probably manage to save this woman's life without ruining everything.

"What are the symptoms?" I asked between groans of pain.

She seemed confused for a moment, and I wondered if I had revealed myself with a stupid question.

"What are your symptoms, I mean," I corrected myself to sound a bit more casual and less like a healer. It was difficult to think clearly as she cleaned my wound. I felt like I would barely have to concentrate for more than a few seconds to heal it, the urge similar to wanting to swallow food at the back of my throat, which was something Eden had told me when it came to her struggles to resist dteria. Apparently it had stuck with me.

"I'll tell you in a moment. This is going to sting," she warned me. I couldn't see what she was doing as I felt a burning liquid being poured into my wound.

I muffled my scream with my closed mouth.

When it was done, she answered my earlier question. "I don't have the fever yet, but I feel like one's coming. I'm coughing and sneezing and finding it more difficult to breathe."

"You're going to get better," I told her with confidence.

"Yes, I'll be fine," she answered absentmindedly. "Hush and be still."

I wondered if there was a way for me to heal her without her feeling it, but even the process of directing my mana into her body might be sensed by her or someone nearby.

"How did you end up here?" I asked. "It doesn't seem like you joined looking for glory and riches."

"Am I that obvious? No, I was given a choice. I could either go with the army or hang for treason. So I went. I left behind my husband and child."

Rohaer must have been in desperate need of water mages.

"I'm sorry that happened to you," I told her.

She dried my wound with a towel and had me tilt to

get a bandage around my torso.

"From how you look, I would've thought you'd be just as bad as most of the others. You're not, though. I can tell you have a kind soul."

"You're right," I answered, knowing it might be a prelude to introducing the real Jon later.

"You're not a sorcerer?"

"No, just a swordsman."

"You must have some skill, especially with one eye, for them not to eliminate you with the others."

Eliminate the others? I had to ponder that a moment to figure out what she meant. I assumed the army had sent off many of their troops, no doubt unable to pay all of them. There had to be some sort of test, maybe even a competition of sorts, to find out who was worth keeping. That meant we really were facing the best they had, as we'd expected.

I could only agree with the water mage so as not to give myself away. "I have a way with a sword."

She gave a hum of agreement.

"What's your name?" I asked. "I'm Peter Welldigger." It was the name on my papers, the name of the dead man who I hoped didn't have many friends able to pick up his name out of the air.

"Sondra," she said. "Sondra Gills."

"Sondra!" yelled someone.

We both looked over. My heart jumped when I saw Davon with a bunch of men around him. He screamed at Sondra again.

"Get over here! Hurry up!"

"Yes, sir. What is it?"

"I told you to fill these barrels before the afternoon! I only see *one* of them full." He gestured at three barrels.

"Yes, sir," she said in a weak voice.

"Hurry up about it." He turned and walked off.

She looked back at me apologetically, for she had left my bandage loose and dangling.

It's all right, I tried to tell her with a wave for her to go on.

I wrapped the bandage around me as every movement sent the feeling of splinters deeper into my back. I could barely take the pain, especially as I felt blood soaking the bandage already.

I gave myself a quick heal, just one second of the powerful spell. It closed the wound just enough for the bandage to stop the bleeding.

Much better.

Over the next hour, Sondra exhausted herself trying to fill a barrel of water—something I'd seen Kataleya do in a matter of minutes. I figured Sondra probably would've finished by now if she wasn't so ill, but she was looking worse with each passing moment as she broke out in a sweat and grew pale.

As I became used to the pain in my shoulder, I began wondering why Sondra hadn't told Davon she was too sick. She shouldn't be anywhere near the water. Wouldn't that lead to more infections?

Then I realized that perhaps that's what she intended. She must hate this army even more than I did. They had taken her away from her family, and now she was likely to die without seeing her loved ones again.

I could see her attempting to hide her cough from here, always muffling her face with a rag that she stuffed back into her pocket immediately after. Unfortunately, she wasn't aware that Davon had returned and saw her cough the next time. He took out his sword as he rushed at her.

"Get away from the water, bitch! Why didn't you tell me you're sick?"

I couldn't hear what she murmured. I had to stop myself from running over to protect her. No one else was going, so I couldn't either. I could only hope that Davon wouldn't kill her on the spot.

Davon kicked over the barrel of water and called for a fire mage to burn the barrel. Meanwhile, he ordered Sondra to the sick ward. Tears streamed down her face as she stumbled over to one of the beds and collapsed into it. At least she was alive.

Someone near me called out to Davon that he needed a healer, gesturing at the bandage around his leg that was soaked with blood. Davon turned and conversed with a group of men who seemed to be following him everywhere, many with decorated uniforms. It didn't take long for one of them to walk off and come back with Valinox.

I instinctively wanted to hide, worried he might be able to sense me even if I dared not use my mana. The demigods had told us this was impossible for him to do, but I still had my fears.

He looked as if he had recovered completely from his fall. I didn't get a chance to see what had happened to him, though I figured he had been knocked unconscious before he was carried off by his people.

What is it going to take to kill him? I didn't know if it was feasible, or if we would have to win this war without slaying him. How long would he keep fighting if we secured victory? Would he be vengeful and foolhardy, or would he fly off to start a life elsewhere?

He pointed in the direction of me and the dozens

of others who were injured, and Davon headed toward us, no doubt following the demigod's command. Davon walked right past me without bothering to look at me or any of the other injured as he stopped among us.

"I've been informed that another water mage will be here shortly," Davon announced. "Tend to yourselves until then."

He walked back the way he had come, leaving a number of people murmuring in what sounded to be frustration and confusion.

I didn't know if it was because of their unexpected battle loss or because dteria had sapped their ability to reason, but I was pleasantly surprised at how disorganized our enemies seemed to be. I could only imagine what the camp would look like after I finished what I came here to do.

To get away with it, I had to wait for nightfall, which was many hours away. I figured I should try to get some rest while I could, but I was too interested in finding out what else I might be able to see. I sat up and looked around the encampment for a long while.

Sondra had stopped coughing and seemed to be asleep. The poor woman had clearly exhausted herself trying to fill a barrel of water in what had looked to be an attempt to infect others. I still had no idea how I was going to help her, but I needed to.

Unfortunately, what I soon noticed was going to make everything even more difficult.

CHAPTER TWENTY-SEVEN

There was one man among the sick who stood out from everyone else. He might've been the largest man I had ever seen, but there he lay in a bed, not moving, without the faintest hint of strength.

I knew I should not go over there. I was supposed to remain unnoticed until night. There were greater things at stake.

Evening came and went. Someone brought by a cart with bowls of cold barley soup and stale bread for the injured. It might've been the most unpleasant meal I'd had in the last year. Had I not closed my wound partially, I would've been in too much pain to eat by my own power. It seemed that many others were in this position, the injured beckoning each other for assistance in getting down their soup. However, most people wanted to keep their distance because of the sickness.

The same meal was provided to the sick, but as the cart went around, hardly any sat up to partake. It seemed as if Valinox cared little about these people who might recover with a bit more assistance, and soon I saw why that was.

A group of hundreds entered the encampment from the south, no doubt new recruits in fresh tabards of black. Among them was a man who turned out to be the new water mage, though I soon found he was even less experienced than Sondra as he spent the rest of the day clearly overwhelmed with the number of injured he had abruptly become responsible for.

Valinox did not care if these people lived or died because he did not expect them to recover soon enough to be worthwhile. That told me something else. Whatever he had planned would likely happen in the near future. He did not want to draw this war on for long.

At least I could relax somewhat while waiting for nightfall. It didn't seem like I would be found out. Through my hours of observation, I discovered that all food originated from northeast of my current location. I couldn't see where it was stored, but I knew there had to a locked shed close to the mountains. Our spy had told us this.

I waited a few more hours, until most everyone who could sleep was already out. There were a number of injured who were in too much pain to stay asleep for long stretches at a time, but I doubted they would care about one of us getting up and walking over to the sick ward.

I completely healed the wound in my shoulder, then made my way over to the huge man. I knew I shouldn't, but I couldn't stop myself. A few torches burned around the camp, providing just enough light for me to locate him among the hundreds of sick who coughed and wheezed endlessly.

I stood over his massive form. "Mr. Craw, I'm a friend of your son, Graham," I whispered.

He did not respond as he wheezed and struggled to breathe. I could faintly see the mark of pox on his neck. He looked and sounded like a monstrous beast in this dim light.

"Mr. Craw," I tried a little louder this time and gave his shoulder a little shake.

He did not respond. Perhaps he was too far gone, but not for my mana.

Somebody mumbled something nearby. I turned around to face him, but he was just someone else murmuring in his sleep, pain in his voice.

I closed my eyes and put my hand over Graham's father to let my mana investigate this sickness. It made one of Valinox's curses look like child's play. The infection ran deep. It had brought out a fight response from his body. A war still raged in his chest, but it was nearly over, his body weakened and on the brink of defeat. If I was going to bring him back, I needed to do more than get rid of his infection, as there was damage everywhere.

The only reason I knew my mana was up to such a task was because I had healed that terrible sickness in the stomach of that young man in Kataleya's town of Livea. I knew how to do it.

My only concerns were that this might not be Graham's father—though it was unlikely someone else was this big—and the other was what Graham's father would say when he awoke. I had to remind myself again that there was much more at stake than this man's life, and I still planned to help Sondra.

There would be time for her after. If I was going to save this man's life, it had to be now.

I knew in my heart what I was going to do. I might as well not delay.

I started the long process of ridding the sickness within this man's massive body. Had he been a child, I was certain I could finish in half the time, but he was the size of a bear. I was glad when he did not wake until later, sitting up with a startled gasp.

I stopped healing immediately. "Listen to me."

"What are you—?"

"Listen to me!" I whispered more harshly. "I'm saving your life. You want that, don't you? If so, you'll be quiet, or you'll get us both killed. Put your head back down and I will finish healing you, but only if you will be quiet."

He stared at me for a long moment. The moon hung in the sky above the forest, the cold wind whistling by. I could hear his breathing had returned to a more normal sound, but pox still covered his skin. Getting rid of it would be last.

"Who are you?" he whispered.

"I met your son, Graham, recently. He told me you were here. You are his father, right?"

"I am. They didn't recruit him, did they?" he asked in an ominous tone.

"No, he is safe in Drayer for now. You will start your journey there tonight and see him by morning."

"I am too weak," he said with a breaking voice.

"Because I haven't finished healing you yet." I handed him the piece of bread I had saved from supper. "Don't eat this now. Wait until you are safely out of the encampment. I recommend you sneak out as soon as I'm done healing you, before the commotion I will cause, because afterward they will be looking for a traitor."

He did not reply.

"Do you understand that you were going to die had I not intervened?" I asked with building frustration.

"I do."

"They don't care about the sick or the injured. They have brought in new recruits. They plan to decimate the land as they pillage and rape. You understand that, yes?"

"I do."

"Did you know that they ransacked your hometown and raped many of the girls there?"

His breathing became heavy. "No. My wife?"

"I don't believe she was targeted." *Probably because she's bigger than most men.*

"I know you," he said with a gasp. "You are the healer from Lycast they've been talking about."

"I am. I'm here for a task, but I came across you. I recognized you from your son's description. I couldn't let you die."

He took my hand. "Thank you. Thank you so much."

"You can thank me by defending your town after you get back there. Davon tried to return with his men, but we stopped them. Your son will explain everything."

"Bless you."

"I will finish healing you now. Try not to make a sound, as it will hurt."

"I will be completely silent."

He kept to his word as I spent a few long minutes getting rid of every last trace of the infection, then moved on to the pox on his skin. I was quite tired by the time I finished, as I hadn't eaten very much that day, but I knew I had enough in me to get everything done.

"I think you should change out of your clothes and wash well before getting close to anyone in Drayer," I said when I was finished. "Otherwise, you might spread the sickness to others. I should be able to heal them later, but it's better to be safe. I don't care if you enter your hometown stark naked and go straight to bathe. It's better than infecting anyone, but you can probably leave your undergarments on if you must."

"Can't say my wife will be too pleased about everyone seeing my shame, but I do agree with you." He offered his hand. We shook. "I'm in your debt, healer."

"I might hold you to that debt as this war goes on."

"Of course. Good luck."

He started to get up as I left him and made my way between the sick. There were so many dying, so many lives I could save, but how was I to know who were dark mages corrupted by power? Sondra was the only one I could be sure of.

She was asleep when I came to her bedside. I had gotten used to the sickening stench in the air by now.

I gently took her hand. "Sondra."

She stirred, then coughed. "What are you doing here?"

"I'm going to save your life."

*****

The conversation I had with Sondra before healing her was nearly the same as with Graham's father. It took very little to convince her to trust me, as I figured it would. When life became precious, desperation was in abundance.

Her home was much too far away for her to get there easily on her own, but I wasn't about to risk my life taking her deep into Rohaer. We came up with a compromise.

She agreed to wait for me in the forest straight west of here. She would sneak there as soon as I left her bedside. When I was done with my task, I would find her and take her back to my fort. I had wanted her to join us, as water mages were especially valuable in times of war, but she told me that Davon had threatened the life of her family if she was to flee from her duties.

"I must get back to them, as difficult as it will be."

"If Davon's promise is real," I replied, "then you will not be safe even after you reunite with them. You should bring them to Drayer. If you cannot make a new home for yourself there, then you should bring them a little farther north to our fortress. We will keep you and your family safe."

"Yes, I will try Drayer first, if I can get back to my family."

It would be a difficult and dangerous trek back and forth for Sondra, but she had to do it without our assistance.

Fatigue and hunger made me sluggish when it was finally time to carry out my task. I especially worried that I did not have my Induct stone of dvinia. If the fight went on long, I might run out of mana and find myself captured, or worse. I had to prevent that at all costs.

Very few people still roamed the encampment at this late hour, which made me quite conspicuous as I searched for the food shed. I felt like every footstep was thunderous as I walked around groups of tents.

I had left my eyepatch on my injury bed. I needed both eyes to see as well as I could in the dark, and no one was going to recognize me in this dim light, even if someone held a lamp up.

I figured it would be better to lose some of the

disguise, anyway. A man with an eyepatch would be too conspicuous once they knew I was there, and the changes I had made to my face and hair should be enough. It wasn't like Valinox had spent a lot of time getting to know how I looked.

I had a sword with me, though it was made of steel that Davon could melt. I had little idea where he was sleeping, but I figured he, along with many others, would soon be aware of me.

Let Davon come.

It was Valinox I was more worried about.

I made my first stop where two barrels of water were stored, lids secured on top. I took Sondra's disgusting, moist rag from my pocket—I had borrowed it from her after I left her bedside—and wiped it all around each lid. I wasn't sure how effective it would be at spreading the sickness, but I figured it was worth a try. I put the rag back in my pocket.

Eventually I came to the shed where the spy had told us food was stored. It was large, about the size of my room at the castle, with a big lock on its door. There was no way to know just how many days' worth of food it contained, but if it was at least half full, I estimated it would provide the army with a few days of meals or more.

Suddenly losing that amount of food could devastate their plans to remain here because, while a few days of meals for one person were easy to come by, the thousands of pounds of food required to sustain these people put an unbearable strain on their kingdom.

I knew because the same thing was happening in ours. It was how I first came up with this idea, when I feared someone might sneak into our camp and destroy our supply. It would devastate us.

Only one man seemed to be guarding the shed. He was most likely put there to protect it from ransacking by his own people, which meant he was probably a skilled sorcerer who could defend himself better than most.

Rohaer knew neither Souriff nor Failina could get to this shed without Valinox sensing them, and I supposed they figured I would never risk my neck flying into their encampment in order to destroy it. That was true. I wouldn't fly in.

I was glad for the dark night as I skulked over to the outskirts of the camp. I walked along the mountainside, deep in the shadows.

I crept along until I was close enough to the shed to see its backside. Then I lifted myself with dvinia and hovered up behind it and across the roof in complete silence.

I slowly let myself down behind the man guarding the shed at its front. There was just enough room for me to fit between him and the locked door behind me.

He looked as if he was falling asleep, his head drooping, as I prepared a ring of dvinia.

I closed my dvinia around his head, face, and mouth as I pulled out my sword and ran it through his back.

His scream was muffled by my dense energy as he tried to make a run for it, but that same dense energy held him in place as his feet slipped out from under him.

I made a quick decision to twist and pull the energy the opposite way from his momentum, cracking his neck. He fell limp to the ground, but I wanted to be sure he couldn't make a sound. I plunged the tip of my sword into his heart and decided not to look at his face as I held my energy in place for a moment longer.

Remorseful, but bound by my duty, I pulled him up by his arms, just enough to get dvinia around his chest to slow his bleeding and help me drag him away. I lifted him much easier with my sorcery, guiding him mostly with my mind as I walked around the shed to the back again. I set the body down, leaning it against the wooden wall.

I still could hardly call myself a fire mage, but I had enough skill to at least get this job done. It was much more difficult to find the three notes of fire compared to the four notes of dvinia that had become as comfortable as breathing, but soon I had them ready.

I pushed out the spell with my mind, mana spewing from my hands and turning into a jet of fire.

It roared louder than I would've liked as it quickly caught the uniform of the man I had killed. I stopped and walked to the edge of the shed and listened, but I heard no sounds of commotion. I went back to check on the fire.

"Come on," I whispered, as the flames danced against the wood but refused to catch.

My hand stung from the heat of the spell, but I ignored the pain as I pushed out more mana in another spell of Fire, this time aimed at the wood right above the dead man's head.

In roared and cackled, my skin singeing. I wasn't sure I would ever have the same control with fire as I did with dvinia, but I didn't care right now so long as I had power.

I pushed harder, transforming more of my mana into fire. The flames finally caught the wood. I hissed in pain, quickly healing myself as the flames spread along the backside of the shed.

I turned away and covered my face with my shirt, keeping my mouth shut as my body tried to force out coughs. I moved toward the corner of the shed and unleashed another jet of fire, burning my hand once again in the process. The flame took to the wood, though it did not look like it would spread very quickly. I needed more, so I moved over to the other corner and did the same.

By the time I had healed my hand again, flames covered most of the back wall. The heat was too intense for me to stay so close. I hurried off, temporarily blinded by the bright light and hoping no one had noticed the fire yet.

I made my way over to the siege weapons. It was a bit greedy to set one of the catapults on fire because it would temporarily take me away from the burning shed, but I thought it was worth the chance.

The flames caught the wood at the base of the catapult quickly. There was one more beside it. I rushed over and set it on fire as well.

It took me about a minute. By then, I heard someone screaming in the distance.

"Fire! Fire!"

I rushed toward the burning shed and away from the siege weapons behind me. Troops began rushing out of their tents in their undergarments and thin shirts. I joined their panic as I ran toward the burning shed.

"Where's the guard?" I yelled. "How did this happen?"

I blended into the crowd as dark mages ran close and tried to smother the flames with dteria. I watched in dismay as it seemed to be working. The flames stretched high over the shed and crept over its top, but the dark mages forced it to the back wall, where it looked to be struggling against the invisible energy.

"Get the water mage!" Davon yelled from the middle of the crowd as he pushed two people in the direction of the injured. Then he turned and ran toward the large tent. "Valinox!"

The demigod was already on his way, now landing in front of me and many of the dark mages attempting to smother the flames.

"Is it Failina?" Davon asked.

"No," Valinox said. "I would've sensed her presence as soon as she was close. It must be Jon. It doesn't matter. I'll have this out in a moment." Valinox moved his hands about as if preparing a spell, but I wasn't going to let that happen.

In the span of a breath, I formed a wall of dvinia and hurled it into the lot of us. I screamed in feigned confusion as we all tumbled away from the shed, Valinox included.

He picked himself up with dteria and marched toward the group of frightened-looking men who had not been disrupted by my spell. "Jon is here!" he seethed. "Where is he?"

They all looked at each other as the fire roared.

"Where?" he screamed.

I pretended to look around with the others, many mumbling that they didn't know what I looked like. It was difficult not to smile.

Valinox swept his arm through the air at a group of men. They somersaulted away. Then Valinox pulled his hands down in the direction of the shed, smothering the flames with dteria. As powerful as he was, however, he couldn't squelch the fire on his own.

"Help me with this until the water mage gets here!" he yelled at me and dozens of sorcerers around me.

We rushed back to his side. I prepared another spell of dvinia and hit all of us again. We tumbled back the way we came.

Valinox was first on his feet, his teeth gritted in a sinister look with the shed half on fire behind him. "Where the fuck is he?" he yelled.

His glance swept right over me. I might've enjoyed this game if it wasn't for the look on his face. It seemed like he was thinking about murdering all of us right here and now if it meant getting rid of me.

"The siege weapons!" I yelled as I pointed at them in the distance. I could already see a group of soldiers running toward us from that direction, screaming for Valinox, so pointing out the fire only served to make me look authentic.

At the same time, the male water mage arrived.

He cursed in front of the massive flames. "I can't do anything about this!" he claimed. "There's too much fire."

Valinox threw his arm at the shed, pummeling the wall with a powerful burst of dteria. It cracked the weakened wood. He repeated the spell, shattering the side wall almost completely. I watched, stunned, as he cast over and over, destroying most of the shed in a matter of a minute. A small fire still burned on the far side, but there was now a large opening where we could see within.

Fortunately, most of the bags, boxes, and barrels were already on fire, and Valinox had destroyed many of the others. "Put out the fires and salvage everything you can," he instructed as he took off toward the siege weapons.

The water mage and the dteria sorcerers rushed toward the shed as I slowly backed away. I broke into a run, passing by a few people who looked at me with confusion.

"I'm going for water," I told everyone I passed, hoping they wouldn't think much about it. I looked back after a little while to find that no one was checking on me. Back into the darkness and away from the fire, I took into the air and headed into the forest. I wished I could stick around and find out just how much of the food I had destroyed and what damage I had done to the catapults, but that was a risk I wasn't willing to take.

I figured it would be sometime the next morning that someone pieced together what I had done when they noticed the eyepatch sitting on the bed I had used.

CHAPTER TWENTY-EIGHT

After I landed in the forest and called out for Sondra a few times, we eventually found each other. She got on my back so I could take her north to the fort for the night. But first, we needed to do something dreadful. This was the part I had looked forward to the least out of everything I had to do tonight. I veered toward the river instead of the fort.

We disrobed to our undergarments and tossed our clothes in the freezing river to get rid of them. She had grabbed her bag on her way out of Rohaer's camp. It contained soap that we were both grateful for. We washed our hands and faces. I hoped it would be enough, as I couldn't imagine submerging my body in the river at this temperature and making it back to our fort before we turned to ice.

With both of us shivering, she climbed on my back when we were done and I took her to the fort. I landed near my tent, where Hadley and Remi awaited. They were expecting me and had a fire going, though I could see both were surprised when I landed with a mostly naked woman on my back.

"I'll wake Byron, unless there's an emergency?" was the first thing Hadley asked.

“Wake him,” I replied. “Everything went well.”

She gave one quick glance at the woman shivering beside me before rushing off. Sondra and I stood close to the fire with our hands out as Remi handed me the dry clothes I had given her earlier in the day.

“I’ll get something for the lady,” she said as she rushed the opposite way as Hadley, toward the girls’ tent.

“It already feels much different here than in Rohaer,” Sondra said.

I lent her my coat as we waited for Remi and Hadley to return. Eventually they came back, Byron with Hadley. Failina and Airinold surprised me when they came out of the darkness to join us.

“What happened?” Airinold asked. “Who is this?”

“This is Sondra,” I said. “She was the only water mage in the whole encampment, but she fell ill to the sickness. I cured her along with someone else who’s now on his way to Drayer, the father of a friend. He was too large for me to carry.”

No one voiced any questions, so I continued.

“While I was there, I burned their storage shed and two of their catapults. Valinox arrived, as expected. He and others tried to put out the fire, but it was too strong by then. So he destroyed the shed and told his people to salvage what they could. I wasn’t able to stick around and see just how much food was left, but I would guess at least half of what they had stored was destroyed. I imagine the catapults are unusable too, at least for a while.”

The night was so cold that most of us shivered even as we stood near the fire, bundled in our furs and cloaks. Byron nodded in my direction. “Good work, Jon.

I will inform the king. Sondra, I'll have you introduced tomorrow. You can sleep with the young ladies in that tent nearby."

She turned to me and lowered her head in gratitude. "Thank you, healer. You saved my life."

I gave a nod back.

"I'll help you get situated in our tent," Remi said and guided Sondra away.

I put my hand near my face and healed all the damage I had done to myself.

Airinold asked, "Why do you believe we can trust this water mage from Rohaer?"

"Because all of Rohaer's sick and injured, including her, were left to fend for themselves," I said. "They're ignored and barely fed. If they don't have the strength to eat, then that's it for them. Sondra never wanted to be there in the first place. She was threatened with death if she did not cooperate, so she went with the army and left her family behind. Tomorrow, she's going to start her journey back to them in hopes of getting them out safely."

I still didn't know much about the territory of our enemies. I didn't know which city she aimed to get to, or even the names of any of them. However, I didn't need to know that right now. We could win this war just by stopping Rohaer from getting into Lycast.

"They must not have very many water mages," Failina said. "Did Valinox know it was you who set fire to their food storage?"

"He did, but he didn't recognize me."

I told the tale, skimming over a few details about how I'd killed the guard on watch. I could feel everyone's pride in me as they grinned my way, except for Failina, who appeared worried.

"Knowing Valinox, he's going to retaliate in frustration," she said.

"Do you have a guess as to what he will do?" Byron asked.

Failina glanced at Airinold. Neither seemed sure, judging from their expressions.

"There's no telling with him," Failina said.

"We will discuss it more in the morning," Byron said. "It is too cold. Everyone get to sleep."

As we dispersed, I took Hadley and pulled her to me. She kissed my cheek and wrapped her arms around me.

"Will you sleep with me?" I asked.

She gasped.

"Beside me, to keep me warm," I specified. "You're always as hot as a furnace, even now. I'm sure the other boys will be fine with it, so long as we keep quiet."

"Yes, I think I can manage to melt away your frost."

"You always do."

"Oh? What do you mean by that?" she asked.

"I mean I can rely on you to dissolve whatever's keeping me down, whether it is something as easy to fix as the cold or as difficult to snap out of like a lackadaze."

She pulled on my shirt to bring my lips down to hers.

*****

Over the course of the next day, Souriff and Failina watched Rohaer's camp for signs of movement. I took the time to fly to Drayer to check on Graham's father. Apparently he had arrived in the morning while most of the townspeople were out and about. He had walked into town in his undergarments, too exhausted and famished to care too much about the many looks he got.

By the time I had arrived, Mister Craw had already spread word across the town about what I had done. A few people came up to me when I was visiting Graham. They asked to be checked for sickness, none with any symptoms to report, just a natural fear. None had it. The sickness didn't seem to have reached the town again after I had gotten rid of it the first time.

Graham thanked me profusely for saving his father's life, and so did his mother. They wanted me to stay for a meal, but I explained that I had to get back. I let them know that a water mage by the name of Sondra might come through their town at some point on her way to retrieve her family. I explained her situation, knowing word likely would get around that she might need assistance.

Sondra was already gone from the fort by the time I got back. I wasn't sure I would see her again. I hoped she and her family would be safe.

A number of changes had been made to the fortress after the events of last night. We no longer allowed camps around the outer wall. That area was to remain clear as we prepared for an attack, setting up a palisade with wooden spikes pointed outward.

We also got to work digging a trench around the palisade. Now that food was probably scarce among Valinox's army, and we had already proven we could stop them on the road, it seemed likely that they would come right at us or try to get around us by venturing deep into the forest.

I wished I had an idea of Valinox's thoughts. The other demigods spoke about his rage as if it was legendary. They expressed shock that he had not come yet.

There was little chatter at the camp throughout the day, as our troops trained and worked. We all knew a storm was coming.

Eventually supper came and went. I ate with all my friends in the now-crowded fortress. We had a table to ourselves. That didn't prevent many other soldiers from approaching us, mostly to talk to the girls in overly flirtatious ways, some of these men a decade older. All were sent away with reproach. This was not the time or place.

Formations had to be practiced, and there were a number of duties that needed to be done, each more unpleasant than the last. Washing, cooking, guarding, transporting, and latrine duty were some of the more common tasks I'd witness from hour to hour. I wasn't the only one who would rather this ended sooner rather than later, even if it meant an attack led by Valinox himself.

After I had undone all the cuts I had etched into my face, I still looked very different without hair on my head or chin. I had never cut my hair this short. It was often cold where I grew up. The only men showing this much scalp didn't do it by choice. And although my short and somewhat shaggy beard was more of a recent development, I felt less like myself without it.

Around sunset, Failina and Souriff returned from scouting. They landed within the fort and walked into the king's tent. I figured I had earned enough clout to walk in and listen, but I decided to wait outside for news with my peers. I could be patient when there was no need to rush, though it was difficult.

A short time later, the demigods came out of the tent. All of our leaders exited behind them and dispersed. Harold Chespar and his son, Trevor, went one way. Kataleya's brother, Alecott, went another, with Kataleya breaking off from our group and hurrying to catch up to him. Byron and the king approached us as Leon and Jennava seemed to appear out of nowhere. Leon ripped off some bread with his teeth as he casually rested an arm on Michael's shoulder.

Michael seemed confused by it, but I figured it was Leon's way of showing endearment.

"The bastard finally on his way?" Leon asked Byron, his voice muffled by bread. I figured he was referring to Valinox. He stepped away from Michael and let his arm hang down.

"Yes, with their remaining siege weapons," Byron confirmed. "Jon managed to destroy two of the catapults he set fire to, which leaves one catapult and two trebuchets. They might stop short and attempt to draw us out by using them against us, or they might plan to weaken the walls with them before they charge."

"The ballista could shatter those weapons," Michael said. He faced Leon. "You should've let me practice more."

"How are you going to practice when every shot is likely to destroy the massive bolt it's firing? Besides, you have good enough aim already."

Michael showed an excited smile. "So that means I do get to use it?"

"If you promise to wait for my order to shoot, and aim at the targets I tell you to."

"I promise."

"Good. I'll defend you."

Michael beamed with joy.

"Don't get too excited," Leon said. "This is not a

game."

Michael set his mouth flat.

"What about the rest of us?" Aliana asked.

"You'll be with the most skilled archers we can fit on the ramparts," Byron said. "You will use a technique developed by Endell Gesh in coordination with sorcerers."

I asked, "From when we defeated him in the forest?"

"Yes."

That battle had occurred after Valinox, while invisible, had stolen four of my peers from the tavern in Koluk. He had held them captive and threatened to kill them if we did not leave the city, but we attacked him instead.

The cousin of Kataleya's father, Endell Gesh, was Valinox's leading officer at the time. He had organized a cluster of archers to shoot at us from the center of the small army. Cover for them had been provided by powerful dark mages who'd kept up walls of energy for the archers to shoot over. It had worked very well against us until I chucked one of Hadley's curse stones into the midst of them.

"Have we confirmed if Valinox has a witch with curse stones?" I asked. The spy had mentioned nothing of witches, but being a basic foot soldier, he probably wouldn't have been privy to that information.

"We have not been able to confirm that," Byron said.

The king spoke. "All of you must mentally prepare for a sorcery-stopping curse at any given time, along with many other things. I will now go over what I expect of all of you during each possible scenario. No matter what Rohaer is planning, we will hold them off."

"That is our goal?" I asked, hoping there could be some way of defeating them here, instead.

"It is all we can hope for right now. They still have nearly double our numbers."

"Can't one of the scenarios include us getting around them to close in on them from behind?" I asked. "That way we can kill almost all of them if they try to retreat."

"We do not have the advantage to press," the king said. "Trying to maneuver into a position like that is likely to lead to our defeat."

I felt a stone in my stomach while about to disagree with the king, but I had to voice my opinion. "But we might have success, and it wouldn't take a lot to be prepared for them to run. I can be ready to take Leon with me, and Souriff and Failina can take one each."

The king seemed to catch Byron looking at him with raised eyebrows. "It could work in scenarios three and four," Byron said.

"And it could mean the loss of Jon or our demigods," Nykal replied. "No, we will not prepare to intercept Rohaer if they retreat. We do not need to risk the lives of our strongest sorcerers because forcing a retreat will be a massive victory on its own. I'm sure we will manage to kill many of them by chasing them down, like before."

"Then sire…" Byron uttered. "The other thing…."

The king looked at Byron for a long while, almost daring him to speak.

"I will tell them if you don't," Byron said. "Punish me if you like, but I can't let it go unsaid."

The king scowled and let out a sharp breath. "Fine. I will tell them." Addressing us, he said, "There is a chance that the Chespars or the Yorns might use the chaos of battle to create an attempt on my life. It is something all of you should be aware of, but I will be guarded by many soldiers, and I will have a callring to signal Failina for help."

"What if she's busy?" I interjected. "I should have a callring connected to one of yours as well."

"Jon, while your devotion is appreciated, you will only be shouted for if someone in my family suffers a grievous injury that needs healing immediately. I want your full attention on finding a way to slay Rohaer's metal mage. He has the potential to turn the battle in Rohaer's favor as much as Valinox does. Davon will be heavily guarded and most likely will end up getting close enough to our archers to melt the tips of their arrows and render many of them useless. He must be stopped as soon as possible. We do not have enough sorcery to hold off Rohaer, even within this fort, if our archers' weapons are dismantled. A number of arrows are equipped with heads of obsidian, but not enough to hold off the horde."

"Who's going to take on Valinox?" Michael asked.

"His siblings, but they may need support."

"From my ballista," Michael said.

"No, there aren't enough bolts to waste on a demigod who can most likely block the strike if he isn't already moving too quickly to be hit. The ballista is reserved for the siege weapons that dare to get close enough, like flame-throwing weapons of a large scale or an enemy ballista if they have something like that which we haven't yet discovered."

I heard Michael mutter something that I couldn't quite make out, but it sounded like, "We'll see about that."

We spent the rest of the evening discussing strategies.

CHAPTER TWENTY-NINE

I stood with our most skilled archers on the ramparts, the blue tabards of Lycast worn by all our comrades. While I would've been comfortable with a bow in my hands, I felt even better with just my sword, my armor, and my sorcery at the ready.

It would be up to me, Leon, Jennava, and Eden to keep up walls of energy that would shield us and our archers from incoming fire of all kinds. Michael stood at the ballista with guards of his own, Reuben and Kataleya, and Leon nearby. Remi took her spot in one of the turrets. It gave her a view of both east and south. Byron took position in the same turret as Remi. He and Leon would issue orders to everyone in the vicinity during the battle.

All of our soldiers crowded together within the fort. That included the Yorn and Chespar army of foot soldiers. The king noted to us that he had been in discussions with Harold about where these foot soldiers would be when the battle began. The king would've preferred for them to guard the outer walls of the fortress, for there were sure to be breaches without them there, but Harold Chespar had demanded that they stay within and keep our enemies off the walls.

I was a little disappointed that the king didn't seem to have the power to order this other army into a position of his liking, but Harold had been adamant in this decision, and the king wasn't about to throw us into a fight against each other as our enemies marched toward us.

All of us waited in near silence. Hadley had already done enough by imbuing a bunch of moonstones with the mana break curse made from the essence of a corrupted soul, but she still insisted on staying near me on the ramparts where she could weaken troublesome sorcerers with curses during the bout. She had a number of ingredients with her, including the blood of Valinox and several feathers of Gourfist. The feathers, huge in size, she had tucked into her belt, which drew many looks from the soldiers around us.

Charlie had not become much braver since the last time he was in combat and stayed off the ramparts, down with many of Harold's foot soldiers. The king, knowing he could be at risk just about anywhere he put himself, remained in his tent with his family, heavily guarded by men we trusted, including Rick.

There had been some contemplation about bringing his family back to the castle now that Valinox would be distracted, but that meant Souriff, Failina, and I might not return in time. It was not worth the risk. Besides, the king needed to be here, he said. There was no telling what was going to happen, and he wanted to be in a position where he could lead.

"Valinox is coming," Souriff warned us.

We looked to the sky. The demigod descended down onto our eastern ramparts in his familiar suit of armor, but this time he did not carry a sword. Instead, he wielded a massive wooden mallet. He crushed one of our archers with his feet as he landed and blasted away a dozen more with dteria. It all happened so fast, I don't think anyone was ready.

As Valinox started attacking our archers with his mallet, smashing through the leather armor of one and sending the man's broken body flying over the wall, it was clear to me that he no longer cared about his oath. He looked too pissed off for that.

"Charlie!" Leon called out. "Get beneath him."

"Got it!" Charlie said as he pushed through Harold's soldiers moving the opposite way, putting themselves farther from the demigod. Charlie could do nothing about Valinox's mallet, but he could take away his armor if he was close enough.

Failina and Souriff took to the air. The demigod of dvinia sent a spell at Valinox while Failina unleashed a jet of water. She wouldn't use fire because of the risk of setting the ramparts aflame.

Valinox countered his sisters by making a wall of energy around him, blocking dvinia, water, and arrows that caught in his thick barrier of dteria.

"They come!" Byron shouted from the turret nearby. A swarm of Rohaer's sorcerers in black darted out from the trees and into the clearing around our fort. Davon ran with them near the front, a few men with wooden shields surrounding him. Rohaer's army still had to deal with the trench and the palisade, but they did not charge on horseback. They would get to our fort eventually if we didn't have the time to stop them. That meant we had to get Valinox out of here so our archers and fire mages could shoot without distraction.

There were too many ally archers between me and

the demigod for me to do anything from where I stood on the ramparts. I lifted myself up and hurled myself at him as he continued to block fire, dvinia, and arrows coming at him from nearly every angle. Charlie was one of many people thrown away from him as he cast at everyone nearby.

I tried to surprise him by dropping down on him from overhead and striking him with dvinia, but he glanced up at me and punched the air. Dteria struck me in my armored chest. It tossed me tremendously high into the air, the fort shrinking rapidly as pain radiated through my heart.

With a slight dent in my armor, I let myself slowly cease to rise and begin to fall as I healed my chest. At least from here I was blessed with a view of the whole fort and its surroundings. Rohaer had reached the trenches, putting down planks of wood to get across with ease.

They needed to be shot and those planks burned, and it seemed as if Byron had given the order to do so and ignore Valinox for now. Our archers rained death on our enemies, killing dozens of them in a matter of seconds. A large fireball I figured came from Remi struck a packed group of them, knocking the wooden plank off the trench as bodies spiraled away from the explosion.

I wrapped dvinia around my body and slowed as I fell back toward the fort. As I pushed myself forward to descend back on top of Valinox, I witnessed him throwing his hand in Souriff's direction and striking her with dteria. Her head whipped back as if she'd been struck in the forehead as she flew off the ramparts and down into our fort. Failina had given up on water and obviously decided to risk setting fire to our fort. She hovered above the archers and propelled a jet of fire down at Valinox. I could feel its heat as I soared toward the back of Valinox's head.

He punched the air toward Failina, his dteria rippling through her fire and striking her hard enough to send her spiraling deep into the forest. I could see Airinold pushing through our archers in his attempt to get to Valinox. I readied my sword over my head as I came toward Valinox's back from the other way. As if sensing me, however, he fell flat to avoid me. My body splashed against the ramparts and bounced off. I was about to fall on a few of our men, but I caught myself with dvinia and pulled hard with my mind.

Floating, I turned to face my enemy. Valinox was looking right at me and threw his hand in my direction. I could only create a rudimentary wall of dvinia with the time given. His spell broke through and struck me in the head.

I awoke, dazed, with my ears ringing as Charlie pulled me up. "Heal yourself," he seemed to be telling me.

It felt like not very much time had passed as I healed my head and shook out my dizziness. Valinox had cleared most of the ramparts by then, with nearly all our archers now running to get away from him. It was because we had no way to defend them any longer. Only Airinold remained in front of the ballista, where Michael still stood with Reuben and Kataleya.

Airinold, the huge demigod he was, lowered his body and turned his shoulder as Valinox cast at him. The powerful spell looked weak against the former demigod of dteria, Airinold's resistance holding up. Valinox cast again, and Airinold slid back a few feet toward the ballista. Before he could cover the ground he'd lost, Valinox cast a third time and sent his brother back even farther. Then there was a fourth spell, and Airinold stumbled into Reuben trying to catch him. The demigod was too heavy, and they fell off the ramparts together.

Valinox marched toward the ballista with his massive mallet up, ready to destroy the weapon in one swing. But that was the least of our problems.

"They're getting through the palisade!" Byron called out. "We need more arrows and fire."

Leon called out a reply, and I saw him standing on the ground near me. "Aliana, with me. Jon, you distract Valinox until the other demigods are able to help. Archers, back to your post now! Do not let them get through the palisade no matter what!"

Kataleya showed off her power with a huge blast of water, but Valinox seemed to barely put any effort into blocking it with a shell of dteria. The water splashed off and rained down on many of us below. She gave up as Michael pulled her out of the way.

"If he wants the ballista so badly," Michael said, "let him have it!" He fired the huge bolt at Valinox.

The demigod made a thick wall of dteria. The bolt pierced through, but the wall must've taken most of its speed away because although it struck Valinox with a loud sound of metal clanking, it did not pierce his armor. At least the force was enough to knock him back a few feet and onto his rear. I came down on top of Valinox while driving the tip of my sword at his face.

The bastard was quick, though, rolling out of the way. My weapon got jammed between the planks of wood that made up the walkway of the ramparts. I gave it two good yanks, but I couldn't get it out.

Seeing Valinox about to cast at me while lying on his back, I didn't bother trying to block him. Instead I fired my own cluster of dvinia at his face. I struck him in the nose, blood spurting out, and sent him rolling off the ramparts while he got me in the stomach. My Valaer steel absorbed most of the blow—the normal chainmail under my armor helped as well—but it still sent me over the wall.

I caught myself in the air and tossed myself with my mind so I would land on the ramparts again. I witnessed Valinox just below me smashing one soldier with his mallet and then another, shattering their bones through their leather armor.

Airinold rushed him and tried to block an attack with his sword, but the mallet was too powerful. It visibly broke Airinold's arm as it went through his blade and struck him. Failina had returned, her face bruised and bloody. She landed in front of Airinold and drenched Valinox in fire, but he protected himself with dteria.

At least it gave Charlie enough time to sneak up close enough and begin turning Valinox's armor into liquid with his outstretched hand. It took a while for Valinox to notice that Failina was only distracting him as he looked down in shock at his armor melting away. I thought he would turn and go after Charlie, so I landed in front of our metal mage, but instead Valinox struck Failina in the mouth with a blast of dteria—her teeth shattering as she spun away and seemed to be unconscious.

Valinox then appeared to notice something I hadn't.

Michael almost had another bolt loaded in the ballista. He swore loudly as he saw Valinox look up at him. Valinox flew up and landed right in front of him, the entirety of his armor left behind as a silver puddle.

"Now, Hadley!" Byron yelled.

Hadley chucked a curse stone at Valinox and ripped the curse out as the stone hit the ramparts at his feet. Valinox looked down at it, then up at Hadley with a wicked grin.

"Think I need sorcery to destroy all of you?" Valinox said. "You've just made it even easier for me."

Leon bravely rushed him from behind as Michael—far more nervously—readied his sword for melee combat. I ran to the ramp to get up there myself, using my two legs for once.

The mana break curse might've made it easier for Valinox to kill us, like he claimed, but it was our only chance of getting through his defenses. He had dismantled our entire defense on his own. The curse should have been used as soon as he landed on the ramparts, but we had underestimated him.

Michael attacked as Leon arrived on Valinox's other side. Valinox turned to face both of them as best he could, his back to the spiked wall. He blocked Leon and dodged Michael, then kicked Leon away as Michael attacked again.

Valinox grabbed the hilt of Michael's sword with one hand and swung his hammer with the other. My friend barely got his arm down in time to block it as it collided with his ribs, but I was certain it still broke his bones as I heard a sickening crack, sending Michael tumbling over the wall.

When I made it up to the ramparts, I could see Rohaer was in the process of destroying the palisade as they held up shields to block our arrows and fireballs. Michael lay between them and our fortress, looking like he wasn't able to move.

"Help!" I heard Callie shriek. "They are trying to kill the king!"

It couldn't have come at a worse time.

A glance over my shoulder showed me the king's guards on the ground with blood around them, but I couldn't see into his tent to know what was happening. At least I didn't see Rick among the injured or dead.

Souriff still hadn't gotten up, and now Airinold held his badly broken arm as he crouched over Failina, who, like Souriff, also didn't seem to be moving.

Leon engaged Valinox on his own as I tried to get there. He somehow outmaneuvered the demigod and managed to stab Valinox in the leg, but Valinox aggressively and without regard for his own defense used the chance to slam Leon with his mallet. There was another gruesome crack as it hit Leon's side and he tumbled over the wall in the same fashion that Michael had.

I couldn't decide between attempting to engage Valinox, going to the king's aid, or attempting to get Michael and Leon out of the path of our incoming enemies before they were certainly killed. I was compelled to help the king because of my oath, but I knew that he —along with the rest of us—would likely die if we didn't stop Rohaer's invasion.

With his mallet, Valinox struck one of the spiked tree trunks that made up the wall of our fort, knocking it loose from the others and causing part of the walkway of the ramparts to dip as if it would soon collapse. I would deal with him quickly, get to my comrades, then help the king. I was about to rush him to prevent him from destroying more when something stopped me.

"Fire!" Byron ordered, and a slew of arrows came from the other side of the ramparts. A few embedded themselves in Valinox's unprotected body. He didn't seem to be in pain as he yelled in anger.

Showing his teeth like an animal, he began pulling arrows out as he hopped off the ramparts, finally.

With the curse still disabling mana around here, I jumped over the wall and rushed toward Michael and Leon on foot. Michael seemed to have one side that wasn't injured, his right. He stood guard over Leon with an unsteady stance as Valinox charged at the both of them, arrows sticking out of his body.

I ran after Valinox and soon felt that I could use mana again. But so could he. Valinox put up a wall of dteria that caught a few arrows fired from our archers retaking their positions on the eastern ramparts. Then a massive bolt from the ballista drove into the ground just behind the demigod, startling me. I looked up to see Reuben behind it and cursing himself for his poor aim.

"At the army!" I heard Byron yell. It turned my attention to where parts of the palisade had broken down completely and enemy sorcerers began streaming through.

Michael tried to push Valinox away with wind, but Valinox deflected it with dteria. Lifting his mallet overhead, Valinox rushed Michael, who looked ready to defend himself and Leon from the attack. But it wasn't necessary as Leon, seemingly unable to get up from the ground, blasted Valinox with a fireball. Valinox must've thought Leon was too injured to cast, as he looked to be having trouble breathing.

The force of the fireball somersaulted Valinox's

arrow-filled body backward toward me as he left a trail of steam behind. I thrust myself at him with a lift of dvinia and descended upon him with my sword.

Something struck me midair hard enough to hurl me into the wall of the fortress, dislocating my shoulder from the extreme impact. One of Rohaer's dark mages, no doubt. They were close!

I healed myself as I ran toward Michael and Leon. They limped in my direction, moments away from a stampede of sorcerers and soldiers about to trample them. I hurled myself over and landed near them. "I'm getting you both out of here at the same time, but you have to cover me!"

They turned and made a barrier of wind and water respectively. Sorcery, mostly in the form of dteria, along with a few fireballs, slammed into their walls as I wrapped my arms around their injured torsos, feeling bumps of broken bones where skin should be smooth.

Both screamed in agony as I clutched them tightly and hurled myself back into the fortress. I had to use just about all the strength I could muster to get the three of us over the wall, and I didn't have it in me to ease our landing in the slightest bit. We slammed down among our troops, Leon and Michael screaming in pain.

I looked around for my peers and found none of them here. The only minor victory we could claim was that Valinox was probably too injured to continue the fight for a while after absorbing many arrows and Leon's fireball, but I saw signs of Rohaer having reached the wall as fire roared up over the edge from below, forcing back our archers. We needed casters there to protect them.

I healed Leon first. It took a precious whole minute

to mend his broken bones and the other damage to his organs. Then I started on Michael; all the while we heard a woman yelling for help from the king's tent. I wondered if it was the queen.

"Jon," Leon was telling me as I healed. "See what's happening in the king's tent. Michael, you and I have to stop them from burning down the walls at all costs."

"Got it," I said as Michael and Leon hurried toward the ramp.

A few more men than before lay dead near the opening of the king's tent, while others nearby were in the midst of a sword combat. Unable to recognize who fought to protect his majesty and who didn't, I hurled myself between all of them, knocking over a number in the process and flying into the tent.

A crowded brawl like in a tavern was the confusing scene before me. Many wounded lay against the sides of the tent, awkwardly attempting to stop their bleeding by themselves as their backs pulled on the fabric and stretched the roof.

Screams filled the air, too many for me to make out anything in particular. There was little room to draw swords, many of the soldiers brawling with their fists or wrestling on the ground. I heard the sound of water on the far end of the tent and noticed splashing above many heads in the way.

"Kataleya?" I yelled as I started to push through.

"Stop the healer!" someone called, and soon many turned my way.

It then became clear how outmatched the king's men were when at least a dozen men split off from beating our soldiers senseless to charge me. I charged right back at them with a barrier of dvinia around me. I plowed through men and overturned furniture as loyal soldiers to his majesty rejoined the fray. It didn't take long to reach the other side of the tent, where I witnessed Kataleya and Hadley standing in front of the royal family.

Callie was desperately in need of healing as she sat against the corner of the tent. Her mother and father held their hands over her neck as blood seeped out. They all faced the same man, Kataleya's brother, who looked to be having trouble standing as he crouched on one knee and his chest heaved for breath.

He pushed himself up as he saw me and picked up a bloody sword from the ground. No doubt the weapon had been used to cut Callie's throat when she had defended her father against him. Rather than attack me, he turned and cut a deep tear across the wall of the tent. Then he hopped out.

"Jon, look out!" Hadley warned.

I turned and jumped away from two men trying to end my life with their swords. Like everyone else in this tent, they had on a blue tabard of Lycast. But they were not our men.

Kataleya blasted one back with water as I finished off the other with my sword. When the one she had struck got up, he turned and fled out of the tent. It seemed to start a trend of them giving up, as many other soldiers ran out after him. Soon all that were left were the men who had attempted to defend the king, and many showed life-threatening injuries.

I started to heal Callie. The cut across the side of her neck was deep. I was certain she would've bled out soon without my intervention.

"What happened?" I asked. Perhaps the answer

would tell me if Alecott would soon make another attempt on the king's life.

"I rushed in as soon as I heard the princess scream," Hadley said. "Kataleya's brother had already gotten through the guards."

"How?"

"With dteria," Hadley said.

So he's another goddamn dark mage.

I finished healing Callie and glanced at Kataleya. She watched the opening in the tent as if expecting her brother to come back at any moment.

"I tried to stop him," Callie said, holding up her burned hand that I had failed to notice. "But he's very powerful. He suspended me with dteria and cut my neck. He would've killed my father had Hadley not arrived."

I healed her hands as Hadley seemed to be looking around for something. She marched over and picked up one feather of Gourfist.

"I had to use one along with Valinox's blood just to stop Alecott," she said. "I have feathers left, but no blood. They won't be any good without more of it."

"Your curse stopped his dteria?" I asked.

"It just weakened him. He tried to finish what he started, but Kataleya came to our aid."

Just about everyone else in the tent had made their way over to us by now. I could see many more needed healing, but there wasn't time. "I can only heal those who are about to die," I said, pushing through those who had walked over because they would all clearly live.

There were two men nearly passed out from blood loss. One was Rick. I closed his many deep cuts and repaired his internal damage.

"Thanks, Jon," he said.

"You must hurry back to the fray as soon as you're done," the king told me as I started healing the other.

"I will guard the royal family and be ready to call for help," Kataleya said. It was the first time I had heard her speak during this whole ordeal. I figured she was just as shocked as the rest of us at finding out her brother was a dark mage.

At least I hoped she was shocked. If not, then that meant something even worse than her brother betraying us.

First her cousin, now this.

I left the tent and glanced around.

"Oh god," I muttered in horror.

We were about to have a lot more to worry about than an attempt on the king's life, unless I could do something about it.

CHAPTER THIRTY

With the mana break curse no longer hanging in the air over the eastern ramparts, we might've been able to hold off Rohaer, but they had climbed up onto our ramparts by then. Davon stood in the middle of the walkway, heavily guarded by sorcerers in metal armor. It appeared that nearly all of our archers had given up, and I saw why as I charged in.

The tips of their arrows had been melted off—many dozens of bolts were lying on the ground without a head. Only a few archers continued shooting, and these were men—and Aliana—who had been given arrowheads made of obsidian. I watched Aliana shoot her arrow into the face of a man—the only opening in his full suit of armor. I then witnessed another ally cast a fireball that blew off a second dark mage protecting Davon. However, more came over the wall to take their place.

Flames grew near the edge of my vision. Screams pierced the air. Byron was descending from the turret with Remi, who burned two men trying to get to him. Byron kicked another away and yelled for those with wooden spears to take out the metal mage.

I didn't believe it would work with Davon and his nearby guardsman armored in steel, but I wasn't sure what else we could do.

I wanted to hurl myself at Davon, but I would need

help if I was going to have a chance of getting through so many dark mages and their barriers of dteria. As I looked around for a demigod or possibly another sorcerer of the king, I noticed a blade suddenly swinging at my neck. I ducked under it and launched the attacker away from me. It was a man I didn't recognize, wearing our colors.

"Not the healer!" yelled Kataleya's brother as a few more of his men closed in on me. "We need him to drive back Rohaer. Kill the king."

A large group of them rushed toward the tent. I blasted some away, but there were too many for me to stop alone. I trusted that our soldiers I had healed, as well as Kataleya, could keep the king protected, because Alecott was right. Without me, it looked like our fort would soon be overrun.

I cursed the traitors inwardly as I checked the ramparts again to find two of my allies near the ballista—Leon and Michael—completely overwhelmed. Leon cast a spell I had only seen him make one other time, to show us what could be done with wind.

The tornado he formed was small but powerful, whirling around at about ten feet tall. It picked up and tossed Davon high into the air as it plowed through Rohaer's people, throwing some over the wall and others onto the ground within the encampment. Then the tornado made a sudden turn, clearly out of Leon's control, and headed toward a number of our own men trying to get up the ramp. It threw them off as it picked up some of the looser pieces of wood from the walkway, which tilted and looked as if it would collapse at any moment.

There was a loud snap, then a clank as Michael

shot a massive bolt from the ballista upward. It caught Davon flailing through the air, impaling him and taking him far away from the fort.

With the metal mage gone and Valinox still recovering elsewhere, I helped my comrades slay the sorcerers of Rohaer who had fallen into the fort from Leon's tornado. Then I lifted myself up to the cracked walkway. It suddenly sank as I landed, nearly causing me to fall off as I flailed my arms and regained balance. I thought it was going to break, but it held, at least for now.

"No more on the walkway!" Byron yelled.

Just Leon and Michael were left with me.

We kicked off the ladders Rohaer had put up while we blasted anyone who attempted to climb up on their own. I tried to keep up a barrier of dvinia to catch all the arrows fired at me, but some made it through. Most missed as I moved too quickly for my enemies to hit me, but a few started to clink off my armor. Then one stuck in my arm. I started to pull it out, but another scraped my cheek. There were too many archers and not enough targets for them.

I was about to warn Leon and Michael that I needed to jump off, but I could see they were already ducking below the spiked wall because they, too, were overwhelmed by arrows. With us unable to push away the ladders slamming against the outer wall, soon Rohaer's soldiers started to climb up and over.

Archers stopped firing. I pulled the arrow out of my arm and healed myself. I was about to engage an enemy on the ramparts, but there was a loud crack as the walkway fell apart in a chaotic mess.

I pulled myself away with dvinia to land on my feet

as I watched Leon and Michael fall with the debris.

"Fire!" Byron called out.

Out of the swarm of arrows, many found new homes in the faces and bodies of Rohaer's soldiers. Remi burned another as Michael blew one back with wind. I checked behind me to find that, surprisingly, Harold's footmen were not solely attempting to kill the king. In fact, most of them fought to hold back our enemies as Rohaer streamed in through a hole in the middle of the burning gate. They must've broken through with fire and a battering ram.

I rushed over and prepared to blast them back, but Charlie called out to let them come. I halted my magic and readied my sword instead.

Every man who rushed into our fort had his weapon melted by our metal mage. Charlie could only disable one at a time, but he was quick. Each sword only took a couple of seconds to melt across the hands and arms holding it.

There were so many soldiers pouring in, but we had the opening well-guarded. Fighting beside these traitors left me confused and constantly looking over my shoulder, but everyone seemed to be on the same side for now.

There were moments when some of us were taken back by sorcery, but just like our enemies, there were many more of us ready to take the place of those removed from the front line. Rohaer tried to get into the fort over the wall, but Byron, Leon, and even Harold Chespar directed all of us to the sections of ramparts that needed more support. There was a surprising amount of organization, but still I feared for the king's life.

Bodies began piling up around the burning gate of the fort, all of them belonging to Rohaer. Charlie must've melted hundreds of pounds of armor and weapons in just a few minutes of hard fighting.

Then all stopped. No more seemed to be coming.

There was a strange quiet. The only sound was the fire blazing and wood cracking as our gate and walls burned. I lifted myself up to find that our enemies had begun to retreat.

"They're running!" I called.

Our soldiers charged out after them. I took a risk by flying ahead of everyone to blast the wooden planks off the trenches that Rohaer had laid out earlier. All of them seemed too focused on running for their lives to worry about me. I thought about landing and disrupting their retreat, but I had the king to worry about.

I soared back to the king's tent to find that there was no battle here. Kataleya remained in front of the royal family with Rick and a few dozen of our soldiers standing guard.

"Where's your brother?" I asked her.

"I haven't seen him since his initial attack."

I flew back outside the fort and found him among the others, his decorated armor making him easy to pick out. He cut down our enemies as they piled up in and around the trenches. I opted to stay in the air and watch him, as I had no idea what he planned now that that it was clear we had won.

I didn't know of his capabilities with dteria. Perhaps he could lift himself like I could, which meant he could return to the king's tent in a matter of moments.

During that time, I must've seen hundreds of Rohaer's troops cut down. They had shown no caution by attempting to infiltrate our fortress and decimate us with their superior numbers, and they had paid dearly for this rash decision.

Among the dead was Davon, with the thick crossbow bolt pinning his body to the ground. It had broken through his armor and split open his chest, the contents within spilled out around him in a pool of blood.

Word of the traitorous attack on the king spread quickly, first among my peers, and then among the archers employed by the king. Those loyal to us gravitated toward the eastern side of the fortress, where the ramparts lay in rubble. The wall was charred in many places, with some of the pointed trunks leaning away from each other as if they might soon break off and fall down. It looked as if a strong wind could topple an entire wall.

We surrounded our king as we faced our new enemies, the soldiers and sorcerers of Harold and Alecott. I stood at the front of our smaller group, with Leon and our three demigods at my sides.

Apparently, Souriff had been unconscious until recently, while Failina had been too injured to offer much assistance. It looked as if she was fully recovered now, with her teeth having grown back.

It was disconcerting that Valinox, alone, had nearly killed the demigods of dvinia and erto, while Airinold hadn't been able to provide much support. But we had won and slain a good portion of Valinox's army, many of their bodies still within our fort. I saw very few of our men among the corpses spread all around.

Harold Chespar's soldiers, all of them men, gathered behind him and took up much of the rest of the fort. Harold stood with Kataleya's brother at the front, with his son, Trevor, on his other side. An invisible line was drawn between our armies. Harold looked to have four times the numbers of those loyal to our king, but I doubted they would attack us. They needed us, just like we needed them.

"How could you attack your own king?" Airinold accused Harold, the demigod's deep voice forming a hush over the murmurs. I wasn't sure if he had witnessed it or just heard about it later. Either way, I doubted he could appear any more disgusted than he did now.

Harold replied without answering the question, "I will be taking my army north to the castle. Lycast will be under my control from now on. If any of you wish to challenge that, you can do so here."

"You would sacrifice all that is good just so you can put a crown over your head?" Nykal asked incredulously.

"I have done and will continue to do what's necessary for Lycast. That is why I fought Rohaer even after the plan to remove you failed. We share the same goal, but you have the wrong methods of leadership. Every step you take brings us closer to our demise. You've put all your coin and focus into training a select group of sorcerers. They are strong, but eventually they will fall and your army will be nonexistent. That is why I must lead. You have good intentions, Nykal, but you are too nearsighted. You have focused solely on Rohaer when your people in Lycast suffer. You may wish to help all of your people, but you don't have the means. The Chespars and the Yorns do. We will fix Lycast *and* win the war, and I refuse to let you take all the credit for something you will hardly be part of."

"What's in this for you, Alecott?" Nykal asked. "The Yorns already have more land and riches than any family in Lycast. If you are not to wear the crown, then what? Why attempt to kill me with your own sorcery unless you have something to gain? And *dteria*, nonetheless. You are disgusting. It must be greed that drives you, especially given that your own sister stands beside me. But then, why let Harold wear a crown that you could one day take for yourself? It doesn't make sense."

Alecott opened his mouth, but Harold spoke up first. "Alecott is a godly soldier in the making. He will one day be richer than all of us, I'm sure, but he doesn't have my experience. It is my family who overcame the economic problems caused by Oquin Calloum. The people of my land have accepted the differences of their beliefs and have come to understand the importance of hierarchy. There is no crime and no thieves or corruption running rampant like in Newhaven and Koluk, the cities you oversee. With Alecott's help, we will instill the same ideals across all of Lycast even before the war's over."

"That's a bunch of horseshit," Leon said.

"How could you do this, Alecott?" Kataleya snapped.

"We are Yorns, Kataleya. Everything we do is for the good of our people," her brother answered. "When you ran off to pursue your own dreams of becoming a water mage, I worked with our father to build our empire. You are the one who betrayed us."

"You have lost your mind!" Kataleya lifted her palm at him as if she didn't want to waste all of our time with her brother's nonsense. "Trevor, don't tell me you knew about this from the beginning?"

"You're making it out to be much worse than it is, Kat. Our families wish to unite to *save* the kingdom. You can still do that with us."

"I would never!"

"You are the traitor here," Alecott accused. "The Yorns raised an army with our people in mind. As did the Chespars. Nykal cares about Lycast, but a man's intentions don't make him a good king. It is the power of his wit *and* the army he can raise. The Lennox family is weak in both regards."

"I was the one who formed and led an army against the corrupt king, Oquin Calloum!" Nykal growled viciously. "I spent all of my coin to ensure we were successful, and it's because of me that our kingdom didn't turn out like Rohaer is now. I did not tax the people afterward. I only sought help from the nobles who had not spent their own coin, like I had. Now you claim that I don't know how to lead? It is because of me that we still have a kingdom that hasn't fallen to dteria.

The king pointed at Harold as he continued, "You had your chance less than two years ago, Harold. And so did your father, Alecott. I told them what needed to be done, and they agreed with me, but how much were they willing to spend to ensure we won? How much were they willing to sacrifice? Hardly anything compared to what my family did. The Lennoxes have always done what's right and will do so again."

"You can prove your dedication not by speeches but by weakening Rohaer while we fix the problems you left behind in Lycast," Harold said. "When you fall or give up, we will be in a strong position to defend the kingdom after I have given order to Lycast. If you come to me then and dedicate the soldiers and sorcerers you have left to our cause, I will give you back your old land before you became king, but only if you bend your knee and show that you can follow my lead. If not, you and your family will be put to death."

Nykal held Harold's gaze in a glare for a long moment, both refusing to look away.

"You may usurp the castle and take over the north," the king said. "Cherish it the way a gambler cherishes his last coin; when everyone knows that it will soon be gone. I will take it back from you after we deal with Rohaer. That's what you're really anticipating. You knew that even if you had killed me, my sorcerers wouldn't focus their efforts on you until Rohaer was defeated. You know we have enough to stop them. You do not return north to bring order to the land but to prepare to face me. Stop lying to your men and call this what it is. You are traitors making a play at the crown, and you are going to lose."

"If they are not going to help us fight Rohaer," Reuben muttered, "then I say we kill them right now."

Alecott made a wall of dteria as other sorcerers stepped forward and made barriers of the same energy. A few fire mages prepared balls of whirling flames that hovered over the heads of the packed soldiers.

"We are not going to kill each other here," Nykal announced. "Only because we need everyone we have on my side to beat Rohaer. Harold knows this. He knows that we care too much about Lycast to waste lives fighting our own traitors. Not until after this is done."

I was horrified when men started walking out of our ranks, across the division, and joined the larger army on the other side.

"What do you daisies think you're doing?" Leon

asked.

Many looked ashamed as they kept their heads down, but they did not return to us.

It was only a few, at first, but soon more started walking across. All sorcerers let their spells come to an end as Harold sported a proud smile above his double chin.

"You can see what's going to happen when we return to Lycast," Harold said. "Everyone knows to follow a good leader when they see one."

We lost more and more men. I thought of many insults for these cowards, but Reuben and Eden called them out before I could. The more that we lost, the more nervous the rest appeared. Someone had to say something that wasn't just insults.

Byron announced, "Their army might be bigger, but Nykal has the support of the people who matter." People finally stopped changing to Harold's side as all seemed to be listening. "Nykal has the backing of nobles all across Lycast, even if they aren't standing here right now. Don't make a foolish choice based on what's in front of you. Nykal recruited the young sorcerers who are responsible for victory. That wasn't a mistake. It wasn't nearsighted. It was because of Nykal's brilliant decision that the sorcerers are here, and it is because of them that Rohaer smells defeat in their near future. If you wish to become the best version of yourself, then stay and pledge your allegiance to the rightful king. You will see great rewards once this is done. If you stand against us, on the other hand, we will kill you like we have a thousand sorcerers of Rohaer. You can either be part of the change we are making or you can get in our way."

I looked back over our army. No one else left after that. There might've been only a couple hundred of us remaining, but I believed in these people, and I believed in myself. I hoped they did as well.

Harold turned and ordered his army out of the fort. We watched in silence, carefully checking to ensure they went to the proper storage shed for their tents and supplies and did not impose on ours. A few of the men who had been on our side just a moment ago looked as if they were about to open up our shed and start rummaging through our things, but I flew over and slammed the door shut.

"I don't care if anything in here used to belong to you. It doesn't any longer."

A number of men started to come over to surround me, a few drawing their weapons. Souriff and Failina landed at my sides, and quickly the men turned away.

At least we would have more resources than before—the one upside to many of our men leaving while some of their belongings stayed behind. We also had all the livestock except the horses, it seemed, because the rest of our group had gone over to protect the pen as some of Harold's men started sniffing around as if they might take some with them. I imagined their journey back to Lycast would be difficult, but I was certain most if not all would make it there alive.

It was probably going to become a very different place once we had the chance to return later.

Eventually, we had the fort to ourselves. We remained in a large group, waiting for direction. I could see everyone's exhaustion from all the drooping shoulders and heavy eyelids. We had fought and argued through the night, orange rays of the morning sun now peeking over the trees. As tired as I was, I felt hope in the air. The betrayal many of us had feared was over, and the king was still standing.

CHAPTER THIRTY-ONE

There was much to do, but many of us needed food and rest before we could even think about being useful. At least there was consolation in knowing that the traitors must feel even worse than we did, and they didn't have the fort. Even though it didn't offer nearly as much protection as it had before last night, when all of its walls and ramparts were still intact, we had everything required for a hearty breakfast and a peaceful sleep.

Just about everyone ate at the same time. The sleeping part would have to come a little later.

I went with Michael and many others to check the corpses of Rohaer's fallen for anything valuable. We would stack the bodies to be burned later, if people from Rohaer didn't come with wheelbarrows to collect their dead for burial. There was fear that some of these bodies might carry the sickness, even if none of their skin showed pox, but having already healed it from two people, I did not fear it would spread through our small army.

Perhaps we would be lucky and the sickness would not only take out many more of Rohaer's soldiers but also some in Harold's army. Then again, that meant the rest of Lycast could be susceptible to infection after

Harold led his troops back and took control of the cities.

It was a confusing time, made even more so by my fatigue.

I noticed Michael looking around. “What is it?” I asked.

“Where’s the metal mage? Did you see, Jon? I shot that fucker with the ballista!”

“I saw—”

“It was a good shot, too! He was moving through the air when I got him!”

“I know, I saw.”

“Did you?”

“I did. His body is way over there.”

“Show me.”

Michael was not at all disgusted by the sight of bloodied bodies. In fact, he seemed particularly proud as we came to stand in front of Davon’s impaled torso.

“Look at that! It went through his armor and everything! Good god, what power!”

“Mmhmm.” I didn’t share his enthusiasm for the ballista, but I was pleased Davon was dead.

“Dah!” Eden called out loudly as she playfully grabbed Michael’s sides from behind.

He squealed like a young lass, clearly startled.

Eden and I laughed.

“I told you I was going to make sure Jon heard one of your screams,” she said.

“At least now I don’t have to worry about it anymore.” He looked at me almost arrogantly. “So I scream like a girl when I’m startled. It’s nothing.”

“If you say so,” I teased.

Eden skipped off. Michael stared at her as she went, and she seemed to realize he was doing so as she looked back and made a flatulent noise with her mouth. He chuckled.

"How is she doing with dteria and all?" I asked.

"Much better. I don't know what Jennava did, but I think she's over it. Eden knows it almost took her to a place that she couldn't recover from. She'll be careful not to let it do that again."

"Does that mean she has to use it more sparingly than she'd like during a battle like last night?"

"I don't believe so. It's not so much a matter of usage as it is a mentality toward the power. She could use it all she wants so long as she remains in control."

I figured my attitude toward dvinia and the power it granted me could be described in the same way. If that was true, then I shouldn't have anything to worry about so long as I never abused the power.

We left Davon's corpse for now and went back to searching the bodies and then piling them together. Eventually Reuben and Charlie came up to us, I thought to help, but Reuben started talking to me without moving toward one of the many bodies near him, and Charlie just stood there as well.

"Jon, have you realized that we must give warning to our allies back north, like my father?" Reuben asked. "He and others in the capital must be evacuated before Harold arrives, people like Barrett. They need safe transport, not just on your back. They have many valuables that need to reach us so they are not pillaged when the capital goes to hell."

"Have you spoken to the king about this?"

"I figured he might've told you his plan already."

"I haven't spoken with him since his speech last night." He and our officers, including the demigods, had been in discussions since Harold left with many of our men.

"When can we sleep?" Charlie asked with dangling arms and drooping shoulders. "I don't want to be awake any longer."

"Charlie, you were great toward the end of the battle," Michael said as he put his hand on Charlie's shoulder, but Charlie looked too tired to care.

"Thank you," Charlie muttered.

"Were you afraid?" Michael asked.

"At first, but—when can we sleep? I want to sleep, then I want to hear a lot of praise."

We chuckled.

"I'm sure it's fine if you sleep now, Charlie," Reuben said.

Especially if he's just going to stand there complaining about how tired he is instead of helping us, I decided not to say.

Charlie shuffled off like the living dead.

"You should probably rest as well, Jon," Reuben told me. "I imagine you're going to be needed a lot in the coming days."

"He's right, Jon," Michael said. "Let the rest of us take care of this mess."

"Are you sure?" I asked.

"Yeah, go ahead," Michael said.

"Thanks."

"Hey Reuben," I could hear Michael saying as I walked off, "did you see what happened to that metal mage? I shot that fucker with the ballista!"

"I heard about it, but I didn't see."

"Let me show you."

I was thankful that some of our people had spent

the morning putting up tents, knowing all of us needed rest. I spotted an empty one across the camp, but I stopped on my way over to poke my head in the king's tent.

"I'm going to rest unless I'm needed," I told the group of officers and demigods.

The king waved me in. The demigods parted so that I could join everyone.

"Jon, we wouldn't be where we are today without you," the king said. "I know the reason you put yourself at risk over and over again is for more than just riches and my good favor. You believe in this cause. In fact, you would probably let yourself die for it. But we need you alive now more than ever before. I'm ordering you to take better care of yourself. You do not need anyone's permission when you want to take time for yourself. You are still young, barely nineteen. Look out for yourself during times like now, and you can bet that everyone will look out for you when battle comes, as you have for us."

"Aye," Leon said. "Barrett was right about you from the start. I owe that man an ale after all of this is done. Hell, I owe him a whole pitcher."

It felt like ages ago that Barrett and Leon were arguing about how I should pursue sorcery. It made me realize how much Leon had grown, not so much with his sorcery, as he had been powerful when I'd met him, but in regard to being patient with us.

"Thank you, Leon, and your majesty," I bowed slightly before leaving.

With permission to take time for myself, I knew exactly what I wanted. I had a lovely bath, then I found Hadley asleep in a small tent. She awoke as I entered.

"Is something wrong out there?" Hadley asked as she sat up.

"Everything's fine," I assured her. "I just came to rest."

"Oh good." She lifted up her furs. I nestled next to her and gently put my forehead against hers. She reached up and ran her hand through my short hair and kissed my cheek.

She was warm and inviting and knew just how to melt away my tension. I knew tomorrow would bring trouble, but for now, I couldn't possibly be more comfortable.

END OF BOOK 4

Author and Series Information

The next book will be the last in the series. Then a new series will began in the same world.

To receive an automatic email when the next book is released, go to my subscribe page and enter your email. Your email address will never be shared, and you can unsubscribe at any time.

If you're considering leaving a review, please do so! They are very important to the life of a book, especially for a self-published author. Even a rating is helpful.

If you want to discuss the book with me or just want to say hello, email me at btnarro@gmail.com or look up my Facebook page (B.T. Narro) and add me. You can also visit my website at www.btnarro.com.

For more information about my other books and series, visit my author page on Amazon and check out my "About" section.

Thank you for reading.

Made in the USA
Middletown, DE
17 March 2022